KINGMAKER

By Eric Zawadzki and Matthew Schick

Read more about the authors at
fourmoonspress.com

DEDICATION

To my parents, who gave me choices and chances,
and the knowledge to know what to do with them.

Matthew Schick

To my mother, who helped me stand when I fell,
and to my father, who taught me how to be a man
before I knew what it meant to be one.

Eric Zawadzki

CYCLE 1

CHAPTER 1

I fell.

The shock made Butu's half-risen head plummet to the ground again. He closed his eyes to keep out the sand as his three playmates ran around him faster and faster, jeering and kicking up a tiny whirlwind, all but obscuring them from sight.

It should have been simple — a complete circuit along roofs of all the tents on the perimeter of the town beginning and ending at the top of Sentinel's Finger. No one had ever questioned his ability to run up the side of the fifty-foot granite column that marked the south edge of town, a crooked finger of a colossal golem encouraging enemies to come and fight.

I fell, Butu thought again, disbelief and shame sliding into anger. He didn't even listen to the taunts. *The simplest of routes, and I couldn't complete it. I've done it a hundred times!*

In the dance of a race, Butu saw himself dancing on the wind, like fine sand flying, or flowing like water carving its way through rocks in a rapids, shaped by the route but still its master. He could run up walls, walk on ceilings and stand on water. He could feel everything and everyone around him before they came close enough to touch him — even on the darkest of moonless nights. He had never tripped or crashed before. He hadn't imagined he could fall. The thought was unthinkable.

I fell. He thought it with a finality that ended his shame and rage, just as the scuffs on his knees and hands had faded.

When you fall, you get back up again. They were his foster father

Mak's words, and they had never made sense to Butu before. In the shock that followed the fall, though, Butu clung to them like a miraman talisman. He leapt to his feet amidst his friends' taunts and joined their whirlwind until it rose above the tent tops.

Butu was short for his fifteen years. The long-lived Turu grew tall and lean in their desert home of Turuna, so maybe he would grow someday. His skin was darker than most of the clan members'. Old Pater's blue-black was certainly the darkest, but Butu was close. His shaven head, bare chest and feet and pryud wrapped around his waist were common enough among boys near his age.

From within the curtain of their growing whirlwind, the boys sensed their foster mother coming toward them. The same magic that kept them from colliding or falling down also kept them from getting caught doing things that would get them in trouble with the adults. Most of the time.

Zasbey was thirty years old, but she could still somehow tell when her arrival would be most unwelcome. She and her husband had no children of their own, yet. She sometimes said that it was enough trouble watching the clan's four fosterlings: Butu, Paka, Remi and Hatal.

They stopped abruptly, and so did the whirlwind. As Zasbey appeared, the fine sand rained down on them in a glistening shower. They dusted themselves off quickly under her approaching glower.

"Well, is he alive?" Zasbey called loudly from two tents away. Her stride caught up to them quickly.

Looks passed between the boys, warning each other to stay silent. Zasbey waited with a look that could draw the truth out of them as easily as a small child could draw pure gold from ore.

"He's fine," Hatal said in his small voice as Zasbey's gaze settled on him. His face turned purple in embarrassment. "He fell."

"Fell?" The word came out flat. Her gaze shifted to Butu, brown eyes boring into his forehead. He felt his face heat.

"From the roof," Hatal said, dodging Remi's outflung foot. "We were racing."

"From up there?" Zasbey asked, pointing with a tiny tilt of her chin.

All four boys looked up at the sand-colored tent behind them. It was a supply tent, and therefore one of the largest in Jasper. The canvas wall blocked out half of the sky and all of the sun. At the edge of the sky and the tent, what felt like very far away, was where Butu had fallen from.

He turned back into the full force of Zasbey's grim stare. He gulped, suddenly very thirsty.

With one quick movement, she grabbed at his arm. Reflexively he dodged — into her open hand, which grabbed at his ear. He was loose in a second, scowling at her, but her expression had lightened, from furnace to bonfire.

"Back to your play, Butu," she said, patting his cheek with one sun-weathered, brown hand. "You'll be fine."

Butu touched his ear. He had felt no pain — a small patch of mud-like armor had formed from the air to protect him — but something about her reaction disconcerted him. Maybe it was her tone of voice. She sounded concerned — as if at some point he wouldn't be fine at all. She left, then, not back the way she had come but around the side of the supply tent.

Butu stared after her with a puzzled frown, his hand drifting down from his ear. He looked back at the tent roof, from where he had fallen. If all four boys stood on each other's shoulders, they would just reach it.

"He'll never be fine, he'll always be coarse," Hatal taunted.

Remi laughed, and Paka and he joined the chant.

"Fine then coarse, coarse then fine, come and make our swords all shine! Coarse or fine? Fine of course! Polish, polish, 'til it hurts!"

The boys' laughter interrupted Butu's musings. Hatal and Remi pounded their fists into their hands in a game of rock, sword, cloth — probably to see who would race next. Paka gave Butu a tight smile, which the older boy forced himself to return. Of all them, Paka was his closest friend. He couldn't stand to see his shumi — his foster brother — worried.

Movement in the shadows of a tent entrance nearby caught his eye. Someone else had seen. A girl's head appeared but quickly vanished. Not back into the tent. Butu could see Jani, the kluntra's niece, clearly, though he knew Zasbey would not have known she was there. She gave him a broad, cheery grin, and he returned it full force.

Hatal gave a shout. He had beaten Remi.

"Of course, I'm fine," Butu said. "Fine enough to try again!"

He walked up the side of the tent above Jani, and flipped backward onto the supply tent.

"Let's go, Hatal." Butu jumped down and jogged toward the Sentinel's Finger's redstone bulk. "I'll beat you this time."

The younger boy grinned at Remi. As he caught up to Butu he said, "Same route. Over-under, right? Edges and corners."

Butu nodded, feet crunching the pebbles at the base of the Finger. "Direct or roundabout?"

"Roundabout."

"Sunset or sunrise?" Halfway up the Finger, he could see the sun just at the tops of the mountains.

"Sunrise."

Butu shrugged. "If you want the easier route, you can have it," he said, nonchalantly. "You don't have to give it to me just 'cause I'm older."

Hatal snorted. "Brag later, if you win."

The four paused at the top of the Sentinel's Finger to stare down over Jasper. Hatal and Remi had their heads together, pointing and checking their routes. Paka stood attentively near Butu.

Most of the clan lived in or near Jasper, which was easily the largest town for a hundred miles in every direction. A cluster of stone and clay buildings formed the town's center. The first Ahjea children had raised those buildings hundreds of years ago when the founders came down from Pophir. Permanent structures and landmarks like the Sentinel's Finger mixed with the dozens of tents that made up the rest of the town.

Power started from the center: the kluntra, or clan leader, and his family and advisers, as well as all the youngest children and their families. Single men and childless women, orphans like Butu, fosterlings like his friends, and the elderly lived in the rest of the town. Most of the adults were herders or miners, though a few did what they could to farm the hard, dry soil surrounding Jasper.

Southwest, just at the range of sight, the Ahjea's army made permanent training grounds at Gordney. The cavalry and sordenu there guarded the only road leading through the clan's territory.

At one end was Pophir, the largest of the clan's mining towns. At the other was the shanjin, a burning wasteland of shifting sands. Legends claimed the children of the fallen Urgarun clan cursed the once fertile river valley, sinking the river and raising the sands into mountains. It was one of the best-known miramani — a longlasting magical feat — in history.

The Sentinel's Finger represented another miraman. A great guardian golem had protected the Ahjea from invaders in the dark centuries before the Time of Kings. In order to defeat his rivals, though, King Dinal pi'Kanjea and his sword, Pisor, had buried the golem. Only its finger rose up now, stricken testament to the former might of the Ahjea.

Butu hopped on his feet a bit, relaxing his body. He could sense a new fountain up here, where one would never form without help.

Probably a second-cycler, he guessed. *Who just had a birthday?*

A cycle was six years — how long it took for the four moons to match their orbits. Though a six-cycler and a nine-cycler looked nearly the same age, a 15-year-old and a 12-year-old were visibly different ages. Turu could live twice as long as people of other lands, or so Butu had heard. Some famous, ancient Turu lived 30 cycles or more.

The top of the Finger changed often. A first-cycler's golem — her guardian and protector — might not let her climb its dizzying height. An adult would need ropes or ladders. But every Ahjea child whose golem was gone came here during her third cycle to play. Everyone left their mark.

Butu had come up here first with Jani, whose older sister had left a pool and garden. Zhek, Jani's cousin and the kluntra's son, had transformed it into an arena, complete with clay gladiators to fight. Jani and Butu had made it into a palace with granite thrones. Butu and Paka had cleared it except for a small hut where the boys sometimes came to talk all night. And now, another fountain was the central figure. Hatal and Remi drank from it with a shared grin.

Butu grinned ruefully. *There's the birthday.* It would have happened at some point. He was fifteen years old now, and Remi and Paka were fourteen. Jani was nearly a year older than Butu. Hatal had just entered his third cycle at twelve.

How old were Jani and I when we came here the first time? he thought as he approached the fountain.

Thinking of Jani made him look for her, down at the edge of the tents. She could disappear into anything, but she had not climbed the Finger for several months.

Butu felt his cheeks warm. *We used to spend a lot of time together up here.* They had kept that secret from everyone in Jasper, and for good reason. She was the kluntra's niece, and he was a tem, an orphan. *One day I'll be a sordella and prove myself to the clan. Then her uncle will give his consent.*

"Are you two ready?" Remi said. "Quick, now, before the sun sets!"

Butu glanced at the sun, kissing the mountain tops. Their shadows just touched the edge of the tents. He wondered if he could keep Hatal waiting until the sun disappeared.

Jasper bustled with late afternoon activity. Mule handlers hauled the stubborn beasts down from the mines at Pophir. Women readied fires to toast bread and meat for dinner. Children, almost all younger than even Hatal, played around their tents. A patrol of cavalry rode out to Gordney, in a hurry to get to their own homes.

He pointed out a particularly stubborn mule to Paka, but Hatal wouldn't let him get away with it.

"Come on, Butu, before Zasbey comes looking for us!"

Butu grinned and pulled out a strip of thin cloth, which he tied low over his eyes to block the sun. He and Hatal pressed their backs together. The sun was in Butu's eyes now, but it would be in Hatal's eyes when he reached the end.

"Over roofs and under ropes," they chanted the rules. "Chase, chase and stay afoot. Race round the corner, race round the edge. Don't cross the top or you'll be dead. Go round, go round, roundabout, edge of town, the farthest route!"

"Ready?" Butu asked, eyeing his first rope and corner almost fifty feet below.

"Ready," Hatal responded.

"Go!" Remi and Paka shouted.

With two quick steps, they leapt off the Sentinel's Finger.

CHAPTER 2

Butu's feet barely touched the rocky sand as he landed, already in motion. He ducked under the first rope, hitched his arm around it, and swung up to the tent's roof. There was nothing tricky until the stables, which he had to run over for having to go sunset, but at least by then the sun would be on his side.

Three steps along the roof he dropped down, grabbed the guide line for the tent, and swung underneath it, gracefully landing back on the edge again. One more step to the corner. He dove for it headfirst, grabbed the tip of the pole in one hand and the line in the other, swung a full turn on the line and launched himself for the next tent.

As he turned the first corner, he yanked the cloth off his eyes and risked a glance at Hatal on the other side of town. Of course the younger boy was a good distance ahead, but he hadn't had to think about the sun. Immediately to Butu's right, Paka raced the short ways across the roof, an honest eye to make sure Butu didn't cheat.

He dove off the side of the corner of the tent again, whipped under the line, and touched the gravelly ground briefly. Ahead was a paddock, and Butu leapt lightly to a fence post next to a sad-eyed mule. Butu took in the situation with a glance, then stepped onto the mule's back as smoothly as a hawk glides through the air.

Not enough to run across. I'll have to jump from back to back.

The mule under his feet brayed an objection and tried to shake him off, but Butu had already jumped to the next one. The mules filled the pen with brays and snorts as he went. The handlers showered him with a mix of cheers and curses.

7

Have to touch all corners, he thought, slapping the pine post with his hand as he sailed past it. Paka easily kept up with him despite jogging along the pen's fence. Ahead, the stables. The stables were as big as the supply tent he had fallen off earlier, made mostly of stone, and had a steeply sloping slate roof. Paka would run right up the wall of the stable, but Butu wanted to get a bit more speed. He changed direction, aiming for another tent.

He risked a glance as he picked up pace again. He'd caught up to Hatal, slowed because the livestock were being herded into their pen for the night. The shouts of the handlers rose as the animals lowed.

Butu ran on. He hopped onto the tent's roof and jumped, using it as a trampoline. He landed at the edge of the stable roof, dancing at the very edge as he ran. Halfway to the other end of the stables, a gust of hot desert wind pushed him sideways so most of his body hung over the edge. None of his weight was on the roof anymore, but he was still running, like a top spinning too fast to fall down.

Butu glanced down at the tent, spread out like a safety net.

If I fall, he thought, and instantly fell.

The tent shook as Butu landed in a crouch on it. He straightened quickly, trying to regain his stride. The roof sagged under his foot, sucking at it. He pulled free, but overbalanced. Arms windmilling, he stumbled sideways. Panicking, he tried to jump off the roof, but instead of catapulting him into the air, the support pole snapped.

Butu clung to the tent as the weathered canvas swung inward, drawing the wall down with it and pouring more weight on the rest of the structure. The central support pole knocked the wind out of him as he slammed into it. A few seconds later, the entire tent collapsed.

He didn't move right away, even as cries of outrage rose from outside. He sensed Paka nearby, running closer, not away. Butu's breathing slowed, but now he felt a remarkable and wholly unfamiliar discomfort in his ankle.

First the falls and now pain, he thought as hands began to shift the canvas. *Just like Zhek.* He remembered Zasbey's strangely concerned face, again. *What next?* The pain in his ankle gave one, larger throb, and then vanished.

The canvas whipped away to reveal what looked like the whole clan. Butu sneezed just as a large, strong hand grasped him by the arm and hauled him to his feet. His eyes met those of Jusep al'Ahjea himself. The kluntra's eyes were as granite as the Sentinel's Finger. Butu turned his head to look anyplace else.

Pater al'Ahjea, the kluntra's father, stood watch over the sobbing Paka. A dozen familiar faces and a handful of others — many of them dressed in the colorful robes of the rich — watched with expressions from amusement to scorn.

Jani stood near the back in a fine dress of purple silk. Gold necklaces and rings with large gems hung on her. Her black hair cascaded below her shoulders in two elaborate braids bound with purple ribbons and woven with fine gold threads. Butu couldn't help staring a little. When she saw him looking at her, she turned away quickly as if ashamed of him but didn't disappear the way she usually did.

Jusep was a huge man, broad-chested and tall. He wasn't the strongest man in Jasper, nor the smartest, but he had won his fair share of battles, and few people had bested him in trade. His big arms crossed that chest now as he let go of Butu.

"You should learn to control your kids better," said one particularly round stranger just as Jusep opened his mouth. He held a glass of wine in one hand and a chicken leg in the other and wore a sword with the bull's horns metal crescent of the Kadrak.

Without looking over his shoulder at the fat man, Jusep gritted his teeth, exposing his gold tooth. Zasbey arrived and quickly herded Hatal and Remi into a line with Paka.

When Jusep finally spoke, it was in a loud voice clearly not just meant for the four boys. "I should make it a rule that children are to be in bed by the time the sun reaches the edge of the mountains," he said, sharing his stern gaze among them. "I would think one of you was old enough to know better." His eyes stopped longer on Butu.

Zasbey stood next to the kluntra, looking nearly as severe.

"Take them to their tent," Jusep said to her. "See that they stay there."

Their foster mother tilted her head slightly, and the four boys walked toward the tent they shared. Butu looked over his shoulder. The Kadrak stranger swallowed a bite of chicken and said something to Jusep, whose expression shifted to one of amusement as he replied.

As the crowd dispersed, the kluntra motioned to Jani to come to him. She shot Butu a stricken expression and opened her mouth as if to call to him. Butu abruptly stumbled.

"Eyes forward, Butu," Zasbey said. "You've fallen enough for one day."

He faced front again, met Hatal's angry eyes. He didn't know what to say, not yet, so he looked away.

A circle of children — none much older than one cycle, he was sure — shouted and giggled in a corner where two tents met. A handful of them poked something with sticks. Butu caught a glimpse of a sand adder struggling to escape. They prodded it and sometimes even picked it up and threw it back into the center. While Butu watched, it hissed at them and bit one, but this only made them laugh even more.

When was the last time I played with a sand adder? Butu smiled in memory. *Eventually, one of the adults will put it out of its misery.*

CHAPTER 3

When they reached the tent, Butu went to his blankets and dug out his marbles. Zasbey left with promises to bring back dinner and dire warnings not to leave the tent.

"Let's play," Butu said when she was gone, pretending nothing had happened.

Paka retrieved his own bag and sat in the tent opening, where the evening breeze trickled in.

Paka was a few inches taller than Butu, but he hadn't grown in months. His sharp features and rich, molasses-brown skin would make him twin to his great-uncle, the kluntra of the Kadrak, once he could grow the moustache the men favored.

Remi retrieved a pouch and looked at Hatal, who sat on his blanket with his back to them. The cousins looked a lot alike, though Hatal was shorter. They had cinnamon complexions, round faces and large feet.

Butu grinned as he drew the playing circle and pulled out one of his marbles — an amber, a rare stone for the desert and one of his favorites. The other boys made no move to join him, their pouches of marbles unopened.

"Want to try again tomorrow?" Butu said into the silence.

His friends didn't respond, but a look passed between Hatal and Remi.

"You fell," Paka said suddenly. Remi went very still, and Hatal curled up a little bit tighter. "That means you'll be leaving like the kluntra's son." Tears welled up in his liquid brown eyes.

"I'm not going anywhere, shumi," Butu said, but even he could hear the doubt creep into his voice.

About three years ago, Butu and Zhek had met in a challenge similar to the race. Zhek's father had begun training his son with a sword, and the third-cycler had taught anyone else who wanted to know, so he could practice swords with his magic, which for some reason the trainer wouldn't let him use. He even taught Jani.

Butu was his best student, but because of Zhek's formal training, Butu could not quite catch the kluntra's son. The challenge was like the race — all in good fun, with bragging rights for victory. They fought on the roof of the stables under two full moons — Galdera and Tirlum, the yellow and blue moons. Butu knew the advantage was his. The kluntra's son was a better swordsman, but he couldn't sense things around him in the dark nearly as well. Soon after the fight started, Butu hit Zhek in the back of one knee. Instead of counterattacking, Zhek lost his balance and slid off the roof. The boys had scattered as shouts of alarm rose, leaving their friend.

Zhek never came back, and whenever Butu had seen him since, the kluntra's son glared at him as if he, personally, was responsible for all the world's troubles.

Zhek didn't come back. Neither did Losi or Miter.

Butu put a hand on Hatal's shoulder, but spoke for everyone.

"Zhek was as big as a mule when he fell, though. Of course the kluntra wasn't going to let him keep playing with us. I'm still too small to be a miner or soldier."

Please let them not send me to the fields, Butu thought.

"Paka would make a much better soldier than me." A wink. "At least until I'm taller, and then even Zhek doesn't have a chance against me!"

Hatal snorted, but looked up. Paka wiped his face and grinned. Butu stood and slapped Hatal on the back.

"C'mon, Hatal. Let's play marbles. You name the game."

Remi tossed a leather pouch at his younger cousin, who caught it with a sly grin.

"Do you even need to ask?"

Butu grinned back. "Not really. If I gave you your choice every time, we'd never play anything but Sentinel."

They all laughed, and Hatal unfolded and joined them. He tossed a clear, quartz marble into the center of the circle and dropped six plain, red granite marbles around it. Then he and the other boys dumped all of their marbles on to the sand, outside the drawn circle.

"Sentinel guard our villagers, guard our clan and guard our kluntra," Hatal chanted. "Sentinel stop the pillagers, save the people of Turuna."

His pile of marbles, made from various materials from sandstone to iron to semi-precious ones like Butu's amber, grew into a lumpy, humanoid figure about six inches high. Hatal stared at the others, daring them to question his craftsmanship.

Butu, Paka and Remi said their own chant, turning their marbles into thumb-high soldiers, the invaders to this town of marbles. Butu placed his amber general, a miniature model of himself with no features, at the head.

Each boy took a turn ordering a soldier into the field, and then Hatal advanced his sentinel, his only defense against the triple threat. He groaned as one of Butu's soldiers caught one of his villagers, dragging it away while Remi sacrificed a soldier to defend it. Butu's soldier dragged the red granite marble out of the circle and the three assaulters gave a small cheer of victory, which was short-lived as the sentinel crushed three more attackers with one blow.

The game would be won for Hatal if he defeated all the enemy soldiers, almost three hundred. He would lose if his six villagers or the kluntra were captured and removed from the field. The odds did not seem fair, except his three opponents were not supposed to work together — each of them sought to pull the kluntra or the most villagers from the field. Their soldiers could attack each other, despite the threat of the sentinel.

Eventually, Hatal lost because Remi and Butu worked together. Paka sided with Hatal in moaning about it, so a rematch was set up.

They were well into this game, laughing and panting, the remains of their dinner strewn about, when Zasbey came back to the tent she shared with her husband. She stood in the opening for a minute, watching them. They stared back, Butu hardest of all. He thought she scrutinized him the most. Then she went inside.

"She'll be better when Mak gets back," Butu said as they went back to the game, in which Paka's sentinel struggled to defend its four remaining villagers. "She's all lonely and alone."

"When's he get back?" Hatal asked.

"Another week, at least. Had to go all the way west, to the Nukata."

"So far away," Remi said. "Must be a big trade."

Paka shook his head. "Sounds more like an alliance. Maybe a marriage or a fosterling. It's been a long time since the Ahjea fostered an al'."

The Turu had three-part names. The first part was the name chosen by their parents, and the third part was the name of their clan, but the middle part described their relationship to the tribe's ruling family. An al' was directly related by blood to the clan's kluntra — a son or a father. An el' was a close relative — a niece or nephew, a sibling or an aunt or uncle. An un' was a distant cousin. A ku was a man who had been adopted into the clan after giving up any claim to his birth clan — a rare event — or a woman who chose to pursue a trade of her own instead of marrying. A tem was an orphan or a foundling of the clan.

None of these boys did, but Zhek used to use Butu's tem status as an excuse to boss him around before the rooftop sword fight. Zhek was an al', after all. He would one day rule the Ahjea, while Butu would never be anything better than a laborer or soldier under him.

My parents ... Butu suddenly had the unwilling thought as Paka cheered a successful assault taking out several of Remi's and Hatal's soldiers.

Butu couldn't remember his parents or anything else from before the Ahjea made him a tem. Zasbey had told him simam had killed his parents. The poison wind roamed the shanjin and turned any adult it caught outdoors into a statue that crumbled like a dried out sand castle when you touched it. Because simam never harmed children, though, it left a trail of orphaned babies and children wherever it went.

He didn't question it. Clans thrived because of their children, be they al' or tem. The Treaty of Mnemon, which governed day-to-day life among the tribes, prevented the capturing or kidnapping of children from another clan. But once in a while he would wake from a nightmare of suffocating heat and scratching sand stinging his face.

"It's Jusep!" Hatal hissed to them

By the time Butu came out of his musings and blinked at the board, all but depopulated by Paka's last strike, the other three boys were already on their feet.

Jusep walked silently but made no effort to sneak up on them — not that he could have if he'd tried. The imposing figure, towering twice Hatal's height and four times his weight, clad in robes of muted blues in the moonlight, stared down at them with eyes made whiter for the deep brown of his face. Zheldesa shone off his shaved head. Past the kluntra, a shadow moved near another tent. In spite of the darkness, Butu could sense it was Pater. He knew Zasbey had moved to near her tent flap, as well. He hoped she would not come out.

And is that Jani, behind us somewhere?

Jusep's stern gaze took in the boys, one by one. "That display today could have damaged our relations with the Kadrak." His voice was calm, but it was the tone of voice that used to send Zhek scampering to seek other company. "I hope you've been thinking about that. You need to learn to keep your eyes open."

"Our eyes were open," Butu protested. "It wasn't a rule to run outbound blind."

Jusep's hand moved faster than a snake, and Butu bent out of the way just in time to avoid the blow. The kluntra withdrew and went on in the same terrifying calm.

"You do not talk to me like that, tem." He looked at Hatal, Remi and Paka in turn. "I said keep your eyes open, and that's what I meant. Tomorrow I want you three to tell Zasbey what you think that means. Clean this mess up and go to bed."

Us three? I'm being sent away just like Zhek and the others.

The fosterlings exchanged wild glances with Butu and fell over themselves trying to put away their marbles and disappear. Butu remained standing, chin high, but his stomach twisted.

I interrupted something important. He's sending me to the fields for sure.

Butu scrambled for an apology, an explanation, anything that might change the kluntra's mind. Mining was dangerous and thankless, but it had to be better than the fields, right? He opened his mouth to speak, but a look from Jusep silenced him.

"Come with me," was all Jusep said, and turned on his heel to walk away.

Stunned, Butu glanced into the tent, where three sets of eyes reflected moonlight back at him.

"You'd better go," Remi said softly.

He sensed Pater had gone, and Zasbey was back in bed. Jani had moved closer, and he wanted to go to her, but Jusep was one tent away already and might look back at any time.

The mines will make me stronger while I finish growing. Maybe they'll let me join the army after a year or two, Butu thought, and walked quickly to catch up to the kluntra.

They walked with their backs to the green moon, Zheldesa. The kluntra was also barefoot, but his enormous feet never quite touched the sand or pebbles beneath them. Butu had never noticed that before. He looked down at his own feet, and suddenly gasped as a sharp stone stabbed his heel.

"It's time you were given a job, Butu," Jusep said without turning around.

Butu opened his mouth to plead his case, but the shock of the pain had driven it out of his mind. "A job," he repeated. The pain had left, but he still had nothing to say. "Is this because I fell? Like Zhek fell?"

"Yes," Jusep said, turning around. Butu cursed himself silently. "For tems there's three choices: the mines at Pophir, the fields or Gordney as a sordenu. I don't want you in the mines because your games could cost lives."

Butu's heart sank, but he said nothing. *Maybe if I keep practicing with the sword every night after the farming is done, I'll get so good with it that I'll be allowed to join the army in a cycle or two.*

"I doubt you have the patience for the fields, though that's where I'll put you if you cross me one more time."

Butu stared up at Jusep and blinked. *But that must mean…*

"Gordney!" Butu blurted, despair changing to delight instantly. "I'm to be a sordenu!"

Jusep nodded, but no emotion touched his face. "This is not a reward. You once bested Zhek with a sword, which shows you have promise, and Pater championed you. With any luck, you'll learn some discipline." He leaned forward slightly. "But if you don't, I'll have you in the fields in time for harvest. Do I make myself clear?"

Butu nodded vigorously, grinning. *I'm going to be a sordenu!* It was all he could do to keep from running around Jasper shouting it to everyone.

"Good. Then go to sleep. You'll report to Seargeant Aeklan in Gordney at dawn tomorrow."

Butu walked away, already imagining the glorious victories he would win for the Ahjea. Butu felt Pater join Jusep, and their whispered conversation pricked in his ears.

"He's too small. He won't even survive the first march," Jusep said, sounding weary.

CHAPTER 4

Zheldesa's light made a path down the empty street for Butu, whose back rose straighter with every step he took. He'd have to work very hard, he guessed. The boys who usually joined the guard were bigger and stronger than he was.

And figure out what he means by "keeping my eyes open."

As if by magic, Jani appeared beside him, brushing his arm. As silently as the wind, they disappeared into a narrow gap between two tents. She still wore the dress and most of the jewelry from earlier in the day, the silk smooth against his bare chest as he pulled her to him. She had just enough time to let out a slight squeak before he kissed her.

When he let her go, Jani was laughing. She pushed him away playfully. "What did my uncle say to you? I didn't want to get too close."

Butu struck a heroic pose and grinned. "I'm to be a sordenu! I'm going to Gordney tomorrow."

He moved forward to kiss her again, but she turned her face aside. Butu brushed one of the braids away from where it had fallen across her cheek. "What's wrong?"

"Daren el'Kadrak came all the way from Mnemon to see Jusep, and now they're sending you away to Gordney." Tears glistened in her eyes.

He took her hands in his. "Hey, I'm not going far. We'll still find a way to see each other."

"Oh Butu, you can be so blind, sometimes," she said with a tearful smile. "You don't think my sister married that Zatkuka el' because of his wit, do you? Jusep got a favorable deal on grain trade."

Jusep is marrying off Jani to some Kadrak! A knife of jealousy stabbed Butu. He grasped at her and pulled her against her chest like a child clutching a favorite toy. She was taller than him, but now her wet cheeks rubbed his shoulders.

"I'm sorry. I didn't know," he whispered, kissing her neck.

We could run away together, he thought. *We could leave right now and go to another clan as kus.* They would need a good story, and they would need to stick to it, or no other clan would take them in. The Clanless would more likely look at a pair of lovers as vultures looked at camel corpses. *Not that either of us would want to be Clanless.*

"Who is he?" Butu asked. *If he's just an un', maybe I can find a way to change Jusep's mind.*

She sighed and slumped against him. "It isn't certain, yet, but Daren el'Kadrak means to present me to his brother as a potential bride."

"Which brother?" Butu asked, stroking her hair soothingly, even though he doubted he'd ever win out over an el'.

"Aesh al'Kadrak."

"Their kluntra?" Butu asked, amazement outstripping jealousy, though his heart sank beneath the impossiblilty. *He's the kluntra of the most powerful of the Turun clans. She's not even Jusep's daughter. To get a marriage proposal from Aesh al'Kadrak ...* "You must've made quite the impression on his brother, Jani."

"You're taking this very calmly." She pushed back, and he released her. They played with each other's hands. "I expected you to suggest we run away together and make a life for ourselves as kus."

"You deserve better than that, Jani." Butu swallowed hard. *Aesh al'Kadrak? How can I compete with him?* "I can't say I haven't enjoyed what we've had."

"What we've had?" She snapped her hands from his and hugged herself.

"Aesh is one of the most powerful men in Turuna. Your uncle isn't going to choose me over him!" Butu had intended to sound reasonable, but his exasperation at his misfortune flooded his voice. "We can run away, but where would we go? Aesh will make sure every clan knows I'm a tem who betrayed the Ahjea, and then no one will take us in. How does that help you?"

"Butu, you're shouting," Jani told him softly.

He flushed, took a quick breath, and continued in what he hoped was a more neutral tone. "Jusep is your uncle, Jani. If you get to Mnemon and decide you can never love Aesh, the kluntra will find some way to politely refuse the marriage proposal."

Jani kept her voice so low Butu had to lean forward to make out the words as she hissed them. "It's not a marriage proposal, Butu! Don't you see? The kluntra of the most powerful Turun clan doesn't marry the niece of a minor clan's kluntra. He wants the Ahjea to do something for him — something Jusep doesn't want to do — and he means to use me as a hostage to increase his leverage over us."

Butu took a step back. "I'm sorry, Jani. I didn't think of that."

"That's because you're just a tem."

The words fell on him like marbles — cold and hard. It was something Zhek would say. She had never treated him like a tem, much less talked about it. In the dim light, she probably couldn't see his hurt expression, but she knew how to read his silences.

"You're right, Butu." Her smile was sad. "I have to figure this out on my own. You can't rescue me. Even if you could, you shouldn't." She vanished from his magical senses as well as from his sight, but her voice floated back to him. "And you won't need to."

"Jani!" he cried, but she was either gone already or pretending to be.

Butu stared at nothing. The absence of her presence like a warm blanket had been pulled off him. He took a deep breath and went out into the street, but he couldn't help but look back into the shadows between the two tents. They had spent a lot of time in places like that, cuddling and kissing like third-cyclers do.

He couldn't help but wonder if he had made the wrong choice or maybe just said it the wrong way. He shook his head and walked toward the fosterlings' tent. Even if her marriage to Aesh never happened, Jusep would never allow Butu to wed Jani.

Unless I can be more than a tem, but to do that, I need to prove myself as a sordenu.

That was also true, and Butu was suddenly grateful to the

kluntra for giving him this opportunity to prove he could serve the clan. Miners and farmers never won glory for themselves the way sordenu could. At least as a sordenu, there was a small hope of becoming an un' or even an el' through blood adoption — a rare event, to be sure, but not an unthinkable one.

"Well?"

Three pairs of eyes became his friends as they stepped out of the tent.

Butu hesitated. *Everything is changing. Maybe Jusep did punish me. He's taken away all my friends.*

"I'm leaving tomorrow," he said, and they gasped.

"Where?" Remi asked.

"I'm going to be a sordenu." He kept his voice firm.

Hatal blew out his held breath and threw a blanket at Butu. "You're not leaving, you'll be right here."

"How often will you come visit?" Butu asked Hatal. "How long before Remi goes back to your family?" It was the way he said family. Paka's eyes grew soft, and the cousins' faces turned bitter.

"We don't care that you're an orphan, Butu," Remi said. "We're your friends."

Butu said nothing, stepping into the tent and going to his corner. He rolled onto his side, his back to them, so they couldn't see his tears. After tomorrow, they'd probably not see him again, or speak to him. It would be years before any of them would be a warrior like he was going to be. Even then, they were of different clans. They would be gone, and not even know him anymore.

If I meet them again, it will be on the battlefield, and we are nearly as like to be enemies as allies.

Behind him, he heard the other boys settle for bed, and he adjusted himself more comfortably.

A hand touched his shoulder. Butu pretended he was asleep.

"I'll come visit," Paka whispered. "If you need a brother, I'll be yours, shumi." Then he was gone, and Butu was alone.

This is my chance to prove that it was worth adopting me. I'll be the kind of sordenu that makes history — another Terzik, the Ahjea kluntra who was also an orphan.

That Jani would no doubt be married by that time, Butu deliberately ignored.

CHAPTER 5

The other three boys were asleep when Butu woke. He quietly gathered his few possessions into his blankets: a shirt he never wore, the pryud, a spare pair of pants, leather strap to use as a belt, his bag of marbles and the small stash of granu — brass coins — he had hoarded over the years. Lastly, he grabbed his knife and sharpening stone, both of which were well-worn hand-me-downs from an un'Ahjea. He made a silent farewell to the flattened, smooth bare spot that had been his corner of the tent for the past cycle, feeling sad yet excited. The next step of his life was about to begin.

He stepped outside, avoiding looking at his friends. He didn't want to show emotion to them, even if they were asleep. The sun was not over the mountains yet, the shadow still laying heavy about them even as the sky turned lighter blue and the stars fading. Zheldesa had long since set. He had barely walked ten paces when he sensed someone behind him.

"Butu." Paka, again.

Butu fished in the small pack and palmed one of his marbles.

"Paka." He turned around.

The boy ran up to him, arms open wide. Butu was surprised to feel the wetness of tears on his face.

"Good bye, shumi," Paka said, stepping back and wiping his face with his hands.

Butu grabbed a moist hand and pressed the amber into it. Paka's eyes widened.

"You can come visit me," Butu said hoarsely, then cleared his throat. "I mean any of you. It's not as though I'm going far away."

Paka nodded. "And when I go home, you can come visit me."

Butu laughed and pushed the younger boy back. "You'll be here for years, yet. I'll come visit you here, if they let me." He nodded southwest, to the training ground. "And maybe they'll let us train together here in Jasper."

"Yeah."

"Yeah." Butu glanced at Zasbey's tent, still dark. "Tell Zasbey I said good-bye."

Paka nodded. "I'll see you around, shumi."

Butu walked in the chill dawn toward Gordney. Jasper turned to tents and then the few fields before the sordenu camp came into view. He felt rather than saw several of the voracious hopping mice that were the bane of the farmers, and grinned at the greenness of some of the wheat, painstakingly watered from a well. The laborers were already in the fields, working though the day had yet to begin. The path turned from gravel to sand as he topped a small hill, and Gordney spread out before him.

Butu stopped next to a lone guard, more than twice his age, rolling a pebble back and forth in his mouth and returning his enthusiastic expression with a bored one.

The guard spat. "What's the message? I'll take it to 'em."

"I'm a recruit."

The guard smirked. "Sure you are. And I'm up for a promotion to first lieutenant."

Butu frowned. "No, really. The kluntra ordered me to report to Sergeant Aeklan."

The man's eyes widened slightly, but he motioned Butu past. Butu started down the hill.

"They're sure recruiting 'em young, lately," the guard muttered behind him, and he felt a pebble bounce off his back. He turned to give the guard a withering look, but the man seemed lost in dark thoughts of his own.

Butu shrugged it off. *I didn't let Zhek get to me, and some stupid guard won't either.*

He trotted into Gordney, staring up at the tents — every one of them bigger than the supply tent he fell off yesterday. Each of the five largest had two poles in the center! One was a long, low open awning that seemed to double as the mess hall and a shelter for supply carts. In one corner, a portable forge ran hot with one sordenu watching it. The smallest tent, still one of the biggest Butu had ever seen, must be supplies, and one near it, with one flap tied up, was the armory.

He paused at the edge of the mess hall, where a few cooks shouted at each other over boiling pots of gruel and the sweet smell of bacon. The guard by the forge looked a lot like the one guarding the road in, and Butu was not sure about talking to him.

I have to talk to someone, though.

The camp slowly came to life, and Butu realized sordenu had been around all along, but he hadn't seen them for the tents. They were all focused on what they were doing and didn't seem to notice him. His palms grew sweaty.

"Um, where's Seargeant Aeklan?" he asked a sordenu woman as she walked by, but either she didn't hear him or was pretending not to.

A man came out of one of the barracks in his pants, his well-muscled frame half-again as tall as Butu. A long scar ran down one side of his face, just missing his right eye, and a short beard clung to his chin like a large beetle. As soon as he saw Butu, he waved. Relief flooded Butu, and he waved back, but the sordenu had disappeared back inside the tent.

Butu approached the barracks, one with a large four drawn on it. The man reappeared moments later wearing the tan sordenu uniform and a long, curved sword.

"New recruit?" the sordenu asked, looking at Butu from bare feet to shaved head.

Butu nodded. He stuck out a clammy hand. "Butu tem Ahjea. Are you Seargeant Aeklan?"

"And I'm Pri…Corporal Blay tem Ahjea." He shook Butu's hand. "Lieutenant Zhek told me about your mirjuva."

"My what?" *He knows Zhek?* Then, *Zhek's a lieutenant?*

"Your fall. How old're you, Butu?"

"Fifteen." He dodged someone leaving the barracks.

Blay nodded thoughtfully and pulled Butu to one side as a half dozen men exited the barracks almost on top of him. Looking back at Blay, Butu placed his age at five cycles. Twice as old as Butu, but less noticeable to him than the gap between him and

Hatal. Butu thought he wouldn't be struggling to keep up with him. He followed Blay to an emptier space near the large training ground.

"Another kid to teach us to chant?" someone muttered behind him, and he turned, but Blay spoke then.

"Mirjuva is the first time magic abandons you." Butu watched the goatee bob on the sordenu's chin. "It means you're now a man, Butu. That's why you're here — to learn what that means."

"I thought it means I'm going to be a sordenu," Butu said dryly, and another sordenu walking past barked a laugh and stopped behind Butu, leaning on his wooden practice sword like a cane.

Butu shifted so he partially faced the new man. He looked to be Zhek's age but seemed much older, somehow. He had a pebble in his mouth, which he rolled back and forth. Dust and sweat covered his skin, making it lighter than it actually was.

"New recruit?" he asked, nostrils flaring.

Butu nodded.

"You don't look a day over twelve." To Blay, "You sure he's fallen already?"

"He wouldn't be here otherwise, Karp."

Karp moved like a sand adder, but Butu was faster. The practice sword was a cane one moment, and the next, three quick swings would have gutted, hamstrung and decapitated him. But Butu dodged, spun and leaned sideways without thinking about it.

He glared at Karp, who grinned back at him, leaning on the sword again. Butu took a few steps away from him, wondering if it he should take the practice sword away and show this sordenu how to use it.

He wouldn't be able to dodge me.

Blay looked about ready to draw his real sword against the nonchalant Karp.

"Leave him alone," he said, instead, voice cold but trembling. "You know the punishment for an unprovoked assault on another sordenu."

The pebble made a few circuits around Karp's mouth. "I know it's not as bad as the punishment for what he just did." He raised his sword and took a defensive stance. "Do you intend to report me to the sarge?"

What did I do? Butu was more confused than angry.

The tremble did not leave Blay. "Not this time. I haven't had a chance to talk to him yet, so he doesn't know. You and I, Karp, will talk later."

"Right you are, corp," Karp growled. He flipped the practice sword onto his shoulder with a flourish and disappeared behind the tent, leaving one more parting shot, "Make sure I'm not there the first time he's caught."

CHAPTER 6

"I'd like to see him try that when I have a sword," Butu growled when the other sordenu was out of earshot.

"You'll have your chance soon enough, but it won't be as easy as you expect. You see how he moves? Karp could cut you faster than the wind even with his back to you, and he could do it in the dark."

"I can move faster."

Blay sighed and straightened, looking around. Most of the sordenu were at the mess tent. "Not for long," he said.

"What's that supposed to mean?"

"It means that next time Karp or another sordenu swings a practice blade at you, let him hit you."

"I thought the point of fighting was not to get hurt."

"That will come later. It will all make sense later. Let's get you to the sergeant."

Butu jogged to catch up, hefting his small pack.

"There are two day watches and two night watches," Blay explained as they walked. "Karp's a midnight sentry, the second of the night watches. He stays up after his shift to spar with some of the veteran sordenu — who rarely take a watch. Most of his shift sleep from dawn to early afternoon and train then."

They passed an attractive but tired-looking woman.

"And Tesa will take the second day shift today," Blay said, goading her with excessive cheerfulness. Her salute included a rude gesture. "She also had the first night shift last night," he confided to Butu.

"How many sordenu women are there?" Butu asked.

"Very few, but it's discouraged. And if you're in the same platoon, it's against the rules."

That hadn't been what Butu had meant, but he couldn't help asking. "Why?"

"It's complicated, but it'll make more sense later. For now, just don't," Blay said in severe tones. He brightened. "Anyway, as I was saying about watches, in the field, watches are different. We're all on watch by day, really, but we have three night watches. Field sentries change from night to night, because even the night sentries have to travel all day. On the march, you usually get good sleep two or three nights out of four. On the other nights or when you're traveling in groups smaller than a company, you sleep a lot less."

"Keep the watch, the watch all night," Butu chanted, quietly, because the childhood rhyme seemed more useful now. "We'll keep the watch, so all be right. Watch all night, the watch we'll keep. We'll keep the watch, through all night's sleep."

"Yeah," Blay said. "Used to do that when I was a kid, too."

"We could stay up all night, waiting on the moons."

"We'd look for when our fathers got home from the Zhekara Contest, the hundred-day war." Blay turned westward, and Butu watched his goatee work his jaw. "My foster father came back, at least. Many didn't." He sighed and looked back at Butu. "Not anymore, though."

"Why not?"

Blay shrugged. "It's not allowed. Besides, I'm in my fifth cycle. It won't work for me."

"Why not?" *Magic wouldn't work for him? You don't have to think about it,* Butu wanted to say, *it just happens!* Then he thought, *but I fell, twice, yesterday. And he asked me if I've fallen. What was the word? Mirjuva.* "Blay, what does mirjuva mean?"

Blay nodded, as if he had expected the question. "Another time. Here comes the sergeant." Blay pointed at the mess tent, at a precisely pressed man striding toward them with two others following him. "His name's Aeklan el'Ahjea, but you'll call him 'sir.' When he gets a little closer, we'll both salute. Don't talk unless he asks you a question, and whatever you do, don't argue with him. He's been at this several times longer than I've been alive."

The sergeant was even older than Pater — twenty cycles, at least. Most of the sordenu shaved their heads, but he had let his hair grow just enough for the gray to show.

Blay saluted, and Butu followed his lead awkwardly, not quite managing to imitate the sharp posture the sordenu adopted. Aeklan saluted back.

"At ease," he said in a gruff voice.

Blay lowered his hand and relaxed his stance. Butu tried to mimic him.

"Is this one of the new recruits?"

"Yes, sir!"

Aeklan looked down at Butu. "What is your name, boy?"

"Butu tem Ahjea, sir," he said, proud he had not forgotten the "sir."

"You're too young," Aeklan pronounced severely. "And you're too small." A pause as the sergeant looked him up and down. "You're also out of uniform."

"Um, I'm sorry, sir," Butu stammered, saluting again in hopes of making up for it. The sergeant grunted.

"I will remedy that immediately, sir," Blay said.

Aeklan's critical glare examined Blay. "You do that, corporal. I would hate to be forced to tell Captain Philbe that his faith in you is misguided."

"Yes, sir!" Blay said, snapping a salute.

Butu mimicked him, and Aeklan saluted back.

"Report to the armory when you have a uniform, recruit."

Butu grinned in spite of himself, but Aeklan's permanent frown turned into a scowl.

"What do you think this is, recruit?" he barked, leaning forward, spittle raining on Butu's face. The boy cringed. "Stand up like a man, boy! You will be a sordenu, you water-starved camel, not some fool performer! Wipe that smirk off you face, or I'll make you think falling down was the best thing that ever happened to you!"

Butu struggled to hold his pose during the tirade, terrified and unsure what to do. But as the sergeant drew to a close, his hand snapped up and he echoed Blay perfectly.

"Yes, sir!"

Once he was sure Aeklan was out of earshot, Butu turned to Blay, even more sullen than after Karp had tried to smack him. "I don't think reporting to the armory means I'll be getting a sword today."

Blay chuckled. "No. It means you're polishing some."

Butu screwed up his face for a moment before he realized what Blay meant. "I'm being given a job to do?"

"Punishment duty," Blay corrected as he led Butu toward the barracks. "For being out of uniform."

"But I haven't been given a uniform, yet," Butu objected.

"It doesn't matter. Ignorance is no excuse among the sordenu."

"Why didn't you warn me?" Butu asked bitterly. "Why didn't you take me to get a uniform before taking me to the sergeant?"

Blay shrugged. "The quartermaster was at breakfast, and no one else can assign you a uniform."

"But that's not fair." *And why haven't we had breakfast, either?*

"Nope."

"So why am I still being punished?"

"Nothing really makes sense for the first couple months after your fall, but I promise you'll understand soon."

"Does everyone know about my mirjuva?" Butu asked sullenly.

Blay shook his head. "Falling down is the most common form mirjuva takes. It's so common that a lot of people simply say 'fall' instead of 'experience of mirjuva.' As someone whose fall was a fall, I can assure you that your experience of mirjuva is not unusual."

"Oh," Butu said, feeling slightly better.

"Now, to find you a uniform."

"Better late than never."

"Be a man, recruit," Blay said sternly.

Butu stiffened. He sounded too much like Aeklan. They stopped outside the supply tent. The flap of the tent was down, and rather than open it for Butu, Blay motioned him to stop.

"Zhepal will fit you for your standard kit." Blay's head swiveled to and fro, searching. "He's very organized, and you'll never want for any necessities in a camp where he's quartermaster." His voice lowered. "That is, if you can ever find him. Ah. There he is."

A man who seemed all arms and legs emerged from the mess hall and jogged toward them, stuffing a piece of bread in his mouth. A large leather knapsack was slung across his back, its straps loaded with pockets down the front. The quartermaster sized up Butu with an expert eye, which Butu's gaze clung to even after he had returned Blay's salute. Zhepal's eyes were like two runny eggs. Butu wanted to poke one.

"Sir," Blay said, "this is Butu. He's ..."

"Another new recruit." Zhepal swallowed his bread. His tone was cheerful, but his face remained flat. "I'll fit him for uniform and kit and teach him the rules."

"Meet me in the mess once you've finished stowing your gear," Blay said to Butu. "We'll at least get you some food before sending you to Kira."

Butu saluted. "Yes, sir!"

Blay grinned like he had been waiting his whole life for this before jogging away.

CHAPTER 7

Zhepal ducked into the square tent, which was barely taller than he was, and Butu followed him. Inside were several trunks. The quartermaster grabbed a long piece of string with knots along its length at regular intervals. He spoke no more than a few curt words as he took the boy's measurements. A moment's search in one trunk produced a pile of cloth that he tossed to Butu.

"Try those on. Do you know how to tailor?"

"There's holes and fraying seams and tears. We'll patch and sew and make repairs," Butu said, repeating the chant as he pulled the sand-colored shirt over his head. It was too large, but they probably expected him to grow into it. The shirt felt rough and uncomfortable against skin not used to wearing shirts.

It could just be the cloth, though.

"A simple 'no' will suffice, if you can't do it without magic," Zhepal said. "As small as you are, you'll learn quickly enough once you start outgrowing your clothes every few months."

"What does it matter if I can't do it without magic if I can do it with magic?" The pants were better, though the legs were too long and too tight, restricting his movement somewhat. He made two thick, deep cuffs.

Zhepal's snort made him wince.

"I'm going to lay down a few rules for you right now, recruit. One. You don't question anyone of higher rank, and you especially don't question the sarge. If you do or say anything Sergeant Aeklan doesn't like, it will be bad for you. Polishing equipment is the kindest punishment he will assign." His watery eyes puckered.

"How am I supposed to learn anything if I can't ask questions?" Butu wrapped the belt around his waist, staring at the socks and boots they wanted him to wear. He had never worn shoes before. "It's not as though I know anything about where anything is, or how it's run."

The quartermaster wiped the bridge of his nose. "The first time you're given an order, it'll be made clear to you who, what, when, and how it is to be done. The next time, you'll be expected to know how to obey." He produced a pebble and lodged it in his mouth. "Two. When you're given an order, you will perform it right away, and as fast as you can. You will do it faster if the sarge gives an order to you."

Butu grinned up at Zhepal as he was pulling on the boots, which, amazingly, fit perfectly. "Don't worry about that. I'm very fast."

The quartermaster frowned back. "Three. No magic in the camp." A pause. "Or anywhere else, for that matter. Sordenu don't use magic. It will be easier for you later on if you learn not to rely on it now."

What? Butu wanted to ask but he kept silent, for now. The quartermaster wasn't the one to ask. Zhepal went to the largest of the trunks. With a grunt, he pulled out a large, bulging canvas sack. Whump! He dropped it at Butu's feet.

"Your kit," he announced, waving his hand dramatically over it. "Bedding, eating utensils, canteen, ration box, sewing kit, grooming supplies, and strips of cloth for pryuds, bandages, and so on."

"When do I get a sword?"

"When you're ready for one, which is whenever the sarge says you are." He adjusted his own pack. "No more questions, or you'll learn what happens if you disobey orders. Take that to barracks four, and then get some food. Blay's expecting you."

"Yes, sir!" Butu said, and pulled at the bag, which shifted slightly. Zhepal snorted, dropping the tent flap as he left. Butu managed to drag the bag out of the supply tent in one good heave. He tried to ignore the stares and comments of the sordenu who noticed his struggles as he tried to get to the barracks.

Suddenly, someone lifted the bag from his hands, almost pulling Butu up with him.

"First day?"

Butu looked up at the man who had taken pity on him. The sordenu was probably less than a cycle older than him, but he was more than a foot taller, with thick arms that held the pack like a sack of marbles. His skin wasn't so much brown as a very dark red.

"Um, yeah." Butu had to jog to keep pace.

"Barracks four, then. What's your name, kid?" he asked. Usually, Butu hated it when adults called him "kid" or "boy," but something about this man's disarming tone made it inoffensive.

"Butu tem Ahjea," Butu said. "Sir," he added, just in case.

"None of that. Name's Tirud ku Ahjea, but call me Tirud. I'd stick to calling yourself Butu. Everyone here belongs to the same clan, and most of us sordenu are tems or kus. Here you are. Upper bunk okay?"

"Uh, sure."

Tirud set the sack down on the upper bunk, and Butu put his personal knapsack next to it with a jingle.

Tirud reached into the small pack and removed the pouch of coins, which he tossed to Butu. "Better keep that with you. We punish thieves harshly when we catch them, but only when we catch them." He held out one calloused hand, and Butu took it. "See you around, kid."

"Nice meeting you, Tirud."

Worried about missing breakfast, he ran to the mess, dodging the working sordenu. He ran to the table where cooks served with ladles from big iron pots. He grabbed a ceramic bowl from a stack nearby and held it out. He saw one of the cooks sneer, but they all ignored him.

"Am I too late for breakfast?" Butu asked, stomach rumbling.

One of the cooks gave a smile missing a couple of teeth. "Oh, no. Not at all. But you don't want any of this." He lifted up the ladle and poured a mix of gruel and ham back into the pot. "I got just the thing for you."

One of the other cooks snickered and walked through a gap in the canvas. Butu felt him rummage through some crates. He returned a moment later with a waterskin, which he handed to the first cook. The first cook removed the stopper and poured white liquid into something behind the table. A moment later, he showed off a skin with a leather nipple on the top.

"Here you are, little one. Still want breakfast?"

Several other sordenu made cooing sounds and babbled at him like he was an infant.

"You're not the brightest recruit, are you, little one?" one with an eyepatch said.

Butu scowled at him without thinking about it and took the bottle. He pulled the nipple off and drank from it.

"No magic in the camp," the sordenu with the eyepatch said severely.

"What do you mean? I haven't used any yet."

"You did when you ran over here. You ran too fast."

Butu stared back the way he had come. Everything from the whole morning rose in him right now. *It's all so unfair. I don't know anything and no one tells me anything, either.* "That was just running! I didn't want to miss breakfast."

"Next time, miss breakfast." This from the first cook, who snatched the skin back.

Butu opened his mouth to shout curses at them all. *I can't just kick sand on it! I may as well count all the grains of sand in Pophir!*

"Come here, Butu." It was Blay, in a calm voice that quieted everyone. Butu stared wildly about, clutching nervous palms. He stepped around eyepatch and sat down, tensely, with Blay.

"Don't take it personally," Blay said, sliding his bowl toward Butu. "Here. You can have the rest of mine."

Butu watched the gruel. "Do they do this to all the new recruits?"

"Only the ones who use magic in full view of the other sordenu."

"I didn't try to use magic. It just happened. That's what magic does. It's not my fault! It seems stupid to ban it anyway."

"I know it's hard to understand it right now, but there's a reason for every rule we have. The Treaty of Mnemon says no clan may use magic in war, so if you're going to be a sordenu, you have to learn not to use magic to fight."

"Why would anyone want a treaty that forbids magic? It

makes no sense!"

Blay's features softened at Butu's outburst. "A blood priest should be telling you this, not me."

Butu stared hard into the sordenu's eyes. "Tell me what?"

Blay stared right back, face hardening. "It's going to go away, Butu. You might have a talent or two that stays with you, but the real reason adults don't use magic is because they can't. In a few weeks, you won't be able to, either."

"The blood priests ..." Butu started, and Blay shook his head.

"Hours of chanting, long rituals, special tools, strict limitations — it's not the same magic as children have. If you learn to live without magic, it will be easier for you to cope when your magic fades away forever."

Butu stood up and turned away to hide the shock on his face.

"I'm sorry," Blay called as Butu left the mess hall without responding.

CHAPTER 8

"You're here to polish equipment?" said a woman's voice.

"Yeah."

It was darker in here than in the desert light, but Butu could feel everything in the tent around him even before his eyes adjusted — the racks of swords and other weapons, piles of armor and boots, and the slim woman in sordenu garb. A flap on each shoulder of her uniform was buttoned back to reveal two square, brass studs.

"It's yes, sir, not yeah," she said, pointing at one of the studs, but it sounded rote, not an attack. "What's your name?"

"Butu, sir."

"Better." She smiled slightly. It didn't make her pretty, but it did soften her face. It was the third-most-friendly face he had seen this morning, "I'm Corporal Kira."

She threw a stained cloth at him, and he snatched it from the air, wincing at the smell.

"Well? You do know armor, right?"

"Yes, sir." *Saying "sir" gets easier the more you do it.* "I've polished swords and mended armor. They like the kids to do that."

"Then start on that pile over there." She pointed to a stack of boiled leather breastplates. "Get to work." There was neither malice nor sympathy in her voice.

It's terrible when the people you consider friendly are simply the ones who don't hurt you, he thought as he hefted the first breastplate and got to work, humming the polishing chant. When Kira slapped him on the back with the flat of the blade, he let it hit him. It stung, but not as much as his first fall had. Butu stopped polishing, and looked at Kira in mild amusement.

"No magic," she said, waving the sword at him. "You have to learn to do these things without magic."

He frowned at the armor. "I only know how to do it using magic."

"Are you going to be useless?" Kira barked harshly. "Are you going to waste my time? Magic is the crutch of the child. Magic is the guardian of the infant. Are you an infant, recruit? Do you want me to send for a wet nurse?" Her tone waxed sarcastic.

Butu kept his mouth shut, staring at her until she settled back from him. The cloth moved restlessly across the leather, oiling it smooth. He knew how to polish without using magic. It was a long and boring process.

The armor weighted down his knees accusingly, and he rubbed harder at it, as though everything today was its fault.

He got slapped again.

"Not so hard. You don't want to wear a hole in it."

I'll bet they can't use magic because they stop practicing it, he thought. *Or maybe they think about it too much.*

When he fell the second time, he had thought about falling. He had known, somewhere, that what he was doing wasn't natural. It was something he didn't usually think about. And thinking back to the first time — he had noticed how the tent roof didn't sag beneath his feet, and knew it should.

So, if I don't think about why what I'm doing works, ever, I'll be able to keep using it.

He got slapped again. "No magic."

Butu put down the breastplate and picked up another one. Kira picked it up to examine it.

"May as well tell me to stop breathing," he muttered, and the boiled leather came down on his head.

"Watch your attitude." She tossed the armor back on the pile. "And do that one again. It's scuffed."

Butu's anger flared, and he dropped the armor and polishing cloth and stood up. Standing, he came up to her breasts. She met his fiery stare with a calm one. The boy stood with fists clenched, unarmed against this woman with a sword.

"I was here for an hour," he vented. "Zhepal wasn't around.

Then the sergeant saw me out of uniform and punished me. Does everyone get treated like camel turds when they show up?" He stood there, breathing hard, waiting for her response.

"Are you done?" Her expression did not change. "I don't care why you are here, recruit. You will follow orders from a superior. You will learn what you can and cannot do. And as your superior, I can extend your punishment for insubordination." She gestured to the armor with the sword. "Work. That is an order, recruit."

She didn't raise her voice, but Butu suddenly understood something he felt was very important. He sat down and began polishing again.

If I'm going to learn anything, he thought, *and I can't ask questions, I'm going to have to watch what other people are doing.* And another thing, "I'm going to have to learn to see."

"Quiet." But no sword came down, and he glanced at her, reappraising him.

After a few minutes of polishing, he felt her draw nearer. "Jusep sends them over with that lesson to learn: You have to learn to see."

He stopped and looked up at her.

She shrugged. "Here's another lesson for you, Butu. If you want to use magic, go right ahead." She nodded as his jaw dropped. "It doesn't matter to me if you polish five breastplates or all of them. You're going to be here all day, either way." He closed his mouth, but she went on, voice as supple as the armor on his lap. "And if you use magic to polish faster, you'll be here tomorrow, too. And the next day, and the next — until you can go a single day polishing without using magic to help you. There's always plenty to polish, and if you polish everything in the armory, sarge'll just find another tedious job for you to do."

Kira smiled coolly, turned her head and spat expertly at his most recently finished armor. "You're better off just doing what you're told and doing it without magic like all the other adults. Are you a man or a boy?"

Butu picked up the piece and scrubbed at the spit, but his anger at the adults he had met today ebbed. No one had tried to hurt him, really. They had just tried to warn him, in brutal fashion. The same way Kira was. He just had to learn to see. And, in the meantime, he would consciously practice ...

"No magic."

He met her eyes and smiled, earning a grimace in return. *This must be why adults can't use magic. The ones who can't use magic anymore force the kids not use magic until they forget how to do it. I'm going to remember, though. If I'm going to prove myself worthy of blood adoption, I'll need every advantage I can get.*

Soon enough he was sweating in the hot tent, and still had a small pile near him. The air reeked of polish. Two sordenu who looked no older than him came in, looking sheepish.

"Phedam. Nolen. Welcome back," Kira greeted them with the sort of friendly air that could only be sarcasm. "The swords have barely had time to miss you. Phedam, you'll do the shields. Nolen, the swords could use more of your attention."

The two young men said nothing as they sat down to polish equipment. Less than a minute later, there was a slap of steel on cloth as Kira swatted the slightly larger one, Nolen, with her sword.

"No magic."

Butu winced, but felt elated. *I'm not the only one!*

"Yes, sir!" Nolen shouted back with exaggerated compliance.

"Don't mock me, or I'll send you to muck out the camel stalls."

"Yes, sir." Almost contrite.

Butu grinned slightly, and Phedam smirked into the shield on his lap. After a second, the newcomer met Butu's eyes and the grin was shared.

"What did you two do?" he whispered timidly.

Kira hit him with the flat of the sword again. "No talking."

Butu turned his attention back to the boiled leather. It was difficult to focus on such a mindless task, but every time his mind wandered, Kira hit him for using magic.

She could not watch all three at once, though, and as the punishment passed, they made a game of making faces at each other behind Kira's back. One of Butu's made Phedam laugh right after Kira had smacked him with the sword, earning him a double-whacking. The face he shot back at them after the second hit forced them both to stifle laughter and pretend to be extremely interested in polishing.

CHAPTER 9

Kira suddenly stood, sheathing her sword.

"Keep working," she ordered when they all stopped. "It's time for lunch. The tent'll be watched, so don't even think about sneaking out. If I have reason to believe you used magic while I was gone, you'll be back tomorrow." She vanished through the tent flap.

They looked at each other in silence, waiting to be sure she was out of earshot before saying anything. Butu felt her leave, and nodded once. The other two stared at him, then Phedam let out an explosive breath and checked himself for bruises.

Nolen spoke first. "I thought she'd never leave. What's your name?"

"Butu. How long've you been here?"

"Three days." Phedam smirked. "We've spent two of them in here."

"We just can't seem to stop using magic. It's such a terrible thing, don't you think?" Nolen asked, dripping sarcasm. "We're from Pophir. How about yourself?"

"Jasper."

"So you're a tem," Phedam declared. Butu's eyes widened. "We're both tems, too. It's rare for boys our age to be kus, yet, or so I've heard."

"I suppose so." It made sense. A ku had to be old enough to desert his birth clan and convince another clan to adopt him.

"Your crime the same as ours, I take it?" Nolen asked. His voice was slightly deeper than Phedam's, too.

"I was out of uniform."

"That's a no, then."

"Using magic got you here?" Butu asked.

Nolen nodded and then smirked. It seemed to be his natural expression. "Plus, I asked Zhepal too many questions. Like why won't they let us use magic."

"Zhepal told us that we'll lose our magic as we get older," Phedam said, picking up another shield and polishing it too quickly.

"Do you believe him?"

"No," Nolen snorted at the same time Phedam said, "I don't know."

"I don't, either," Butu said. He stared at the breastplate on his knees, and Nolen drawing wavy patterns on his sword. He picked up his rag and concentrated on not using magic to clean the leather. "I think they want us to forget how to use magic so they can control us better."

"It's the treaty, I think," Phedam said. "After Mnemon unmade the last king, all the clans agreed to stop using magic in war. Everyone else is bound to attack anyone who breaks the treaty."

They sat in silence for a few seconds, thinking about that.

How great would the Ahjea sordenu be if they could use magic in battle? Butu thought. *If the Ahjea had had magic when the Kadrak had betrayed them, the Ahjea would rule Mnemon. Except the Kadrak would've had magic, too. You can only do it once. Well, you can do it for a generation, because it would take that long to train an army that could use magic. After that, war would change forever. Maybe there could be a way to end wars.*

"I'm never going to stop using magic," Butu told them. It felt good to say it out loud, even to people he had only known for a few hours.

"You'd better get used to polishing for Kira, then," Nolen said with an angry swipe of his cloth.

"There's got to be a way to practice magic when no one is watching," Butu said.

"They watch us pretty closely." Phedam sounded dubious. "But they can't be..."

They stopped talking as all of them felt Kira returning. Butu focused on sullenly and slowly polishing the breastplate. Kira entered the tent with a tray. The smell she brought with her made their mouths water. She set it down on the low table near the back of the room.

"Come eat," she said, smiling coolly. "Quickly, now. There's still lots to polish."

It was nothing remarkable — a large loaf of fresh bread and a pot of bland barley porridge — but all three of them were glad for the food. They ate it in silence, and it disappeared as if by magic.

"Back to work," Kira ordered when she had heard the last gulp.

The rest of the afternoon moved in a lazy haze of polish followed by occasional swats from Kira's sword. Butu's thoughts wandered all over the desert, and so Kira's order to stop surprised him.

"That's enough," she said, standing up. "Get out. I don't want to see you three again."

Butu followed Nolen and Phedam outside. He was the shortest of them, by almost half a hand. And darker, by half the night.

"Which barracks you in, Butu?" Nolen asked.

"Four."

"Same here," Nolen said. "My bunkmate snores."

"So do you!" Phedam objected.

"Yeah, but you snore louder."

Butu chuckled. "Do you think there's any chance we're in the same squad?"

Phedam shook his head. "After the initial training, new sordenu join existing squads. They'll do some shuffling of the ranks to make room for us. It has to do with making sure we're surrounded by sordenu who can teach us as we go."

"And who can make sure we don't use magic," Nolen muttered.

"You meet Corporal Blay, yet?" Butu asked.

Nolen nodded. "He brought us to Kira's tent the day we arrived after we showed up some of the veteran sordenu on the obstacle course. Sarge caught us and had Blay bring us."

"Meet any other recruits?"

"Retus and Lujo gave us a little tour our first day," Nolen said. "They've been here a bit longer."

They reached the mess hall. Sordenu waited in long lines for the evening meal. From their place at the back of the line, Butu couldn't even see what they were going to be eating.

"So, have you two started training with a sword, yet?" he asked hopefully.

Nolen made a dismissive sound.

"It could be months before that happens," Phedam said. "From what I've heard, they'll drill us for a couple months. It'll be really harsh, but it's meant to teach us to obey orders. We won't get swords until they're ready to assign us to a squad."

"Our foster father comes from a long line of sordenu, and all three of his sons are sordenu, now," Nolen added. "Phedam was much better at getting them to talk about the training."

"Which is why I almost stayed a farmer, no matter what General Pater thinks of my potential," Phedam said with a smirk. "But if you're going to endure countless indignities on your path to becoming a sordenu, I mean to be there to see it."

"So, training and polishing, that's it?"

"And pranks," Nolen said with a conspiratory wink.

"Yeah, but pranks get you punishment duty," Phedam reminded him.

"That's certainly why Retus and Lujo spent the day in the armory yesterday," Nolen said. "It wasn't a flattering sculpture, but Lujo got Zhepal's eyes exactly right, don't you think?"

Phedam snickered. "Yeah."

"They weren't punished for their prank," a pimply sordenu in line behind them said. They all turned to him. Irritation flashed on Nolen's face. "They were punished for using magic to do it. And if you get caught using magic, you'll be punished even worse. That's the way it works. The armory is just a warning."

"We heard about the treaty," Butu said, trying to head him off.

"Yeah?" The sordenu on their other side had noticed them. His face seemed to be mostly jaw. "Well, the treaty don't say how you're supposed to stop using magic." He spat a pebble from his mouth to his hand. "Your whole squad gets punished for it. If you keep using magic, your whole platoon gets punished."

"There's not that much armor," Nolen muttered.

"It'd never get that far," the pimply sordenu said. "The reason being, after your first warning, your whole squad'll be against you. Getting caught by your officer is the best thing that can happen to you."

Butu felt queasy. *So if the squad catches me …*

"And one of us *will* catch you before your officer does," the sordenu with the jutting jaw growled. "So quit it now, kiddies."

"Yes, sir," Phedam said drily.

Butu grinned mildly. This morning, he would've beaten the pants off both of those sordenu if they had talked down to him like that. Now, he knew more than when he started.

Kira's punishment worked, he thought, and knew then he'd never go back.

CHAPTER 10

"Have you moved on to solid foods?" the gap-toothed cook asked Butu, who picked at his teeth self-consciously. The cook grinned and handed him a plate piled with mutton.

"That's Retus and Lujo over there." Nolen pointed with his chin at a table where three men sat. One of them looked up and waved them over, one seemed to be talking, and the third one Butu recognized.

"Next to Karp?" He couldn't keep the bitterness from his voice.

"Who?" Nolen asked, leading them to the table.

"Just some phutra I met this morning. Attacked me for no good reason."

Butu looked around and spotted Blay and Tirud together. He thought to go sit over there, but they sat with the sordenu with the jutting jaw. The conversation there looked less than friendly, and Blay's frown only grew when the pimply sordenu joined them. Butu knew no one else here, and though he would meet many of the other sordenu in the coming months, today he wanted to be with people he already knew.

He placed his plate down across from Karp, who looked up and, to Butu's surprise, smiled genuinely, showing off yellowed teeth.

"Hello, again. No hard feelings, right? I was just giving Blay a hard time. I've no quarrel with you."

Butu was not convinced. "Right. You meant to hurt Blay, instead."

Karp snorted and leaned over. "I was just telling your boys

here. Blay fancies himself a born leader. He'd do anything to move up in rank — and don't think he hasn't tried a couple things that didn't work — which is why so many sordenu aren't too fond of him."

Butu kept his mouth shut. *And you're one of them*, he thought. He looked over his shoulder at Blay, who had his head down while Tirud said something.

"Two cycles he's been at it, but he always gets turned down by the higher-ups," Karp went on. "Now he's suddenly a corporal?" He snorted again. "Myself, if I was in his squad, I'd be mighty curious to know what kind of deal he made." Karp stood up and stretched. He spoke a bit more loudly. "Anyway, I wish all of you the best of luck in the sordenu. One final word of advice. Before you use magic, think long and hard about what you are doing."

"He doesn't seem so bad," Nolen said once Karp was out of earshot.

"I'm not so sure," Butu said. *Exactly what should I see in him?* "So, which of you is Lujo and which is Retus?"

Retus had lived his life among the roving shepherds in the foothills of the mountains. He was taller than Butu by a couple inches but was still short for his age. He spoke very little during dinner, and when he did, his voice cracked as often as not.

Lujo came from Kruk — one of the mining towns north of Jasper. He was taller than all of them and wore a small silver earring in his right ear. While not quite as talkative as Nolen, he was much more open than any of them, eager to insert a story into every conversation.

Nolen and Phedam were not related by blood, but they were almost exactly the same height and shared enough facial features to pass for fraternal twins.

"We've been shumi since we got to Pophir," Nolen said seriously, and Phedam nodded. "So when Phedam's mirjuva happened, about a week before mine, he was all set to go work in the fields."

"Too many bad stories about the mines," Phedam said, staring off at nothing.

"I said, hey, let's be sordenu! Training and fighting and protecting and all is gonna be more fun than planting grain."

Retus and Lujo looked uncomfortably at their empty plates, and Phedam and Nolen met each other's eyes.

"Yeah," Phedam said, into the sudden silence.

"I want to know," Nolen said, somewhat defiantly. "It had to be pretty much the same for everyone, right?"

The subject was their mirjuva, and an awkward silence fell over the table. No one's head had turned when magic was brought up, but the mess hall wasn't the place.

"Maybe we should talk about this somewhere else," Butu said. Retus nodded fervently, and Lujo tugged his earring thoughtfully. Nolen and Phedam stood as one, dropping off their plates and leaving. The other three followed. The cooks grinned wolfishly at the boys as they walked by, and the gap-toothed one winked at Butu.

"Where to?" Nolen asked. They looked at Butu, who shrugged.

"The armory will be empty," he said.

"And sealed and guarded," Lujo said with an annoyed edge to his voice.

"Sure," Butu said, "but it backs up against the half of the mess where they store the carts. No one will come close enough to hear or see us."

Nolen and Phedam grinned at Lujo's stricken expression. He recovered quickly, though, and started into a story in which he won a horseless-cart race down a mountain with only two wheels working. They laughed quietly with him, walking and talking like any other group of sordenu.

The spot Butu picked was perfect — carts came through here regularly, so the ground was firm gravel interspersed with a few brown, smashed weeds. They couldn't see the rest of Gordney here.

Retus flicked a scorpion away from him as they stood uncomfortably in a circle.

"We've got about an hour before lights out," Phedam commented.

They murmured understanding, but the silence returned. Butu had the sense everyone was waiting for someone else to say something, first.

Nolen let out a long sigh, and everyone focused on him.

"I fell," he started. "Well, slipped, more like. Broke two bones in my left arm." He held up his arm to show them, even though it was completely uninjured, now. "It...it hurt. A lot. They had to put a splint on it. It kept the arm from bending in the wrong place, but it didn't stop the pain. I cried for all three hours it took for the bones to mend. It still hurt a little the next morning when my foster father told me I couldn't stay in Pophir."

He nodded, looking slightly relieved. Everyone else did, too. Butu began to feel more comfortable. He couldn't sense anyone near their group. Nolen pushed Phedam forward, and Lujo rocked on his heels a bit, looking more confident.

"I fell, too." Phedam spoke next. "Not nearly as bad, though. I had stolen an orange from Basper's fruit stand and was letting him chase me so the other kids could steal more of his fruit. I really don't know why Basper bothers chasing kids, but he always does."

"And it always costs him a lot more of his fruit, in the end," Nolen interrupted.

"It's my story, shumi." But Phedam grinned. "I wasn't even going very fast, because I didn't want to lose him too soon. Then, somehow, I tripped over a tent rope and fell flat on my face. It hurt, and Basper caught me while I was too stunned to get up and run. Instead of carrying out all the threats he always makes when he's chasing kids, he laughed and told me I could keep the orange. The next day ..." He trailed off.

"If it wasn't for me, he'd be in the fields." Nolen smiled at his friend, and Butu felt a stab at the warmth there. It made him think of Paka.

CHAPTER 11

Butu's eyes met Lujo's, but neither of them spoke.

"When it happened, I was helping the other shepherds find water in the mountains."

Butu jumped at Retus' words. The quiet boy smiled apologetically and went on.

"I was sure there was a big spring in a certain place, but they dug and dug and ..." His voice cracked. "After that, Dad told me I could take twelve of his sheep to start my own flock, because I was a man, now. I asked him if I could join the sordenu, instead." He sounded embarrassed. "I've always wanted to do something exciting — maybe just for a cycle or two, not for the rest of my life. I could tell he didn't want me to do that. I thought for sure he'd say no, but he didn't. Instead, he shook my hand and told me ..." He paused, taking a deep breath. Butu patted him on the back.

I wish I had had a father to love me like that.

"He told me that if I ever change my mind and come back, he'd give me a flock then." Retus wiped his nose and put on a brave face.

"You're not a tem," Nolen said.

Retus shook his head. "I'm an un', but my family's not rich."

Butu felt a small stab of jealousy. *He's here because he wants to be. He had a choice.* Lujo looked annoyed.

"I'm an un', too, but my mother was the daughter of an el'Ahjea," Lujo boasted. "If she hadn't married an orphan against her father's wishes, I'd be an el', too."

"How did your mirjuva happen?" Butu asked with a bit of venom in his voice. Their eyes locked again. Nolen and Phedam rolled their eyes.

"You first," Lujo said suddenly.

"Fine." Butu didn't want to fight him. *He'll only exaggerate his story, let him have the last say.* "I fell off a rooftop. It was a race around Jasper. General Pater el'Ahjea told Jusep that I had potential. I once bested the kluntra's son in a sword fight, you see." *Two can play the story game!* He felt his face flush as Nolen sighed.

"How about you, Lujo?" Phedam asked.

Lujo adopted a dramatic tone of voice and raised an arm.

"About a month ago, the foreman had me exploring a cave. It looked natural enough at the entrance..." He put so much emphasis on "looked" everyone leaned in closer. "...But some rock formations a few hundred feet in seemed to've been shaped by magic. It looked like I might find something even more amazing than the tomb of the ancient kluntra." He frowned when Butu groaned. "When I found a labyrinth built of some strange silvery metal, I knew I was right."

He met each of their eyes in turn. "I could just dig through the walls, right, who can't? But there's something about a maze that begs to be solved! This one was tricky. I'm pretty sure the walls moved around just to confuse me. I grew hungry, tired and thirsty, but persevered. Finally, I reached the center — a large courtyard with a silver fountain in the middle. I suddenly realized how thirsty I was. As I approached the fountain, a golem made of the same silvery metal as the labyrinth rose from the floor to block my path. Then a girl who looked to be five or six years old stepped out from behind the fountain. 'Who are you?' I asked. She answered, in a voice as cool as the water behind her, 'Pophira al'Ahjea.'"

He paused, looking to see if the name meant anything to anyone. Butu couldn't help but be as fascinated as the rest. Nodding, Lujo went on.

"I didn't know Jusep had any daughers named Pophira, so this confused me! 'Who's your father?' I asked her. She answered, 'Makhad al'Ahjea.'"

All his listeners burst out laughing. Makhad al'Ahjea had been the last Ahjea to be made King of Turuna — more than two hundred cycles ago.

Lujo took their reaction in stride. "Fine, fine. You don't have to believe she was Makhad's lost daughter. I wasn't so sure myself, at the time, but you understand why I didn't run over to get a drink of water from that fountain, either. It was obviously a mira-man that kept her from getting any older but made her forget to leave."

A bell rang from the direction of the barracks.

"Lights out," Phedam hissed. "We should go."

Nolen waved off his friend. "We can sneak back after Lujo finishes."

Phedam and Retus looked toward the barracks but said nothing.

"So you just left her there?" Nolen asked with a snort.

Lujo grinned. "I asked her, right, if she was angry with her parents! She shook her head with a smile. 'Not anymore. I'm just going to get a drink, and then I'll go home.' I wanted to stop her, but I knew I was no match for her guardian golem. As she finished drinking from the fountain, she looked up at me like she was surprised I was there. 'Who are you?' she asked, as if we had not been talking. I told her. 'Are you thirsty?' she asked. I shook my head instead of lying. 'Are you sure?' she asked. 'There's plenty. 'Yes,' I told her. 'I think I'm going to go home. My family probably misses me,' I said by way of excuse. Then I walked into the labyrinth and left her there."

He threw his hands up in disgust. "Unless someone destroys the fountain, she'll always be there. I didn't think of it at the time, but anyone who marries her will have a stronger claim on the clan leadership than Jusep does. Maybe in a year or two, I'll go back down there and rescue her."

He crossed his arms, daring them to challenge his story.

"And your mirjuva?" Nolen prompted.

"Which you didn't mention?" Phedam added.

"Oh, yes. That was a misunderstanding, you see. When I came home, I found out three days had passed. Half the town was looking for me. They thought I'd gotten lost in one of the caves. Of course, despite my truthful explanations, they all thought it was mirjuva, and even though it wasn't, I couldn't admit it to anyone. I joined the sordenu because I was tired of pretending I had gotten lost. So, I've kind of had a mirjuva but not really. I hope my secret is safe with you."

They all murmured their assurances that it was. Butu suspected they all meant it, too.

If I repeat that story and sound like I believe a word of it, the other sordenu will think I'm the most gullible person they've ever met. He grinned inwardly. *Learning to see has some merits, I think.*

Butu told them what Blay had said about magic. All of them had apparently heard the same thing from other sordenu since their arrival.

"They force us not to use magic. Of course we'll forget how," Nolen said, echoing Butu's suspicions. Retus and Phedam murmured their agreement.

"I'm going to keep practicing," Butu said. "I'll do it in secret, if I have to, but I'm never going to stop using magic."

They all nodded, even Lujo. Butu thought the storyteller would generally be agreeable, if untrustworthy when it came to his stories. He shared a grin with the silver-earringed boy.

How would I look with an earring?

"Maybe we should form a magic club," Lujo suggested. "Once we're done with our training, we'll secretly teach the recruits who come after us to keep their magic, too."

A good idea, Butu thought, then felt something else — a handful of people approaching. *Pater, Aeklan and ... Zhek? The general, a lieutenant, and the sergeant!* A familiar flickering presence trailed them. *Jani?*

The other boys kept talking and gave no sign that they noticed. "Quiet!" Butu hissed. "Someone's coming this way."

They all sensed the new arrivals, now. "Let's go," Lujo said. "We're done anyway. Meet you all back at the barracks!" And he vanished.

"Make sure you split up," Nolen said, voice coming from nowhere. "It'll make it harder to catch us."

Retus and Phedam began chanting. "You seek and search, but never see. I'm hiding, and you won't find me. No sound I make, no shadow cast. No tracks I leave in sand I've passed." They said it again and again, concentrating on the words and remembering the hundreds of games of hide and seek they had played. Of course, even in an open area, winning at hide and seek was much harder when everyone else was just as invisible as you were — including the one doing the seeking.

Butu ducked behind some carts but stopped in earshot. *Jani is here.* He was sure of it now. Even invisible, she couldn't hide from him completely. *Jani shouldn't be here. What's going on?*

Everyone else was out of his senses when the three men appeared. The sergeant looked around as if expecting someone else to be here. Butu ducked behind his cart, trusting the darkness more than his magic to hide him as Aeklan peered intently into the shadows.

CHAPTER 12

"Can we trust him?" Zhek said suddenly, and loudly.

Aeklan snorted. "Keep your voice down, sir."

Pater sounded even less amused. "He's reliable, in his way. The timing of Aesh's proposal couldn't've been an accident. I'm inclined to believe he knows what he's doing."

"They're not going to be ready in time," Aeklan said. "If we do it this way, the Kadrak will suspect the truth, to say nothing of our own troops. I need more time."

Butu froze as he felt another sordenu approaching. *Blay? Is that who they are talking about? Then why is he coming?*

"There isn't any. The fighting has begun. The clans are moving. The Akdren and Nankek are there."

"They're freshly fallen," Zhek said. "If we wait too long, they won't be, and this becomes impossible."

"It's already pretty close to impossible," Aeklan muttered, but the others didn't respond.

"You shouldn't have let her join," Zhek said. "She's your granddaughter."

"It was her choice to make," Pater reminded him. "Besides, it would have been suspicious if I'd denied her request."

"It works in your favor," Aeklan said to Zhek. "You can do what you need to, and she'll be safer that way."

"Only if it works," Zhek said, not sounding so sure it would. "I'd almost rather see her wed Aesh."

Butu felt Blay join them and salute. He risked a glance. The two older soldiers stood at marginal attention, Aeklan a smaller version of Pater. Zhek stood near them but slightly aside. And

Blay, at full attention before his general, looked unhappy.

"At ease, corporal." Pater commanded. "Will your squad be ready?"

"Yes, sir."

"Good," Pater said. "I don't have to remind you how important what you're doing is to the Ahjea."

"No, sir."

"Have you met the final member of your squad?" Zhek asked, stepping closer to the other officers.

"Yes, sir." Butu watched Blay direct a remorseful look on the kluntra's son. "With all due respect, is that wise? This could kill her."

"It won't come to that. I know what I'm about." Zhek's voice was granite.

"And if my grandson fails in his project, I trust you'll make good use of her talent," Pater said.

"But she's ..."

"I'll hear no more about it," Pater said, cutting him off. "Do you want us to find someone else, corporal — someone who doesn't question his superiors?"

"No, sir," Blay said. "I will do whatever is necessary, just like I always do. I will repay the Ahjea clan for taking me in when I was an orphan wailing in the shanjin."

Butu gaped. *Karp may not like Blay, but he spoke the truth.*

The four men left, and Jani hesitated only for a few seconds before heading toward one of the other barracks. *I'm not the only one who heard something not meant for me.* Now to get back to his barracks and let the others know what he had learned. He began the hide-and-seek chant in a low voice.

"You seek and search, but never see. I'm hiding, and you won't find me. No sound I make, no shadow cast. No tracks I leave in sand I've passed."

After a handful of repititions, he began to walk.

What exactly did I hear? What was Jani's choice? Some of the conversation returned to him. *There's a woman in Blay's secret squad. Zhek was concerned, so it must be Jani.* Suddenly he wanted to be in Blay's squad again, and at the same time, he knew he already was. *Blay's probably our corporal — and Karp's right about him. And something very shady is going on that involves all of us.*

Confident he was hidden, Butu snuck toward the barracks entrance. Someone chanted quietly just inside the entrance. Butu felt Karp and three more sordenu he didn't know — one a woman — hiding right there. He paused a few paces away, certain he still wouldn't be seen.

"Don't think about the magic hiding you from me," Karp said, clearly. "Don't think about what'll happen if I catch you. Don't think about another day polishing with Kira. Don't think about the magic hiding you from me."

Butu frowned as he came closer, trying to figure out why the sordenu didn't want him to think about hiding with magic. He understood too late, as an evil grin split Karp's face and a large hand grabbed his shoulder. He looked up at the gap-toothed cook, who had alertly looked anywhere but at his charge.

Butu threw a punch at the cook's mid-section, but it was like hitting a side of beef. His grip only tightened. He opened his mouth to shout a warning, and a calloused hand covered it.

He looked up into the eyes of Tesa.   "We can't stop boys from being boys," she said. "We can put the fear of the desert into 'em, though. After tonight, you won't think of breaking any more rules."

A strip of cloth silenced Butu, and the cook tossed him to the ground next to Nolen, similarly trussed.

Retus' arrival was as quiet and cracked as the boy — the bruise on his head soon faded. Phedam didn't even fight back, just went in mute astonishment at the situation. They waited some more time, and Butu sweated in his boots.

"Tesa, post chanters," Karp barked suddenly, making all four boys jump and someone mutter in their bunk. "We'll deal with these failures."

Lujo never came back, Butu noted as the cook dragged him to his feet and ungagged him. *That or he got here before the chanters.*

Karp and the other sordenu lined up the four boys in front of the barracks.

"You want to run around in the dark instead of sleeping," he said. "I'm happy to grant your wish. March. And keep quiet. Other sordenu are trying to sleep."

They marched, and Butu fumed. He'd been caught before, and punished, but never so often or belligerently as today.

It's probably because I'm still trying to figure out how things work.

Karp and the others flung baby jokes and insults at them all the way to the area behind the training ground, to the obstacle course. Even in the dark, Butu could make out the hurdles, walls, ropes, climbing bars and other traps — including a broad pit filled with cracked sand. Butu grinned, then, earning a warning cuff from the cook.

They think this will stop us? He glanced at the other three, to gauge their reactions, and was surprised to see them looking beaten already. *Come on, guys. The rooftops of Jasper are worse than this!*

"This is Zurburan," Karp said, gesturing to a black-robed figure who appeared seemingly from nowhere. "He's a blood priest. Whatever he says, you will listen. Obey him, or a day with Kira will seem like a night spent playing marbles and eating sweets."

CHAPTER 13

Zurburan stepped forward into a lighter shadow and threw his hood back, revealing long, black hair with strands of gray in it. A neatly trimmed beard surrounded a face carved from the Sentinel's Finger itself.

He could be Tirud's father, Butu thought, then amended, *grandfather, maybe.* He looked around for Lujo, but no one else was around. Retus was practically bent double in humiliation. Phedam and Nolen hung their heads and slumped, each toward the other. Butu raised his chin and straightened his back, determined to protect them.

"The sordenu woke me from a sound sleep," the blood priest said, "which means you boys have behaved very badly." His deep voice carried more weight than any of Karp's lewd insults. "You are wondering, perhaps, how an adult with no magic of his own was able to see you in spite of your magic?"

He's thinking of how Karp caught us.

"The more you understand how magic works, the more difficult it becomes to use it."

"Then I don't want to know how it works," Butu said immediately. "I'd rather run through this obstacle course in the dark."

Zurburan chuckled. He waved a long arm at the field behind him.

"That is exactly what you will be doing if you don't listen to those who have lost their magic, young man. Whether you seek understanding or not, you will eventually understand. You've already begun to think about your magic, else you would not have come to this camp, and Karp's little chant wouldn't have tricked you into revealing yourselves if you had not fallen once before."

The other boys unfolded a little when no physical harm seemed forthcoming. Retus still hugged himself, but he said, "Making us think about it made us unable to use magic."

Zurburan nodded, but Butu growled out a curse immediately, covering his ears. "Shanubu, be quiet!" He rounded on the blood priest. "You use magic, so you have no reason to take away mine. Set me running in the dark. Make me polish armor and boots. Put a sword in my hand and send me into battle. But don't take away my magic."

Zurburan stared at him intently for a long moment. Butu felt his heart throbbing in his neck and head, felt the sweat bead on his back and sides. And he felt the astonished stares of his three friends. Only Nolen seemed to have caught some of his fire, but he said nothing.

"You each have a choice," the blood priest intoned. "Either listen to what I have to teach you now and sleep before midnight, or run through an obstacle course in the dark until the sun rises."

Butu didn't wait for the others to respond before running toward the first obstacle.

I will not forget how to use magic, he vowed as he vaulted a hurdle as high as his chest. He jumped a second one, and then blinked into the night air. *I just used magic while thinking about it!*

His knee caught the next hurdle and he flipped forward over it, landing in time to receive a mouthful of sand. A pair of boots passed him as he picked himself up and dusted off, refusing to look back at Zurburan — certain the blood priest would be smug. He ducked the next hurdle and jumped the fifth.

Perhaps what matters is that I don't think about what I'm doing with magic at the moment I'm using it.

Butu focused his attention on anything else he could hold in his mind. He thought of Jani's mysterious presence. He wondered when his training would begin and whether he would spend another day polishing. He absently noted that Nolen paced him on the obstacle course. He shouted challenges at him, and they raced each other around the circuit.

Each time they passed the start, a whisper of the blood priest's conversation with Retus and Phedam reached his ears, so he took to singing loudly as he ran.

"This is only the first day," he told Nolen. "They can't all be this bad. We just need to be smart about it."

Nolen nodded, chest heaving.

"What's wrong?"

Nolen shook his head, motioning Butu to go on. A few minutes later, Nolen caught him up, breathing normally. Butu didn't press the issue.

As the hour neared midnight, Retus and Phedam left the obstacle course behind and retired to the barracks. Zurburan stood, implacably, and watched Butu and Nolen run.

They fell down many times — mostly brief spills and mishaps as thoughts of magic strayed into their minds. They each slowed, regularly, panting. Then they'd catch another wind and run onward.

Some time later, Zurburan commanded them to stop.

Maybe this was just a warning, like the armory, Butu thought, panting as he and Nolen trotted over to the blood priest. *I'm sure Zurburan doesn't want to stay up all night watching us run.*

The blood priest held out clay jugs. Butu could feel the water inside. Sweat drenched his clothes, and the cold desert breeze made goose bumps rise all over his body.

"Drink," Zurburan said. "Your bodies cannot endure the strains they could when you were children."

They did so gladly, and Zurburan continued talking amicably.

"Though it takes a hundred mortal blows to kill a first-cycler, you must understand you are not of that age. You might survive a mortal blow or you might not. And if you survive one, you might not survive the next. Therefore, you must care for your bodies and keep them from harm."

"Stop!" Butu cried, trying to cover his ears in spite of the water jug in one hand. "You said we could either listen to you explain magic or run the obstacle course all night. We chose the obstacle course."

"You didn't listen very carefully. I said you could choose to run the obstacle course if you didn't want to listen for an hour and sleep before midnight. I never said I'd spare you the lesson."

"Then we'll just keep running until dawn," Nolen announced,

throwing his water jug on the ground so it shattered into clay fragments and running onto the obstacle course.

"Will you drink?" Zurburan asked Butu with a patronizing smile. "Or would you rather remain thirsty?"

Butu growled low in his throat and followed Nolen. After another hour, he was thirsty and tired, again. He focused on that discomfort to keep from thinking about magic. Nolen seemed to do much the same, but they still fell often.

He felt water sloshing around, somewhere, and licked his dry lips. He blinked, looking around. The feeling got stronger, and so did his thirst. Then he passed Zurburan, shaking the jug.

Shanubu, if I didn't have this magic I wouldn't have felt that water. If I didn't have this magic, I'd be blind in the dark.

The course vanished to his senses. Butu frantically tried to remember where he was on it, and leapt, thinking he was at the pit. He slammed into the climbing wall face first, crashing to the ground. He felt blood run down his cheek.

Butu lay there for awhile, dazed more by the blindness than the pain.

If I can't see in the dark without magic, how can Zurburan see us?

He touched his nose and felt a stab of pain from the flat space where his nose had once stuck out. He jerked his hand away and sat up dizzily. He noticed blood had dripped onto the front of his uniform, and then Nolen ran up the wall with only a brief glance.

Butu grinned, wishing for a mirror to see what he looked like. His Turun vision had returned, though it winked out again for just a moment as he thought about it.

He felt Zurburan at his side, offering the water jug.

"It is very dangerous to rely on a magic that could fail you at any moment."

"You did that deliberately." Butu was tired. He could hardly get any accusation in his tone.

"I merely shook a clay jug. How did that make you lose your sight? This is the curse of magic. One stray thought, and it will desert you. If you rely on the gifts Mir gives Turu children, you will suffer worse than a broken nose. The next time, it could kill you."

The next time, I could kill you! Butu thought savagely as he took a long drink from the jug, but he said nothing.

He touched his nose gingerly as he stood up. The blood had stopped flowing, and his nose was back to its original shape. Without waiting for Zurburan to resume his lecture, he dodged around the wall and continued the course.

Stray thoughts, he thought. *The games and rhymes make more sense, now. If I can teach myself to keep my mind from straying, I can keep using magic.*

Butu tasted sand again. Smirking at himself, he picked himself up and continued running.

As the night faded into the dark blue of dawn, the blood priest called them to a halt. Butu and Nolen limped off the obstacle course, exhausted and covered with scrapes and small bruises from their falls. Both their uniforms were soaked with sweat and spattered with blood. Zurburan looked ready to go to a formal dinner. Butu scowled at him.

"You have served your sentence with me," the blood priest intoned. "Do you have any questions before you begin your first day of training?"

"How much time do we have to sleep?" Nolen said, yawning. Butu nodded and yawned also.

Zurburan gestured to the mess, where the cooks had already begun work. A handful of older sordenu warmed up in the training yard. Two others, maybe three cycles older than the boys, appeared on the obstacle course, offering rude comments to Butu and Nolen about their mothers.

"You should eat before you report to morning drill."

"When is morning drill?" Butu asked.

"It begins when the sun fully breaks the horizon."

They looked over their shoulders. The sun's first rays crept toward them.

Zurburan smiled far too sagely. "There are two paths to wisdom — falling down and learning from those who have fallen down. You chose to run through an obstacle course all night long. I'm afraid you've earned this fall."

"But you didn't tell us we'd have to train today!" Butu objected between gasping breaths. The two sordenu on the course, passing by then, laughed at his tired complaint. *When have I ever been short of breath before now?*

"You are men, now," the blood priest intoned. "You will get nothing by whining at me or any of the other sordenu. Those who get caught breaking the rules will be punished. Now, go eat before you must endure morning drill on an empty stomach!"

"Yes, sir," Butu said, saluting.

Is he saying I can use magic as much as I want as long as no one catches me doing it?

He clung to that thought, determined to understand this twist to the rules.

CHAPTER 14

Jani sat in the sand in the training area when Butu and Nolen arrived. Butu barely recognized her without her jewelry and with her hair cut so short it made her ears look much larger than he expected.

Her uniform fits better than mine does, though.

Tirud and Blay stretched nearby. Blay waved to each of them as they arrived before continuing his animated conversation with Tirud. Phedam and Retus barely even yawned in the morning light, and Lujo looked positively cheerful, grinning at all of them but with an eye on Jani.

So he didn't have to work all night. No reason to look all smug about it, or look at Jani like that, Butu thought bitterly, his jaws stretching in another yawn of his own. His muscles were still sore, which had never happened before. *Maybe it will go away in a little while.*

Aeklan strolled toward them from the mess hall, but was still out of earshot. No one else moved in Gordney toward them. Phedam frowned at their small gathering.

"What is it, shumi?" Nolen asked.

"Usually there would be more of us for basic training," Phedam said. His voice dropped as he glanced sideways at Tirud and Blay. "And why are they here? They've already been through this."

Blay stood up abruptly and put a hand on Phedam's shoulder in a reassuring gesture. "Someone has to show you how things are done." He grinned. "You don't expect sarge to demonstrate, do you?"

Phedam opened his mouth, but at that moment Aeklan started

barking orders at them.

The obstacle course was a game of marbles compared with the first day of training. The recruits endured relentless verbal assaults from the sergeant for most of the morning. He cursed their upbringing if they did not salute properly or fast enough. Improperly standing at attention led to comparisons with farm animals, and a speck of dust on their uniforms resulted in even wilder accusations.

And then there were the marching drills. Walking in step, moving in formation, and remembering commands would've been hard enough without being exhausted, and Butu found himself on the ground doing push-ups as often as falling over. The drills were repetitive and boring, and whenever he could, Butu glared into the back of the sergeant's head, wishing for sword training.

The sergeant used Blay to demonstrate the right way to do everything. Although Blay shared the squad's punishment whenever someone made a mistake, he seemed almost glad for the opportunity to do push-ups or run laps.

"Halt! Attention!" Aeklan's roar never cracked. They stopped and stood.

Tirud remained neutral throughout the day's training, producing without effort exactly enough accuracy and fervor to satisfy Aeklan and not a grain of sand more. He didn't hesitate to obey when Aeklan punished the squad, but he didn't pretend to enjoy the extra work, either. And Jani struggled as much as any of them. *She got here yesterday, too,* Butu thought. *I wonder if she's had any punishments yet.*

"At ease, you worthless rugs," the sergeant said, switching his comparisons from domestic animals. "I should have you all hung and beaten with sticks, you're covered in so much dust. Fall out for lunch, recruits."

Butu was as tired as he was hungry, but knew he had no time for sleep. They found a place where they could all eat together, and Nolen laid his head down next to his plate as soon as he sat down. Tirud made some comment about that which had Phedam giggling. Butu watched Jani out of the corner of his eye, where she sat listening to Lujo explain about the giants living in the mountains above Pophir.

Blay joined them, intimidatingly cheerful and energetic.

"Whatever you might think, you're actually doing pretty well, for your first day." He smirked and lowered his voice. "Especially after the late night some of you had."

They looked at him, and Nolen lifted his head to yawn.

"Stop that," Butu said, yawning back.

"I'm sorry." Nolen yawned again.

Blay tipped the bowl of porridge into his mouth and gulped it down quickly. "It's tougher in the afternoon, but don't you worry. It's in no one's interests that you pass out from heat stroke. Sarge'll keep us watered, and he'll likely ease up a bit. All the same, you'll all be asleep before they put out the lamps tonight."

"What'll sarge do if I disappear to take an afternoon nap?" Nolen asked, poking at his lunch muzzily.

Tirud grinned at the suggestion, but Blay's smile drained off his face like sweat. "If one of us disappears, sarge'll have the rest of us looking for you all afternoon. We'll all miss dinner to spend a few more hours training under an angry sergeant who isn't happy himself to be missing dinner. And the runaway will spend another night on the obstacle course."

"It's not worth it," Phedam said, eyeing his shumi for suggesting it. Nolen put his head back down on the table, muttering to himself.

They spent the first half of the afternoon on the obstacle course. At the hottest part of the day, the training was less monotonous and more simply exhausting. Aeklan made them drink water every time he hauled them aside to bark at someone, which was frequently.

Occasionally, one of them would use magic. It couldn't be helped. The punishment after that was worse than others. Aeklan, who appeared to enjoy striping them with words, dove into scatological references for these tirades. Even without magic, Blay and Tirud moved quickly through the obstacle course — not as fast as Butu knew he could, but faster than any of them could without magic. Lujo sometimes outpaced them for a lap or two, but another tirade against magic usually wasn't far behind such displays. Only Jani could manage occasional bursts of speed without using magic to do it, although she wasn't nearly as fast as Blay and

Tirud.

"With enough training, you'll be just as fast. It takes time to develop strength and coordination," Blay said between gulps of water when he saw the others looking at him with something akin to wonder.

"As long as you keep using magic, though, you'll remain useless to the Ahjea," Aeklan added. "Break's over. Get moving! I have shirts that move faster than you maggots!"

I'll get stronger, but I'm going to keep using magic, too, Butu vowed silently as he climbed a wooden wall covered with small handholds. *It doesn't have to be one or the other. It can't be!*

By the end of the day, Butu felt like an empty waterskin. He could barely stand up. Nolen leaned on Phedam, eyes blinking rapidly.

"Right," Tirud said, rubbing his hands. "Dinner, folks."

"Bed," Butu said, though he was hungry. Exhaustion won this time.

"You need to keep up your strength, and Lujo promised us a story. You can sleep later."

"Shanubu, you water-starved camel turd," Nolen mumbled just clearly enough to be understood. "May you find a scorpion in your boots. I'm slithering to my bed, 'cause someone took my legs. C'mon, Butu," he offered, pushing away from Phedam. "Jani, ladies, good night."

They all grinned at him, and Butu and he started walking away.

"Pretty good Aeklan impression," Butu said.

"Marching isn't the only thing we learned today. I think my vocabulary tripled."

"Right." They sluiced some cooling water over their heads in the tent, using wet rags to rub off sweat and dust. Nolen seemed more awake now. "So, Jani."

Butu cleared his throat. "Yes?"

"She recognized you. I could tell."

"What does it matter?" Butu asked, suddenly in a foul mood. He climbed up to his bunk. Nolen sat on his own.

"Not many women join the sordenu," he said, removing his boots. Butu's dropped next to his bunk.

Butu grunted as he laid back, hoping this conversation would die if he stopped contributing to it.

"You have, um, history, don't you?" Nolen persisted.

Butu's sigh betrayed him.

"I knew it!" Nolen said. "Who is she?"

"She's the kluntra's niece."

"Oh," was all Nolen managed, and Butu heard a note of pity there.

When he slept, his dreams filled with Jani's kisses — the flash of her eyes, the feel of her hands around his neck, the scent of her long, dark hair. *Did she have to cut it so short?*

Training the next few days was no better, nor did it change significantly. Butu barely spoke except to respond to the sergeant's orders. It wasn't until the fifth day that everyone seemed to get the marching passable enough that Aeklan stopped them with an incredulous sneer on his face.

"Take a break, men. Corporal, I will speak with you."

Butu watched Blay briskly approach the sergeant, wondering what they whispered about. Blay came back and ordered them to fall in. The sergeant regarded them suspiciously.

"Tomorrow you'll get weapons," he said, and the line broke down in a ragged cheer. He hollered at them until they found order again. "That'll be two extra laps on the course." He cleared his throat. "Tomorrow you'll get weapons, and we'll start your sword training. Some of you may be able to hold a sword without dropping it now."

Butu fell asleep that night feeling exhilarated. *Finally*, he thought.

CHAPTER 15

He woke to a blaring horn and the movement of many sordenu. He looked up bleary-eyed in the dim light of dawn. Sordenu were dressing hastily and pouring out of the barracks. Someone shook the bunk.

"Butu, get up," Lujo said below him. Nolen and Phedam appeared, fully dressed.

"I don't see how you could've slept through that," Phedam said.

"What's going on?" Butu asked, jumping down and rubbing his hand across the stubble on his head. He'd have to shave today. Looking up at the other recruits, he wondered if he would ever grow, too.

"Camp inspection," Blay said, appearing behind them. He nodded at Butu. "General Pater inspects the sordenu once a week. Get into uniform and come outside. Quickly."

Nolen grinned at Butu as he and Phedam followed Blay. Butu had his shirt on and pants up when Lujo finished and jogged after them. Glancing around the barracks, Butu saw he was the last one inside. He ran to the entrance, doing up his shirt as he left. He stepped into line with the other recruits to a stern nod from Blay.

Sergeant Aeklan paced in front of the ranks, occasionally barking orders to stand straighter and otherwise finding flaws in each sordenu's uniform or carriage. Butu heard other voices shouting, as well — sergeants in charge of smaller groups of sordenu.

Aeklan must be more than just a regular sergeant, Butu realized. *Maybe that's why he trains new recruits.*

Butu risked a glance at the sordenu around him. The way they all stood in neat formations made it easier to guess their numbers than he had expected — three companies of about a hundred sordenu each, each divided into three platoons and subdivided into squads of eight or nine. The recruits and Blay stood alone, not a part of any company. Aeklan came by and shouted at each of them, then grumbled to Zhepal about equipping "this small herd of even smaller goats."

The officers rode in from the road, the way Butu had walked in a handful of days ago. General Pater al'Ahjea rode at the head, and not too far behind him, his grandson, Zhek.

"Ah-TEN-shun!" Aeklan roared, and the already stiff army somehow stood up taller.

Pater was his son's girth if not his height, with his carefully trimmed beard completely white. He had ceded the position of kluntra to his son before Butu had been born, and now corrected his son from the side and ran the army with equal efficiency.

The general and his companions rode down the line of sordenu. Pater's eyes bored into Butu when he passed. Zhek also made eye contact, and then looked away — directly at Jani, Butu assumed. The kluntra's son looked back at Butu with barely contained rage.

What's his problem? Butu thought. *He can't blame me for her decision!*

After a few minutes, the horses' hooves picked up their pace and the officers appeared in front of the assembled army.

Pater nodded to someone out of Butu's sight, and then Aeklan shouted, "Recruits! Present! Single line! Hup, hup hup!"

Nolen jumped nearly as high as Butu did, and Blay led their straggling line forward, in between the veteran sordenu and the officers. Aeklan shouted at them until their line was flawless. He turned and saluted to Pater, who had dismounted along with Zhek and the tall, lean man with the most stripes besides the general.

"Sergeant Aeklan, are the recruits ready?" Pater asked. He could have been heard halfway to Jasper.

"Ready and awaiting your instructions, sir!"

"Very good, sergeant." His gaze speared each of the young recruits in front of him one more time, and, staring at Blay, he said,

"Lieutenant!"

Zhek stepped forward. "Corporal Blay!"

Blay saluted. "Yes, sir!"

"You are hereby assigned to lead squad Tem-35!" Butu didn't even know what it meant. "Your charges are Private Tirud! Recruits Jani! Butu! Nolen! Phedam! Retus! Lujo!"

"Yes, sir!"

I thought they'd assign us to different squads, Butu thought.

"I see squad Tem-35 stands before me in its entirety, captain," Pater said, dryly, to the other officer behind him.

"Yes, sir," the captain said.

"Sergeant, you may dismiss the squad."

"Yes, sir!" Aeklan faced them, hollering for them to fall out and return to their company. Blay led them behind the middle company. Butu could see the faces of the other companies, feel their eyes on him.

"I have some bad news," Pater announced. "Ku company will be late coming back from the Nukata. An army of Clanless attacked them just east of the Riphil River. Until ku company returns, all leave is suspended."

Low murmurs escaped from some of the sordenu, but the sergeants quickly silenced them. Pater continued.

"This is only a temporary measure and should last a few weeks. Over the next few months, we will be creating two new sordenu companies in order to deal with this new Clanless threat. The kluntra is sending us fresh recruits from the towns, and the first of them will arrive in a few days. Companies dismissed."

The Clanless must be getting bold if Jusep is raising a larger army, Butu thought as the sordenu dispersed. *I hope Mak is safe.* He had never been close to Zaseby's husband, but Mak had always treated Butu the same as he did the fosterlings in her care.

"Tem-35," Phedam mused as they walked toward the mess hall. "That's the fifth squad of the third platoon of the fifth company. It didn't even exist before."

Tirud smirked. "We're all orphans, now."

"Most of us are orphans," Butu said, and Nolen nodded.

"The Ahjea have five companies of sordenu," Phedam explained, "al', el', un', ku, and tem, which is why the sordenu call the companies dad, brother, cousin, bastard and orphan. I wonder what they'll call the new companies."

"But, orphan," Lujo was clearly worried. "Sounds like we're, um, unimportant."

"Of course not," Blay said. Since the general had dismissed him, his grin had not left his face. The goatee danced in pride whenever he looked at one of his squadmembers. "All the companies are equal, but they have some specific roles. Dad stays in Gordney. Brother's up in Pophir. They're always ready to protect Jasper and the Ahjea's interests. 'Un, ku and tem patrol our territory in six-week marches. Ku was due back at the end of the week."

"And then who goes out?" Nolen asked.

"We do." Blay said with a conspiratorial wink. "Assuming you all finish weapons training in time."

Phedam looked confused. "Aren't we a little new to be in tem company? I thought all new recruits were assigned to dad at least for the first couple years."

Blay shrugged. "Usually, yes, but not always. It will all make sense in a month or two, I promise."

"Who were the two riders next to the general?" Retus asked.

"Captain Philbe el'Ahjea, the commander of tem company, and Lieutenant Zhek al'Ahjea, who's in charge of our platoon."

Retus's eyes widened. "The kluntra's son?"

Butu knew Zhek too well to feel awe, though he supposed it was something of an honor to be a sordenu under the heir's direct command. *Zhek is up to something involving us and especially Jani, and she knows it, too.* He looked at Jani, who shook her head slightly.

"A short lesson, then we'll start our day," Blay said. "You got your officers, right? Lieutenant then captain then general. Then you got your enlisted, sergeant, corporal and private, which you all will be when you get your swords. They don't mix, understood?" He nodded as they agreed. "The officers do the strategy. The enlisted do the day-to-day stuff."

"And what do you do?" Nolen asked.

"His job is to be our friend and rat us out if we screw up," Tirud said.

"He's half right. I'm the voice of experience and the shining example you're all supposed to imitate." Blay said it jokingly, but then he sobered, staring hard at each of them in turn. "I'm here to help you — to teach you how to be sordenu. You're gonna make a lot of mistakes at the beginning, and I don't mind suffering a bit for it. But remember. If any of you gets caught failing to live up to the example I'm supposed to create, the whole squad gets punished, including me. We don't rat each other out. If someone is doing something that'll get us all in trouble, the rest of us put a stop to it ourselves before anyone else finds out. In camp, foolishness gets us polishing duty. In the field, it gets us killed. The sergeants and officers don't police the squad. The squad polices the squad."

They all nodded again, quietly. Butu shared a glance with Nolen.

Who can we trust to practice with us?

A throat cleared. They all turned to see Aeklan standing there, Zhepal at his shoulder.

"Let's go get your weapons, men."

CHAPTER 16

The squad's excitement was palpable as they approached the armory. Even Jani looked as eager to have steel in her hands as the rest of them. Phedam, though, seemed uncomfortable with the situation.

"What's wrong?" Butu asked in a whisper.

"It's too early," Phedam replied. "We've had five days of drill. It's supposed to take months to get our arms. Not only have we already been assigned to a squad, but it's a squad in one of the roving companies. And it didn't exist before!"

"I think you're being paranoid, shumi," Nolen said. "We might be really good." He didn't sound like he believed himself.

Phedam glowered and slowed to talk to Tirud. Nolen looked confused at his friend's silence.

Butu thought of the conversation he had overheard between Aeklan, Zhek and Pater.

If they're raising an army, it means war is coming. And what Phedam said, that we're a special squad, that could mean a special mission. His eyes widened. *A dangerous mission, something the Kadrak won't like. And maybe it's us because our mirjuvas were so recent.*

Butu wanted to share this with the rest of his squad, but he knew Blay and Aeklan were both a part of it. If they overheard him, they'd know he had spied on them. He'd find some other opportunity to tell them what he had heard.

Kira waited outside the armory.

"All of you are here to polish?" she asked with hands on hips and a smile that said she knew full well why they were coming to the armory.

Aeklan came up behind the squad and went into the tent with Kira and Zhepal.

"Nolen'll be first," Blay said. "The rest of you stay close. We'll call you when we're ready for you." He followed Nolen into the armory.

"How much longer do you think we'll have to train before we get our insignia?" Jani asked suddenly.

"Our what?" Retus asked.

Jani pointed to the flaps of cloth on each shoulder of her uniform. Butu missed her braids. "Everyone has a rank insignia to show clan, assignment and rank. Colored squares for company, platoon and squad. Brass studs for enlisted ranks and silver studs for officers."

Phedam nodded in agreement, looking impressed. "From what I hear, it should take about another month to get our insignia." He sighed and gave a small shrug. "But they put us through basic drill in just five days, so I have no idea anymore."

Awkward silence fell until Nolen emerged from the armory. Butu had enough time to note the boiled leather breastplate and the hilt of the sword before Blay called him. He trotted into the tent dutifully, if not eagerly.

Zhepal was there with his knotted measuring string, which he employed as soon as the tent flap closed behind Butu. He called out measurements to Kira, who nodded and rummaged through the neatly organized piles and racks of weapons and armor. She handed a boiled leather breastplate to Blay, who showed Butu how to put it on. Like his uniform, it fit poorly, but Kira promised it was the smallest one in the armory. It was covered with sand-colored cloth much like that used to make sordenu uniforms and protected his chest, belly and shoulders.

"Children can survive almost anything, but your childhood is coming to an end," Aeklan said, the words flattened and measured by many repetitions. "Armor is a burden that can save your life, but it is not as foolproof as youth has been."

Kira handed Blay a steel cap. Butu took off his pryud and took the cap from him. The steel was cold against his shaved scalp, but it warmed quickly. Blay handed him back the pryud and motioned for him to put it on over the cap. It covered the metal completely.

Butu grinned as Blay rapped his own head with knuckles. *They must always wear caps under their pryuds,* he thought.

Kira handed Blay a sword in its belt sheath, and Butu's hands trembled in delight as he put it on, unable to stop smiling. Aeklan droned on.

"Your sword is your most valuable piece of equipment. It marks you as an Ahjea soldier for all to see. In battle, it is your sole hope of survival and your only means of winning glory. To return from battle without a sword — neither your own nor one taken from the corpse of your enemy — is the greatest dishonor you can suffer."

Butu made a motion to draw the sword, but Blay shook his head. Kira handed Blay a large leather pouch, which Butu took from him. It was surprisingly heavy and rattled as if filled with pebbles.

"Sordenu must be versatile," Aeklan recited. "You'll train as hard with the sling as you do with a sword. A sling is as deadly as a bow, and you never need worry about running out of ammunition. Practice with stone. Make war with lead."

Butu nodded his understanding.

"Good. Once I am satisfied you know how to use sword and sling, you'll get your stripes. After that, you'll be a true sordenu. Dismissed."

Butu saluted and left the tent, grinning and eager to start training immediately. Blay called Phedam next. Nolen sat cross-legged on the ground, examining his new sword. Butu sat next to him. A metal sphere on the pommel marked Ahjea blades. Other clans had different pommels. The Nankek had a cube attached by one corner, while the Kadrak had a metal crescent like bull's horns.

He slid the sword — *his* sword — out of its sheath. The slightly curved blade had one edge, and tapered to a sharp point. He tested the blade with a thumb, and it cut him almost painlessly. He sucked it, grinning at Nolen, and the taste of blood filled his mouth for several heartbeats before the wound closed.

Blay called Jani into the tent as Phedam emerged, looking every bit as pleased with himself as Butu felt. Nolen stood up, sword still drawn, grinning at his shumi. Butu wished Paka was here.

I'll never get to see this for him, though. Paka's going to go home before then.

Phedam and Nolen crossed swords so clumsily Butu couldn't help but laugh. After several dramatic poses and a ludicrous spinning attack in which Nolen nearly dropped his blade, Butu could stand no more.

"That's not the way to do it. Here, let me show you."

He squared off with Nolen, who swung the same way, clearly expecting Butu to block the blade with his own, making a nice X with the swords. Butu stepped out of the way of the sword and kissed the back of Nolen's arm with his own sword. The light touch of the blade cut cloth and skin easily, red blood oozing out.

Nolen laughed and tried to counterattack. Butu knocked the blade aside easily.

"Where did you learn to fight like that?" Butu asked, adopting a fighting stance and waiting to counter Nolen's next move.

"Some of us didn't have the kluntra's son as a sparring partner," Nolen said, fingering the cut in his sleeve. The cut had already closed as his magic unconsciously healed it.

How much longer would sordenu survive if they could still heal as quickly as a child!

Butu smirked. "I'm not an expert. I just know a couple things about fighting on roofs in the dark."

Nolen moved much faster this time, and with more force than before. Butu halted the blade before it could do any real damage, but it scraped his breastplate as he parried. He countered just as quickly, and Nolen intercepted the blade the same way he had blocked Phedam's attacks.

One after the other, each with a breastplate and sword, the squad paired off and practiced in front of the armory — though practice was a bad word for the flailing most of them did.

"Aw, look. They're having fun," Aeklan said in endearing tones from the armory's entrance. Zhepal, Blay and Kira stood behind him, wearing frowns.

They all looked up in shock, and Butu winced as Phedam's sword grazed his knee. Aeklan smiled at them until he had everyone's attention, and then his face contorted with rage.

"What do you think you're doing? Do you think those are toys you're playing with?"

"No, sir!" Butu said, sheathing his sword awkwardly while trying to salute with the wrong hand.

The rest of them stared at Aeklan, dumbstruck.

"Sheath them," the sergeant said. "And then you'll run laps until I can think of a worse punishment."

"Yes, sir!" they all said, not quite in unison.

After a miserable afternoon running circuits on the obstacle course, the sergeant relented and began their training. Tirud proved the most skilled with a sword. Butu and Jani were better than the others, but the gap between Tirud and them was substantial. Retus was the worst, and Aeklan yelled constantly at him, until they switched to slings. Whereas the rest of them were lucky to get the bullets to go in the right direction, Retus consistently hit the target.

"Shepherding," he said. "Snakes can kill a sheep really fast."

At the end of the day's training, before dismissing them for dinner, Aeklan called them together. He walked up and down the short line they made in the training area, eyeing each of them severely. Abruptly, he removed two round, brass studs from a pouch and pinned one to each of Jani's shoulders.

"Your training has just begun, but your time training with me is over," he announced gravely as he pinned studs on each of them. "You're not ready, but no training I can give you can prepare you for what you will face as sordenu. You will report to Sergeant Puro at dawn. Dismissed!"

They gave one final salute and headed toward the mess hall, excited about this turn of events.

We're sordenu, now. I should be as excited as everyone else, Butu thought.

He looked from face to face in his squad. Nolen, Retus and Lujo danced with joy around Phedam, who looked as uneasy as Butu felt. Jani seemed more shocked than elated. Tirud and Blay smiled like nothing was strange about this turn of events, but Butu had his suspicions.

There's something they're not telling us.

He ate his meal in silence. He couldn't voice his concerns with Blay around, and the corporal gave no sign that he would leave them alone any time soon.

That night, just before lights out, Captain Philbe el'Ahjea gave tem company their orders. They would be leaving at dawn to participate in training exercises with the Kadrak army.

The rumors told a different story: The Kadrak were now at war with the Akdren, and the Ahjea were sending Aesh al'Kadrak reinforcements.

CYCLE 2

CHAPTER 17

"So I'm left of Rarin, right of ole' Chewlip, and behind a mouse." Whoever said it earned general laughter, but Butu scowled as he adjusted his pack and looked over his shoulder at the grinning man behind him. Lujo struggled with his waist strap. Blay walked over to help him.

"Don't tie it in a knot like this," Blay advised, picking at the twists of leather. "If there's an attack, you need drop your pack quickly. It'll just get in your way if you try to fight while wearing it."

"Hope you're fast, mouse," the sordenu behind Butu said. "I don't want to crush you beneath my boots."

If the rest of this morning had been anything normal, Butu thought, *I might take this as sick humor.* But he didn't feel up to accepting a joke right now. *How often is a new, young squad placed at the head of a company?*

First had come the packs — three times the size of their camp packs, but full of necessary supplies. It was nearly as large as Butu. Then, when they assembled in the yard, Tem-35 at the back of Tem-3, Zhek — *that water-starved idiot lieutenant* — had ordered Tem-35 ahead of Tem-31. Only the captain's brief flash of surprise and the sergeant's sharpening of jaw had let Butu know this was out of line. Butu wanted to explode at someone.

"What're you up to, mouse?"

"Just memorizing your face," Butu said, more calmly than he felt. He looked down at the sordenu's boots. "Your lace is untied."

The man looked down, bending a bit. Butu grabbed his shoulder and pulled. Off-balance in part because of his big pack, the round-faced sordenu fell over to shouts from the other ranks of Butu's platoon. Butu fell on top of the aggressor, under a pile of other sordenu trying to pull him off.

"Leave us alone," he whispered into the man's ear, as Puro's enraged shouts commanded order. "I'll do worse next time."

Blay and Tirud hauled him upright, and the round-faced sordenu's squad helped him up.

"Squad Tem-35 will have the first two watches tonight," Zhek said from atop his horse, when they had lined up again.

Butu twitched, feeling the stare on the back of his neck. Tirud had replaced Lujo to his right. Jani stood impatiently on his left, radiating anger. *Well, why not? Zhek had all but hauled her out of the squad after he moved us forward. Is he punishing me or her?*

He had not seen much of the kluntra's son in the past three years, but Zhek didn't look very different. His stint in the army had visibly toned his muscles, but he looked just as self-assured as ever. *That fall from the roof must have shaken his faith a little, though.* Butu recalled the secret conversation with Pater, Aeklan and Blay. The old Zhek never would have admitted the possibility that he could fail at any project.

Zhek said something to Sergeant Puro that Butu didn't quite catch. Puro saluted and turned to his platoon with a dark expression.

Zhek rode back to the front of the short column, joining Philbe and the other lieutenants. Once the company had mostly resettled into their ranks — the scuffle had not gone unnoticed — the sergeants gave one last inspection. Puro glared murder at Butu and the round-faced sordenu behind him.

"Company, attention!" Philbe shouted from the head of the column.

There was a great clatter as a hundred sordenu dressed in full kit stiffened in unison.

"Forward, march!"

The company marched in perfect step behind the captain. Butu could hear orders being given to the sordenu at the gates and could sense people moving out of the way of the marching column. He had difficulty concentrating on anything but marching, though, because the weight of his equipment was too much of a distraction. With every step, he thought for sure he would collapse, and then Rarin, Chewlip and their squad would cheerfully trample him.

The cool air of the early morning soon gave way to the blazing heat of day, adding a new layer of discomfort. More than once, Tirud grabbed Butu's elbow and hauled him forward as their line bent.

"Straighten up your rank!" Puro shouted.

The sergeant was much younger than Aeklan, but still weathered, and the two sounded exactly the same when he had met the youngest squad in the Gordney. "I didn't ask for you water-starved mice, but you're with my platoon now," he'd said. "So fall in, don't make trouble, and you'll only get second watch for the first month. Move it!"

Glancing down the line, Butu saw only Blay keeping pace with the platoon in front. Jani lagged even behind Butu, and he could see members of the squad behind them grimacing.

"We're all gonna get night watch at this rate," the sordenu behind Butu grumbled. He was called Tak, Butu had learned quickly. The one called Chewlip, who had an ugly scar on his face and was missing part of his upper lip, lisped madly but started every sentence with his name.

"Tak, the lieutenant wanted them to lead."

"Yeah," Tak grumbled again. "What a water-starved camel turd."

"Quiet in the ranks!"

Butu grinned and redoubled his efforts, but his knees shook. His shoulders ached and his fingers were going numb because the straps cut off circulation.

"Focus on keeping up," Blay hissed from Butu's left.

Puro walked backward, facing the platoon as he marched. His stern face swept back and forth through the ranks. After a minute, he turned around.

"Left. Left. Left, right, left," he called in time with his steps, and the platoon stirred as sordenu shuffled their feet to match the sergeant's. "Left. Left. Left, right, left."

Everyone was on the same foot, now. Then Puro did something that surprised Butu very much. He chanted.

"Fought the Kanjea in their orchards green," he called in time with the march.

"Fought the Kanjea in their orchards green," answered the sordenu of the platoon.

"Saw the sweetest fruit that I'd ever seen."

The sordenu answered, and Butu joined them, this time. He heard Jani and Tirud do the same.

"Plucked that fruit right off the tree."

Is this magic? Butu wondered. But the pack didn't feel any lighter. His shoulders and feet still ached. And he was still miserable and covered in sweat.

"Brought it back to camp with me."

The chant isn't done, yet, and sometimes it takes a few repetitions for the magic to work. Butu frowned. Of course, if it was a magic chant, thinking about it might keep it from working. He needed to concentrate on something else. *Like keeping pace with the sordenu in front of me, and keeping ahead of Tak and Chewlip.*

"Ate 'til I could eat no more."

Butu concentrated on that as he repeated Puro's chant.

"Had a pile of seeds and cores. Planted my seeds in fertile ground. Now I've children all around."

Nolen quickly suppressed a laugh, confirming what Butu already suspected. *The chant is about more than just fruit.*

"Left. Left. Left, right, left."

Instead of repeating the first chant the way children using magic did, the sergeant followed with a new chant. This time, the battle was with the Nukata, and the Ahjea carried off all the other clan's ore and heated the ore until it gave all its gold to the sordenu. Each clan had a turn as the focus of the chant, and by the time Captain Philbe called the first halt, the platoon had stolen every other clan's most precious commodities. Butu felt sore, but he also felt better than he had when the march started.

Maybe we'll make it, he thought, grinning at Tirud.

CHAPTER 18

The packs had come off as soon as their feet had stopped. Lujo muttered to Nolen while he massaged his shoulders. Blay spoke quietly with Jani. She shook her head but didn't answer, leaning on her pack.

Butu saw Zhek talking with Puro, though the lieutenant stared grimly at his platoon. The sergeant seemed annoyed.

"Drink," Blay urged her, and she did.

She wouldn't even be here if not for me, Butu thought. *I didn't want to get both of us killed by running away, so she gave up her birthright, and now we might both die anyway in the Kadrak's war.*

"I'll carry the tent," he heard himself say.

Jani fixed her eyes on his and seemed on the point of accepting his offer. She shook her head abruptly. "I don't need your pity."

Butu looked away, flushing, not sure what to say that wouldn't make this even worse. He drank from his canteen to give his hands something to do.

"Jani, Butu is right," Blay said softly but with an air of authority. "If you can't keep up, the whole squad will be punished."

Jani turned her attention back to Blay. "Then I'll keep up, sir," she snapped, biting off the "sir."

"That goes for everyone in the squad," Blay assured her. "Phedam, Nolen, Retus, how are you doing over there?"

"I could stand to carry less weight," Retus admitted.

Blay made a gesture with his hands as if to say "see?"

"Hey, mouse."

Butu growled in his throat and turned to look up at Tak. *He's stupider than Karp.* The thought made him grin. Tak grinned

85

right back.

"Rarin here says you lift your knees too high." Rarin's dark look suggested he had not. Butu stared at Tak. "Use your hips, he says. Just let the knee swing forward." He poked the chocolate-colored man, who glowered.

"Yeah, what I said."

"Mouthe," Chewlip said, "no hard feelingth, right? We all gotta fight together."

"Yeah."

Butu stared at them, feeling Tirud and Jani near him, and Blay not much farther away.

"Yeah," Butu said, holding out his hand. He took their hands, each in turn. "We're all in the same platoon, with a water-starved camel turd for a lieutenant."

Their grins faded fast, and Butu looked over his shoulder at Zhek, fuming and grasping the hilt of his sword. Puro appeared next to him.

"Drop and give me fifty, sordenu!" Puro hollered. Butu leapt to obey. "Shanubu, I've seen smarter piles of snakeskin, I have! Bright as the backside of a dead Nukata, are you? Mir desert you, sordenu, are you gonna take all day?" After a minute and twenty push-ups, he leaned in very close. "Watch your back, kid," Puro said, not unkindly. "I won't always be nearby."

Philbe called for the end of their break, and the company resumed its march.

Butu felt much better — still sore, still chafing — but he worried less about Tak trampling him. Once or twice, when he lost track of his pace, he felt hands pushing him forward, and was grateful.

We have to work together. One person can't do this alone.

Butu watched the captain and the lieutenants, especially Zhek, who spent more time near his platoon than the other, older leaders. Tak whispered to the taciturn Rarin that the kluntra's son was overprotective, but Butu caught his sarcasm.

Zhek made us lead the platoon on purpose. He wanted us to screw it up.

Butu envied them on their horses but held immense admiration for the sergeants. They didn't have mounts. Their packs were as large if not larger than the sordenu's. And they didn't flag or notice the weight. They moved around twice as far as anyone else, dropping back, swinging around, and shouting the entire time.

They are men of stone — like golems sent to torment their charges instead of protecting them.

They were still, technically, on the road, though it was more a wide, flat and very sandy path. The small rocks, pebbles and gravel of Gordney had already vanished. While the occasional green could still be seen, propped against some weathered outcropping, the desert mostly surrounded them.

The captain called a halt for the midday meal, which was hardly enough time to rest, and then they marched again.

"Not quite the shanjin, yet," Tirud said quietly next to him, handing him a canteen.

"I think I can see camels," Butu replied, drinking.

"Baggage train. We wouldn't survive more than a few days out here without them." Tirud hefted his pack. "We'll camp somewhere with a water supply. The Ahjea know every well, oasis and cistern within a hundred miles of Jasper. How're you holding up?"

Butu tried to think. *Arms and legs moving. Ground, moving. Pack, check. It's lighter, somehow. Didn't I take Jani's tent? She's to my left.* He looked over his shoulder. Chewlip grinned at him, and it wasn't ugly.

Butu's leg jerked spasmodically, and he walked. Puro began to chant again, and Butu answered it without thinking. Time slid by in a slow blur. It seemed the day would never end. He wasn't tired or sore anymore. He was simply marching — keeping the line with Blay, Jani and the rest. Tirud complimented him. Butu was bored with marching, though, and wanted it to end, but it seemed it never would.

Butu sensed some of the other sordenu stumbling and struggling to keep up. One of them might have been Jani, but if it was, she definitely was not alone. They paused for water, and many sordenu shuffled items so some packs were heavier than others. Tak and Rarin would hardly look at him, and Chewlip's face was bitter. Butu heard himself offer to carry some of their equipment, but this only seemed to make them angrier.

Zhek rode by, once, face dark. He bent to say something to Puro, who flushed and pointed at the captain.

At last, Philbe gave orders to make camp for the night. Butu couldn't see any source of water, but he could feel one deep underground. A squad dug open the covered cistern. A large part of the company dug trenches around the camp. The sordenu with tents pitched them in the gathering shadows of oncoming night.

Butu walked around the camp, offering to help, but everyone ignored him. Then Blay was there, leading him to a cookfire where Tirud sat. Their tents lined up near it, and their packs lay on the ground there. One tent only had one pack by it.

"Take off your pack," Blay said, hand covering his mouth.

"What?" Butu asked. Then, stunned, he felt over his shoulder. *Shanubu! I offered to help all those sordenu when I'm in full kit!* He groaned and stripped the pack off, letting it drop heavily to the ground. *I hope nobody saw me.*

Tirud pressed something into his hands. "Drink."

Butu did, staring at the tin cup. His hand started to shake, and his legs, and he sat down then. Across the fire from him, Lujo, Nolen and Phedam gave him exhausted stares.

"I'll get you some food," Tirud said. Then to someone else, "Blay, check on Retus."

There was a dry laugh. "He's not the one I'm worried about."

Butu felt suddenly very alone. He could sense sordenu around him, but they seemed miles away.

"You don't belong here." It took a moment for Butu to realize the voice was an external one instead of an internal one. It felt like Karp. "You used magic. Your whole damned squad used magic. We all seen you do it."

"I had no choice," Butu murmured. His body had stopped shaking. Someone put a plate in his hands — stewed barley, carrots and meat, a biscuit to sop it up.

"Shut up," Tirud said.

The snort was familiar, and angry. "Whatever you do, don't let the Kadrak catch you. The Ahjea will punish you, but the Kadrak will kill you."

"Leave him be, Karp," a new voice growled. It might have been Blay's.

"Look at them. This is why the clans signed the treaty — to prevent this from happening."

Butu ate mechanically. The food was warm and invigorating. The boots crunching around him, shifting the sand by the fire, were a tiny distraction from his focus of the plate.

"What's really going on, Blay?" Karp asked quietly.

"I have my orders. It's an experiment." Butu heard the strained tones Blay's voice took when he didn't want to explain something. "If it doesn't work out, we'll go back to the old way of training sordenu."

Karp sounds worried. That's strange. Didn't he see Zhek put us in that position?

"Don't feed me that load of camel chips!" Karp snarled, though he kept his voice low. "The rumors are true, aren't they?"

"Which rumors are those?" Blay asked with an innocent expression.

Karp turned his back on Blay and walked away.

CHAPTER 19

Second watch had been easy, using a chant to stay awake. Lujo, Nolen and Butu had convinced each other no one would be able to find out. The problem came when they woke, exuberant and ready to go, somehow having slept better than even those squads who'd had no watches.

"Squad Tem-35 will have second watch for the rest of the trip!"

Sergeant Puro had lined them up in front of the platoon in full kit. Even Tak didn't have a sympathetic look for Butu, who felt angry and ashamed at the same time. Zhek smirked from the side, but this time the punishment had not come from him.

"It's not fair," Butu heard Lujo mutter as they got back in line, and someone touched the bottom of his pack, forcing him to take a few steps forward or topple onto his face.

"No hard feelingth, mouthe," Chewlip said when he stumbled back into line after an irritated bark from Puro.

During the day, keeping up was subconscious. Butu tried to think about magic and march as they wanted him to, but he still finished the day feeling only marginally exhausted. That night, the other sordenu in the platoon took it upon themselves to wake up members of Butu's squad every hour or so. Even the ones who went to bed dragging their feet, like Jani.

Butu watched her doze off regularly during their watch. Blay came around a lot, as well, to wake her.

This is harder on her. She's only a year older than I am. When did she fall, and why did she keep it a secret from me? How much of this is really our fault, and how much is because of Zhek's project?

On top of this, at the end of the third day of marching, Philbe

90

announced that scouts reported the well at the next camp had gone dry. They would need to carry enough water for two full days instead of one. Zhek passed on the command.

"Squad Tem-35, you are assigned to carry the extra ration of water for the platoon."

A low whistle escaped Tak's lips, and Butu resisted the urge to turn.

The squad absorbed this like hard earth soaking up rain. Retus comprehended it first and burst into tears. Blay quickly bent down and spoke sharply to him before Puro could speak.

"That's not fair!" Nolen burst out of line. "We're barely keeping up as it is! You have no idea what you're doing to us!"

"This sordenu will carry water for the lieutenant, as well," Puro said sternly, as Lujo and Phedam jerked him back to line. "You may fall out. Corporal, come see me when you have time."

"Sorry, mouse," Tak said as they fell out.

Butu sighed.

"Bein' punished for using magic is one thing, we understand that. But this? It's too much." He nodded to Rarin, who scowled.

"Yeah."

"It's Zhek," Butu blurted. "He's making things way tougher for us. You saw him on the first day, making us lead the platoon."

Tak shook his head. "All recruits get hazed on the first march, hey? But not by their lieutenant." He snorted. "Good luck tomorrow."

They disappeared to find their squad. Tirud looked at Butu.

"I think you're right," Tirud said. "But we can't do anything about it."

Butu and Tirud joined their own squad, in time to hear Nolen say murderously, "I hate him!" Butu assumed he was talking about Zhek, until Blay spoke, scratching his goatee.

"Sarge has a job to do. If a sordenu in his platoon questions orders, it's part of Puro's job to punish him for it. You can't talk your way out of a direct order."

Sometime during the day, they had climbed down a steep ridge covered in prickly pear cacti and leading into a kind of forest of the tall, multi-armed spires of the zahuara cacti. Rocks stuck up a lot here, but the sand grew thicker about the base of everything.

Butu sat on one.

"But he's making us work harder than everyone else," Nolen objected. "It's not fair."

"Beyond being unfair, it doesn't make any sense," Phedam said. "Why single us out?"

Blay shrugged. "I'm afraid it is quite common for sordenu to give the newest recruits a tough time, especially if they've already been punished for using magic. The platoon punishment is next, remember."

Phedam considered this for a moment. "Maybe you're right, but something tells me there's more to it than that."

Butu glanced at Jani, whose downcast eyes were eloquent. She polished her sword intently.

Blay shrugged.

Nolen cleared his throat. "Whatever they throw at us, we'll take. We have to. We'll be rocks in their river, and ignore them."

Phedam shook his head and frowned slightly, and Nolen frowned back.

Lujo spoke up. "One time, me and Bran made a bet to see who could carry the most rocks. So he went first, picking up boulder after boulder and stacking them on top of each other until he seemed to hold everything in town. I said, you're impressive, Bran, and he said, I know, you can't do better. I walked up to him, offering to shake his hand, and he did, and lost his balance so all the rocks fell.

"You know how I won, then? I picked up a handful of sand. He said, that's not rocks. I said, yes, it is. Look at them closely. Sand," he let some trail through his fingers, "is just worn-down rock. So I held countless rocks."

"Does this mean anything?" Nolen asked.

"Well, maybe we should think of ourselves as water, not rocks. Rocks get broken down, but even a river that's divided is just as strong."

Butu watched Jani, and thought about the conversation he'd overheard in Gordney.

Maybe Zhek wants to convince her to give up on trying to be a sordenu. If she asks him to give her back her birthright, he can give her to the Kadrak as a potential bride for Aesh when we get where we're going.

It made sense, really. They were here for training exercises with the Kadrak. Maybe the training exercises were just an excuse to deliver Jani to the Kadrak so they could take her to Mnemon.

But it will only work if they can convince her before we get to where the Kadrak are waiting for us.

Butu considered telling this to the rest of the squad but quickly dismissed it. Maybe they would stand with Jani, but they might help Zhek, instead. Why should they choose to suffer because of her? Whatever else Butu felt for Jani and in spite of Jusep's threats, she was in his squad now.

And she'll stay in it, too, if I have any say in it.

CHAPTER 20

The first water break the next day was a welcome relief. Butu couldn't tell if his strength was growing, but he had no problem serving himself and helping Lujo, who gulped at the water between panting breaths while grinning at him. Everything they drank made their loads a little lighter.

Jani looked much worse off. Her face was ashen, and deep grooves marked her wrists where she had tried to hold some of the water's weight off her shoulders.

If the adults are telling the truth about magic, no wonder she's having such a hard time.

Based on the annoyed stares of the other sordenu, Butu already suspected he'd blatantly used magic again. The other young sordenu had the same benefit. Blay and Tirud had their adult strength. Jani hadn't had enough time to get as strong as the other sordenu, and yet she lacked the advantage of a child's magic, so she struggled to keep up.

"Jani," Butu whispered, leaning toward her. "Let me carry some of your load."

"I don't need your help." She was too tired for her voice to carry any venom.

"I know what Zhek is doing and why."

She stiffened, then, and nearly fell over. He grabbed her arm.

"Look, I'm sorry about before," he whispered. "You're my squadmate, now, and you're going to stay my squadmate."

She looked at him like he was an oncoming rockslide. "I'm getting all of you in trouble just being here. Why do you want to help me?"

"I know you, Jani. Any help I give you now you'll repay a hundred times over later."

"I'm not weak," she said firmly, but her eyes told him she wasn't so sure.

Butu bent close to her ear so only she could hear him. "You're not, but you've got no magic left like we do. If I can avoid thinking about it, I think I can carry any weight they make me carry." He squeezed her arm when she tried to protest. "I can't help it. I'm too weak to do it with body alone."

"It could fail you at any moment."

He grinned. "Wouldn't that be piss in their well — the rest of the squad crushed under abuse while the sordenu they're trying to convince to quit keeps marching."

That convinced her. Butu's pack was soon too heavy even for him to lift without her help. Then the sergeants called them to resume formation, and Butu focused on the marching chants, letting the world blur into a nimbus of pain too far away to really hurt him.

"Look at the mouthe," Chewlip said behind him.

"What mouse?" Tak said. "I just see three days worth of water!"

Butu's pack got lighter, and then lighter again, and then, after a grunt from Rarin, lighter a third time. Tirud looked back over his shoulder at them, then grabbed another ration off Butu. Butu grimaced inwardly.

I'm trying to help Jani, and they're only helping me. Why didn't they try to help her?

Captain Philbe called the halt for lunch, and then surprisingly, ordered the company to make camp for the night. The sordenu began digging trenches in the stony ground around the camp. Zhek sent Butu's squad to their tents to sleep. The sordenu would not march any farther today, and their squad would have the second watch, as usual.

Butu laid his bedroll on the rocky ground under the canvas of the tent and sprawled onto it. He thought it might take some time to sleep with all the noise of the camp, but his eyes closed almost immediately.

"Do you still want to try to keep using magic secretly?" Lujo asked suddenly.

Butu snapped awake, disoriented. *How long have I been asleep?*

It was still light, and from the sounds around the camp, it had probably only been a few minutes.

"Yes," he answered.

"I've already talked to Nolen. He's in." Lujo went on, but Butu was already asleep.

He woke in the dark as the heat of the day drained away into the chill of the desert night. They were the only squad on watch, so as soon as Butu was sure the sergeants and officers were asleep, he turned to Nolen and Lujo, who shared one of the three watch fires with him.

"Ready?"

Nolen looked nervous but nodded.

Lujo held out an eating knife from his ration box. "It's no good for hide-and-seek, but there are still some things we can practice."

"What about Phedam and Retus?" Butu asked, feeling guilty he hadn't thought of it before.

Nolen shook his head sadly. "If we get in trouble, I don't want Phedam involved."

"And Retus said no," Lujo said. "Come on. You want to take first watch, Nolen?"

They all knew what he meant. When they practiced magic, someone had to make sure none of the other sordenu caught them, and that meant looking alert in case anyone checked on them.

Nolen nodded after a second's hesitation, then stood up and looked alert.

Butu took the knife and chanted, eyes closed. "Steel is sand and sand is steel. This knife has tasted its last meal. Sand is steel and steel is sand. Blade will bend against my hand." He had to chant it several times before the knife bent. He and Lujo shared a grin as he handed the knife to his friend.

"The desert cold will make you shiver, and steel looks like a flowing river. The desert heat will burn your skin, but by that time this game I'll win."

Lujo repeated the chant a second time, and Butu tried not to blink as he watched the knife. The blade didn't bend. It simply changed. One moment its blade was bent in on itself, and the next, it was nearly straight except for a gentle ripple like the path of a tiny metal stream. Lujo opened his eyes and looked at the knife, grinning.

"I'll watch next," he said. "Butu could use some more practice. Show him how it's done, Nolen."

Nolen took the knife and held it up to the firelight. He didn't close his eyes as he chanted.

"Crescents, rivers, shining stars. Blade is mine that once was ours. Cacti, snakes, and blazing sun. Show them that this game I've won."

He repeated the chant a dozen times with no change, and then the blade snapped straight. Nolen held it out to Butu, who held it up to the fire. Carved into one side of the blade were two crescent moons and a sky of night stars overlooking the banks of a river. The other side showed a desert by day, complete with three kinds of cacti and several snakes.

"It looks like it belongs to an officer," Butu said, grinning. "Can you do mine?"

Nolen grinned back.

Butu sensed movement near one of the officers' tents. He tapped Nolen and Lujo as he walked around the fire. They said nothing, but the knife vanished up Lujo's sleeve. The shadow came only a few yards closer before Butu identified it.

"Zhek." he whispered.

They saluted as the lieutenant came within the fire's light. Zhek returned the salute half-heartedly. He looked like he would rather be anywhere else, tonight.

Butu looked more closely. *Has he been crying?*

"Butu, collect the rest of your squad and bring them here. I need to speak to all of you. And no shouting 'Yes, sir,' either. Just do what I say."

Butu saluted in silence and went to find Blay. He sat at the second watchfire with Jani, and Butu could sense Retus nearby.

"Blay," he said, quietly, from the edge of the firelight.

Jani stiffened and stood up quickly. "Why have you left your post, Butu?"

"Sorry. Zhek wants to speak to us all." Butu said it loud enough for Retus to hear, and the shepherd came closer.

"While we're on watch?" Retus asked, unbelieving. "What if someone attacks while we're away from our post?"

"Zhek's our lieutenant. We do what he says. No questions," Blay said in severe tones.

Of course, whatever this is about, Blay already knows about it.

"I'll tell the others," Butu said, leaving them.

"Isn't that dereliction of duty?" Phedam asked, putting away a bag Butu knew to contain marbles.

"It's an order from our commanding officer," Butu said. "Blay's already gone to him."

Tirud frowned thoughtfully but nodded.

The squad formed a ragged circle around the first watchfire. Zhek made no comment. In fact, he looked around as if to make sure no one was watching or listening to them.

"We are sending an important delegation to the Nankek's main camp at Tranugal," Zhek announced exactly loud enough to be barely heard. "This is a secret mission, and requires the utmost security. Even our Kadrak allies must not learn of it. Therefore, we may not use the main road to Tranugal, which would go through the oasis at Pophir. We will need to pass directly through the shanjin."

"Shanubu," Retus murmured, forgetting himself for a moment.

Blay shot him a warning look.

Zhek either didn't notice the outburst or didn't care. "Squad Tem-35 will scout ahead to make sure the envoy has no trouble. You'll also identify and mark as many water sources as you can find as you travel. The escort will have horses, and horses need a lot of water. I've seen you work." He gave Tirud a tiny smile that vanished as quickly as it showed. "And I have every confidence that you will not lead us astray."

"When do we leave, sir?" Blay asked.

Zhek's perusal of them had stopped on Jani, who deliberately avoided meeting his eyes. His gaze flicked to Blay and then back again.

"Tonight. Now. Don't return for your gear. You'll find several camels tethered at the eastern edge of the camp. They've already been provisioned. Take them. Dismissed."

They saluted. Distracted, he saluted them back. Butu hung back, stepping up to Zhek after the squad had departed.

"You don't want Jani to go, do you, Zhek?" he said, gently.

The kluntra's son looked down at Butu and banished the uncertainty and pain from his expression.

"This is your fault," Zhek said angrily, "and you'll regret it."

"She made the decision," Butu said, stepping away a little bit. He sensed Tirud, not so far away, but just out of firelight. "I'll protect her as best as I can."

Zhek gave a dismissive snort as he turned and left. Butu watched him go for a minute. He caught up to Tirud and passed him wordlessly.

"Remind me to check our waterskins when we get to the camels," Nolen said when they were well out of Zhek's hearing. "I want to make sure they're not filled with sand."

Butu snorted. At the southern edge of camp, the rest of the squad waited. They marched out with little optimism for the tough road ahead.

"You're sure you can lead us there?" Blay asked when Tirud caught up to them.

Tirud shrugged. "Assuming we survive, yes."

Nobody laughed. The shanjin was a desert so inhospitable that even in a nation of deserts, it was a wilderness. Its name meant "fire sands," though that was only half true. While the temperature soared daily among its shadeless dunes, it was as cold by night as it was hot by day. The sand of the shanjin was fine and dry, so even a slight breeze created clouds of dust. Sandstorms were not uncommon. Halfway to the horizon, mirages — illusions of water or landscapes — blanketed everything beyond in a cloak the color of a desperate traveler's hope.

Lizards, snakes, scorpions and other poisonous creatures made the shanjin their home, eating each other as often as the unsuspecting rodent that ventured in. More terrifying, though, were the Clanless — nomadic outlaws who preyed on lost travelers and on each other. The tallest dunes in the area, nearly mountains, concealed the contents of the valleys on their far sides. A traveler could stand on a high dune within a mile of a nomadic camp without seeing it — a fact the Clanless used to their advantage.

"It must be nice to have sordenu who are so loyal they don't question your orders," Nolen muttered as they unhitched the camels. "We should have gotten some explanation of all this."

"The most important part of what he said is that this is a secret," Blay said.

"You think the whole trip out here was planned just to let us slip out in the middle of the night like deserters?" Butu asked.

"Not likely," Phedam said. "The Ahjea and Kadrak drill together quite regularly."

"I don't think we'll have time to think too hard about our orders once the sun comes up," Nolen said. "We'll be lucky if we can find enough water to keep us alive in the shanjin, much less enough for everyone."

"I don't get it," Butu said, stopping in his tracks. "Why send the least experienced sordenu squad on a scouting mission? This whole thing smells like last month's mutton."

"Keep marching," Blay ordered.

"Do you want to explain it, Blay, or should I?" Tirud asked breezily, as if he didn't care one way or another.

Blay stopped, turning to everyone. They all stopped and spread out themselves, to see everyone.

"Our squad is an experiment," Blay explained. "Most of you are freshly fallen, so you still have your magic, and Tirud knows the way to our destination."

"What about Jani?" Lujo asked with his usual lack of tact.

They all looked at her, though Butu looked away quickly, not wanting to make her any more nervous than she already was.

"I gave up my birthright as the kluntra's niece to become a sordenu," she said. "Zhek wanted me to give up my new life and beg to come back to the family."

"He ordered Puro to give the squad a hard time," Blay said. "The sergeant wasn't your enemy there. Neither, by the way, is the lieutenant. You brought enough trouble on us by using magic." He hesitated. "Though, of course, Tem-35 must use magic on this mission."

CHAPTER 21

"Before the Treaty of Mnemon, the kings of Turuna recruited children as soldiers." They marched, now, slowly, and Jani's voice carried in the cool night air.

"My great-uncle says magic was a weapon of war, then. I've thought about it. I'm sure all of you have. What could an army, even a squad of second-cyclers, do to one of our current armies? Only the king had such an army, however, and he called the members of that army sordellas." She paused, and Blay took up the story.

"After Mnemon el'Nankek disappeared, Pepis pi'Kanjea the Tyrant ruled with fear and terrible power for a hundred years. When he finally died, the clans disbanded the sordellas. They signed the Treaty of Mnemon to prevent anyone from creating another army of children. In the thousand years since, any clan breaking the treaty by recruiting children has been crushed by the combined might of all the other clans."

"You forgot to mention Pisor — the Sword of Kings," Lujo commented. "We all know Mnemon el'Nankek, the last kingmaker, took the sword with him. But, well, when Dinal pi'Kanjea — Pepis' ancestor of seven generations — was king, his sordellas brought him the swords of his enemies, at his command. He kept them as trophies.

"One day, they gave him a sword that lacked a pommel. When Dinal took the unadorned sword, he regained all the magic he had possessed as a child, but his very life became bound to the sordella who had given him the sword. 'I am the kingmaker,' said the boy soldier. 'You rule until I no longer wish it, and then you die, and I will choose a new king. If I die, so do you. If anyone other than the king or me touches Pisor before I die, he too shall die.'"

Tirud snorted while drinking water, and they all laughed as he choked.

"How trite!" Jani said.

Lujo went on as if the interruption had not happened. "Dinal did not believe the sordella, so he had the kingmaker killed and died for his folly. One of the other sordellas took Pisor from the dead king and became the next kingmaker — creating and destroying kings. Mnemon el'Nankek was the last kingmaker, and soon after he made Pepis the Tyrant, he vowed never to make another king so long as he lived."

"In Pophir, they say Dinal had the blood priests forge Pisor," Nolen said. "It had the power to drain children of their magic and to bestow that magic on an adult. The kings used it to create the blood priests' magic. Instead of unmaking the king he had made, Mnemon stole Pisor from Pepis and fled into the desert with it."

"There are many stories," Lujo said.

"But I thought using magic in war wasn't allowed," Retus said. "Is it?"

"No using magic," Blay said with a severe expression, pointing his finger at Lujo, who flinched.

"What ... ?" Lujo sputtered.

Blay laughed and pointed his finger at each of them in turn. Chaos erupted as they ducked and cursed. A thin stream of water hit Butu in the face before he could escape. It wasn't a lot — less than a mouthful, but more than a bead of spit.

"What was that?" Nolen said, wiping his face with the back of his hand.

"You know how us adults'll tell you that most Turu keep a magic talent even after they grow up? That's one of mine." Blay grinned. "So now my secret is out."

He sobered, absently patting the camel next to him. "The most common interpretation of the Treaty of Mnemon is that you can use magic as long as no enemies are close enough to notice. No one is going to care if a sordenu survives a trip across the desert by sucking water from his finger. If you use a hide-and-seek chant to help you ambush an enemy army, though, you've just broken the treaty, and the Ahjea will disown or kill you and all your accomplices if anyone finds out what you did."

"You only get in trouble if you get caught," Butu said, remembering what Zurburan had said.

"Exactly."

Tirud shifted, and Butu thought he saw him open his mouth to object.

"How much water can you make like that?" Retus asked.

"Enough to keep a man alive from day to day," Blay said. "Useful enough to me but not especially useful for the sordenu as a whole, I'm afraid."

"Jani's would be more useful," Butu mused. "But it would also violate the treaty."

"Oh? What can you do, Jani?" Lujo asked.

"I can still hide whenever I want," Jani said.

"Wish I'd had that talent the night before training started," Nolen said, laughing. "It would've saved me a night on the obstacle course. What's yours, Tirud?"

The tall sordenu shook his head. "I have none."

"Surely you must..." Butu began.

"I don't," Tirud growled. "Not everyone is so lucky as Jani and Blay. The closest thing I have is being a bit taller than most, but that's got nothing to do with magic."

Nolen and Butu exchanged disbelieving glances. Even Jani seemed mildly surprised.

"The first night, when Phedam and I met you behind the barracks," Nolen said, "how did you sneak out?"

This was a story they hadn't mentioned to Butu before. *This was probably why Nolen and Phedam spent so much time with Kira.*

"You didn't have to use magic to get out, you know. I walked out like I was about proper sordenu business." Tirud grinned. "Most times, people don't look at you twice if you seem to belong, but that isn't magic."

You have to learn to see, Butu thought. *Whoever was guarding the barracks assumed Tirud knew the rules better than they did.*

"Enough," Blay said, cutting off Nolen's next question. "You think practicing magic will keep it from fading, Butu? Well, all of you will have plenty of chances to practice soon enough. You're a squad of green sordenu, now. The only way to season you is to send you into the field. Some lessons can't be learned from old blood priests."

The younger sordenu all grinned at the prospect, but Tirud looked grim.

"So, we were picked for this mission because we can still use magic," Nolen reasoned. "That makes it more likely we'll be able to find water. I was the oldest kid in Pophir to win the water-finding contest two years running. This won't be so hard."

"It isn't as if you're doing it for honey cakes and the thrill of victory," Tirud said. "It's different if you have to find it to stay alive, much less if you just have orders. I've crossed the shanjin before, so it can be done, but it won't be easy."

This must be why he knows where we're going, Butu thought. *Maybe Tirud is more than just a sordenu.*

CHAPTER 22

At night, the shanjin didn't seem as deadly as the stories told. A light breeze blew the cool, dry air around them as they plodded between two dunes twice as tall as Tirud. Overhead, Zheldesa and the stars marked their travel, and sometime just after the sky began to lighten, the red-skinned sordenu led them up the side of one.

They paused at the top. Nothing broke their view to the horizon except for progressively larger dunes. Their route would take them straight across it. The sky was crystal clear, brightening to their left.

"The shanjin," Tirud said. "We should travel by day, from now on."

Blay nodded. "We'll stop at the base of the dune for a few hours of rest, and this'll be a short day's march." He led them down the slope.

"Why don't we go on in the night?" Nolen asked, sounding peeved and tired. "Won't it be cooler?"

"Night is when the dangerous things are most active," Tirud said. "Snakes and lizards, and the cats that come down from the mountains to eat them. Night is when other Turu will be traveling, and bandits can lay ambush in the dark. We'll be less seen for traveling when it's most bright."

"We should be able to see in the dark better than any Clanless," Butu said.

"Not all of us," Retus said, but grinned.

"Also, we'll be able to see signs of water by day more easily than at night," Blay said. "Remember our mission, sordenu. We don't know how big this delegation is or whether they're going to want to stop during the day for water. We can't afford to miss any sources of water in our path."

"We won't," Butu said, confident in his ability to find it. He had tried, a few times along the way, and though he had sensed the camels, the squad, a few snakes and the water on their packs, he had not sensed any under the ground.

"You already have," Blay said gravely.

They all looked at each other disbelievingly.

"How do you know?" Nolen demanded. Phedam shook his head at his shumi's irritated response. "You can't use magic."

"I was out here barely a month ago, and I had to find water to survive the trip to Gordney," Tirud reminded them. "There are at least six water sources within a day's travel of the camp. We walked right past half of them last night, and none of you felt anything."

"We just need a chant," Retus said. "That's what Zurburan said. Really young kids can use magic without thinking about it. When they get a little older, chants help them focus on what they want instead of thinking about using magic to get it."

"Chanting might help," Blay said. "But we travel by day until you can prove that you can find water using magic."

"It'll give me a chance to show you how to recognize signs of water even without magic, too," Tirud added. "One day, you'll have to rely on that, instead, so there's no harm in learning to do it the boring way."

"We'll try a chant later," Jani said. "The corp's right. We need to sleep."

"One other order of business," Blay said with as severe an expression as he could manage. "We need to set a chain of command in case anything happens to me. The person highest in the chain is always in charge, and I expect all of you to obey him as you would Sergeant Puro." He paused, looking a lot like Puro right now, until everyone nodded. "Tirud is my second. Then it's Jani, Butu, Nolen, Phedam, Retus, and Lujo. Is everyone clear on that point?"

They nodded.

"Good. Get some sleep."

The sun appeared over the horizon, then, bathing the great

sands of the shanjin with fire. Brilliant orange, the sun ascended in the cloudless sky, the endless hills sitting like waves frozen in amber. Butu and Nolen stared at it with awe, and all motion in the camp stopped.

"'This, our beach on the sea of death,' " Tirud quoted from the blood priest chant that opened their healing ritual. "This is the last time we'll have natural shade for several days. With magic or without it, we'll really have to work to find water."

Butu had volunteered for first watch, and so sat a little way from the tent while the other sordenu went to sleep. The beauty of the sunrise quickly faded into stifling heat, and the light breeze only moved the hot air around oppressively.

"I'll keep the watch, the watch all morn. You see, I've sworn to keep the watch," he chanted softly, concentrating on watching the wind kick up dust and trying not to let his mind wander to what the chant was doing.

He practiced other chants, as well. He changed the shape of a knife blade, polished his sword, turned sand into sling bullets, and most of the other chants he knew that didn't require any movement from his spot.

I need a water-finding chant, he thought.

Butu composed and discarded several possibilities, but he didn't feel the familiar tug of nearby water except from their camels, where their waterskins were. He still hadn't found any sources of water when the time came to wake Nolen for his watch. Butu returned to the tent he shared with Lujo.

Two hours after dawn, and I'm already starting to sweat. He willed himself to sleep, and, as if by magic, did fall asleep.

Unwelcome visions of losing all his magic like Tirud had filled his dreams. When he woke, sweat drenched his clothes. Butu wanted to roll over and go back to sleep, but it was far too hot for that now. Lujo was gone, and Butu could see the blazing orb of sunlight even through the tent's roof.

He staggered out of the tent, stripping off his uniform shirt. Tirud was on watch, his eyes scanning the sands ahead of them. The rest of the squad was sitting in a circle in the shade of a rock, eating. All the other tents were gone, and the camels turned their heads to Butu expectantly. He flapped his shirt at them.

"Good morning, sleepyhead," Retus said cheerfully as Butu approached.

"I hope I didn't oversleep."

"We were going to wake you in a few minutes, but you've gotten up at a good time." Blay handed him a canteen.

Butu drank from it deeply. The water was as hot as the air, but at least it was wetter than his mouth. After drinking several mouthfuls, he offered it back to Blay.

The corporal shook his head. "Drink it all. You'll need it."

"Yes, sir." When the canteen was empty, he sat at the edge of the circle. "How long've you been awake?"

Nolen shrugged. "I've kept the watch, the watch all day." He winked conspiratorially.

Tirud muttered under his breath.

"I couldn't sleep, right? It was too hot."

"You'd better not fall off your camel while we're looking for water," Phedam warned.

"Let's finish up and get moving," Blay said, standing up. "Lujo. Stow your tent. Jani and Phedam, ready the camels. Retus, pack up the rest of the camp with me."

CHAPTER 23

"I'll bet I can find more water than you and Lujo," Nolen challenged Butu soon after they broke camp.

Butu saw where this was going. "You really don't have a chance of winning that bet. Out here in the open like this I can feel everything for miles around."

Lujo snorted a laugh. "Everything except all that water we walked past last night, of course. If you want a game, though, I'm happy to beat you both at it."

"What's the wager?" Butu asked.

Nolen shrugged. "Losers take the winner's next two watches."

"You're on," Butu said. "I could use a nice night's sleep."

"I'm in, too, Nolen," Lujo said. "I give you two days before you learn how to sleep whenever you have the chance, heat or no heat."

"Are you alright with this, corporal?" Jani asked.

Blay shrugged. "I'll tell you three what. I'll let you make your bets as long as you find more water than Tirud does."

Tirud smiled knowingly as he slid off his camel and walked away with water marker in hand. Butu noticed the slightly darker patch of sand only after Tirud placed the marker near it. Groans answered his broad smile when he turned back.

"Come here, squad." They obeyed.

"You need to develop a keen eye to find water in the shan-jin," Tirud lectured amiably. "Sand color varies, so a change in color doesn't always mean water, but if you see a spot that's a different color than any other sand in the area, it's usually worth a look." He prodded the darker patch with the toe of his boot, revealing lighter sand underneath and a long, slim root.

"Bitterroot," Retus said, voice cracking. He made a face.

Tirud nodded. "Dark green and almost flush with the ground to hide from desert grazers. The plant isn't good to eat, but it means water hidden not far underground. The bitterroot has a long root, but Turun shovels can burrow much deeper. The delegation will dig a well here, whether it's a trickle of a spring or something larger."

I didn't even feel it, Butu thought. *And it was only a few dozen paces away. I need to try harder.*

"Valleys are usually the best places to look," Tirud continued. "Green is a dead giveaway, but pretty much any color other than brown is just as clear a signal. As you can tell, though, even brown doesn't always mean there's no water nearby."

"Better think up some good rhymes," Blay told them with a smirk.

More groans and taunts as they mounted their camels. Tirud led them up the side of a dune, and they plodded along its ridge for a short distance before returning to a valley.

Butu, Lujo and Nolen repeated a water-finding chant as they rode, while Blay, Jani and Tirud looked for other signs of water along their route. Retus and Phedam swung back and forth between chanting and keeping watch, changing their approach whenever someone found some.

Once they had made it a game, Nolen, Lujo and Butu had no trouble feeling nearby water. After Tirud's initial find, Nolen sniffed out the first two spots within an hour of each other just before they halted for a break. Lujo found one a mile later. Tirud's next find was the biggest Butu had felt all day. Three hours before they made camp, Blay found his first source, crowing like a second-cycler himself.

Then, near the end of the day, Butu sensed an underground stream deep under a dune. At first, Lujo accused him of trying to get out of watch duty, but Nolen felt it, too. After some chanting, even Lujo had to admit he had overlooked a large reservoir of water.

As the sun touched the horizon, Nolen uncovered a cactus at the base of one of the dunes, barely concealed by blowing sand.

"Are you sure this is the shanjin?" he joked. "That's three for me, today. I'm beginning to wonder if we're actually marching next to the Riphil River."

Lujo urged his camel forward and wiped his face with his pryud. "The curse of the shanjin — a major miraman. Those children flipped over an entire river valley, making it vanish."

"You mean there's a river underneath us?"

"It's all true," Lujo insisted. "You'd be amazed how much stuff is true."

"He's right," Tirud said. "The Clanless use the underground rivers to navigate the shanjin."

"That's what you're using to guide us, too, isn't it?" Jani asked.

Tirud shrugged, but his smile betrayed the truth.

"That's enough for today," Blay announced. "We'll stop here for the night. We'll replenish our own water supplies here. Butu and Nolen will dig the well. Jani, Phedam, Lujo and Retus will stand the night's watches."

Butu and Nolen rolled their eyes, but they unloaded shovels and got to work as the rest set up camp. The water wasn't deep, and they soon had enough of a pool to refill the waterskins. The sunset wasn't as spectacular as the sunrise, but the cool air made them all sigh in relief as they settled in for an evening meal.

"You've done some impressive work today," Tirud congratulated them. "It'll get harder as we get deeper into the shanjin, though."

Nolen yawned. "I'm much more exhausted than hungry. I'm going to turn in now."

"Drink your water, first," all of them said at once.

They all looked at each other for a moment and then burst into laughter. Nolen smirked around another yawn and took the canteen. When it was empty, he tossed it to Butu, who caught it easily and shook it. Their eyes met.

Second watch will be Lujo and Retus, Butu thought. *I can practice with them. That's probably why he didn't get any sleep.*

"Good night, shumi," Phedam said, quietly. He looked down at his hands.

We should invite Phedam. He and Nolen haven't spent much time together lately. Butu thought of Paka, remembered times when he didn't see his shumi for most of a day and how lonely he felt. And today, Butu and Nolen had worked together while Phedam had struggled.

I know how you feel, he thought silently to Phedam. *I'll try to help.*

CHAPTER 24

Blay picked up the canteen from Butu and idly stuck his finger in it.

"Any idea what the delegation wants to discuss with the Nankek, Blay?" Lujo asked. "Didn't they kidnap the last Ahjea who came to Tranugal? I hear they kept him in a mountain tower so high it rains all the time, and the only reason he didn't die of hunger is because his three sons sent their pet eagles to him with parcels of food. Even then, the Nankek shot down his youngest son's eagle. The first-cycler was so upset that he and his brothers crossed the shanjin and rescued their father. Otherwise, he'd still be there."

Stunned, disbelieving silence answered him. Lujo spread his hands. "I said some stories are true, not all of them. But I still want to know, don't you?"

"There was a reception for an emissary from the Kadrak, a few months ago," Jani said quietly. "And we've been guesting an el'Nankek — the kluntra's wife's first cousin — for almost half a year."

"Are you sure he's just a guest?" Lujo asked. "Maybe he's a prisoner. I heard about …"

Blay jumped in. "Speculate as much as you want, but understand it's not your place to know. We're sordenu, and we will follow our orders."

Tirud glared at Blay. "You should tell them now, corp." He sat forward a little more, gesturing with his knife. "The problem with secret missions is that if something happens to the ones who know about the real mission, the people who don't know better might complete the wrong mission."

He leaned back again, picking at his teeth.

"The other sordenu probably think we're deserters," Jani said, earning a scowl from Tirud. "If I saw another squad abused the way Zhek and Puro ..."

"It was just Zhek," Butu said quietly. She spoke right over him.

"... treated us, and then they vanished during their watch, I wouldn't have trouble believing they deserted."

"I wouldn't blame them," Retus muttered.

"That won't stop them from doing their duty if they catch us," Phedam said. "They execute deserters."

"But we didn't desert!" Retus objected, looking suddenly afraid. "We're following orders."

"Phedam is right," Tirud said with a vicious smirk, eyes glued to Blay. "If the mission fails and we get caught, Jusep can claim the Ahjea had nothing to do with our actions. It also means we have to succeed no matter what."

"I hadn't thought of that," Butu said.

"Of course not, mouse." Tirud's smirk faded. "Because if you knew..."

"Tirud, why don't you check the camels?" Blay said, a twinge in his voice. Butu's head snapped his way. The corporal's face had flushed.

"But I haven't finished ..."

"Now." The corporal's voice was harder than any other time Butu had heard it.

"Yes, sir!" Tirud stood up, saluting half-heartedly, and loped off. Blay watched him until he was over by the camels. Tirud stood there, knife still out, staring back at them. Butu shuddered.

Lujo swallowed the last of his water and stood up, stretching. "I'm going to rest my eyes until it's time for my watch. I'll definitely find water tomorrow."

"Night," Butu called to him. He glanced back at Tirud, who had disappeared behind the camels. Blay leaned back, staring up at the stars, canteen on his finger. *There's too much to pay attention to,* he thought. "I'll be turning in soon, I'm thinking."

Blay waved at Butu as if shooing him. "Go practice your magic before Nolen falls asleep. We all appreciate that you've been so careful not to get caught, but we're in the middle of the shanjin, though, so it's a bit ridiculous to try to keep it secret from us."

Only Phedam looked surprised by this exchange. Butu flushed, ashamed for letting Nolen keep their secret from him.

"The rest of you are welcome to join us," Butu suggested.

"I'm kind of busy here," Blay told him, pulling his finger out of the canteen to show the stream of water flowing from it.

"And I'm too old," Jani reminded him.

"You're younger than you seem to think," Blay said, sitting up again. One of the camels brayed. "Tirud and I will watch the camp. The rest of you practice until it's time to sleep."

"What's the point, if we're going to lose it?" Retus asked.

"I'm still young enough to enjoy watching you use magic. A bit jealous, too, maybe, but it brings back many happy memories. Besides, I've already told you our squad was chosen for this mission because most of you can still use magic. Start with hide and seek." Blay smiled wistfully. "That's an order."

They saluted. "Yes, sir!"

Butu, remembering his promise, asked Phedam to go get Nolen, but Jani pulled him away because he had shown some talent with hide and seek chants. Shrugging, Butu went and kicked his friend awake, and Nolen became more excited than even Butu was. He ran out of the tent as if he had a full night's rest, catcalling until Blay shouted at him to be quiet. Tirud had come back to camp, and the two of them spoke with heads together by the fire.

They played hide and seek, using chants. Butu was caught first, making him seeker, but when he found everyone instantly, even Tirud's interest grew. Butu tried to explain it.

"It's a lot like sensing water or minerals. Bodies aren't like anything else. They feel really different. In a town like Jasper, though, where there are a lot of them together, it's hard to feel the ones that are far away because there are so many nearby. But out here…" Butu screwed up his face as he tried to think of a better way to explain it.

"A town is like a mess hall with a bunch of smells competing with each other?" Lujo suggested. "And the shanjin is freshly baked bread in the kitchen when nothing else is cooking?"

The metaphor clicked. Butu nodded. "Yeah."

Lujo shrugged. "It's like that for me in the mines, sometimes. It's easier to find a vein than to follow it."

They practiced that, failing often, until Blay finally said they had to sleep.

The next three days passed in a haze. Get up with the sun, look for water until about noon, eat lunch, and then plod on — sometimes over dunes, sometimes around them — until the sun nearly set. Make camp, eat dinner and then practice magic until it was time to sleep.

Tirud and Blay seemed to have come to some level of compromise, and everyone seemed a little more relaxed. Phedam trailed Nolen and Butu more, now that everyone practiced magic, and their friendship seemed on the mend. Jani smiled more often at Butu, and he sometimes wondered if the rules against them reliving their past were as flexible on this mission as the one against using magic.

That's not really our interest in each other anymore, though, is it? Butu thought as he watched her help Tirud water the camels. Maybe it was the long marches or the secrecy of the mission, but Butu was having trouble thinking too hard about the future, these days. *Strange that this might be the only chance we have of getting away with it, but neither of us is making a move.*

Butu had once known exactly what Jani wanted from him, but now he wasn't sure he did. *Whatever the next cycle brings, no one will tell us whether or not we can be together. The choice is ours in a way it never was.*

CHAPTER 25

Their search for water led them to sand-covered stones, lone cacti in the valleys between two dunes, and patches of dry-caked mud buried under three inches of the yellow sand they crossed day in and day out.

"I think I can feel water from farther away when we all chant together," Butu commented to Blay as they made camp on the fourth night. "If you explain that, will it make it stop working?"

Blay grunted as he pounded a tent stake into the powdery sand. "I don't think so. I know when the blood priests perform the healing chant in groups, they can heal more serious injuries more quickly than if they were chanting alone. Maybe it's something like that."

"Are you saying we're becoming water priests?" Lujo asked with a smirk as he sat sharpening his sword nearby.

Blay pulled the tent he shared with Tirud and Retus into position. "Maybe. The stories say that until Mnemon took Pisor away, only a king could make someone a blood priest, but that might have been political."

"How do Turu become blood priests now?" Retus asked, handing him a waterskin.

Blay shrugged.

"Then where do they come from?" Retus's voice cracked.

"That's a carefully guarded secret," Tirud said from their fire. "Which is why some clans don't trust them — no matter how well they might treat the blood priests."

"I've heard the blood priests aren't Turu at all," Lujo said, staring at the fine pattern on his sword. "They're like the golems that

117

protect children, except they protect adults, instead. Kids just need golems to keep them safe, but adults need golems to keep track of the history and lineage of the Turun. The blood priests' history scrolls also tell the story of all the events that haven't happened and all the Turun that haven't been born, yet, which is why they never teach anyone how to read the secret language they're written in."

"Haven't happened?" Nolen muttered, sharing a grin with Butu.

"The blood priests taught me to read and write," Jani said. "The children of all els and als learn history from those scrolls."

Lujo didn't let it ruin his theory. "They only taught you enough so you could read about the past. You need to know their secret code in order to read about things that will happen in the future."

"Secret code?" Butu raised his eyebrows, and Nolen giggled.

"I had to read and memorize all the histories, as a girl."

"The future might be written in the same place as the past," Lujo persisted, "but the same words that mean one thing in the Turun language might mean something completely different in the blood priests' code. That's why you didn't notice them." He thought for a moment. "Either that or the blood priests' magic made you forget the future. I hadn't thought about that. Kids don't find as many uses for magic as adults can think up, but adults who keep their magic would find hundreds of creative uses for it."

He just contradicted himself, Butu noted. Nolen chuckled into his hand, too.

"Maybe if we keep practicing magic together, we'll keep our magic, too," Butu said. "Having to chant in groups is better than not being able to use magic at all."

Jani tossed her bedroll into the small tent she had to herself before joining them. Blay stood up, dusting his hands off.

"If it was that easy, there'd be a lot more adults than just the blood priests who could work magic together," Jani said. "Since there aren't, I'm guessing there's more to becoming water priests or sand priests or hide and seek priests or whatever than just practicing magic together as kids."

"Maybe it's just that no one ever thought about it before," Butu said casually. "Ever since I joined the sordenu, everyone keeps telling us that our magic is going to go away, so there's no reason to practice using it."

She shook her head slightly.

"There's no harm in hoping," Blay interrupted. "If you're right, you'll be the first of a new breed of Turun magic-user. If you're wrong, it's not like trying to hold onto your magic costs you anything, provided..."

"As long as no one outside our squad knows," Butu and Nolen said.

"Exactly."

Tirud snorted from by the fire. Butu noted that Phedam and Retus had shown up, showing something to Tirud.

"We should experiment," Lujo said.

"Experiment how?" Butu asked.

"How about turning sand into glass? Nolen is slow but detailed, so we'll say his chant with him. If it takes him less time, it means you're probably right."

"Good idea."

"But after dinner," Tirud said. "We've got a special treat tonight. Look what Retus caught for us."

"Is that a sand adder?" Lujo asked, squinting at the headless serpent in the dim light.

"It most certainly is," Blay said immediately before either of them could answer. Butu looked at it with interest. He had never examined a dead one before. Blay had warned them to watch out for the dull-scaled snakes. First-cyclers might laugh off the bite of a sand adder, but the poison could kill a full-grown man.

"We spotted it on a rock at the edge of camp," Phedam said. "I bet him he couldn't hit it with his sling, but he proved me wrong."

"Is it safe to eat?" Butu asked. "I mean, its bite is poisonous, so maybe it's not good to eat, either."

"Safe enough, as long as you don't eat the poison sacs," Nolen assured them. "The adults in Pophir eat them all the time."

They explained Lujo's experiment over the dinner of snake adder, prepared by Tirud. The meat was gamey and dry, but a welcome change of pace as far as Butu was concerned.

After they had eaten, Lujo, Nolen, Butu and Retus practiced making glasses out of the fine, dust-like sand of the central shanjin. Once they felt they had an idea of how long it took them to create a goblet, they recited Nolen's chant together as the sordenu from Pophir held the sand. The results were less impressive than any of them had hoped. The glass wasn't as beautiful as Nolen's usually were and took longer to make than Lujo's normally did.

"We could have made two glasses in the same amount of time," Nolen muttered after the first combined chant. "Even Butu would've been halfway to a new goblet."

"Not quite," Lujo countered. "I can't make glasses this complex, and you can't make them this quickly."

"So what?" Nolen persisted. "It's still three times the work for less than twice the effect."

"Let's try again without Butu, this time," Lujo suggested. "Retus, come here."

"Thanks, guys," Butu said sarcastically, but he stepped aside, clapping Retus on the shoulder.

"Sorry," Nolen said.

Lujo and Nolen began the chant anew. This time, the glass was much more elaborate, but it took just as long as Nolen working alone. They tried letting Retus hold the sand while the other two chanted, but the glass was lopsided and slow.

"You sure you're not thinking about what we're trying to do?" Lujo asked him.

"Concentrate on not concentrating on anything," Nolen advised. They brought Butu back in, to do the same thing they'd asked Retus to do.

They chanted until they were hoarse. They chanted until the sand did nothing, and came no closer to proving anything. Lujo finally tossed the handful of sand to the ground, grimacing.

"The more you understand magic, the less it works for you," Tirud reminded them from his spot by the fire.

"Shut up," Nolen snapped.

Butu joined him. "Just because you've lost all your magic doesn't mean we have to."

Tirud shrugged. "Adults have a different kind of magic, and it works the opposite way as yours." He picked at a stone in his boot. "The more you understand it, the less it works on you. Ever wonder why the corporal keeps encouraging you to think about magic while we're wandering in the shanjin? He doesn't want you to get bored with the daily routine of looking for water and sleeping."

"What's wrong with that?" Butu demanded, tired. He wanted to think about what they had learned, not about what Tirud said.

"Nothing, except the more you think about magic, the less you think about anything else. Such as why we've been going due south for the last three days when Tranugal is southwest of Jasper."

"No we're not," Lujo objected. "I would have noticed if we'd changed directions."

"Oh really? The way you would have noticed if we passed close to water that first night?"

Lujo didn't answer.

"If we're going the wrong way, it's your fault," Nolen said. "You're the one who's supposed to know how to get to where we're going."

"You're right, but my route is taking us to where we're supposed to go. I guess that means where we're going is different from where you think we're going."

No one said anything.

After a long moment of silence, Tirud smiled in triumph. "Look, here come Blay and Jani. Ask the corp where we're really going."

Butu was surprised that he hadn't felt their approach. He looked toward the camels where Blay and Jani checked their supplies. They were not, in fact, coming toward them, but while his head was turned, he felt Tirud walk away from the fire and toward his tent.

Tirud is a ku, Butu reminded himself. *He has not always been an Ahjea. Can we trust him not to betray his adopted clan the way he did his birth clan?*

"Where did he go?" Lujo growled when the rest of them realized the deception.

"To his tent," Butu said.

"What's his problem?"

"I have no idea," Nolen said severely. "But I mean to find out."

"Is that such a good idea?" Lujo asked. "Blay told us it wasn't our affair."

"He doesn't like it when we ask questions," Retus said in a low voice. He looked nervously at the camels.

"Don't worry," Butu told them. "I'm keeping watch."

Lujo breathed a sigh of relief. "Thanks, Butu. Sorry the glass chant didn't..."

"Don't mention it," Butu said.

"It's kind of a dilemma, isn't it?" Nolen said. "Here we have a corporal who lets us use magic as much as we want, even though every other adult tells us we should stop trying, and now we're worried that he might be keeping some kind of secret from us."

"Do you think the blood priests' magic works the way Tirud says, or do you think he just made that up?" Retus asked, and Butu couldn't help but laugh.

"You mean can blood priests use magic on each other or on themselves?" Nolen asked. "I've never heard otherwise, have you?"

"Have you guys started?" Phedam called from the entrance of the tent he shared with Nolen. Butu felt him coming toward them through the darkness.

"He's right. We should practice magic while we still can," Lujo said.

Nolen gaped at him. "Are you saying you don't care that Blay might be leading us all to disobey orders? You heard what Tirud said about failing secret missions."

"It's also possible Lieutenant Zhek lied to us about our mission," Retus suggested. "Maybe Blay knows the real mission and has orders to keep it a secret from us."

"Either way, Blay's lying to us," Nolen said.

Lujo shrugged. "Blay seems like a loyal Ahjea sordenu. If he has orders to keep our real mission secret from us, who am I to try to convince him to disobey his instructions?"

"What're you talking about?" Phedam asked them as he stepped into the light of the fire.

"Blay's keeping a secret from us," Nolen announced.

Phedam held one arm out over the fire and rubbed it with his hand to warm it against the chill of the desert night. "So, what's this secret?"

"We're not going to Tranagul like we thought," Nolen said gravely.

Phedam didn't look impressed. "So? Remember when we were second-cyclers and the adults took six of us out to the hills east of Pophir? Sebem el'Ahjea told us we were out there to play a game," he said for everyone else's benefit. "The adults had hidden some gold, silver, iron and water out here, and it was up to us kids to find it. Whoever found the most would get honey cakes."

"Of course I remember," Nolen snapped. "What's your point?"

Phedam rolled his eyes. "None of us found anything, but they gave us all honey cakes anyway. That's because they never hid anything out there. If we had found anything, it would have been a new vein of ore or a new well."

Nolen leaned back, looking thoughtfully at his shumi.

"You think there isn't any delegation," Butu said, voicing all their thoughts.

Phedam nodded. "Exactly. It sounds like a test to make sure we can learn to follow orders and survive in the shanjin."

"Then why does Tirud seem so upset about it?" Nolen demanded. "Unless the test is to see if we'll notice whether our leader is lying to us."

"They're coming back," Butu warned. "Let's practice magic. Maybe we'll find a way to convince him to tell us."

Phedam had created his first glass with Nolen and Butu's help before Blay and Jani stepped into the light of the fire.

"How goes the experiment?" Blay asked.

"Slowly," Lujo admitted.

They tried different combinations of chants and chanters. Butu couldn't concentrate on it at all, which meant he had an easier time turning sand into glass than he usually did. None of the other sordenu dared comment on it for fear that Blay would ask him what he had on his mind instead of magic.

CHAPTER 26

The next day, the wind picked up, blowing sand into their faces as they traveled. They rode with pryuds wrapped around their heads, leaving tiny slits for their eyes. Blay stopped them before too long to tie all the camels together with a rope. Tirud cursed and shouted at him about sandstorms and shelter, but the corporal ordered them to move on.

They hadn't gone much farther before they could barely see the camel in front of them, and Blay ordered another halt.

He appeared at Butu's shoulder. "Move up to the lead, next to Tirud," he ordered. "Listen to what he says, and lead us. You're the only one who can see in this mess."

"Sir, shouldn't we get some shelter?" Butu asked. "Will this get worse?"

"No and no, sordenu. Move to the front. That's an order."

Butu did so, urging his reluctant camel forward until he was next to Tirud.

"We'll keep to valleys," the red-skinned sordenu shouted at him. "If the corp's going mad, he's picked a fine time to do it. Shanubu."

Butu agreed, but led them anyway. Blay had made it an order. They stopped again when Nolen shouted he had found water, and Tirud barked a laugh. Only Butu was close enough to hear him mutter, "Why didn't I think of that?"

They circled the camels while Blay checked Nolen's find, then he ordered them to ride again.

"We should wait for the storm to die down," Tirud said, and everyone held their breath.

"We'll ride on," Blay said. "This isn't much of a storm."

There were grumbles barely louder than the howling wind. They could barely breathe in this, even with cloths over their mouths. Their eyes watered too much to bother opening them anymore.

"Yeah. A real shanjin sandstorm would've ripped the flesh off our bones in minutes," Nolen said with a nervous laugh.

"And we don't have a lot of time to get where we're going," Blay added without acknowledging Nolen.

Butu made a dismissive noise. "At least we're just suffocating. It's not like it's simam. One minute you'll be in a light breeze, the next, you'll have baked in your own clothes. If the heat doesn't kill you in an instant, the dust will, because right behind the broiling front is a wall of the finest sand there is, and you're bound to breathe it. Even shelter won't save you."

"Nevertheless," Blay started, trying to regain control, but Lujo picked up the thread.

"The reason it's so rare is because it's not an ordinary storm," Lujo confided. "It's a golem created by the curse of the first-cyclers King Dinal pi'Kanjea ordered killed. It chased down his entire army and killed a thousand of them without the soldiers realizing they were dead."

"Shut up!" Blay roared. The camels started braying.

"Corporal!" Tirud shouted, as the wind grew stronger. "If we keep going, we will get lost, and that's a death sentence in the shanjin. We have a mission, corporal!"

Blay froze, eyes locked somewhere above Butu's head. His eyes were shut, and his fingers curled and uncurled at his sides. Finally, he crossed his arms, gripping his biceps.

"We have to move on," he said, firmly. Tirud seemed ready to leap on him, but Blay forged ahead. "We don't have to stay in this storm."

Butu shared a look with Nolen. He hadn't thought of that. *If we could find a way out of the storm ...* Tirud held the pommel of his sword as if one less madman in the desert would make up for killing his corporal. Blay was just as tense, leaning forward slightly in the wind.

"I have an idea," he said at the same time as Nolen, and everyone looked at them, even the camels. Nolen waved for Butu to go.

"I can see through this mess," Butu said. "And Nolen's the fastest. If we can move sideways against the storm, we might find a way out sooner. It might be off the route, but it makes more sense."

"No, it doesn't," Tirud said hotly, but Butu only watched Blay, who still hadn't moved. "Split us up in this? Corporal, we need shelter."

"There isn't any," Butu said as calmly as he could. "We'd have found it by now! This is the fastest way out. We don't lose any time."

"We lose time," Tirud's voice was hoarse with shouting, "looking for his sorry ass after the storm dies down. If we're still alive, waiting here for him!"

"Do it," Blay said, into the enraged silence.

"What?" Tirud's disbelief cut the wind.

"Nolen, go, find the closest way out that isn't back the way we came," Blay said, sounding more sure of himself. "It came from the west, so that's your best bet."

"Good idea," Nolen shouted, dismounting and handing his camel's rains to Phedam. "Wish me luck."

He vanished into the cloud of sand, though Butu could still feel him getting farther and farther away, hastened by magic. Butu adjusted their route to follow him, though the camels were much slower than Nolen. Tirud rode near him, grumbling.

Only a few minutes passed before Nolen stopped running. Butu could sense him only half a mile ahead of them. He yelled the news to the rest of the squad.

"We must be at the edge of the front," Blay said, sounding more and more confident. Tirud's grumbling grew louder, especially when the trail led them up the side of a dune.

They traveled in silence for a quarter of an hour, and yet the wind and blowing sand didn't die down. Butu felt Nolen at the bottom of the dune as they reached its peak. He called for a halt, and the rest bunched up behind him. He told them what he felt, with the wind whirling around them.

"Something happened," Jani said. She cried out over the howling of the approaching storm. "Nolen! Where are you?"

Tirud groaned. "We need to get out of here!"

Butu checked the rope holding his camel to the rest, and prodded the irritated beast down the steep slope, knowing he could find Nolen.

"Butu, wait!" Blay shouted. "Shanubu! Tirud, loosen his rope!"

It was too late. The side of the dune shifted, and he slid faster and faster toward Nolen. The rope jerked on the camel, which fell, screaming, and Butu barely leapt off its back before it rolled over him.

Suddenly, he danced on a wave of falling sand, riding it as it carried him down to the valley below. Then he sensed Nolen, buried to his chest in sand. Butu knew this second wave of sand would finish burying him, so he concentrated on getting to him first.

"Raise your hands!" Butu shouted as he ran closer.

They grabbed arms, hands touching elbows, and Butu heaved, making what use he could of his momentum. Nolen didn't come completely out of the sand, but when the wave of sand swept over him and pushed Butu back several yards across the valley floor, he was no worse off than he had been a moment before.

"Butu!" Nolen shouted.

"I'm here! I'll be there soon."

Butu came to him. After some grunting and straining, he extricated Nolen from the sand. They huddled against each other in the driving wind, sand piling up against their backs.

"Tirud was right," Nolen muttered begrudgingly.

Butu snorted. "We should get back to the squad. They can't find us in this weather."

Nolen shook his head. "The dune is too unstable to climb. We need to find shelter and hope they listen to that ku and do the same. Can you run?"

Butu didn't like the situation. Leaving the squad felt like desertion, but going back for them was suicidal. "Even faster than you can, if I want. And I don't even fall down dunes."

"Oh yeah? Let's see you keep up with me."

They ran across the rest of the valley and up another dune before Butu realized it was getting lighter.

"The wind's not blowing as hard over here."

Nolen said nothing, but half a mile later, they emerged from the cloud of powdery sand that had obscured their vision all morning long. It was much hotter here.

As they reached the top of another dune, Nolen pointed. "Look! I'm glad we didn't decide to go back into that."

From their vantage point, they could see a great, swirling brown mass of sand roiling half a mile behind them. Butu tried to sense the rest of his squad, but he felt nothing in the storm.

They might just be too far away for me to sense, he thought hopefully.

CHAPTER 27

"What now?" Butu asked.

"I don't know. You're ahead of me in the chain of command, remember? What do you think we should do?" Fear tinged Nolen's words.

I'm scared, too, Butu wanted to say, *I'm scared for us and for our squad.* But saying it wouldn't help. He watched the storm for a few seconds, trying to ignore Nolen's murmurings.

"We don't know where we are or where we're going," he said, thinking aloud.

"And we don't have much water. I don't feel any nearby, either," Nolen added, sounding a little better.

"Right. We've lost our camels, too. In any case, we can't stay out here for long." *Time to make a decision.* "We're going to wait until the storm blows past. Then we'll go look for the rest of our squad."

"What if we can't find them?" Nolen asked, and added, "Phedam."

"Right now, let's assume we'll find them."

He sat down on the sand and pulled some dried mutton out of his pack, adjusting his pryud. They ate in silence, watching the storm as it lashed the desert where their squad was lost. The sands shimmered with the sun's heat, and sweat poured down their faces before the meal was finished.

"We should get out of the sun," Butu said. "Help me set up the tent."

Nolen obeyed wordlessly, glad for something to do.

Anything to keep our minds off the people we can't help. He's worried about Phedam, I'm sure.

As they worked, Butu tried to avoid thinking about his own

worries about Jani, but this only made the sand swirl into images of her face drawn in shades of brown. For a moment, he cursed his own magic for conjuring up uncomfortable phantoms. He had known her since they were first-cyclers, and he couldn't imagine her not being a part of his life.

"He followed us around, you know," Nolen said, somewhat bitterly. "Like a puppy."

"Who?" Butu said, distracted.

"Phedam." Nolen took a deep breath. "He never was happy. He doesn't argue with me, but if he did, he would've said he would rather be a farmer."

"Right now, I agree with him."

Nolen stiffened, then sagged a bit and barked a laugh. "Yeah, right? Shanubu, when I see him again, I'll follow him around like a first-cycler."

Butu laughed. "I'd like to see that. You two will walk in circles."

Nolen laughed. Butu made up his mind.

"From here on, we'll travel at night."

"But Blay said..."

"That was when we were still looking for water. We don't have much water, and we'll need to drink less if we stay out of the sun. We have to wait until the storm passes anyway. Let's get some sleep." He lay down in the tent and suited his own words.

"Shouldn't we keep watches?"

"I'd feel anyone before they got close, even in my sleep," Butu lied. They were both exhausted from heat and fear and worry. *And it's not like anyone else is likely to be out in the middle of the shanjin after a sandstorm,* Butu thought. *Even the Clanless must have taken shelter.*

The tent offered some shade from the heat, and Butu fell asleep more quickly than he thought he could. Nolen shook him awake just before dark.

"The storm's done," he said. "Eat. I'll take care of tent."

Butu didn't argue with him. The sand was still warm with the day's heat when they set out, but it cooled quickly as darkness seized the shanjin. They were both glad to walk. The exertion would keep them warm. Nolen could not see well in the dark, which made running too dangerous. Butu cursed himself for forgetting that. He certainly didn't want to risk another avalanche of sand. They crossed down one dune and up another, pausing at the top to look around.

"None of this looks familiar. Are you sure this is the way we came?"

Nolen pointed at a bright star ahead of them. "Terpul's Lamp leads north, and we were headed south earlier, right? Maybe the sandstorm reshaped the land."

The slid down this dune, walked along it for a few minutes, then scampered up the side of another. The desert looked no different up here.

Nolen made a face. "How long before we run out of water, you think?"

"A couple days, probably. If we can retrace our steps and find the water markers we left, we'll be fine."

"And if we can't?"

"Shanubu, Nolen. You're starting to sound like Tirud. We've been alone in the shanjin for half a day, now. It's a bit soon to be abandoning hope, don't you think?"

"You're the one who thinks we're lost."

"I didn't say we're lost. I just said..."

Nolen burst into laughter before Butu caught himself. He sighed and shook his head. "You got me, that time. It's been a rough day."

We've still got magic, he thought. *It might not be perfect, but it should be enough to survive the shanjin for a few days.*

Another dune, another empty view. Butu watched Terpul's Lamp suspiciously, feeling that it had moved.

"Let's talk about something else," Nolen said, a note of pain entering his voice.

"Magic?" They marched along the top of the dune this time, keeping eyes open.

"Not that, either. The more we think about it, the less it works."

"What, then?"

"I've been thinking about this mission, and it doesn't make any sense. People don't travel across the shanjin just to discuss secret alliances. It's too dangerous. The only people who go into the shanjin are the kind of people who don't want to be found."

"So? Phedam thinks it's a test, and Blay would just tell us not to question orders."

"I think we're supposed to find someone who doesn't want to be found." Nolen's voice became more adamant. "I think we should find Blay and make him tell us what secret he's been keeping from us."

"We're looking for Blay right now," Butu said testily. He stopped and looked at Nolen. "First things first. We can ask him once we ..." Butu felt the familiar touch of a person nearby. He stopped, looking down the dunes.

"What is it?"

"I felt someone." *I can't find them again!*

"Where? Which direction?"

"I don't know." He felt worried. "It's gone, now." *More Turu might be out here than our squad.* Suddenly he felt very afraid.

"The person?"

"Just the magic, I think."

Nolen took the lead, sliding down the dune, and Butu followed, eyes as wide open as they could be, staring in every direction so much he slipped and fell.

"Stop it," Nolen said, picking his way up the next dune. "Do you think the rumors are true?"

Butu crawled to his feet. "Which rumors?" He struggled to keep up.

"The ones about the Kadrak going to war with the Akdren."

"It's possible. The Ahjea wouldn't recruit two hundred miners and farmers unless they really needed more sordenu. It's not like there are two hundred third-cyclers in the entire... Wait. There it is again. Two of them."

"Keep walking, this time," Nolen ordered, letting Butu take the lead. "What happened to ku company? Was there really a battle, or are they still on campaign?"

"I hope they're safe." Butu said, following the feeling of nearby Turu without thinking about it. "My foster father is in that company."

"I have friends in it, too."

"There," Butu said, pointing to the floor of the valley below them.

CHAPTER 28

They descended in silence, carefully picking their way down the side of the dune.

"Hello!" Butu called. "Who's there?"

No one responded, and the Turu did not move. He thumbed a bullet into his sling, and Nolen drew his sword. They nodded to each other, and spread out a little ways, Nolen leading.

By the time they reached the bottom, Butu could see a pair of sordenu lying on the open sand, but he didn't recognize them. Nolen drew up short as one raised his head. They did not recognize him.

"Who goes there?" the sordenu said in a weak voice.

"Ahjea sordenu. Are you friend or foe?" Nolen said.

The sordenu who had spoken scrambled to his feet and drew his sword with a curse at his motionless companion. Despite the parched look to his face, the sword was rock steady in his hands.

"We don't want trouble, and you're in no condition to fight us," Butu said.

The sordenu hesitated, turned more toward Butu. Nolen stepped in a little closer, as quiet as a snake on the sand. The sordenu turned back to Nolen, though. Just enough starlight would let them see each other.

"Stay back!" Butu shouted, hoping he didn't sound as frightened as he felt. "We don't want to hurt you."

The sordenu crept toward Butu, eyes locked on Nolen. "You've sharp eyes, but you're no match for me. Put down your weapons and surrender, and I'll see to it you're treated well. No one has to hurt anyone."

"Keep back, I say." Butu's heart pounded in his ears as he took up a ready stance, the sling hanging heavily from his fingers. "We don't want a fight."

"Deserters," the older sordenu said. "Run away from us, too. Run!" He shouted, and Butu nearly did.

I must do it now!

Butu took a step forward with his back foot and swung the sling over his head the way he had been taught. When his arm was still high above the level of his shoulder, he loosed the leather cord to unleash the bullet.

"Shanubu!" the sordenu cried as the missile flicked past his head.

He charged Nolen, sword held high. Nolen dodged the blow and came up between Butu and the stranger even as Butu started whirling a second shot. Half a second later, Nolen dodged again and was behind the man, and the sling bullet missed wide left.

He has to stand still. This isn't going to work.

Butu dropped the sling and drew his sword even as the stranger's blade glinted briefly and Nolen gave a surprised shout and fell.

"Nolen!" Butu cried and charged the stranger, who had bent to look more closely at his combatant.

"Shanubu! Two of you," the enemy sordenu said as he flicked Butu's overhand blow aside and struck him in the chest with his other hand, sending him sliding backward. Butu rolled to one side and leapt to his feet, ignoring the pain in his chest.

That was just from his fist! He eyed the other's sword warily.

Someone on the ground groaned, and both fighting sordenu turned.

"Amber?"

"Nolen?"

They looked back at each other, and then, as if by magic, the man engaged Butu. And, like magic, Butu dodged and parried his flurry of blows, dancing around on the loose sand as if it was firm ground. He felt the sting of the blade, though, at least once. Finally, his opponent stumbled on the shifting sand and Butu's sword, caught in a parrying motion, slid past the guard and sliced something off.

The sordenu's sword fell from his hand and he fell to one knee, but as Butu approached to help, a dagger appeared and thrust at him, sinking into his shoulder. His whole arm immediately went numb and he let go of the blade. It didn't fall to the ground because it was stuck in the man's chest.

"Stupid," the other man said. He fell on top of Butu, who blinked past a wave of dizziness.

"Nolen?" he said feebly, rolling the sordenu off him and lying on his back, teeth clenched against the pain in his shoulder. He could feel the blade resting there, lodged in the bone. The smell of blood filled his nostrils, and then the smell of vomit as Nolen got sick nearby. Butu felt something in the back of his throat, and he rolled over to cough.

"Shanubu," Nolen cursed, spitting. "Why did he have to fight us?"

Butu barked a laugh, relieved that his friend was still alive. "Are you hurt?"

"My arm's bleeding a bit, but otherwise, I'm fine." He appeared in Butu's vision, and whistled lowly. "How are you?"

"I'm fine," Butu said automatically, noticing the dark strip of cloth on Nolen's arm and missing pant leg. "Just have to do something about this dagger."

"Yeah, and the cut on your belly."

"Cut?" Butu felt faint.

Nolen leaned in. "I'm going to get something to light." He looked at their attacker, lying with Butu's sword inelegantly stuck from his chest. "Is he dead?"

"I hope so," Butu said. "I don't think we could fight him again."

Nolen grunted. "I'll be right back."

Butu fought of a wave of dizziness and nausea, and then a brilliant light shone forth, banishing the darkness. After a few seconds, it faded somewhat, and Nolen appeared with a glass containing flaming camel dung. He whistled again, and Butu leaned forward a bit to look at his belly.

"Stay calm," Nolen said. "It looks shallow. Let's get you out of that armor."

Butu nodded and did his best to let Nolen remove the breastplate. Despite the pain and blood, Butu felt strangely calm. He knew he should be panicked, or at least worried. Kids could survive just about anything, but he knew he might not be as resilient.

How can I practice recovering from injuries? Butu thought as he let Nolen inspect the injury. *I can't very well cut myself to make sure I still heal, can I? What happens if I lose my childhood healing and hurt myself so much I can't heal?*

"Would you stop poking around in it?"

"It's shallow," he said, blowing out a long sigh. "Let me bind it, then we'll take out the dagger."

I might be dying, but he sounds more worried than I feel.

Somehow, they sat Butu upright. His whole right arm was numb, and blood oozed slowly from the wound. Nolen, who thus far had been fairly calm, started sweating.

"I know it's going to hurt," Butu told him. "But just get it over with."

Nolen nodded and, with a pained expression, gripped the handle firmly. Just that motion set Butu's teeth on edge.

"On three, right? One, two..."

Butu's howl cut off abruptly as he fainted.

CHAPTER 29

"Don't move."

Butu surfaced from the darkness into the pale light of pre-dawn, moaning. The pain had only subsided. He still could not feel his arm.

Nolen appeared next to him. "Hey, how're you feeling?"

Butu tried to sit up, but his stomach knit in agony. Grunting, he rolled onto his side and with Nolen's help got into a kneeling position.

"I guess you weren't talking to me," he said. Someone else sat with them.

"She's tried to run away three times," Nolen said. "I took her weapons from her and tied her up." He flushed. "And gave her some water and food."

The girl wore a sordenu's uniform, but she couldn't have been older than Butu. Her skin was brown like sugar, and her defiant eyes were deep brown. Her hair was braided as Jani's used to be.

"Her name's Amber," Nolen offered. "She won't talk. Look at this."

With his good arm, he dragged a sword over to Butu, who fingered the pommel. A four-sided pyramid with the Riphil etched on each side. *She's an Akdren.* The Akdren controlled much of the Riphil Valley, but the river was hundreds of miles west of the shanjin. They were also the second most powerful clan, behind the Kadrak.

"What are you doing here?" The question was more to himself, but she looked sullenly at her knees.

He fought a wave of nausea and stood, looking around him.

Maybe I still have a child's resilience, after all. The dead sordenu was half-naked and sitting in a pool of something brown. Nolen followed his gaze and grimaced.

"Our sordenu's last desperate assault," Nolen said. He checked Butu's bandage. "I've heard that sometimes happens when a man dies. There." The cloth tightened around Butu's side.

"Thanks. I feel better already," Butu lied. "How are you?"

Nolen touched his arm. "I can barely move it." He handed a waterskin to Butu.

Butu nodded and drank the warm liquid. He approached Amber, motioning with the skin. She nodded and tilted her head back as he tipped the skin over her mouth. She kept her eyes tightly shut, ducking her head and swallowing. The skin felt very light in his hand.

"Did they have any water?" Butu asked.

"No," Nolen said. "I'd say they were much worse off than we are." He frowned at their prisoner. "Might be the Ahjea aren't the only ones who send sordenu to the shanjin to look for water." He laughed without humor.

"You were right. There's something very strange going on that no one told us about."

The Kadrak are the allies of the Ahjea, and they hate the Akdren, so that makes her the enemy of my ally. There's no reason to help her. Except we did already.

Keeping his back straight, he crouched down next to her.

"It's time to answer questions, Akdren," Butu said. "But we'll do this fairly. I'm Butu and this is Nolen. Are you Amber?"

Her eyes were darker than the stone she was named for, but they glittered as she finally met his gaze. They dropped to the sword at Nolen's belt, and then she nodded.

"We're sorry about your friend," he said, feeling stupid. *If he hadn't attacked us, we would have gone away.* Something flickered across her face, but he wasn't sure what it was. "We're from the Ahjea, on a mission..."

"To scour the shanjin for orphans," Nolen interrupted, and Butu looked over his shoulder, hoping he looked as nonchalant as Blay did when Tirud spoke over him.

"We were chasing Clanless," the voice was low and soothing,

though colored dark by fear. Butu turned back to look at Amber, who swallowed. "They raided a town at the edge of the Riphil."

She's speaking very quickly. She must be lying. But, then again, so are we.

Butu nodded, noting the square button on her shoulder, matching the brass stud on his. "And the rest of your squad? Was he your corporal?" Nolen took the hint and went to check. Butu shifted his feet and winced. He flexed his right hand. It moved but the arm was still numb.

"I could ask you the same," she said, shifting a bit herself. "What are two young — very young — Ahjea sordenu doing alone in the middle of this trackless wasteland?"

Trackless wasteland? Butu sniffed, causing her to bridle a bit. "And have you fallen yet, Amber?"

He said it with no real malice, but her back stiffened even further. The bonds snapped behind her and she leapt to her feet, almost immediately falling over as blood returned to her legs again. Butu leapt with childlike speed, regretting it instantly, and they tumbled across the sand.

"He's not a corporal," Nolen called. "Hey, what are you doing?"

"Hold still," Butu whispered to her, using all his strength to hold her down. She froze. "I'll let go of you if you promise not to run, right?"

Amber hesitated before nodding. Butu slid off her, clutching his belly. She turned to him with something akin to worry on her face.

"Butu," Nolen said, appearing. "He was a sergeant, I think."

"We're out here for different reasons," Amber cut in. "But we're in the same position. Why don't we head back to where the rest of my platoon is? There'll be water and help for you there."

"We're not going to some stinking Akdren camp!" Nolen cried. "Shanubu, you know what they'd do to us?"

Her smirk told them quite well she did know. "Come peacefully," she said sweetly.

Butu had to laugh. "You are our prisoner," he said, slowly and firmly, "not the other way around. If we go anywhere, it's to our squa — platoon. Besides, I don't think your platoon is anywhere near us."

"It's ..." She stopped, eyes narrowing. "Have you fallen?"

He laughed again, knowing what they should do, and Nolen looked at him nervously.

"You'll come with us," Butu said. She opened her mouth to object, and he shook his head. "If you could've found water or your platoon, you would have done it before now. Some of our platoon is less than a mile away." He nodded at Nolen's gasp. "Yeah, I just felt them."

He looked back at Amber. "Anyway, I like talking to you." He grinned at her gasp.

"Well, then," she said, standing up and brushing sand off herself. "Maybe it's because you like listening to me. And my brother Terril says I can talk the ear off corn, so you have made a lousy bargain."

Butu laughed again, then wheezed, then coughed, and Nolen helped him to his feet.

"Let's go," he said. "The corp will want to meet our Akdren companion."

She frowned at that, but moved when Nolen prodded her.

CHAPTER 30

Two tents and a fire awaited them two valleys away, along with an exhausted Blay, Tirud, Lujo, Phedam and Jani.

Phedam saw them first, shouting joyfully and racing toward them with Lujo close to his heels. Jani stood up, arms across her chest, wiping her face. Butu guessed she'd been crying. Blay rose with a fierce grin. Only Tirud seemed unsurprised. He disappeared into a tent.

"What happened?" Phedam asked after initial greetings. "Are you well?"

"Do we look well?" Nolen grumbled. His feet had dragged more and more as they traveled, the weight of the extra sword heavy on his back.

"Who's this?" Lujo asked, meeting the tired but defiant eyes of Amber. Her mouth was blissfully sealed shut.

Amber, true to her word, had rambled nonstop for the entire trip. She only paused when she drank, and Butu had grinned when Nolen suggested they drown her. She spoke of the Riphil, where she was raised. She spoke of farming — dirty, boring work — and her brothers. She had four, all older, and all fat, boorish mules the way she said it. She talked about alligators and how the river was worse than the shanjin, which earned her an earful from Nolen. Butu noticed she listened to them as diligently as she spoke, and he wondered how calculated her ramblings were. Nolen didn't seem to give anything away, but who knew what she listened for?

And should I find something in hers? He tried to listen more closely, but feeling his friends nearby was distraction enough.

Now they were here, and he could pass her off on Blay, and

get some sleep.

"Where's Retus?" Butu asked.

"What did you two unearth out there?" Blay asked before Lujo could answer.

"Sir, this is Amber, an Akdren from near the Riphil." He gave a short account of her capture while Tirud looked over Nolen's arm. "I didn't want to leave her to die after we saved her life, so we brought her with us," he finished, wincing as Tirud removed his sticky bandage.

"I was fine," Amber said tartly, garnering everyone's attention. "If you two had just left Beker and me alone, you'd be fine and so would we."

"He was exhausted and water-starved," Butu countered. "Anyone could see that you weren't fine. If he hadn't threatened us, we would have helped you and everyone would've gone their own way."

"Yeah, well, he's dead now, right?" Her lip trembled, and suddenly she was crying. Jani jumped to her side to comfort her, despite Blay's order to stand aside. After a few seconds, he commanded Tirud and Butu to follow him behind the tents.

"What are we going to do with her?" Tirud asked as soon as they were out of earshot.

"I haven't decided yet," Blay said.

"I hope she's not out here for the same reason as we are, but it certainly looks that way," Tirud said.

"What are you talking about?" Butu asked. *I know we're young, and we're out here because we can still use magic, but does this mean Blay's going to tell us why we're out here, then?*

Blay shook his head. "Tell me everything she talked about, Butu. And everything you said to her. We need to find out what she knows."

Butu nodded, back on firmer ground here. *I guessed he'd ask this.* So he recounted the events more thoroughly, to nods from Blay and a frown from Tirud. They met each other's eyes when he spoke of Nolen's outburst, and Butu wondered what they thought of that, but Blay motioned him to continue. When he finished, Blay clapped a hand on his good shoulder.

"How's that arm?"

"Fine," Butu lied. It twinged when Blay touched him. "I'll be holding a sword tomorrow, no problem."

"Good. Get some rest, Butu. Use my tent. We'll stay here the rest of the day." He turned to go. Tirud had already disappeared.

"Sir, what happened to Retus?"

Blay stopped and placed his hand on his sword. "Clanless caught up to us, after the storm. A handful, really. Tirud and I took care of most of them, but one slashed open Retus' side. He blocked a sword with his arm, and that's not even scratched. He'll be fine — the magic of youth saved him." He looked over his shoulder at Butu. "Be careful, Butu. That slash across your belly would have killed anyone else." He returned to camp.

Butu touched the bandage around his stomach. The pain was gone. Slowly he unwound the blood-crusted cloth, exposing unmarred, unscarred flesh. The wound was gone. The one in his shoulder still hurt, and he tried not to think why one would heal and the other still hurt.

He went around to the front, where Jani had used water and a towel to tidy Amber's face. Lujo watched the prisoner warily and obeyed only reluctantly when Tirud ordered him to sheath his sword. Phedam kept watch in front of the tent where Retus rested. Phedam seemed stunned by everything, and Butu couldn't help but feel the same. He crawled into the other tent, where Nolen already lay comatose. A few seconds later, Butu joined him in dreamless sleep.

He woke to the flickering light of fire through the tent flap. Voices filtered through the canvas.

"How did you survive the sandstorm?" *Nolen.*

"Lujo saved us," Phedam explained. "He made a dome of sand to protect us from the storm."

"That was nothing." Lujo almost sounded embarrassed. As if to illustrate this, he launched into a story about an arena that appeared and disappeared in the desert, with more characteristic tones.

Butu sat up and crawled out of the tent.

"Oh, you're awake," Jani said softly from near the tent mouth. She smiled slightly, childlike, into her hands. "Look what I found."

He moved closer, the better to see what she held. When his

head was near hers, she leaned in to kiss his cheek. The hands were empty.

"What's this?" he asked, a little embarrassed at this sudden affection in front of their squad.

"I'm just glad you're alive," she said. "We thought you and Nolen were lost. We were nearly killed ourselves." She wiped her face, and Butu could see she'd been crying. "That's all."

"Jani," he whispered, but she stood and left. Blay replaced her.

"Good, you're awake. Let's look at that arm again."

Everyone except Amber was at the fire, fending off Lujo's ridiculous tale. Tirud lounged, but his eyes dug into a third tent with such ferocity Butu was surprised it wasn't set aflame.

"Where's Amber?" Butu said, staring at the tent.

Blay slowly unwound the stained bandage. "She fell asleep in that tent over there right after we fed her. She hasn't used magic since I explained the consequences, so don't worry." He whistled at the wound. "Tirud, bring the medicine over here. You and Nolen did good, Butu. We'll learn a lot from her."

"And then what?"

Blay gazed intently at Butu.

What aren't you telling me now? Butu thought.

Tirud arrived, and with barely a pause, sloshed acrid-smelling liquid onto Butu's shoulder. He winced as it stung him.

"Infection," Blay explained. "That's why it's not healing as fast. Nolen had the same thing. You can't just use anybody's torn clothing as a bandage."

They wrapped clean cloth around the wound again, and Butu joined the rest at the fire.

CHAPTER 31

"How do you feel?" Lujo asked.

"Better," Butu said cheerfully. "I'm ready to dodge your helpless swordwork."

Nolen snorted. "I still don't think I could pick up a sword."

"Good magic, there," Tirud said. "A slashed arm doesn't just heal itself, once you're an adult. Well, not overnight."

"It could've been much worse," Blay said, but he sounded proud. "You two fought for your lives and won. If you had lost your nerve or forgotten your training, that wouldn't have happened. Fast healing aside, that makes you more than just lucky. It makes you experienced sordenu."

"He's right," Phedam said. "We ran away, and Retus still nearly got killed." He glanced at Retus, who looked pale but was upright, devouring a meal.

"Only because they were mounted and outnumbered us," Lujo said.

"I still want to know what the Zhekara were doing out here," Nolen said.

"Blay said they were Clanless," Butu prompted.

Blay simply pointed at the tent where Amber slept.

"We ran into a pair of Akdren, alone in the shanjin," Nolen continued. "And there's another clan, on horses, in the shanjin. Why is everyone here?"

"Come on, corp," Lujo said. "You have to tell us, now."

"I had orders to keep it a secret for as long as possible, but it's not possible anymore, is it?" Blay said.

"There was no reason to keep it quiet from the squad at all,"

Tirud muttered, arms crossed. "I knew from the start, and Jani figured it out before we even left Gordney. As long as one of us knew, the curse would keep us all away, and if the curse is breaking, it doesn't matter if we all know."

Butu mouthed "curse" but waited for Blay to explain.

"I still don't think this curse of yours has anything to do with it, Tirud," Blay said.

"The Akdren, Nankek and Zhekara already have troops in the shanjin, and the Ahjea and Kadrak are preparing for war," Nolen said angrily. "Why are we here? What are we looking for?"

Blay stared at the stars, avoiding the questions again. Tirud stood as if to walk away. He stopped, staring at the tent where Amber slept. Jani crossed her arms, gripping her shoulders as if cold. Everyone else watched Blay. Butu's mind played hide-and-seek with the answer.

There must be something I haven't seen, he thought.

"Pisor," Phedam blurted, and they all looked at him except Blay. "Everyone's here to find Pisor."

Heads slowly turned back to Blay, who had ceased his study of the stars.

"The Nankek have found Urgaruna," he said gravely.

"So?" Nolen demanded. "A thousand lost Turu have found it, but few ever find it on purpose, and no one finds it twice."

"I was told that Nankek scouts found it not once, but five times in the last year."

Nolen cursed. Jani frowned. Tirud seemed unimpressed. The others gasped in amazement. And then, "What's Urgaruna?"

Shocked faces turned to Retus, who looked embarrassed. Phedam and Lujo burst into laughter.

Jani answered first. "Urgaruna was once a great city at the heart of what is now the shanjin — built inside a huge, free-standing rock nowhere near anything else. Stories say the Urgarun, master artisans of stone and metal, carved out its heart and sculpted a magnificent city made of diamond deep underground. The clan, which was not as loyal as it pretended to be, forged Pisor for the sordellas, the king's child soldiers."

Lujo scowled at her, tossing sand on her lap. Jani brushed it off and kept talking.

"After Dinal pi'Kanjea slew the first kingmaker and died himself, his successor sent sordenu to Urgaruna to find a way to free himself of the kingmaker's power. The Urgarun would not break the bond between king, kingmaker and Pisor. The king ordered the Massacre of Urgaruna. As the Urgarun first-cyclers watched their families butchered by the king's soldiers, they unleashed the Urgarun Wail. As the king used Pisor to kill the Urgarun children, the first-cyclers levied a great curse that sank the river and raised the sands, creating the shanjin."

Lujo spoke into the silence. "The curse killed all the king's soldiers, and only he returned to tell the tale. Part of the curse makes it almost impossible to find Urgaruna, and even those who find it by accident can never find it again."

"That story is a thousand years old," Blay said. "And even the curse of a thousand slain first-cyclers must break eventually."

"When Mnemon fled with Pisor, he fled into the shanjin," Jani said, snatching the story back. "Some think his destination was Urgaruna. He hoped the curse would keep anyone from finding Pisor."

"The quest for Urgaruna is the quest for Pisor," Phedam said. "Whoever finds it has the power to make a new king."

"And whoever is king gains the magic of a first-cycler, including miramani," Lujo added.

Blay nodded.

"It would mean an end to the Treaty of Mnemon," Tirud said, looking grim. "Whether what replaces it is better or worse depends on a king who can impose his vision on everything and everyone. He could be a benevolent lawgiver or an all-powerful tyrant."

This fearful vision made them all take a breath. Nolen broke the silence.

"What's our part in this? They don't expect us to find Pisor and bring it back to Jasper, do they?"

"No. Our orders are find out which clan claims Pisor and bring word back to Jasper. And, if possible, make sure the Akdren and Nankek don't find the Sword of Kings," Blay said. "Or any other clan, for that matter."

"That's it?" Nolen asked. "We just have to keep all the other clans in Turuna from finding the one thing they want most. Shanubu, we could probably manage that with just half our squad!"

"Where an army fails, send an envoy," Lujo murmured, quoting a Turun proverb.

"Why not send an army? Why just a squad?" Butu murmured.

"The army is behind us," Blay said.

"Jusep is no fool," Jani said suddenly before Blay could flesh out his excuse. "He's not going to send his entire army into the shanjin to bleed in a free-for-all war between the clans."

"Then why send us at all?" Nolen asked. "If the mission is strictly recon, why the impossible order to keep the other clans from finding Pisor?"

"Isn't it obvious?" Jani asked. "The kluntra wants us to steal it for him."

"This keeps his hands clean if we get caught," Tirud said. "Zhek surely told the rest of our company we deserted during our watch."

"Whichever of us gives him Pisor becomes the kingmaker," Phedam observed so softly Butu barely heard him.

"Very clever," Lujo said. "And if we're deserters, the Treaty of Mnemon doesn't apply to us."

Blay fidgeted in obvious discomfort. "Technically, we're still bound by the treaty. If one of the other clans catches us using magic, they'll kill us horribly. If we somehow succeed and bring Jusep the Sword of Kings, it won't matter if we used magic to do it."

"We'll just have to be subtle," Nolen said.

"But we don't even know where Urgaruna is," Retus objected. "Even if the curse has broken, we can't search the entire shanjin for it."

"Tirud knows the way," Blay assured them.

"How?" Retus asked.

Blay hesitated as if considering how little truth he could reveal to them, but Tirud spoke first.

"I was spying on the Nankek's second expedition to Urgaruna. As soon as I found out the curse was breaking I came back to Gordney to warn Jusep. I've been there before, and I can lead us there again."

CHAPTER 32

"Tell us what you and Beker were doing alone in the shanjin," Blay said.

They had slept, or kept watch, most of the night. The sun had just risen and the darkness entirely left the sky now. A breeze blew from the north, bringing some sand. Lujo and Jani scouted — an idea Tirud suggested since the area was more crowded than expected.

Amber looked rested and healthier for the food and water. A plate of food was on her lap. She gazed at Blay with crystal eyes.

"Clanless raided one of our towns, and our company was sent to chase them down." The story was the same as she had told Butu and Nolen. "The platoons split up, and then there was the sandstorm. Our squad got separated. We found a group of Clanless, and only Beker and I escaped. The rest is your sordenus' fault."

Blay put a hand on Nolen's knee as he bridled.

"Nolen says Beker was a sergeant."

"So?" she said with a shrug. "Growing up, we had a dog named Sergeant, and ..."

"You said your platoon was nearby," Blay interrupted.

"Probably. Then. It probably moved since then. It might be closer. It might be farther away. Do you want me to go look for it?"

Tirud snorted. "You're not going to learn anything from her," he said. "We might as well kill her and get moving."

Blay stiffened, and Amber's face became three large circles. Nolen's face almost matched Amber's.

"We're not going to kill her!" Butu blurted. He cleared his throat and turned to Amber. "We're not going to kill you."

149

She looked slightly less alarmed as she held up her tied hands. "Why don't you just let me go? I'm no threat to you."

Blay looked thoughtful. "She doesn't know anything that can help us, but she knows the Ahjea are nearby."

"All eight of you, and all children." She rolled her eyes. "Big threat, right?"

Blay glared at her, forcing Butu to smother a smile. *I wouldn't mind having her in our squad, except she's an Akdren, and the Akdren are our enemies. She reminds me of Nolen on that first day with Kira.*

Except Kira hadn't threatened to kill any of them. Butu was torn between grudging respect and pity. *She's been very brave even though we killed her clansman. She's just like us, making the most of being used by someone else.*

"Tirud, how close are we to Urgaruna?" Blay asked.

"Not far," he said, glaring at Amber. "Maybe two days' march north of it."

Amber said nothing, but the flicker of recognition followed by confusion betrayed her. Tirud looked smugly satisfied, and even Blay's expression showed some pleasure.

"You were headed to Urgaruna, then?"

Frustration played across her face, followed by worry. Then she sighed. "Which one of you is going to be made the king?"

Butu didn't know what he would do in this circumstance. *Talking seems to make it worse. I'll just answer yes or no if I get caught.*

"What are you talking about?" Nolen blurted.

She rounded on him, tears in her eyes. "Beker was chosen to be our king. When we got to the rock, I'd steal the sword and make him king. And now he's dead, and I'm captured. We failed our clan."

Butu held himself back from reaching out to touch her. *I don't know what you've been through, but I don't want to hurt you anymore.*

"The Akdren wouldn't send out one pair like this," Tirud commented. "Amber and Beker were not alone."

Blay nodded. "She's lying to us. Again." He smiled at her shock. "Well, I think that's all you know, truthfully. I'd like to know how you and your sergeant got lost in the shanjin, but we've got more pressing concerns." He stood and nodded at Tirud. "Go round everyone up. It's decision time."

"Yes, sir," Tirud said, and Butu thought he sounded surprised.

"What's going on, sir?" Butu asked. "What are you going to do to her?"

"Amber will stay with us, for now. Maybe we can use her to save ourselves if the Akdren catch us. Of course, if the Zhekara do, she's on her own." Blay smiled again at her again as Butu helped her to her feet. "Do you know if any of the other clans are around?"

"The Nankek, of course," she said. "It's their rock."

"How about the Zatkuka or the Kanjea?"

"I wouldn't know one of them from an Ahjea."

Blay searched her face again. He nodded. Butu wondered what the last comment really meant. *It sounded like she didn't know, but then again, she didn't know any Ahjea were around until just now.*

Tirud arrived with everyone else, the camp stowed behind them. They had three tents and five packs. The flight from the Zhekara horsemen had cost them all the camels and most of the provisions, Butu noted.

We're not going to get back to Jasper with this amount of provisions.

"Tirud. You and Jani and, um, Lujo," Blay said. "You will go to Urgaruna and reconnoiter. Do not attempt to obtain Pisor. Find out, if possible, who has it and where it is." He lifted Amber's sword and gave it to Tirud, who took it, handing over his own. "You can usually get away with leaving rank insignia covered, in the desert, and most soldiers will only glance at your pommels to determine your clan. Lujo, can you make yours and Jani's look like Tirud's?"

Lujo nodded.

"Good. As long as you're passing through a camp, you're not likely to cause comment, but if you spend too much time around the same group, someone will ask. Jani, Lujo, stick close to Tirud and do exactly what he does. If anyone can lead you safely through this, he can."

Lujo and Jani nodded, looking nervous.

They probably feel the same way I did when Nolen and I were alone in the desert, Butu thought. He frowned at the back of Blay's head. *I don't think anything Amber said prompted this decision.*

"Don't use magic unless you absolutely have to, and that means only use it to save your life," Blay advised. "If you have to use magic, use it to escape. Once the Akdren suspect an enemy clan has violated the Treaty, they'll tear up the whole desert looking for the culprit so they can make an example of him."

"That goes double for you, Jani." Butu blurted.

Jani looked irritated, but Butu knew her well enough to spot the fear in her eyes.

"Butu's right," Tirud said. "Soldiers treat treaty-breakers bad enough when they're men. They're even … harsher to ku women."

Jani's lips were pressed together so hard they were almost white. She nodded mutely.

"You get two packs, and no tents," Blay said. "Try to come back with everything."

"Let's get going before it gets any hotter," Lujo grumbled, strapping a pack to his shoulders.

"Sands and sun willing, we'll be back in a few days," Tirud said.

"Good hunting, and come back safely," Blay told them. "We'll be following your trail until the first time we find a good camp."

Jani nodded in silence. She glanced once at Butu, and then, as if by magic, she vanished into the shanjin. Butu stared after her for a long time and with growing unease.

CHAPTER 33

Blay barked some order at Nolen and Phedam, and Butu turned back to see Amber staring hard at him. Retus stood to one side, in charge of watching her.

"Corporal, can I talk to you a moment?" Butu heard himself ask.

"Of course, Butu," Blay said. "Let's take a little walk."

Butu obeyed mutely. *He sounds like he expected this.*

"Why aren't we all going? That was the plan, wasn't it?"

"Was, yes, but not anymore," Blay said with a dismissive wave.

"Why not?"

"Do you think I shouldn't have sent Jani, or are you wondering why I didn't send you?" Blay asked.

Butu noted the subject change and understood its meaning. He shrugged and tried to sound nonchalant. "I don't feel good about her risking her life while I sit safely in camp." He glanced at Blay, then forced his gaze back to the dunes. "But I think you made the right choice with regards to the three you sent."

"Thanks," Blay said drily. "I am in charge, you know."

Butu went on as if he hadn't spoken. "Lujo needs to be there in case they meet another clan, because he's the only one who can change the pommels at a moment's notice. Magic or no magic, Tirud knows how to handle himself when there's trouble. Jani is your best scout because you can count on her to get away to tell us what the three of them learn. Of the three, she's the most likely to get back alive. If you're going to worry about any of them, I'd worry about Tirud. He's got no magic to help him escape."

"Tirud is very resourceful."

Butu turned around, watching Retus look pained while Amber rambled on about something. *She's a lot like Lujo, that way.*

"I still think you should have sent me with them. I can feel people farther away than they can see me, and that might've spared us some trouble."

Blay nodded. "For the same reason, I want you here. They won't run into patrols, they'll run into armies. We might run into patrols."

"That's not the real reason, though, is it?"

Blay snorted a laugh. "I have no idea what you're talking about, and you don't either, do you?"

Butu shrugged. "I'm just trying to see, corp. If I'm not allowed to ask questions, I suppose I'll just have to guess." He walked away and went to help Retus.

"... into a trench, you dolt, that carries water to the fields. You don't think it gets there by itself, do you?" Amber threw her tied hands up in the air.

"Butu," Retus said faintly, "she won't be quiet. I don't want to know about agriculture."

"Do you know he raised sheep?" she said indignantly. "Do you know what they do to crops?"

"No," Butu said as Blay caught up to him.

"Butu, you're in charge of the prisoner. I don't want her to be out of your sight. Where you go, she goes. When you're on watch, she's on watch."

"Yes, sir," Butu said tiredly, taking the rope that worked like a leash from Retus, who looked apologetic.

"They eat them! All the way to the roots! You have a sheep near the river, and a month later, you have a river in your backyard. Sheep are vicious, thuggish brutes ..."

The familiar tug of water distracted him from her talk, so Butu followed it, dragging Amber behind him. She let out a squawk and nearly fell.

"Be more careful," he said. "I don't think any of us could carry you."

She bent over to dust sand off her legs. "I'm not going to walk very well with my legs tied like this."

Butu sighed, looking around. Nolen and Phedam had returned, laughing and with full water skins. Retus strapped a pack with a tent on himself — since the first few days of the march, he had grown the most, and now he lifted the heaviest pack with as much ease as Blay did. Blay called to Butu to come join them as Phedam attached a skin to Retus.

"I should help," Amber said. "I can carry my own water."

Blay said she was my charge, Butu thought. *I'm responsible if she doesn't keep up, and I'm responsible if she escapes. So this is my decision, not his.*

He knelt down and untied the ropes around her ankles, standing up. She was very close to him, and their eyes were at the same level.

"Thanks," she said, softly. He stepped back and started toward Blay's command, earning a squawk from her as he nearly dragged her off her feet.

They marched into the rising sun all morning, stopping for water breaks. Butu didn't let Amber carry anything. It could all be used to try to escape. Nor did he practice his magic, and, during a whispered conversation with Nolen, he relayed that request to Blay. *If she doesn't see us use magic, she won't really think that's why we're here.*

She talked. All the time. About her home on the Riphil, and farming. She didn't ask any questions of Butu, but if he did speak, she listened so attentively he felt himself telling more than he intended. Blay suggested she be quiet because keeping her mouth open so much would only made her thirsty, and she made comments about his generalized ineffectiveness as a leader that had Nolen and Phedam grinning ferociously behind their hands.

Early in the afternoon, they reached the summit of a particularly tall dune and Retus gave a shout, pointing south.

The first thing Butu saw was a patrol of a dozen men on horses. The second thing he saw, at the very edge of the horizon, was a featureless mountain that looked like it was floating above the shanjin.

"Urgaruna," Nolen said in awe.

"Zhekara," Blay said. "Let's disappear."

Butu already had bundled Amber partway down the slope before she could cry out for help.

"I won't cry for help to Zhekara," she said indignantly. "Shanubu, Butu, don't you know anything about the political situation?"

"No," Butu said, somewhat sullenly.

"You should ask your corporal about it sometime. I'll bet he knows more than he's letting you know."

Yeah, right, Butu thought, but he said nothing.

CHAPTER 34

Halfway down the slope, Nolen announced he had found a large, shallow source of water. Butu glanced at Amber, who didn't register any surprise at this obviously magical feat.

"My feet hurt," she complained. "And my wrists are chafed."

Blay glanced after the patrol, which had still been quite far away. He nodded to himself.

"We'll make a camp down here. It's as good a spot as any." Blay gestured to Retus. "Help me set up camp. Nolen, Phedam, look for that water."

Amber adjusted her pryud and held out her hands to Butu. "Off," she commanded.

"Now listen here, Akdren," Butu said, trying his own hand at indignation. "You are my prisoner. I will make the decision to untie you when I'm ready to."

Her hands did not move. "Off," she repeated.

"No," he said, firmly.

"Off."

"No!"

"Off."

"Shanabu, Butu!" Blay said. "If you're worried about it, tie up her ankles and remove the rope from her hands." He glared at Amber. "I've never heard anyone more annoying than you. Makes me glad I don't have sisters." He turned away.

Butu jumped then — he felt the large source of water Nolen had spoken of. Amber complained, but he dragged her after him in search of Nolen and Phedam. They crouched near a small circle of rocks sticking out of the sand a few hundred yards from the camp.

"What've we got, Nolen?" Butu called as he approached them.

"Looks like an old well," Nolen called back.

"That'd be a welcome break from the taste of sand in my mouth."

Phedam and Retus were at the center of the circle, ladling sand out of it with makeshift spades crafted from their swords by Nolen. Phedam kept digging as Butu reached them, but Retus left the circle to drink from his waterskin.

There was a loud tchunk as Phedam's spade struck something beneath the sand. "Looks like they were even kind enough to cover it for us," he announced.

"Excellent." Nolen grinned. "The less digging we have to do to get it, the sweeter this water will taste."

"Oh, water," Amber mumbled through chapped lips.

Retus lowered his waterskin and shook it dramatically to show it was empty. "Let's finish the job, then. I'm still thirsty."

Phedam's spade scraped across the wood, pushing sand from it. Retus lowered his skin and stepped forward to work again Then, with a crunch, Phedam disappeared. A collective gasp later, they heard a splash.

"Phedam!" Nolen shouted, scrambling to the side of the well. "You all right?"

"Yeah," Phedam's voice echoed back, dazed but not worried. "You were right about the water, Nolen. It's not deep, but it sure tastes good."

Nolen chuckled. "We'll have you out of there in a minute. Try not to drink so much that we can't lift you out."

"I'll get rope," Retus volunteered, jogging back to the camp.

Butu nodded, and he and Amber joined Nolen at the edge of the well. He could just make out Phedam's silhouette against the glimmer of flowing water. He clung to something on the wall.

"You should be careful," Amber said. "In the Riphil, there's giant crocodiles and fish that eat people."

"Thanks," Phedam said drily, then yelped.

"What's wrong?" Nolen called, frowning.

"Something bit me," Phedam complained. He sounded afraid.

"Hold tight," Butu told him in what he hoped was a reassuring voice, though he had doubts.

"Trying to."

"Snake!" Amber cried, leaping back and nearly jerking the rope from Butu's hands.

Then Phedam began to howl in pain. The sound was chilling and the echo made it worse, and Butu felt hairs rise on the back of his neck. They could hear Phedam thrashing in the water.

Butu screamed over his shoulder, "Retus, run! Bring Blay!"

Phedam was panicking, now. "They're everywhere! Help me, quick!"

Nolen pressed the makeshift shovel into Butu's hands, his eyes wide with fright. "I'm going down after him. Pull me out with this."

Before Butu could react, Nolen was gone with another splash. Phedam's cries were weakening.

Retus ran up, tossing a coil of rope at Butu. "I got it. Blay's coming."

Butu dropped the spade and grabbed a loop of the rope. He flung the rest down, then called, "I'm lowering a rope!"

For a long, breathless moment, nothing happened. Then someone tugged on the rope.

"Pull!" Butu cried, putting all his strength into the endeavor.

Retus was there immediately, and Blay arrived a moment later to help without asking any questions. The surprise was Amber, closest to him, pulling with as much strength as she could. Nolen's arm came out first, followed by his head and shoulders. He looked wet and worried, more than anything. He held Phedam under the shoulders with his other arm, and Butu would have marveled aloud at this feat of strength if he hadn't seen Phedam.

Phedam's face was swollen where red bite marks marred it, and his whole body was limp. Retus gasped as the unconscious sordenu flopped onto the sand. Blay examined the injuries on Phedam's face before checking the rest of his body for similar marks.

"Did you see the snakes that made these?" Blay demanded. Nolen shook his head.

"Is he going to be all right?" Retus murmured.

Blay shook his head, his face a mask of worry. "If those were sand adders, there's nothing I can do for him."

"What about magic?" Nolen asked desperately, panting. "Can magic save him?"

"He's in his third cycle, same as the rest of you. He might not have any magic left in him."

"Butu and I can use magic."

Butu nodded, not even thinking about making sure Amber didn't know.

"Kid stuff doesn't work that way. Phedam needs a blood priest, and even if we had one, he might not live long enough."

Nolen shook his friend. "Phedam! You've got to fight it! Wake up!" He himself shivered a lot.

Butu and Blay exchanged glances. No one should be shaking that much just because they were wet.

Blay laid a hand on Nolen's shoulder. He spoke in a rush. "Nolen, did anything down there bite you? I can't help him, but I might be able to help you."

Nolen shook him away and continued shaking Phedam. "I'm fine." His teeth chattered.

"No," Amber said. "Look at his leg."

Blay took a step back and looked at Nolen without speaking. At last, his gaze settled on a tear in the younger sordenu's pants. Butu followed his gaze and saw blood and venom oozing out of it.

The corporal spoke in a measured tone, but his voice shook. "Nolen, it is very important we tend your wound right now. Sand adder or water thief, whatever bit you was poisonous."

Nolen covered the bite with one hand and said nothing, not looking at them.

Blay shot Butu and Retus an intense look, and they both nodded. A moment later, Nolen was kicking and screaming as his squadmates held him down on the sand and stripped off his pants. Blay cut open the wound and poured water into it to flush out some of the poison. They tied a strip of cloth tightly around Nolen's leg and took turns sucking out the poison. The taste of blood made Butu gag.

Before they were done, Nolen was drenched in sweat and shivering as if freezing cold. Not far away, Phedam moaned softly, and they all hesitated to look at him. He was still unconscious, but he looked better off than Nolen.

"We can't help him," Blay reminded them. "But we can help Nolen. Butu, let's get him back to the tent. Retus, do we have anything left to burn?"

"I'll find something," Retus promised, running off.

Butu and Blay lifted up Nolen's limp body and brought him to the tent. Amber trailed after them. Blay rummaged in his pack. He only spared Butu a glance.

"Go watch over Phedam. If he wakes up, bring him back here."

"Is Nolen going to be..."

"I'll do everything I can," Blay growled impatiently. "Now go!"

Butu nodded. He suddenly remembered Amber. He turned around, expecting her to be gone, but she was right behind him. Wordlessly, she handed him her leash, which he had dropped.

"One of my brothers ..." She stopped. "He got better, though, and I think you're younger than he was."

"Thanks," he said, and led her back to the well.

CHAPTER 35

Phedam had shifted slightly, but his face and limbs were still swollen, bloody, and dripping venom. Butu sat in the sand near him and took a swollen, sweat-slick hand in his own. Amber knelt nearby.

Either he lives or he dies. There's nothing I can do, he thought. The knowledge did not comfort him.

He's like my parents, that way.

The idea came unbidden and unwelcome. First- and second-cyclers could survive the sandstorm that leveled a town and killed everyone else — toddling across a desert of tears and hunger until they reached a clan that would adopt them. With their magic, which couldn't save anyone but themselves, no snake's bite would poison them. The sun's powerful heat would not parch them. The angry, windswept sands could not strip their skin from their bones.

Yet, if the legend of Urgaruna held any truth, children could die by the sword — even if it took a hundred mortal wounds to do it. And if they could die by the sword, why not by accident or exposure? The shanjin was full of things that could kill an adult, with not a town for several days of forced march. Who could doubt the shanjin could deal a traveler a hundred mortal blows before his escape?

Especially one as fearless and naive as a child.

"This, our beach at the sea of death," Butu murmured, recalling the healing chant of the blood priests. "Endless motion til we rest. Cling and strive til our last breath. Mir's mercy, grant our request."

Butu stopped. He knew there was much more than that, but he couldn't remember it. He looked at Phedam's swollen face and quickly looked away.

Even if it doesn't help, it cannot hurt.

He repeated what he could of the healing chant until the sun was high in the sky and the sands shimmered with false water.

Why a beach? He knew a beach was the place where the land met the sea, though he had never been to the sea, which was far to the south of the Ahjea's holdings, nor even to the Riphil, which was the river that cut Turuna in half. *We need water to live. If I'm standing on a beach, which is the sea of death — the water or the land?*

He glanced at Phedam. The sordenu's face and limbs were still swollen and bruised, but the wounds had closed. Butu wasn't sure whether it was his magic or Phedam's at work, but he kept chanting to be sure.

"This, our beach at the sea of death. Endless motion til we rest. Cling and strive til our last breath. Mir's mercy, grant our request." The faint echo was Amber. He had forgotten her again.

Both are seas of death. Turu cannot live without water, but nor can they live without the food they get from the land. Our beach is the place of the living, but it is surrounded by death. My body is a beach — a perfect mix of sand and water surrounded by the shanjin, which is as close to being a sea of death as anywhere.

Butu felt Phedam squeeze his hand. When he looked, the injured sordenu's eyes were open and alert. His face remained slightly puffy, but his breathing was stronger.

"Water?"

Butu shook his head. "They'll have some at the tent, if you feel strong enough to walk."

Phedam lifted himself up shakily. "Help me up."

Butu stood up and hoisted Phedam to his feet. Butu put one of Phedam's arms around his shoulders, and then Amber was there, propping him up on the other side. Phedam looked at her as if he didn't recognize her.

"Where's everyone else?"

"Nolen was bitten, too, but not nearly as much as you."

They walked for a long moment before Phedam spoke again. "They left me for dead."

"Blay said there was nothing he could do to help you."

"You used magic to heal me. I heard you chanting."

Butu felt his face heat. "I tried. I'm not sure if you healed on your own or because of me, but Blay said even a blood priest wouldn't have enough time to save you. The chant takes hours. I could only remember the beginning."

"How's Nolen doing?"

"He looked pretty bad, but you looked a whole lot worse."

Phedam said nothing, but he walked faster. Retus waited outside the tent, prodding the remnants of a fire with a dagger. He looked up as they approached, and his eyes brightened when he saw Phedam.

"Phedam!" Retus cried.

"How's Nolen?"

Retus took a deep breath. "I don't know. Blay's been with him, but he sent me out after I helped him."

"I want to see him."

Retus shuddered slightly. His voice dropped to little more than a hoarse whisper. "I've seen too much, today. I've seen death before. Every shepherd does. But this? Let me know if the swelling's gone down."

Butu looked at Amber, who turned her gaze away. Wordlessly, he handed the leash to Retus, who frowned at it. But she just sat down near the remains of the fire and stared at her bound hands.

Butu and Phedam slipped inside the tent. Even before their eyes adjusted to the dimmer light, the almost sweet stench of sickness assailed them.

Blay's voice was a weary croak. "Phedam, you're looking better."

Butu couldn't see either of them, yet, but he could feel Blay kneeling by Nolen's still body. The younger sordenu's breathing was quick and far too shallow. As Butu's eyes adjusted, the sight made him want to turn his head, again, but he suppressed it.

Nolen lay undressed except for the wrapping around his wounded leg and a wet cloth on his forehead. The affected leg was swollen to twice the size of his other leg, and the skin from his knee to his chest looked like a huge, angry bruise. His lips and face were slightly blue, and his eyes tightly shut.

"There's nothing more I can do," Blay said sadly. "This was a sand adder's bite. Only a blood priest could have healed it."

"Nolen has magic, too," Phedam objected.

He didn't seem to have any trouble watching his shumi and had quickly taken up station across from Blay. He took Nolen's hand, making Butu feel slightly embarrassed.

I can't even look at him, and we've become so close.

"His chances are the same as yours, now," Blay said. "Either his magic heals him and he lives, or it doesn't and he dies. If the poison paralyzes his breathing, he loses this battle. I'm sorry."

"But his magic is so much stronger than mine," Phedam persisted. "He can actually still use it."

Blay opened his mouth as if to refute this, but after a moment's consideration, he thought better of it. He left the tent, touching Butu's shoulder lightly as he did so.

Butu moved, then, taking up Blay's place beside Nolen. He watched Phedam instead of their wounded friend. Neither of them spoke for several minutes.

"Will you chant with me?" Phedam asked timidly.

"Of course," Butu said at once. "I only remember the first part of the healing chant, though."

Phedam said nothing, so Butu took Nolen's other hand and began the chant. After he had recited it a few times, Phedam joined in, weakly at first and then stronger. They chanted in low voices for a long time, and at some point, Butu noticed Nolen's chest was still.

Just a little longer, he thought. *For Phedam. Because for a while there, I was to Nolen what Phedam used to be.*

Butu said nothing. He simply continued the chant. The sun was low in the sky, and their voices were hoarse before Phedam noticed Nolen's hand had grown stiff and cool in his.

He stopped abruptly, and Butu did the same. Phedam threw himself on his dead friend and let out an agonizing wail. Butu looked on in numb silence, dumbfounded by his own lack of emotion.

Nolen was my friend, too. Why aren't I crying?

He had no answer, so he laid a comforting hand on Phedam's back. Blay and Retus joined them after several minutes. After a moment of silence and with great tenderness, Blay pulled Phedam away from his shumi long enough to cover Nolen's face with a cloth.

Phedam leaned on Amber weakly as they used the swords-turned-shovels to dig the grave. Once they had lowered Nolen into the pit they had dug, Blay asked Butu to transform Nolen's makeshift shovel back. This was the way a sordenu ought to be buried, Blay explained. Butu obliged, but he felt wholly inadequate burying Nolen with such a plain-looking sword. Nolen had always created beautiful decorations on the blade of his sword — new designs a couple times each day.

The sorrowful duty done, the four sordenu and their prisoner returned to the camp. Phedam lay down in a tent in absolute misery. Nolen had been his shumi, as close to a brother as most orphans could have. Blay helped Retus practice his sword while Amber watched. Their sparring was silent except for the clang of sword on sword and the crunch of sand beneath their feet. Butu sat near the grave marker.

Long before the sun set, their valley had sunk into shadow. Butu offered to take the first watch, and Blay and Retus, tired from their relentless afternoon of swordwork, did not argue.

Butu watched the last of the light vanish from the top of the dune on the other side of their camp. He looked up the valley, toward Jasper and his home, and thought about Paka, Remi, Hatal, Zasbey, and Mak.

Feet crunched on the sand behind him. He knew it was Amber but turned anyway.

"Get some sleep," he ordered. "It'll be a long day tomorrow."

She nodded but sat down near the fire. "Blay said if you're on watch, I'm on watch."

Butu snorted and walked down to face the direction Urgaruna would be in.

"My brother was bitten by a water thief," she said. "We stayed up all night with him, just like you and Phedam did with Nolen. By the time the blood priest got there, though, my brother was sleeping peacefully."

Butu stared at her. "How long ago was this?"

"Four? Five years ago? It didn't make much sense to me. I had probably been bitten myself, and nothing like that had happened." She shuddered. "Not that I like snakes."

"Nolen and I had known each other for only a few weeks," Butu said, guiltily. "We practiced, a lot, together. Magic," he added hurriedly. "The idea was that if you keep using it, it won't go away."

"That's not true."

"Yeah, I guess we found that out." He sat down across from her. "He and Phedam grew up together as shumi, in the mountains above Jasper. Phedam came because Nolen asked him to." He moistened his lips. "Nolen and I, we got along a whole lot better than them at the end. Now my friend is dead, and his shumi is alone."

She remained silent for a time before speaking. "You can be his friend."

"Yeah," he said and felt no relief. *She was the only person I could talk to about that, though. It had to be her.* He looked at her, puzzled. "You could've escaped today, several times."

"Yeah." She looked down at her still bound hands, and Butu watched the ropes untie themselves.

"All of your magic hasn't gone yet. You're younger than me. All this time you could've escaped and you didn't. Now, when you go, you'll tell them where we are."

She gazed out over the desert. "Beker and I were lost — he thought we were east of the rock. If you and Nolen hadn't shown up, we would've died." She leaned toward him. "If I make the king, I'll remember who helped me, and I won't let him hurt you."

Butu shook his head. "I don't think it'll work that way, Amber. I think if Jusep was made king, he'd destroy anyone who had opposed him. I can't trust your king that much."

"Then trust this," she said, holding something out in her hand. It was a marble, crystal clear on the outside, and inside colored orange in the light. "Let this be my promise to you that I'll find a way to help you if you ever need it."

Butu took the marble. He remembered handing his amber to Paka, a token of friendship. He looked Amber in the eye. She didn't turn her gaze this time.

I have to learn to see, he thought, and nodded mutely. They rose to their feet together. *She didn't set out to spy on us. She'll keep her promise.* He nodded again, and she ran off into the night, south, in the direction of Urgaruna.

"I'm learning to see," he mumbled, staring after her. He felt Blay approach.

"You fought to keep her with us," Blay said, "and then you let her go. She'll tell them where we are."

"I don't think she will," Butu said, clutching the marble. "She'll have other things to worry about. But when she gets back, they'll have their kingmaker again."

"All the more reason we should've kept her." Blay's voice trembled.

Butu thought of Amber, who owed her life to Nolen, and of Phedam, whom he had died rescuing.

"Punish me if you want, corp, but this is what Nolen would have done."

Nolen's grave stared back at him. In a few days the shanjin would wipe it away, erasing the last traces of his brother-in-arms, his shumi, forever.

Whether I will fall in battle or by accident, one day, I'll be buried with my sword.

Butu touched the hilt of his weapon.

I can't choose how I die, but I can decide how to live.

CYCLE 3

CHAPTER 36

Butu sensed Jani, Lujo and Tirud returning shortly before the three ghosted into camp, their faces streaked with frustration and exhaustion. Jani slumped across from him without a smile, and Tirud retrieved a waterskin from his pack, which he tossed to her. Butu grasped Lujo's hand in mute welcome. Despite the exhaustion in his face, Tirud paced.

Butu broke the silence. "What happened? How many are at Urgaruna?"

Lujo grunted, but Tirud nearly exploded.

"That place is a fortress and will be impossible to get into." He stopped and dropped onto the sand near Lujo. "I would rather cross the shanjin without a waterskin."

The outburst woke Blay, Phedam and Retus, who joined them.

"Were you followed?" Blay asked tensely, sitting next to Jani. He relaxed after Tirud and Lujo shook their heads. "What did you see?"

Tirud answered. "Akdren sordenu, at least four companies. One company of cavalry, I think. No fewer than three platoons scouting around the rock." He poked at the sand next to the fire, making a map. Lujo took one look at it, and the image drew itself. Tirud snorted and continued. "There are two Nankek sordenu companies and no cavalry camped east of the rock."

The map grew as they spoke: the rock, in the center, and entrance on the north face; guarding the entrance and part of the north wall, the Akdren; controlling the east and rear, the Nankek;

and Nukata and Zhekara cavalry, hovering on the west and north. The Kadrak themselves, a blob maybe a day west.

"There will be blood when the Kadrak run into the Zhekara," Tirud said, strangely mild, glancing at Jani.

"Aesh requested Jusep send me to Mnemon as a potential bride," she said. No one seemed surprised. "Aesh wanted assurance that Jusep and the Ahjea would support him as king, that if they found the sword first, they would give it to him. I was ... part of the bargain." She turned her head.

Blay tugged his goatee. "He'll be furious Jusep didn't deliver on his promise."

"Did they expect her at the exercises?" Phedam asked. "They couldn't have known she'd been there."

"I don't know," Blay said, and Tirud snorted.

No reason to believe him, Butu thought. *Could be more orders.* He said, "If the legends are true, and we got the sword to Jusep before the Kadrak got to him, they could come with everything in the country, and the Ahjea would still win. With Pisor's power, the kluntra could bury all of Mnemon."

"If they're not true," Jani countered, "we need to get the sword back to Jasper before Aesh loses his patience." Butu found the courage to look at her. "Jusep can explain that I gave up my birthright, and Aesh will have to forgive him, so long as we give him Pisor. If Pisor is just a symbol, he'll need the support of the Ahjea to claim and hold the title of king."

"Well, no one's made a king yet, right?" Retus said. "We'd know, right?"

Tirud nodded. "The battle at the rock hasn't started yet, but it will soon. The Akdren may not be able to get out if everyone sides against them."

"Maybe they don't have a kingmaker," Phedam said.

Blay grunted. "Maybe their kluntra, Philquek, isn't there yet."

"Maybe they haven't found the sword," Butu suggested.

"We didn't sneak inside to find out," Lujo said. "It's a fortress with one entrance and everyone's watching it."

"For which we are grateful," Blay said. "Or else you might not have gotten back." He stood up, looking to his tent.

"We have to leave tonight," Butu said. "We have to get there before the Kadrak do."

Tirud gave him a strange look, and Phedam and Retus yawned.

"It's too late for that. Too many clans are involved now," Blay said. "Our orders were to find out who has Pisor, and we've done that."

"We know who holds Urgaruna, not who has Pisor," Butu pointed out.

"You seem to have forgotten who gives the orders here, Butu." Blay said tensely. "This is not your decision. Finish your watch. The rest of you, get some sleep."

"Blay's right about one thing," Tirud said quietly. "We have to sleep now."

Butu opened his mouth to argue, but Tirud settled a paralyzing gaze on him. Almost like magic, his mouth shut, and Retus and Phedam hauled Lujo to his feet as Blay disappeared into his tent. Jani warmed her hands in the fire, eyes downcast.

She probably thinks Blay and I are still fighting because of Amber, he thought, glancing at the moons. *How could she know that it's because of Nolen? She doesn't even know he's dead yet.* A hollow pit formed in his stomach as he thought of who might have to tell her.

That left Tirud, staring at him questioningly.

"Nolen's dead." He gave a terse explanation, gesturing to the pile of snakes by the well. He fought to keep tears from his voice, tried to stick to the death itself and not the arguments from it. Jani gasped but didn't move. Tirud's expression softened.

"And Amber?"

Butu wiped his face. "I let her go. She wasn't a spy, and we were low on supplies. She promised she wouldn't tell anyone, and I trusted her."

Tirud nodded. "Probably stupid, but since we're not going back anyway, it doesn't matter."

Butu frowned. "We should go."

"The corporal said we shouldn't." Tirud sounded too casual. "We have orders."

"Do you think it's worth a war?"

Tirud didn't speak right away, and Butu wondered if Nolen's death had shocked the red-skinned sordenu beyond the power to speak. But, at last, "It's expected of us. What I think doesn't enter into it."

"Treaty or king — what does it matter who rules? Why are we fighting over this?"

"The third cycle is filled with questions, Butu. We've all asked ourselves questions like that. Be grateful these worries did not trouble your second cycle."

What would you know? Butu thought, but held the question. One did not ask a ku about his past. Kus abandoned their birth clans for a reason. But Tirud looked haunted, and words spilled from his lips, gaining strength as he went on.

CHAPTER 37

"You Ahjea are used to thinking of Turuna as a vast desert with mountains at the edges, but that is not true along the Riphil, and the southern coast has forests and orchards." Tirud nodded to himself, sounding like Lujo. "As Ahjea children shape steel and sand, so Kanjea children command branch, leaf and fruit. Most of the fruit is nothing special to a Kanjea, but some have magical powers." He held out his hand as if plucking something from a tree.

"One of these is lej. If you eat a piece of that bitter fruit, you see yourself as you would if you were looking back on yourself a cycle from now. It isn't seeing the future, but it distances you from the present enough to put the current crisis into perspective. When you look back at the things that were important to you a cycle ago, you'll find that most of them don't matter to you anymore."

He frowned, his face green in the setting light of Zheldesa, large against the horizon. Galdera's pale sliver and a thousand stars soon would be the night's only light.

"Lej is dangerous to those who try to gain too much perspective by eating a lot of it. Many merely lose hope, but some fall into a sleep from which they never awaken. Turun children are the most vulnerable, though, and the adults try to keep the children from eating it. Some Kanjea keep it a secret from the children, while others warn them not to eat it. You see, a single bite of lej robs a child of magic forever. However, he's immediately aware of how foolish his actions were."

Tirud fell into a long silence. The green moon set.

Adults have a different kind of magic, and it works the opposite way as yours. The more you understand it, the less it works on you. The more you think about magic, the less you think about anything else.

He'd been hinting at Blay's deception, at the time. Butu suspected this was another of the tall sordenu's subtle warnings, but he couldn't find any connection between the story of lej and their present situation.

Why hide his meaning at all? We're all in the same squad.

"Is this your story, or are you trying to tell us to obey Blay's orders?" Butu demanded, not really in the mood for parables.

Tirud smiled mysteriously.

"Either you want to answer my questions or you don't," Butu said. What's the point in getting me to ask questions if you're not going to answer them?

Tirud stood up, brushing the sand off his pants. "Some questions are more important than their answers, and many questions have no answers."

"What's that supposed to mean?"

Tirud winked at him before strolling back toward the tent. "Now you sound like a child who might reach his fourth cycle."

Butu muttered several choice words at Tirud's back. He supposed it was possible Tirud had told his own story. There was a certain comfort to that. It was much easier to imagine an unfortunate childhood misunderstanding had caused Tirud's lack of magic, and not a stroke of bad luck that could yet strike Butu.

I will keep my magic, Butu vowed silently, and suited action to thoughts, grabbing a handful of sand and crafting marbles. About half his attempts were acceptable. He considered racing out into the night, dancing over dunes as lightly as the wind, but the memory of Nolen pressed down on him. He felt suddenly afraid of the darkness, afraid of stepping on a snake, afraid of falling down a dune in an avalanche of choking sand.

One of us is dead, he thought, *and we didn't do anything. We just found out several clans have gathered at Urgaruna. Our corporal wants us to leave without finding out if they have Pisor.*

"He was talking about Blay," Jani said suddenly from her place near the fire. Butu jumped. She hadn't even made herself invisible, and he had forgotten she was still there.

Butu frowned. "But Blay still has his magic."

Jani sighed. "It's not directly about Blay, of course." She looked annoyed, exhausted, and sad all at the same time. She collapsed into the sand near him. "Blay thought he was a born leader when we left Gordney, remember?"

"Yeah. Karp tried to warn me about him, but I didn't listen." The words were bitter. "His lack of judgment nearly killed the entire squad in the sandstorm. It did kill Nolen!"

"You said he did everything he could to save Nolen," she said gently. "No one died because of him."

Butu took a deep breath. *She's right,* he thought. *I can't blame Nolen's death on Blay. But I can blame the lies on him.*

"Fine," he snapped. "His decisions didn't kill Nolen. I'm tired, Jani, of being told one thing when we're doing something else. For all we know, we're actually going to Urgaruna in the morning. That's our corp for you. He calls us men and treats us like children!"

"He's scared, Butu. He's under a lot of pressure from Pater and Zhek. He's never done anything like this before, and it obviously isn't going well."

"It would have gone a whole lot better if he'd listened to Tirud sooner and told us the truth."

She shrugged. "That's what Tirud was talking about just now. People make mistakes because they don't know they're mistakes, at the time." She picked up a handful of sand and let it trickle through her fingers.

"Well it's not like Tirud didn't spend the entire march here practically shouting at Blay to just tell us what was actually going on, you know. Ku or not, Tirud has some idea what he's doing."

Jani didn't look his way, watching the sand fall from her fingers, instead. "The adults warned Tirud not to eat lej, too, and you see how well he listened."

"A second-cycler doesn't get put in charge of making life-and-death decisions for a squad of sordenu, Jani," he countered.

Jani fell into a fidgety silence for several minutes. Butu stared into the shanjin.

"I think I know what Blay is going through," Jani said abruptly.

Butu turned to look at her, but she had turned invisible. She flickered back into view after only a moment. She looked embarrassed.

"Butu, we need to talk." Her voice cracked a little like Retus', though Butu knew it wasn't because her voice was changing.

His heart pounded in his chest as he considered all the possible meanings that one sentence could have. He nodded mutely.

"I joined the sordenu when I did partially because I wanted to be in your squad."

Partially?

"Yeah. I know," Butu said softly, taking her hand. "The night I left you in Jasper, well, I kind of know how Tirud must have felt after eating lej. My world ended."

"Mine too," she said. She slid her hand out of his grip. "But not for the reason you probably think it did."

He glanced at the withdrawn hand. "Jusep was sending you to Mnemon. I was joining the sordenu. You didn't know if you'd ever see me again."

"I was being selfish, Butu," she said, sounding miserable. "I'm so sorry. I didn't mean to hurt you like this!"

"Hurt me?" He leaned back and looked at her searchingly.

"I wasn't chasing you. I just wanted to be in your squad because you were familiar. After everything else I lost, I just wanted one thing from my old life that I could trust."

Magic senses or not, if a Clanless raid approached right now, Butu wouldn't have noticed it. "Oh," he managed after the initial shock had passed.

"Oh?" she repeated, looking even more miserable.

"Well, um, I'm glad we're talking about this, actually." Butu rolled one of the marbles between his fingers nervously. He was almost certain he didn't look glad. "When I found out you'd joined the sordenu, I thought it was all my fault for refusing to run away with you. I thought you were going to die during that first march."

"So did I," she murmured with a faint smile.

Encouraged, he plunged forward. "But I meant what I said, too. During the march, I mean. I'm glad you're in my squad. I was kind of glad for the rule, though."

Jani looked puzzled. "Which rule? Not the one about magic,

of course."

Butu hesitated. *Maybe she's chasing me but doesn't want to admit it. Maybe she isn't but won't believe me if I tell her I'm happy about it.* His stomach knotted again as he blurted, "No romance within the same platoon."

Jani laughed, and all her tension melted. "I should have known."

He managed a small smile of his own. "We both should have. We snuck plenty of kisses behind the backs of your family. No reason why some sordenu rule would have stopped us, right?"

"As if they didn't know exactly what was going on," Jani reminded him. "I think Jusep decided it was better to just let us think our doomed little romance was a secret. It kept us from running off together before our mirjuvas."

Butu digested this. "You know, you never told me about your mirjuva."

She shrugged but looked embarrassed. "You remember when Jusep took Zhek and me to negotiate that trade deal last year? It happened during that. I tripped and fell while Zhek and I were playing hide-and-seek with some of the Kadrak kids. I was so embarrassed that I didn't want to tell you about it. By the time I stopped being embarrassed about falling down, I was embarrassed for not telling you as soon as I got back, so I just kept it a secret."

Butu nodded, remembering the awkward mirjuva conversation in Gordney. "I can understand that."

Jani relaxed again. "Still friends?" she asked in a cheerful tone.

He nodded vigorously, and they hugged warmly. Butu felt a small, irrational pang at losing her again, but it was weaker now than it had been in Jasper.

"I should get to bed," Jani said with a yawn as she stood up. "I've been marching all day."

A wild thought came to Butu. "Jani, wait."

She turned, watching him in the firelight. "Yes?"

"We should go get Pisor," he said in a deadly serious tone.

She stared back, her face a set of O's. She didn't object, though.

"The corp won't take us to the rock," Butu explained quickly, recreating Lujo's map in the sand. "He thinks there's too few of

us, but I think there's too many. If just you and I went in — you to
be invisible and me to see — we could snatch it from them before
they knew." He paused. "Look, Jani, if we go back, they'll find a
way to marry you to an el'. We'll all be branded as deserters whatever Blay says. And if he says we won't, I still don't believe him."

She was shaking her head.

"You think I'm crazy, don't you?" he asked sheepishly.

"No," she said slowly. "We have to bring Lujo."

"What?" But Butu could already see how useful he would be.

*Phedam can heal himself, and Retus has his armor. Tirud and Blay
have no magic. Lujo, though, can transform rock and metals. He could
hide Pisor once we get it.*

"He could create a tunnel for us where there wasn't one," Jani
said, as if echoing Butu's thoughts.

"So we're going to do it?" he said, excitedly.

She nodded. He stood up, dusting himself off.

He went to wake Lujo while she snagged supplies for them.
Their exhausted friend was easily persuaded that they could protect him, and that they'd die without him. It was another prank to
their perennial tale-teller, and an exciting one at that.

They left the camp as Galdera set, the stars spinning overhead
their only light. Jani's mouth was a bitter line, and Lujo's yawn
swallowed the night. They'd travel all night, Butu explained, and
when they were inside the outer line of patrols, they'd rest. Lujo
didn't complain for four hours, and Jani never once opened her
mouth as they backtracked toward the rock.

Finally, as they marched partway up the side of a tall dune,
on the idea that patrols would look at ridges and valleys and not
in between, Butu felt nothing around them for at least half a mile.
He poked his head over the top. Torches on Urgaruna had been
visible the past two hours, and now, as a thin blue line promised
the start of the day, the rock loomed before them, less than a mile
away. He thought about Pisor as he watched the three distinct
camps in front of it, soldiers moving like ants from this far away. A
squad of cavalry thundered out on patrol, their hooves just reaching his sensitive ears.

"I'll take first watch," he said. "You two sleep. Two hours,
then I'll wake Lujo. Then two more for Jani, all right?"

"Can we stay here that long?" Jani asked. "The Zhekara patrols came out this far."

"Farther," Butu corrected. "They're behind us already, about a mile back. And if we're not fine, we'll have plenty of warning. Besides, when Lujo's on watch he can build us a shelter and no one will notice us."

Lujo was already asleep, half-buried in sand. Jani did the same, staring around her wildly.

"Do you think they followed us?"

"No," Butu lied. *Someone had seen us leave, I'm sure of it. Blay would be waking right now. It's easy to track across this. Would Blay follow us, or go home?* He was certain Blay would command them to go home. *Will Tirud argue?* He couldn't decide.

Well, he's done nothing but ask us to question Blay's authority.

The thought startled Butu. *Did Tirud lead me to make this choice? Is he as much of a liar as Blay?*

He crawled back up to stare at Urgaruna as the sun broke the horizon.

It was a mountain, no doubt about it. This close, it rose into a shadowy knife of black rock stabbing the sky. Steep slopes met narrow ledges to riddle the structure with places to hide and false entrances to the tomb beneath — the legendary city of Urgaruna, lost for a thousand years.

He ducked his head as he felt a cavalry patrol come by, headed to the rock. The ten horses trotted through the valley below him, and he chanced to look at them again.

Zhekara, he thought. *Of course they'd come back to camp somehow.* He cursed himself for thinking they'd be safe here.

But the squad went by without even looking up, intent on getting home, and he coughed out a sigh of relief, leaning back and drinking from his waterskin. He took a deep breath and concentrated on keeping watch. Time passed quickly, and he woke Lujo from a sound sleep.

Lujo held up well on little sleep, Butu had noticed as his tentmate, and after two hours here, he was alert.

"We saw it," he had said, when Butu had asked him to come. "The rock, the armies." He had hung his head in his hands. "A lot of people are going to die for this sword. Maybe if we take it, no one will fight, because there'll be nothing to fight over."

It was a second-cycler's comment, Butu knew, but he didn't dissuade his friend.

We're all here for different reasons, he thought as Lujo's tent went up to hide them. *He's here for a noble ideal, while I'm here because of Nolen.* He fell asleep thinking about Paka, though. *I wonder if I'll see my shumi again before I die.*

Jani woke him with the sun high in the sky and a faint rumbling, far in the distance. Lujo was already at the rise, and he and Jani joined him.

"Shanubu," he breathed.

CHAPTER 38

The chaos of a battle raged below them.

"Everyone's moved," Lujo commented breathily, and Butu, who could hardly tell an Akdren from a camel, looked more closely.

A large force of Akdren densly packed sordenu defended the entrance. Cavalry lurked behind the lines of infantry. Suddenly, the ranks of sordenu opened, and the horsemen rushed out into the melee, kicking up whirlwinds of sand wherever they went. The mounted archers loosed arrows at the enemy sordenu without waiting for the dust to settle. Then a horn blew, and the Akdren sordenu ranks parted to let the cavalry fall back to prepare for the next skirmish.

The Akdren fought a force of three armies, which Jani said were the Zhekara, Nukata and Nankek. The armies had many more cavalry, and used them to try to chase down the Akdren cavalry, except for two flanking platoons. Butu wondered what they were for when a horn sounded, and the near side of the attacking sordenu gave up a grudging retreat. Akdren sordenu pressed forward, creating a gap in their line, and another horn announced a cavalry charge, neatly nipping off the line.

Thunder and sand announced the cavalry, but the ringing of steel on steel echoed loudest. The sordenu fought in close quarters. The cavalry's dust obscured most of the melee from view, and from what little Butu could see, he considered it a mercy.

A sword plunged into someone, who embraced it and smashed the hilt of his own blade into the other's head. A man rose up behind another and chopped off his head in one great blow. Butu thought he could see the blood trailing from it as it flew. The cavalry were not immune. Many riderless horses raced into the desert, away from the battle, to die on their own. Sometimes one galloped out dragging a corpse.

"I think I'm going to be sick," Lujo said.

Butu felt the same, but he said, "I thought the Nukata and Nankek hated each other."

"Pisor has forged new alliances," Jani said solemnly. She pointed at another camp, a bit back, where sordenu lined up but didn't join the fight yet. The Kadrak and Ahjea. "And when this battle ends, another will start."

"The Akdren must've said they have it," Butu said. "We have to go down now." Jani handed him his pack without comment, and Lujo led them down the side of the dune, angling slightly away from the battle but on as close to a direct line to the rock as possible.

"The goal is to find Pisor," Butu said as they jogged. "We need to get inside, locate it, and get out." He took a deep breath. "Only one of us needs to get out."

"We're all going to get out," Jani said.

"Since Jani can conceal herself, Lujo, we need to get the sword to her if possible."

"It's not going to work like that," Jani protested.

"You know it's the best way."

She did not respond, and as they topped another dune, nearly abreast of the fighting, Lujo said, "We don't want anyone to know we're Ahjea. We'll have to lie, sneak, and break the Treaty to do that."

"That's why we brought you," Butu said, grinning. "You can change our pommels."

"Jani already has an Akdren pommel."

"We might need a Zhekara one before we're through."

"Drop!" Butu ordered, and they did, Lujo drawing sand over them as a thundering cavalry maneuver came too close. The captain reared his horse and turned his men around back into the fray.

"Over there," Jani said, and they ran to some boulders. They stood in the shadow of the looming rock. The sand had ceased to be the fine, yellow stuff of the shanjin and was more of the beige, gravelly quality of Jasper's roads. More and larger rocks were strewn about them. But no plants, yet, and Butu could sense nothing larger than an insect within a few hundred yards.

Lujo fished out a waterskin and passed it around.

"Jusep would give the sword to Aesh," Jani said. "We can cut out the Ahjea and give it directly to the Kadrak, and we'll be safe."

Butu gripped his sword. "Zhek might be with them. I'd rather get back to Jasper. If Jusep is king, he can handle the Kadrak."

"If the legends are true. If they're not, the Kadrak would crush us."

"If they're not, how soon will we know?" Lujo asked. "But maybe there's more to think about."

They looked at him as he started talking, and Butu began to see what he meant.

The kingmaker gained so much power it frightened kings and kluntras alike. This was why Dinal pi'Kanjea had killed his kingmaker, and died himself for it. A kingmaker and a king needed to understand each other, because their lives were tied together. When a king died, the kingmaker didn't long outlive him, because the king protected his kingmaker from enemies. A new would-be king would rather choose his own kingmaker.

"True or not, even if we make a king and promise to make Aesh later, Aesh might still kill us to get the sword back," Lujo finished.

"And the Ahjea are history," Jani said. "We must bring the sword to Aesh, then."

"Fine," Butu said. "If we can escape, we'll head out to the Kadrak. Let's go."

Not much farther on, Butu placed his foot on the first hard basalt. Lujo paused, gazing up their path, and Jani nudged him and pointed out a way for them to climb.

"What are we looking for?" Lujo asked as Jani took the lead.

"I think we need a cave," she said. "A false entrance. Up here, no one will see us and we can rest and think."

The thunder had nearly died away completely, and Butu could feel no one nearby. *The rock itself is a good cover, and since everyone is on the field, who would look out here?* A couple of hours later, a black chasm appeared between two rocks, and after some testing, Jani lowered herself into the covered gully. Butu and Lujo followed to where it opened into a fairly sizable cavern.

"Lujo," Jani said, "can you feel the tunnel beneath us?"

"It's not quite beneath us," he said. "But it's close."

Butu raised an eyebrow. *Of course,* he admonished himself. *Lujo can drag us through the rock.* "The tunnel here is full of Akdren."

"There's a side tunnel. An air shaft, I think. It's useless to the Akdren so they're not using it. That one is almost directly below us."

Jani grinned at both of them, and Butu caught some of her excitement.

"When you're ready, then," he said. "I think we can rest here for a bit."

A cheer rose from outside, and they all met one another's eyes. Butu closed his eyes, trying to feel so many people moving. The two large groups had separated.

"I think Akdren held them off, and the other clans are retreating," he said.

"That'll make things easier," Jani said as Butu slouched near her. "They'll be tired, most of the army will be outside rebuilding, and no one will be looking for a handful of intruders."

"Thieves," Lujo corrected, and recounted a tale of how a desert thief kidnapped him and forced him to seek water and riches for many years.

Butu let him talk. Lujo was trying to relax, and they would need him to be focused soon. Besides, they'd do well to let the Akdren get some rest and be more complacent.

Lujo finally wound down. Jani passed him the waterskin, and they all stood.

"There's no turning back from here," Lujo said. "If we go in, we have to find Pisor."

"There was no turning back when we left the others," Butu replied.

Jani and Lujo nodded, and Lujo laid his hands on the black stone of Urgaruna, which slowly melted away into a shallow cave and then a short tunnel and then a longer tunnel, sloping downward gently.

Butu kept a watch on the entrance while he worked, and Jani watched Lujo. A patrol passed by above them, a squad of sordenu who watched the outlying sands more than the rock beneath their feet. A part of him thought he would feel so much safer with the rest of the squad nearby — Retus and his sling, Phedam with his knowledge of armies, Tirud and his secret information.

Even Blay, despite his lies. *What did Jani say about familiarity? I'd rather be with people I know.* He snorted then. *If wishes were water, the shanjin would have its river back.*

A hand clasped his shoulder. Butu turned. Jani stood there.

"It's finished," she said.

"I wish the others were here," Butu said. "Even Blay."

She nodded. "There's safety in numbers, right? But like you said, maybe three can do what seven couldn't."

Butu knew she was right. With one final glance over the ledge at the entrenched Akdren army, Butu followed Lujo and Jani out of the shanjin and into the rock.

They traveled in darkness and stale air. Lujo sealed the entrance behind them to prevent any enemies from discovering their means of getting inside Urgaruna. Butu felt the weight of the stone around him, and for the first time in as long as he could remember, his vision was limited to the narrow pathway ahead of him.

"What if we run out of good air before we reach a larger tunnel?" Butu asked nervously.

"We'll slowly fall asleep and die. Miners often bring children with them, and not just to help find ore. If there's an accident, the children can usually get them out. 'Stay calm and breathe slowly,'" he recited part of a chant, "'Panic only hastens a miner's death.'"

"Have you ever seen a miner die?" Butu asked suddenly, trying not to pay attention to his queasy stomach and lightheadedness.

Lujo didn't answer right away. "Yes," he said at last. "In peaceful times, even a soldier's life is safer than a miner's. As a child, I led more men to safety than I watched die, but I couldn't always save them."

Butu had no response to this. The children in Jasper found water, polished and sharpened weapons and performed countless other chores made easier by magic. He supposed that these were essential to the survival of the adults in the town, but the adults never mentioned their importance to the children.

The path was smooth, but Butu lost track of time without the sun to help them. He felt as though hours had passed before Lujo stopped them. A solid wall stood before them.

"What's this? I thought we were joined to another tunnel."

"I stopped it before the tunnel, so you could try to sense what was beyond it," Lujo said. "Wouldn't want any patrols to come up on us, right?"

"Good thinking," Butu said, fighting off panic.

We're sealed in a pocket of air. If Lujo's magic fails us, we'll die here.

His breath quickened, and he desperately tried to sense if anyone was nearby.

"I can't feel anyone. I don't know if my magic is working."

"Then we'll have to chance it." Lujo removed his hand from the wall, and Butu saw a fist-sized hole there connecting the bubble with a larger tunnel. To his right, Jani breathed a sigh of relief.

The hole vanished briefly as Lujo pressed his face to it. After a moment, he withdrew.

"Take a breath," he told them. "The air out there isn't great, but it's better than in here."

CHAPTER 39

After they each took a deep breath, Butu confirmed no one waited for them. Lujo put both his hands in the hole and pulled. The stone melted around them, creating an opening big enough to slip through. Butu took a deep breath of the cool, musty air, welcoming the more open space. He clapped his hand quietly on Lujo's shoulder.

"See anything around us?" Lujo asked. "I can feel the tunnels, but not any people in them."

Butu shook his head before recalling the futility of the gesture. At this close range, he could see Lujo as if the sordenu were carved of stone — enough to make out facial expressions but not enough to note fine details or colors. Lujo, he knew, couldn't even see that.

"Not much. I can see through canvas and sand, but not rock."

Lujo frowned, but he said, "At least the same is true for our enemies, even if they share your talent."

"What about Pisor? Can you feel it?"

Lujo smirked and tugged his earlobe. "I'm afraid not. There's way too much metal and rock in this mountain. I wouldn't be able to tell Pisor from a vein of silver down here until I'm really close to it."

"This is going to be a lot harder than we expected," Jani said.

She and Butu laughed bitterly.

As if we'd expected it to be easy.

"My sense of stone is flickering like a torch, too," Lujo confessed with a nervous laugh. "I can move the rock, but I can't always feel through it. That's why I was sent to the sordenu, you know."

187

No boasting, this time. He's too terrified to invent a story.

Butu laid a hand on Lujo's shoulder. "We must hold onto our magic for just a few more days. After that, we'll have Pisor and be well on our way back to Jasper."

"Then let's get going," Lujo said, and started down the tunnel, one hand brushing the smooth wall. Butu grabbed Jani's hand and followed him quickly.

"How do you know it's this way?"

"It slopes down, and the rock that way feels different," Lujo explained. "Not basalt, like the rest, but something lighter." He paused, lifted his hand from the wall, and then put it back. "This wall isn't natural."

We should be quiet, Butu thought as they marched. *I can't see through the rock, but sound carries even in the dark.*

Jani's hand gripped his in the darkness, palm sweaty. He squeezed it reassuringly.

"I don't like not being able to see," she whispered.

"I'll be your eyes," Butu whispered back. They stumbled along on the uneven floor.

"The mountain above us is riddled with tunnels," Lujo whispered after a few minutes of silence. "Tunnels in basalt! Even with the magic of first- and second-cyclers, it must have taken centuries to carve them all."

"Basalt is the black rock outside, right?" Jani asked.

"Yes."

"And what's the lighter rock you say we're moving toward?"

"I don't know for sure, but it isn't basalt. It's not even directly under the mountain."

"Then why are we going this way?" Butu asked. "I thought Pisor was in Urgaruna."

Lujo's excitement was palpable. "Because legends of Urgaruna describe a city made of crystal, and you're not going to find a lot of crystals in a giant slab of basalt. The rock up there is just the gatehouse. We're looking for a city."

Urgaruna was described as a city made of crystal, but why would someone hollow out a mountain to build a city? Butu thought. *Living underground, with no sun — they'd have no idea of the time, and what would they eat?*

A sensation of people moving interrupted his thoughts, and he grabbed Lujo and Jani and pulled them to one side. Jani grunted as she hit the wall, and Lujo opened his mouth to speak. Butu let out a sharp hiss, and they fell quiet.

Torchlight blossomed a few yards away, and a head appeared from a crack in the wall. Someone muttered something, and then the torch vanished and continued on.

Butu blinked the spots from his eyes, and crept to the crevice. Tensing, he stuck his head through. He took a quick look before pulling back.

"They're gone," he said. "This must be the main tunnel."

"Which way did they go?" Jani asked.

"Up. We won't have to think about them." He stepped through the crack, followed closely by Jani and Lujo. He glanced after the guards, then looked the other way. The tunnel obviously bent downward here. "There'll be guards at the end of this."

"Maybe," Lujo said. "Maybe not. The army is behind us, and they'll expect no one to get through that. Let's go." He sounded less than enthusiastic.

"Wait," Butu said. Something that had nagged him came to the fore. "I feel water up ahead." As soon as he said it, he lost the feel of it.

"How far?" Lujo asked.

"I don't know. It felt like a lot of water, though — more than we saw anywhere in the shanjin."

"The Urgarun Wail," Lujo murmured, inhaling deeply. "We're practically there."

Butu caught a whiff of brine in the air. He felt the water again, flickering briefly in his awareness, just around the bend in the tunnel.

Enough water to support a town the size of Jasper, Butu thought. *Maybe even enough to water a city.* The feeling passed as soon as he acknowledged it.

Lujo started walking, hand dragging against a wall and feet shuffling slowly. Butu followed, guiding Jani as best he could.

Lujo cleared his throat. "When the king's army killed the last defenders of Urgaruna, the children of the city wept without stop for many days. By the time the soldiers reached the city, they found it surrounded by a moat. The army was thirsty from the march and siege, so they filled their waterskins from the moat. It was not until they began to drink that they learned the water was salty — a sea made from the tears of the children whose parents the soldiers had so mercilessly slaughtered. Many died of thirst, because salt water only makes you thirstier."

"Shanubu," Jani breathed.

Butu shuddered at the thought of drinking from a pool of tears — especially the tears of children the soldiers later helped their king murder.

We are sordenu. Would we disobey our kluntra if he ordered us to kill children?

"I think the tunnel curves to the right," Jani said.

Butu blinked. *She can see?*

"Yeah, I think you're right," Lujo whispered.

"There must be light up ahead," she said, keeping her voice low.

Butu frowned. He couldn't tell a difference. "It must be very dim. I still can't see color. Or is everything down here still black and grey?"

"We're out of the basalt and into the first layers of limestone, now, so it's probably a slightly lighter grey," Lujo said softly. "I definitely feel crystal up ahead, though, and I'm pretty sure it's salt."

"In the water?"

"No. I can't feel salt dissolved in water. This is rock salt — lots and lots of it."

"I thought the city was made of diamond," Jani said.

Lujo shrugged. "Maybe it was. Maybe the curse changed that, too."

"And the light?"

"I don't know, but it's getting brighter."

Butu could see a difference, now. Beyond having a sense of his surroundings, he could see the slight sparkle of tiny crystals covering the surfaces of the tunnel. The air became distinctly salty as the passage opened into a vast cavern. The ceiling vanished high above their heads, and the path they followed became a rounded, stone bridge over black waters glittering below.

CHAPTER 40

"Miramani," Jani said softly. The three of them fell into an awed silence.

A hundred feet away, on the huge island beyond the bridge, a great white gatehouse and a wall ran along the water's edge. Within the walls, eight tall, broad columns rose to the top of the cavern, glowing with a pale white light. They could hear voices, raised in argument, echoing from somewhere.

They hurried across the bridge, the silent black waters stinking of brine below. Butu couldn't sense anyone, but he felt very exposed here. Lujo and Jani followed as he ducked into the gatehouse's shadow. His shoulder scraped the sharp wall, breaking some of it off. He bent to pick it up and paused to look at the wall itself.

Spiky rivers of brittle, shaped crystals formed the wall. Left and right, up and down, the entire city seemed built of the stuff. The crystal spikes were built of cubes, stacked over and over again on edges and points. Butu pocketed the chunk in his hand.

"Salt," Lujo murmured with some satisfaction, snapping off a piece. "The legend is true."

"You didn't believe it?" Jani asked.

"I believe all the legends. It's one thing to talk about them. It's another to see them."

Butu certainly couldn't argue with him there, and he didn't know as many stories as Lujo. The voices had quieted, and the steady plip ploop of water dripping into the Wail grew loud in his ears.

Almost like the first-cyclers are still crying, he thought, and shuddered.

"Come on," he ordered, ducking through the gatehouse and

191

into the city.

The great gates lay broken and shattered, relics of the forced entry the ancient king's army had made. Square buildings of solid crystal lined the street ahead of him, themselves untouched by the violence the gates had seen but looking half-melted under the salty growths on them. Tiny crystals grew on the path ahead, too, many of them worn down in what looked like a recent attempt to clear the path. But that wasn't what made them stop.

Jani gasped, and Butu tried to cough quietly into his hand. Dozens of shriveled corpses littered the square beyond the shattered gate, all dusted with glittering crystal. Many of the mouths were open as if screaming, and the limbs stiffly grasped the air in front of them to ward off whatever horror had silenced those cries.

"They're still whole," Butu said.

"It's the salt," Lujo whispered back, taking the lead and crossing to a side street, where fewer corpses waited and the path wasn't cleared. "I have heard that the Kadrak wrap the bodies of their dead in linens soaked in salt and herbs to preserve them from rot. The process comes close to turning bodies into sand. In the time of kings, whenever the Kadrak were outnumbered on the battlefield, their children would quicken the corpses to fight alongside the living soldiers. They haven't done it since the Treaty of Mnemon, of course, but they still keep the old tradition of preserving the bodies of their dead."

"You just made that up," Butu accused, stepping gingerly over a low wall of salt growing over the bones of someone.

Lujo shrugged. "Believe what you want."

"He's telling the truth," Jani said, wiping her gloves on her legs. White dust rolled off them. "At least, he's telling a story I'd heard before he told it."

"Those were too big to be the first-cyclers," Butu said. "Where are all the children?"

Lujo paused in a doorway. Inside, the furniture, protected from the dripping, wasn't salt-covered. He went in, drew his knife, and chipped at a corner of a chair. The blade barely scratched it. He shook his head. "The king turned them into salt statues, and they crumbled at his touch."

"Like adults killed by simam," Butu said, the hair on his neck prickling.

"Yeah." Lujo pointed at a collapsed building that looked like a sand castle after being doused with a bucket of water. "They could be as much a part of the city now as those."

"Can you feel Pisor?" Jani asked, sounding faintly nervous.

Lujo swallowed and shook his head. "No, but there are lots of swords over there." He pointed.

"Which clan?"

"I'm not sure. Sorry."

"I guess we'd know if they had Pisor already." Jani said.

"There," Butu said, pointing at a building several stories taller than its neighbors. "We'll climb that. Maybe we'll see a good place to start looking for Pisor."

Jani nodded, and the three sordenu crunched to the building and started up the stairs. The steps were cracked in a few places, making the footing a bit treacherous at times. Two more corpses lay face-down on the first landing.

"The city is salt, but its foundation is marble. That's why it hasn't all melted into the moat," Lujo said.

Butu grunted and continued up the next flight of stairs. At the top of the fifth flight of stairs, they reached the top of the tower. There were signs of recent visitors here — stale crusts of bread and an empty wine jug — but no one was there now.

They looked over the side of the tower, and were granted a perfect picture of the city.

Once, Urgaruna had stretched out in perfect squares. Glittering white streets connected uniform blocks of crystal buildings, all glimmering in the columns' light. Scattered here and there were empty courtyards decorated with crystal statues. The whole city had a clear geometry — perfect cubes arranged in perfect squares arranged in perfect squares arranged in perfect squares.

Now, many of the buildings were mere ruins — piles of wet, melted salt. Where the buildings hadn't melted, salt had grown up and around them, creating spikes of cubes. Many of these lay shattered, collapsed under their own weight or shaken by a quake, their fragile shapes destroyed more easily than the crystal city they grew on. Hundreds of darkened mounds littered the streets like rocks in the desert — the bodies of the Urgarun, forever preserved by the tears of their children.

The tears of the children have never stopped, Butu thought, staring up at the twinkle of light rain falling from the ceiling. *The Wail will never dry.*

"Why so many squares?" Butu wondered aloud.

Lujo shrugged. "Salt is a cubic crystal, so it would be the easiest shape."

"And where is that light coming from?" Butu asked. *It wasn't always salt, though,* he didn't say.

This time, Jani answered, shaking her head, "The wishes of children a thousand years dead, I imagine."

"Do you think it was brighter back then?" Butu asked, imagining a bustling city below him, like watching Jasper at sunset from Sentinel's Finger. No one answered.

"The swords are that way." Lujo pointed to a spot near the city's center.

Wide staircases led to a great palace, easily the size of Jasper and Gordney combined. With pillars and towers and giant, square windows and balconies, it must have been a great seat of power, once. The strange terror of seeing mummified people had kept their eyes focused low, but this building dominated the city even more than that. Guards littered the steps but were barely recognizable from this distance.

"It's in there if it's anywhere in this city."

Butu considered this. *Mnemon ended the Age of Kings. Why would he put it somewhere so obvious?*

But Jani spoke first. "There's only one way we're getting into that without being noticed."

Butu felt her vanish even as she spoke.

"Jani, wait," he said, but Lujo had begun his hide-and-seek chant, and she didn't respond. Butu felt a little uncomfortable, but also confident they'd be able to magic their way out. He began the chant himself and followed Lujo down the stairs. They passed the crumbling remains of buildings and sometimes had to take detours around salty pools. Butu looked around at the ruins as they walked.

Urgaruna was supposed to be something so wondrous, but it's really very sad. A drop of falling water brushed the back of his hand. *Kind of like Pisor's history, I guess.*

CHAPTER 41

They ghosted up the huge flight of stairs that led to the looming salt palace. This close, they could see the massive entrance hall, open on the roof. Sharp pillars of salt made a labyrinth of its own, and Butu counted at least a dozen Akdren sordenu guarding the entrance. Their lips moved in a steady cadence, but the irritated voices that rang from behind them drowned out whatever they said.

Jani's hand brushed Butu's hand, and he tried not to think about the reason he stuck his fingers in his ears. He focused on the space around him and walked more quickly. He could see motion through the crystal walls of the building in front of him, but he couldn't feel through them. It was a novel experience.

The sentries never looked at him, and he soon left them behind. He removed the fingers from his ears. He could hear the argument more clearly now.

"Our enemies have surrounded Urgaruna's rock and have withstood our attempts to break the siege," one man's voice argued. "It could take a month for another kingmaker to arrive!"

"Then we will hold out for a month, Sorjot," a second voice said, and then he launched into a coughing fit.

Deeper into the ancient great room of the Urgarun palace, the spiky salt pillars had been systematically leveled, and fine white dust piles rested in corners. A whole platoon of sordenu camped here, dicing in earnest or joking a bit uneasily, staring at the great crystal walls around them.

Behind the sordenu, in front of the white back wall of the room, a great crystal throne sat on a shallow dais. A gaunt man in rich robes with Akdren embroidery sat on the throne, coughing into a handkerchief. He was so old he could be confused for one of the salt-mummies, and deep bags under his eyes suggested he had gotten no more sleep than Butu in the past two days.

That must be Philquek, the Akdren kluntra, Butu thought. *And the tall one standing next to throne must be Sorjot al'Zatkuka, the Zatkuka kluntra.*

Sorjot wore a Zatkuka officer's uniform covered with medals. He watched the coughing with a concerned look, as if he knew Philquek might not last another month, siege or no. But Butu saw a flicker of a smile there that suggested Sorjot might not mourn his ally's death.

An arm's length away from the throne was a column of translucent white crystal the size of a large man's leg. Butu could make out a shadow in the crystal.

"The Clanless don't attack armies looking for plunder," Philquek grumbled when the fit had passed.

Sorjot shrugged. "Clearly someone betrayed us. We don't have the resources or the time to scour the shanjin looking for her. What is important is my nephew is here in Urgaruna, and he is young enough to make you king."

"Do you take me for a fool?" Philquek demanded in a voice every bit as strong as Jusep's and as accustomed to command as Pater's. "I will not be made king only to be unmade."

"At least let him remove Pisor from this crystal, kluntra," Sorjot persisted. "There will be casualties, but we can escort you back to Philen to be made king there."

"No, Sorjot, and I'll tell you why." Philquek looked directly at an empty place near the short column of crystal. He raised his voice. "Don't think about your magic."

Lujo flickered into view, his hands moving to cover his ears too late. Butu turned at the rattle as the platoon of sordenu rose as one, swords drawing with a rasping hiss. He glanced around looking for a way out, but sordenu covered all exits. He looked up. Far overhead, the rocky ceiling dripped salt on their heads.

If only I could fly, Butu thought.

Several heads turned his way.

"Shanubu," Butu said, and an instant later the soldiers disarmed him.

Philquek must have my talent, Butu thought, but then he noticed the fine powdered salt scattered like dust on the floor and saw Lujo's footprints. *Not magic at al!. Jani must have noticed it before we reached the chanters, but I misunderstood her warning.* At least they hadn't found her, yet, so there was hope.

Beefy Akdren sordenu lifted Butu and Lujo to their feet and then forced them to their knees at the foot of the dais.

"You see I have no shortage of thieves who fancy themselves kingmakers," Philquek announced to Sorjot with a gesture at them. His eyes bored into Butu's and then turned to Lujo. "You have broken the Treaty of Mnemon. You changed your pommels, so you've likely torn off your insignia, too, but you are no Akdren. Which clan sent you?"

"We won't tell you," Butu growled, even as Lujo shouted, "The Nukata!"

The Akdren kluntra chuckled. "What brave young sordenu we have here! One defies me, and the other takes me for a fool." He brushed some water off the crystal block near him. "You know the penalty for breaking the Treaty of Mnemon, don't you?"

Butu saw no reason to answer that question, but Lujo spoke in a hoarse voice, "Death."

"Death," Philquek said, waving a wet finger in their faces. "The shanjin gives us some very interesting means, but our favorite is to bury you up to your necks in sand at sunset and leave you there overnight."

Lujo looked faintly confused, but Butu felt the blood leave his face.

The wrinkles on Philquek's face crinkled even more. "I see you've heard of the speckled snake."

Butu made no motion for fear of betraying himself further, but a trickle of nervous sweat threatened to bead in his eye.

"This rock is crawling with them," Philquek said. "We have buckets of them, which we've put near many other treaty-breakers like yourselves." He frowned slightly. "They hate the cold of the night so much, they will burrow into any crack or hole that promises to keep them warm, or maybe just a convenient ear or nose. They're all quite deaf, too, so shouting doesn't make them go away."

Lujo looked ready to faint, now. Absently, Butu noted Sorjot shared the same expression. Philquek sighed, facing smoothing as he looked up at the ceiling.

"Don't be afraid, you won't be alone up there. We have plenty of friends for you."

"You're insane," Butu said, struggling against the sordenu holding him. "The Treaty doesn't call for such methods of death." Inwardly, *Stay hidden, Jani! No matter what happens, stay hidden!*

"You've read it?" Philquek's eyes blazed. "Then you know it only says, 'shall be put to death.'"

The soldiers' hands held fast, and Philquek laughed. Sorjot slunk back to Philquek's side while the Akdren kluntra kept speaking, his voice suddenly hard.

"I am not without mercy, though. If you tell me which clan sent you, I will have my sordenu behead you both right here."

Butu and Lujo answered only with stony silence. If they told the truth, all the clans would band together to destroy the Ahjea for breaking the Treaty of Mnemon. Since the Treaty was passed, six clans had been wiped out, most in the first century. Only the first-cyclers were spared to be taken in as orphans. A handful of others had fled into the shanjin, and the luckiest of those survived to become Clanless. *The Akdren are probably strong enough to do that without any help*, Butu thought, and the Ahjea were not a minor clan like the Kanjea or Zatkuka, but nor were they a powerful one.

After a minute without an answer, Philquek snarled, "Spit on my mercy, then. Sorjot?"

The Zatkuka kluntra clasped his fingers before his chest. "They are not Nankek, because we know they never came down here. They claimed to be Nukata, yet want to keep their clan secret, so they are not them."

We have nothing to fear as long as we say nothing, Butu reminded himself. *Lujo can dig us out of the sand, and we can slip out under cover of darkness.*

Sorjot smiled thinly. "They have neither the ruddy faces of the Kanjea nor the fair complexions of the Zhekara. They are not Zatkuka. That I can vouch for."

Philquek's tone could've ground gravel. "If they are, Sorjot, you'll think the speckled snakes would've been a nice way to die."

"That would make them either Kadrak or Ahjea," Sorjot said after a short cough and a nervous twitch. "No other clans is connected enough to have heard of our find so quickly. The Ahjea are the tools of the Kadrak, so either way, they're here on orders from the Kadrak."

No more than the Zatkuka are the tools of the Akdren, Butu thought, sweat beading his lips.

Philquek shook his head, turning his attention back to his prisoners. "Is he close to the oasis? The Kadrak are powerful, so the clans would dislike punishing them for violating the treaty, but they would have no trouble making an example out of a weak clan like the Ahjea. My enemy's ally is my enemy. So, like it or not, you're both Ahjea." He rode over Lujo's protest.

"Take them out to the desert and bury them with the others."

CHAPTER 42

Butu and Lujo struggled, but their captors lifted them easily. A sordenu captain prodded them once or twice, and they started through the salt columns.

Shanubu, Butu thought again. *Could things have gone any worse? Even if we escape, we can't sneak past the Akdren again.*

"Wait," Philquek ordered when they were nearly out of earshot. "Return them to me."

The sordenu obeyed, forcing Butu and Lujo to their knees, again. Philquek leaned forward between them boys' heads. He smelled faintly of rotten meat.

"You don't have to die, you know. Nor must harm come to the Ahjea."

Butu craned his neck to look at Philquek, who continued speaking.

"We found Pisor. Mnemon would've destroyed it, if he could, but because he couldn't, he made it impossible for an adult to reach it."

The kluntra gestured at the block of crystal. A soldier looked to Philquek, who nodded once. The sordenu swung one of their confiscated swords hard at the crystal. With a spark and a crack, the sword shattered against it.

"Diamond made with Turun magic." Philquek sat down on the throne, steepling his fingers as he leaned back. "If you help me retrieve it so I can bring it back to Philen, I will release you back to your clan the moment I am king."

If Mnemon wanted to stop anyone from making a king ever again, Butu thought, *why would he go to all the trouble of crossing the shanjin and searching for Urgaruna only to put it in the most obvious possible place?*

Sorjot looked on the point of objecting, but thought better of it. He smothered a momentary smile. "You will make a just and merciful king, kluntra."

He almost sounds sincere, Butu thought as he leaned closer to Lujo.

"If you touch the sword, he'll kill you for being kingmaker," Butu whispered.

As a soldier pulled them apart and slapped him, he saw Lujo's grave nod.

At last. He understands.

And then, someone shouted, "Kluntra! It's the kingmaker. She's coming up the stairs."

The widening of Sorjot's eyes and the press of his lips told Butu everything he needed to know about who was responsible for the attack on Amber's escorts.

You're the one who betrayed Philquek so you could trick him into using your nephew. He probably knows it, too.

Philquek's coughing grew at the news, though he waved everyone away and sat up, visibly trying to control himself. When the fit passed, he hid the kerchief but not before Butu saw the bloodstains on it. The kluntra brushed a hand over his hair, which did nothing to the flimsy strands.

And then Amber rushed in, breathing heavily. She glanced at Butu and Lujo but betrayed no surprise at seeing them. "Uncle Phil!" she squealed, practically throwing herself into the kluntra's lap to kiss him on the cheek. "I came as fast as I could, but between the armies and the ladder and the tunnels, it was a long way to run. I hope you weren't worried."

Uncle? Butu thought.

Philquek's face softened immeasurably. "I'm just glad you're safe, Amber. They told me you were lost in the shanjin."

"Oh, I was!" She wheeled to stare at Butu again. "But these sordenu and his squad saved me after the Clanless killed my escort." Her expression turned pleading and she grabbed one of Philquek's hands in both of hers. "I ... was frightened when I left them. They were nice to me, but they're not Akdren, and I didn't want you to hunt them down thinking they kidnapped me."

Butu couldn't suppress a smile. Amber returned it, blushing. Philquek frowned at Butu, but his smile returned as soon as Amber turned again.

He knows we're here to steal Pisor, but he doesn't think she does, and he doesn't want to tell her. Butu felt disgusted. *How many times did Blay hide the truth from us because he didn't think we'd understand it or because he didn't trust us to keep it a secret? It always made matters worse! We never told Amber why we were in the shanjin. I never told her the truth, and Philquek won't, either.*

"Amber, we were sent here to find Pisor," Butu blurted.

She winked at him. "I knew that. I have eyes to see and ears to hear, and I can pretend to be asleep when I want to." Then to Philquek, "Uncle, what were you planning to do with them?"

The kluntra weighed the question carefully before speaking. He couldn't help but notice the expressions Butu and Amber shared. "The punishment for breaking the Treaty of Mnemon is death, my pomegranate."

Her eyes widened in genuine shock, but her voice was firm. "Show mercy to them, for my sake."

"How can I refuse you anything, Amber?" Philquek's free hand brushed her cheek.

He can't, and she knows it, Butu realized suddenly. *She is his kingmaker. The king is the sword, but the kingmaker is the sordenu who wields it. The king must do what his kingmaker wishes, for the king's life is tied to the life and whim of the kingmaker.*

"Then you will release them and treat them as honored guests?"

"Of course, shining jewel of my brother's son." If it pained Philquek to submit to her, he hid it well. "But until I am king, I can do no such thing. The treaty forbids it."

"Tell me what to do."

The kluntra made a motion with one hand, and the soldiers holding Butu and Lujo released them.

She's amazing, Butu thought, smiling in sheer exuberance.

Philquek touched the block of crystal again, and Amber stepped up to examine it. She crouched down, peering into it, one hand wiping away the salt dusting it.

"Is that ...?"

"Yes, my dear. It's Pisor." He took a step back. "Take it from the stone and present it to me. If the legends are true, that will be enough to bind us together as kingmaker and king — granting me the magic of a child."

Amber nodded curtly and walked around the block until she faced Butu and Lujo. She reached out her hand confidently, but her fingers struck the diamond with a click as one of her nails cracked against its hard surface.

She expected to pass through the crystal without resistance.

Amber frowned at it, and the Akdren kluntra's frown matched hers.

"Try a chant," Lujo suggested.

She glanced up at him for a moment before turning her attention back to the crystal. Amber put her hands on the stone and closed her eyes, whispering a chant. Butu's feet hurt from standing up by the time the crystal cracked. The sword tumbled onto the floor with a hollow clatter.

Pisor was a plain sword — nearly a perfect match with Butu's own, but it had no blade decoration. *I could make something that simple in a few minutes of chanting.* It matched the legends perfectly, though, in that it had no pommel, just a plain steel hilt not even wrapped in leather.

His breath caught. *It's right there. I could seize it and run before anyone could stop me, and then I could turn myself invisible and sneak outside.*

He could sense the soldiers leaning in to watch, too distracted to remember their prisoners.

But they are faster than me, and they'll catch me, unless my magic works. The instant he thought it, Butu regretted thinking it. *I can't trust my magic, right now. Even if I escape, they can track my footprints in the salt.*

In the moment of hesitation, Amber picked up the sword. "Sorry," she mouthed silently at Butu, turning around.

Philquek rose to his feet when she faced him, his eyes following the blade, wrinkles deepening. Her hands shook, and Butu was sure she meant to do something unexpected — strike down Philquek, make the wrong person king, break Pisor with her magic. He gulped, throat suddenly dry.

After a thousand years, you'd think the first kingmaking would be more interesting than this.

Amber reversed the sword and held the hilt out to Philquek.

The words came out in a single breath. "Philquek al'Akdren, kluntra of the mightiest Turun clans, I, Amber el'Akdren, daughter of Melik el'Akdren, son of Piquel al'Akdren, brother of the kluntra, Philquek al'Akdren." She inhaled loudly and then paused as if stuck.

A great uncle, Butu realized. *I thought he looked too old to be just an uncle.* It was common enough for Turu to call great uncles, great great uncles, and great great great uncles simply "uncle" — just like most people didn't bother distinguishing one generation of cousins from another. Turu lived so long that anything else wasted too much breath.

Apparently no one told Philquek it's a waste of time, though.

After a long moment of concentration, Amber continued. "... Do choose you and make you King of Turuna, granting you all the power and ... responsibility of that position."

Her face contorted in the ensuing silence. Philquek held out his hands but didn't take Pisor, which shook in Amber's nervous hands.

She's going to do something, Butu thought, leaning forward eagerly.

After a minute of silence, Sorjot spoke in her ear. "May your rule," he prompted.

Relief flooded her features. "Oh, yes. May your rule be long and filled with wisdom, and may your power bring unity and order to the clans."

"I accept this burden you offer me, Amber el'Akdren," Philquek said impatiently, grabbing the hilt.

CHAPTER 43

The onlookers held their breath.

"How do you feel, your majesty?" Sorjot asked quietly and fearfully, the question echoing in the chamber.

"I feel nothing," Philquek announced, clearly displeased.

"I ... I'm sorry, uncle," Amber stammered.

"She's had her mirjuva since we left Philen," Sorjot suggested, a note of desperation creeping into his voice. "She is no longer a child, where the Sword of Kings is concerned, or maybe we've overlooked elements of Pisor's legends."

"Or maybe I was right to question your counsel." The Akdren kluntra sounded like a man who had been up all night running an obstacle course only to learn at dawn he would be expected to march across the shanjin that day. "The blood priests' histories are clearly false, and Pisor is but a symbol of the old kings."

"But your majesty, what of the Urgarun Massacre?" Sorjot asked, leaning close to Philquek. "Why would a king ..."

"The Akdren have bled much to find the Sword of Kings," the ancient kluntra said sternly. "Our scouts report the Kadrak will attack at dawn, and we are too weak to defeat them."

"Perhaps there is a delay between the making and..."

Philquek spoke over him, and reared over him, as well. "Or perhaps the Zatkuka have betrayed the Akdren."

"Never!" Sorjot cried as he took a step backward, stumbled and fell.

At a gesture from Philquek, two sordenu rushed forward to seize the Zatkuka kluntra. "One of your agents confessed to attacking Amber's escort. You'll find him buried with the other spies, traitors and treaty-breakers."

Sorjot's face froze in fear, a white smear of salt fading as he sweated.

Philquek raised Pisor until it was right in front of Sorjot's face. "Your bad counsel and lust for power have cost my clan dearly, and for that I will make good on my threats. The Akdren will fall upon the Zatkuka and devour them."

Sorjot wrenched his arms from the sordenu and flung himself at the feet of the Akdren kluntra. "Have mercy, kluntra! I had no way of knowing..."

Philquek didn't move the sword away from Sorjot, but he turned his attention to Butu and Lujo. "Captain Bephis, please take these young sordenu outside and find them a tent on the east face of the rock. Give them food and water."

"Yes, your majesty," Bephis said, saluting.

Philquek looked on the point of correcting him but thought better it. He smiled at his niece. "Amber, accompany me back to the camp. You must be tired. I must plan our strategy for our battle with the Kadrak." He turned his attention to Sorjot, who was a sobbing wreck on the floor. "As for you, Sorjot al'Zatkuka, you have until we reach the surface to convince me you are innocent."

Bephis stepped between the kluntras and the Ahjea, blocking Butu's view of the weeping Zatkuka. Butu could still sense Sorjot scraping on the ground in front of Philquek.

Is this a worthy king — a ruler who makes his subjects weep? Butu remembered the story of the Urgarun Wail with a shudder.

"Come with me," Bephis said in a voice used to giving orders.

Butu stopped his arm from saluting and followed Bephis and several Akdren sordenu out of the crystal palace. Before he reached the first step, he glanced over his shoulder into the other half of the dead city. The water damage was even greater, there, and the light far weaker. More buildings were destroyed back there, and the salty rain seemed heavier.

They began the descent. Butu felt a hand briefly touch his neck, though he couldn't sense anyone.

Jani reminding me that she's still here, assuring me she is safe, Butu realized.

They passed slick streets and encrusted buildings filled with dead men and women whose faces and bodies were twisted with the pain and terror.

But not even one child.

"Doesn't this prove there's some truth to the stories about Pisor?" Lujo asked softly.

All this over a sword, Butu thought sadly. *All this because a king was angry at a kingmaker he was afraid to kill.*

"None of this makes sense," Lujo whined. "What went wrong?"

Butu said nothing. He had his own suspicions but thought it best not to voice them, yet.

It should be easy to get back to the city. Lujo can dig us another tunnel. Amber was helpful, there. We're not prisoners. Part of him questioned that. Philquek — king or kluntra — did not seem the kind of man to abide by such an agreement.

When they reached the tunnels beyond the bridge out of the dead city, one of Bephis' soldiers lit a lantern to guide them. Compared with the gleaming light of Urgaruna's columns, the flickering red light was hardly illumination at all. Very quickly, they passed the crack Lujo had widened for them to get into the city.

Lujo suddenly gripped Butu's arm and spoke softly in his ear. "It's gone." Butu could hear the fear there. "I can't feel the stone, anymore."

His magic is fading, too. I'd better think of a way to get to the city without magic.

"Quiet." He couldn't think of anything else to say. "Later. Keep your eyes open."

Lujo tilted his head, confused, then nodded and kept his silence. The tunnel sloped upward, but there were no branches this far down.

Like a road, Butu thought. *It's designed to let adults get up and down easily, so that should be pretty easy to follow, again.*

Eventually, the straight path became a series of meandering, branching tunnels. Butu watched the sordenu, trying to figure out how they found their way out. Someone had marked the ways with a white, chalk arrow. The darker, charcoal arrow must be the way down. Butu could just make out the marks in the lantern's light.

He yawned. *I'm going to need a lantern, then, or some other way of knowing which way to go.*

Once they passed out of the lower levels, the caves widened into large rooms connected by tunnels. Butu quickly lost count of the Akdren soldiers they passed along the way.

I can't count on invisibility to get past all of them. Tirud's trick might be the only way through.

At last, the light of lanterns seemed dim in the tunnels. They reached a wide cave mouth guarded by sordenu and archers. Great bonfires lit the tops of basalt battlements at the lip of the cave, which provided cover from enemy attacks. One of the guards on watch lowered a rope ladder off the ramparts, and Bephis' soldiers took turns climbing down. When Butu's turn came, he looked down and felt a momentary pang of terror seize him.

It must be a hundred feet to the bottom. Without magic, I'm not getting back up here unless they throw down the ladder.

"Shanubu, is it second watch yet?" asked one of the Akdren sordenu. "How long have we been underground?"

"Second watch begins in an hour," someone answered. "We'll see battle against the Kadrak, tomorrow. Aesh al'Kadrak himself leads a force of ten thousand. Our scouts report they've brought the Ahjea heir with them."

Zhek! Tirud, Blay and the others will probably be with them, too.

"How many men did the Ahjea bring?" the sordenu asked, snorting a laugh. "I'm guessing three squads of sordenu and an old man leading a camel."

Butu clenched his teeth and continued his descent in silence. If he had felt terribly tired knowing he'd had less than four hours sleep in the past two days, the effort of gripping the rope ladder made it even worse. At the base, he stood next to a yawning Lujo.

"Better a night's sleep under the sun than a day's march under the stars," Bephis murmured, apparently quoting some saying Butu didn't know. The two boys looked up at the stars. Then, more loudly, "Come with me. I'll show you to your tent."

Butu felt lighter as he walked, almost as if the smallest gust of wind would blow him away like a cloud of dust. In the gathering darkness, they led the young sordenu toward the heart of the eastern camp through pools of light cast by fires. At last, they came to a small tent surrounded by lanterns on poles.

Bephis shouted orders to a nearby sordenu and led the pair inside. He smiled at them. "Food should be here shortly. Try to rest. This part of the camp is the farthest from the battle lines."

Farthest from the safety of our own clan, you mean, Butu thought but murmured thanks.

Lujo stifled another yawn as they went inside. "I don't know if I'm going to make it to dinner."

Butu felt Bephis and his sordenu as they left. The captain headed back toward Urgaruna, while the sordenu immediately congregated with several others by a fire. None were close enough to overhear them.

"Jani?" Butu whispered to the air.

"I'm here." She didn't appear, but her voice came from a foot in front of him.

"No one's close," he assured her.

"Perhaps, but others in the camp might share your talent."

"Oh." Butu paused, considering what to say next. Lujo had already curled up on the rocky ground, arms stretched out under his head like a bony pillow. Butu sat down near him, leaning forward on his knees, flexing his wrists. He had a good view of the tent flap.

"We need to get back to the rest of the squad and let them know Philquek has Pisor," Jani whispered. "That's the mission. If we do that, Blay can't say we're deserters."

"How are we going to get out without the Akdren catching us?" Butu asked. "Our magic has already failed us once."

"Who cares if they catch us? We're honored guests, remember? Philquek can't have us killed. Otherwise, Amber will unmake him," Lujo said. He yawned. So did Butu.

Jani sighed heavily. "No. Butu's right. You're only guests so long as you let yourselves be held captive. If you give the Akdren soldiers a reason to think you're spies, they're going to kill you without asking Philquek for permission. The kluntra can easily claim innocence, punish the ones responsible, and offer his insincere apologies to Amber and the Ahjea."

"That doesn't force her to accept his excuse, though. She can still unmake him."

"She won't. Philquek might be a son of a washerwoman, but he's still Amber's blood. Jusep and Zhek have done a lot of things to make me angry, but I wouldn't kill them for something someone else in the clan did."

"Maybe she's different from you," Lujo persisted, propping his head up on one hand, the elbow digging into the rock. "Some kingmakers have unmade their kings for much less."

"She won't unmake him," Butu said. "Because she can't."

CHAPTER 44

Butu wished he could see Jani's face. He grinned slightly at the mouth-open astonishment on Lujo's.

Jani's voice was steady. "You're saying Philquek is right. Pisor's legendary powers are a myth. If the Sword of Kings doesn't grant the king incredible magic, it probably also doesn't give the kingmaker the power to unmake him."

"No," Lujo said, shaking his head. "We saw what happened to Urgaruna. The legends must be true."

The silence stretched.

"The legends are true, but Amber is not the kingmaker," Butu said.

Lujo spoke first, this time. "How is that possible? We all saw her take Pisor from that diamond and give it to Philquek. He accepted it, so he's king, and she's kingmaker."

Jani spoke from near Lujo, causing him to jump slightly. "I've read about it. Anyone young enough to use magic can make a king by giving Pisor to someone who isn't. There's no ceremony. You can be tricked into it, for that matter. One story told of a kingmaker who tried to hide Pisor, and some farmer adult found it and became king."

"Kerik pi'Zhekara," Lujo whispered. "He rode into Memok driving a wagon, to sell pots his sons had made." He shook his head in bewilderment.

"You know the name?" Jani was incredulous. "No, wait, no, don't tell me. Butu, Amber's the right age. Turu as much as a month past their mirjuvas have made kings. I see no reason at all why she wouldn't be the kingmaker."

"Amber isn't the kingmaker because the sword isn't Pisor," Lujo murmured. He sounded amused.

Butu's smile broadened, his certainty growing. "Mnemon wanted to put an end to kings forever. He risked his life to cross the shanjin, seeking Urgaruna. He hoped the curse that made the rock so difficult to find would hide the sword. If anyone did find it, they'd have no water to get home with."

Lujo nodded. "To find the city, it would take an army making an organized search or a lone explorer making a hundred trips, but the curse prevented more than one person at a time from finding Urgaruna as surely as it stopped anyone from finding it more than once."

"Exactly," Butu said. "But it wasn't enough for Mnemon. He knew someday the curse might fade."

"He must have found his way in the same way we did," Lujo said, getting excited. "He could have used that same talent to put a sword in a block of Turun diamond."

"Yes!" Butu tried to keep his excited voice low. He and Lujo exchanged grins. "That would preserve any sword for as long as needed, but Pisor wouldn't need it!"

"So, you think the sword Philquek has isn't Pisor, but you think it's still somewhere inside the city of Urgaruna," Jani said, sounding more like she believed him.

"Yes," Butu said. "And I need you to tell Blay and the others what we've seen. That way we're completing the mission and not deserting. We can't sneak out of the Akdren camp, but you can."

"And you mean for us to stay here and enjoy the treatment afforded honored captives, right?" Lujo asked, but he didn't sound like he believed it.

Butu shook his head. "We can't. If Philquek doesn't come to the same conclusion we did, some other Akdren will. We need to find Pisor before they do." He didn't say, *I'm certain we're not as honored as we were told we were, either.*

"You just said we can't sneak out of the Akdren camp," Lujo objected.

"No, but maybe we can sneak deeper into it. They think they have Pisor, remember?" Butu hoped he sounded more confident than he did. "Besides, all we have to do is get to the rock, and you can do the rest." He grinned. "We'll go back in the way we did the first time."

Lujo moaned a little.

He's worried his magic will fail, Butu thought. *I don't blame him.*

Lujo yawned and shook his hand, irritated at being tired. "Can't Jani just sneak inside, take the sword and take it to the Ahjea? Why do we have to be involved at all?"

"I can't do it alone," Jani said before Butu could respond. "I doubt Mnemon would have left it out in the open, and I can't tunnel through rock like you can."

Lujo looked crestfallen. "I'm worried about my magic," he muttered.

"We'll get past that," Butu said firmly, trying to believe it himself.

Jani took a deep breath and released it. "I'll let Blay and the others know. Be careful though. Our mission is to keep any of the clans from getting Pisor, and that fails if you lead Philquek right to it."

"Of course," Butu said, and Lujo agreed tiredly. He felt Akdren coming toward the tent. "You'd better be going, now. They're bringing us some food."

"See you soon," Jani whispered, and then she was either gone or pretending to be.

Eight sordenu to bring food for two guests? Butu wondered, frowning as the soldiers paraded into the tent with bowls in their hands. *Empty,* he noted, and leapt to his feet a second before they drew their weapons. He suppressed a cry of fear.

"Don't make any sudden moves," a sordenu suggested in a husky voice. Butu recognized him as one of those who had been with Philquek in the crystal palace of Urgaruna.

Six had swords out, but the other two held slings at the ready. If he ran, they would kill him.

Unless my magic protects me. His doubts mirrored Lujo's, though, and he didn't trust that it would.

The sordenu stripped them of the rest of their weapons and armor, leaving them standing in their coarse and sweat-soaked uniforms. They searched the pockets of the clothes, and hooted when they found Butu's small pouch that held some of his coins and the marble Amber had given him. Taking the coins, they tossed the pouch back at him, muttering something about kids playing at soldiers.

"What is the meaning of this?" Lujo demanded. "Philquek al'Akdren himself commanded we be treated as honored guests."

"There's been a change of plans," the familiar sordenu said. "You're both spies and treaty-breakers, and you will be punished accordingly."

Butu thought of the speckled snake and briefly tasted of bile. He forced himself to calm down. *Lujo can dig us out easily, and we can slip out when no one is watching. This actually makes our mission easier.*

Lujo seemed to suddenly shrink, but it took Butu a fraction of a second to realize he was sinking into the ground. Too slowly, though. One of the sordenu grabbed Lujo by the front of his uniform and lifted him out of the sand.

"It looks like we'll have to kill this one the other way," another said with a laugh.

A shrill whistle rang in Butu's ear — two long notes. He wasn't sure what was the source of the sound, but because he could sense no movement, he guessed it was a whistle made with tongue and teeth.

Another squad of sordenu came to the tent, swords drawn and ready. Lujo tried to kick free, but they quickly dragged him outside.

"Lujo!" Butu lifted his arm heedlessly and knocked the swords away from his throat, surging forward. Someone shoved him from the side, and he sprawled to the ground. Three sword points were leveled at him, and the captain's eyes were tiny white specks above him. His arm stung, but the cuts were shallow.

All the sordenu were larger and stronger than he was. In moments, they were carrying him squirming on their shoulders like the hero of the day. Some of them had shovels. Not many sordenu were awake at this hour, but enough were to make nasty comments at Butu as they marched him past.

Lujo's cries moved farther and farther away and then vanished in the general midnight camp noises. Not long after that, Butu lost track of Lujo's location.

Maybe they took him inside Urgaruna or behind a dune where I can't sense him, Butu thought, clinging to hope. *If they're not going to give me a simple death, they won't to him, either.*

CHAPTER 45

The cold darkness of the shanjin wrapped its lonely arms around them as they left the camp. The first crescent of Tirlum — the blue moon — rose in the northeast, skirting the northern horizon from east to west. Butu could sense round shapes sticking out of the sand, barely visible in the moonlight. At first, he thought they were stones rounded smooth by the wind, but the stench as they came closer betrayed the horrible truth.

The heads of other spies killed the same way I'm about to be killed.

They set him down, and pressed a shovel into his hands.

"Dig," someone growled. "It must be deep enough for you to stand in."

Butu stared at the shovel in wonder and terror. He looked at the ground and smelled the rotting stench of death in the air. He suddenly gagged on it and vomited on the sands.

"He's too weak," another soldier said, voice low and deferential. "He'll never finish before sunrise."

"Then the water-starved tem will face the sun before he faces the speckled snakes." The soldier cuffed Butu. "Get digging."

Butu stuck the tip of the spade into the sandy ground and threw the first shovelful aside.

The longer I delay, the more likely I'll survive long enough for someone to rescue me.

With that in mind, Butu took his time. The soldiers shouted and occasionally hit him, but he only dug more slowly. Eventually, the squad's leader lost his patience.

"Coward of a spy — and all spies are cowards by nature!" he raged, snatching away the shovel and tossing it to one of the other soldiers. "You three — dig this coward's grave for him. You thought you'd delay death, but you've only hastened it," the soldier snarled in Butu's ear.

Butu said nothing as he watched the Akdren soldiers dig the deep hole that would become his grave unless a miracle occurred. It took them far less time than he had hoped it would.

When it was done, a peremptory, "In," was snarled in his ear. Butu hesitated, and several strong hands grabbed him. He fought as hard as he could, dragging his feet, kicking, and squirming to stay out of the hole. Curses rose as he smashed someone's nose with his knee, but with a strong twist to bring his legs together and a jerk downward, he plunged into the hole. His splayed arms creaked as he slammed down on them. As he gasped in pain, a swift lift of his collar and kick to the chest drew his arms in, and they dropped him again.

He coughed and tried to climb out as sand was shoveled around him, but someone put a booted foot on his head to hold him down until only his head stuck out of the ground. Panting from exertion and the pressure of the sand against his chest, he howled in misery. The stench of death was overwhelming, now, almost as if the earth itself was a decaying corpse. Butu fought down another wave of nausea.

"I've nothing against you personally," someone said, looming over him. "But this is for making my job harder than it had be."

Butu suddenly heard the sound of water splattering on the ground a moment before a stream of liquid poured over his shaved head. The smell of urine as it ran down his face made him gag. Moments later, more streams of piss watered him until he could feel it soaking into the ground around his neck and chest.

Butu wasn't sure whether to be angry, ashamed or disgusted, but nausea suddenly turned into wracking sobs. The sand around his chest seemed to tighten with every quick, involuntary breath. Then, one-by-one, the streams of urine faded away, and the soldiers left him to die in a puddle of their reeking piss.

If I had the right talent, I could shape the sand away from myself and escape. It's far enough away from the camp that no one would see me in the dark.

He didn't have that talent, though. He had his own, which for once was more of a terror than a blessing. He sensed dozens of tiny snakes sliding across the sands, steering clear of the commotion, for now.

Our mission will succeed, at least, he thought, trying to hold back tears. *And even if Lujo and I don't survive, the others are as safe as they can be. Maybe the Kadrak will win the battle before Philquek finds out the truth about Pisor. At least the king will owe his throne to the Ahjea.*

He found he lacked the ability to care.

Butu sighed heavily, and the ground squeezed his chest a little tighter. The cold night air made his skin prickle. His stomach growled suddenly, and he snorted in misery — what was the point of hunger at a time like this? He had never felt as alone as he did right now.

Something brushed his right ear. Butu jerked in instant terror. *Why can't I sense it? Is my magic fading?*

He tried to shake his head to keep the speckled snake from crawling inside, but the sand held him tightly. The touch vanished for a moment and then its source landed on his shaved head with a click.

A beetle. Only a beetle, he thought, weeping with relief. *It's too small for me to sense.*

It walked around, tickling his scalp until it itched like mad before taking off, again. Butu's stomach growled again. He heard a soft moan, and for a moment he thought it was his own voice. Then he heard it again, not far behind him.

"Hello?" Butu said, but all he could manage was a whisper. It was comforting to think he was not dying alone. The face was vaguely familiar, but not familiar enough that Butu could identify him.

The other man didn't answer except to moan again.

Maybe he didn't hear me.

Before Butu could suck in enough breath to speak again, though, the moan became panicked breathing. Butu needed no magic to know the snakes had found the man.

"Get away! Leave!" the man cried, voice weakened by the earthen fist closing around his chest.

Sorjot al'Zatkuka, Butu realized in sudden amazement.

The desperate anger became frantic terror. "No! No! Aaah!"

Sorjot began to scream, and Butu closed his eyes, wishing he could plug his ears to block out the horrible sound. It wasn't even very loud. He wouldn't even have heard it if it hadn't been so close.

It wouldn't matter if I was deaf. I can still feel them.

Butu sensed several speckled snakes coming toward him.

Maybe if I chant...

The more he spoke, though, the harder it became to breathe, and the ground gave no sign of releasing him. The closer the snakes got, the greater his urgency, and the more he thought about how the magic had to work, the less it would work.

Butu suddenly felt something slide along the back of his neck — something small and scaly. Behind him, the doomed kluntra's screams grew muffled.

They're plugging his nose, Butu noted, and a moan escaped his lips without his notice.

Butu felt something tickle his earlobe and then vanish. He tried to shrug, but the sands held him fast. The tickling sensation touched the back of his ear for just a moment and vanished again. Butu heard the soft whisper of scales against sand at extremely close range.

Every muscle tensed uselessly against the sand around him. When the tickle touched the delicate bones of his ear around the opening, Butu roared at the speckled snake, but all that came out was a hoarse whisper, and the sand fist tightened around him. He tried to take a deep breath to shout more loudly, but his chest couldn't expand. His breath was shallow and quick just to keep him from suffocating, and the pounding fear was not making it any easier for him to catch his breath.

His eyes bulged as a tiny reptilian head no wider than his finger slid into the canal of his ear — no deeper than he could reach when picking his ears. Silence suddenly wrapped around him. For a moment, he thought the snake had stopped up his ear and blocked the sound, but then he realized the Zatkuka kluntra had stopped screaming.

Butu's head was light, and he felt slightly giddy as spots danced in his eyes.

It won't be long now.

He giggled hysterically and then broke down into breathless sobs, his mouth opening and closing uselessly as he tried to breathe. His ear crackled as a tiny tongue probed its depths in search of a warm place to curl up.

I'm going to die.

The fist of the earth crushed out the last of his breath. A shadow passed over his eyes, blotting Tirlum from sight as he struggled without success to take another breath.

CHAPTER 46

The speckled snake by his ear suddenly retreated. Its scales scraped the sand as it slithered away. For a moment, he was certain the Akdren sordenu had come back to urinate on him some more, but then he recognized the man standing over him.

"Tirud!" he gasped, his whisper barely audible even to him.

"Hush," Tirud said, sitting down in the sand and shoveling it aside with his hands. "The others should be here soon."

Others? Butu thought.

Then he felt Phedam and Retus approaching. A moment later, they all shoveled sand away from him, seemingly oblivious to the rancid smells. They chanted softly as they dug, but it didn't seem to speed up the process.

Like the marching chants, Butu thought as the fist of sand around his ribs gradually loosened.

Once they could reach under his shoulders, Tirud and Retus pulled Butu out of the hole. He took in a gasping breath and coughed violently where he lay on the sand.

Where are Jani and Blay? he thought, too busy breathing to speak.

"Blay and Jani went to rescue Lujo," Tirud explained before Butu had enough breath to ask. "The Akdren tied him up and hung him upside down for the vultures. They do that to spies who can escape from holes like these."

Not far away, Butu could sense a speckled snake burrowing into Sorjot's eye, but the Zatkuka kluntra was no longer screaming.

If Tirud had found me a little while later... Butu shuddered.

"Can you walk?" Tirud asked.

Butu nodded. "Thank you," he croaked.

Tirud and the others led Butu to a larger tent near Urgaruna. He felt Lujo and Blay inside long before they reached it. It was a mobile armory — spare swords, slings, pouches of bullets, breastplates and helmets. Two Akdren sordenu lay unmoving on the ground. They stank of blood.

Blay stood with his arms folded, stony face resentful. Butu grimaced and cast his eyes downward.

"No accusations," Tirud said quietly into their standoff. "We must work as a squad."

Butu nodded sullenly, and then Blay uncrossed his arms with some finality.

"Arm yourself," Blay said in a low voice. "Quickly. It will be sunrise soon, and we must get into the rock with the others."

"Yes, sir," Butu murmured, looking through the equipment for a breastplate that would fit him.

"Any trouble?"

Tirud shook his head. "No one was watching the prisoners. Philquek can't win in the field without the power of the old kings. The Akdren will withdraw into Urgaruna and force the Kadrak to besiege them."

"We've cut his supply lines."

"He has shelter from sun, sandstorm and simam. We don't."

The poison wind could wipe out the entire Kadrak army — including Zhek's company and the Kadrak kluntra. Butu shuddered at the thought of seeing thousands of soldiers standing frozen in the shanjin, crumbling to dust at a touch. He drew out a breastplate only slightly too large for him.

"The Akdren can still win this battle," Blay said.

"The Kadrak had heard the Akdren had made a king," Jani said, helping Butu strap on the armor. "Aesh and his soldiers were relieved to hear Philquek's Pisor is false."

Butu nodded thanks to Jani, but said nothing. The next words spoken weren't entirely unexpected, given who said them.

"Because of that, we have new orders," Blay announced quietly.

"Retrieve Pisor and bring it to the Ahjea," Phedam guessed.

"Close," Tirud said. "He wants us to bring it to Aesh. The Kadrak's kluntra will be the new king. He's even brought a king-maker of his own — some third-cycler fostered by the Ahjea, which gives our clan a little bit of leverage, still."

"Paka," Jani said.

My shumi, here? Butu thought and suddenly felt guilty. It meant Paka was supposed to be kingmaker, but it also meant his friend was in danger, if the battle or the shanjin turned against them.

"Actually, that's secondary," Blay said, tugging his goatee. Butu groaned inwardly. "Our first task is to make sure Philquek doesn't gain the powers of a king. Maybe Pisor is still somewhere in Urgaruna, or maybe it takes time for a king to regain the magic of a first-cycler, but either way, we must not let the Akdren make a king."

"If we find Pisor and keep Philquek from getting it, we'll know he's not the king, and can't become one," Jani said.

Blay shook his head. "Zhek believes that will take too long. Without a kingmaker, there can be no king. Zhek has ordered us to kill Amber."

Butu's stomach clenched.

Jani spoke in a measured voice. "But we're not going to do that, right?"

"She's barely more than a child, corporal," Tirud said.

Blay didn't meet their gazes. "She's a kingmaker, or Philquek wishes her to be. We know she's the only one in Urgaruna he trusts to make him king." He was visibly shaking, now. "Otherwise, he wouldn't have waited for her before seizing Pisor."

Is this what it means to be kingmaker — that everyone who opposes the king wishes to kill you? Do I want that to happen to Paka?

"This is wrong, Blay," Butu said, hoping he sounded calmer than he felt.

"If you hadn't let her go, it wouldn't be necessary," Blay snapped, rubbing his temples. "You and Nolen should have left her in the shanjin to die."

He wants it to be my fault? "We thought she was a sordenu. We didn't know she was Philquek's kingmaker."

"That didn't stop you from killing her cousin." The words

were sharp and precise — as if he'd known the argument would go this way and had prepared them.

Guilt stabbed Butu. He remembered Amber's tears for Beker — tears for a kinsman as dear to her as Nolen had been to him. He clenched his hands into fists so tight the fingernails dug into his palms. "He attacked us. He would've killed us, if he could. Perhaps if we'd had some way of knowing we didn't have to kill him, we wouldn't have done it."

Sweat on his forehead, Blay whispered harshly, "And perhaps if I'd known you'd defy our orders to my face, I'd've left you to the snakes!"

There was a loud crack as Jani slapped Blay hard across the face. She moved a knee, and Blay grunted and fell on the ground, writhing in pain. Lujo spat on the corporal, and Phedam snarled several curses under his breath. Retus looked on in shock.

"Don't we have enough enemies already without fighting ourselves?" Tirud said, stepping between Blay and the rest of the squad.

Jani turned away, though Butu couldn't tell whether she was angry or ashamed.

Which am I? he wondered. *I had no choice. Beker would have killed both Nolen and me!*

Tirud grasped Blay's hand and hauled him to his feet. "Blay is still our corporal. It's his job to see that we obey orders."

"If I'd intended to do that, I wouldn't have had to sneak out and follow you," Jani said bitterly. "Zhek would've given Aesh my hand on the eve of battle, if I'd stayed."

"You're a ku," Blay said in a weak voice. "He can't."

Jani turned to face him. "In case you haven't noticed, our lieutenant doesn't care what he can't or shouldn't do. He sent us into the shanjin with very little training on a suicide mission to find a lost, cursed rock, which we can only do by violating the Treaty of Mnemon!"

"Don't forget the part where he tried to force you to beg to marry Aesh by putting you in our squad and punishing us constantly," Butu growled.

Jani continued as if he hadn't spoken. "And now he's ordered us to kill a ... a child. And you thought we'd just go along with that because that's what you've been doing the whole time?"

"It's our duty to follow orders, not question them," Blay said weakly.

"I don't disagree," Tirud said. "On the battlefield, all you can do is obey orders. The officers don't share the strategy with us, so we don't know enough about their plans to discern their desires. But I am a spy by profession, and this is not a battlefield. I see a critical flaw in Lieutenant Zhek's plan that prevents us from following his orders — beyond questions of right or wrong."

"And what is that?"

"Can't you see?" Tirud steepled his fingers. "Philquek thinks like Zhek. He'll expect an attempt on his kingmaker's life."

CHAPTER 47

A horn sounded from the direction of Urgaruna.

"They're calling in their rear guard," Phedam interpreted.

"We'd better join them, then," Tirud said. "In the press, no one will doubt we are Akdren."

"Can't we just dig a tunnel the way we did before?" Butu asked.

Everyone looked at Lujo except Jani. Lujo shook his head, staring resolutely at the tent wall. Blay looked down at the sand.

Something's eating him. What happened to him, last night?

"Corp, what are our orders?" Tirud asked.

Blay met Tirud's eyes. The red-skinned sordenu saluted. Slowly, everyone else did as well, and Butu forced himself to do the same. *Tirud is right. We'll need the whole squad for this, and that includes Blay.*

Blay nodded and saluted back.

"We'll try it Tirud's way first." he announced. "But if we can't find a way to the city, we might have no choice. This way, the option is still there."

"Only if we need it," Retus said, his voice not cracking.

"Only if we need it," Blay agreed.

"Let's go," Tirud said. "The Kadrak army will be here soon, and..."

Butu completed the sentence. "And if they catch us, they'll execute us as deserters."

Blay and Tirud didn't answer, but the squad filed out of the tent in the predawn light and joined the lines of Akdren soldiers ascending rope ladders into Urgaruna. Butu couldn't quite shake the fear one of Philquek's guards would recognize Lujo or him, but he sensed no familiar people nearby.

The Ahjea walked with the confidence of a squad of sordenu who knew exactly where they were going, and no one questioned them. Butu and Lujo guided them through the maze of rooms, each filled with Akdren soldiers — eating, gambling, sleeping, or doing all the other things soldiers did between battles.

They don't have enough food and water to survive a long siege, but there's little they can do except wait.

At last, they neared the tunnels down. No guards patrolled back here. As far as the Akdren were concerned, everything important had been removed from Urgaruna.

"We'll need a lamp," Butu said quietly when he was sure none of the Akdren could hear them.

"I thought you could still see in the dark," Lujo commented, hugging himself as if cold, though the air was slightly warm. "Have you lost it?"

"No, but the way to the road down is marked, and I can't see the marks without light."

Blay and Tirud nodded. They passed through a dark room filled with sleeping Akdren. Retus grabbed the extinguished lantern with the most oil and a piece of flint. They could easily use a sword for its steel. At the entrance to the winding tunnels, he lit the lamp and handed it to Butu, who gestured to Blay and Tirud.

"The chalk marks the way in. The charcoal marks the way out," Butu explained, holding the dim light up to the wall so they could see.

"So, you've learned to see," Tirud said, clearly pleased.

Butu blushed at the compliment. *I have, haven't I?* "I wouldn't have claimed to know where Pisor was if I couldn't take you to it. This wasn't just a ploy to keep us from having to kill Amber."

"I never said it was," Blay said defensively. He glanced over his shoulder.

"Second thoughts?" Tirud asked.

Blay shook his head but said nothing.

They traveled single file through seemingly identical, narrow corridors carved through grey-black basalt by the magic of children. Butu led, holding the lantern.

"We should've brought extra oil," Jani said, pointing to their rapidly dwindling supply. Only about half remained.

"It's too late to go back for more," Butu said. "The road should be just ahead, and there aren't any more branches after that. We'll have to make do with whatever we can find in the city to get back. Maybe some of Philquek's men left lamps behind."

"Maybe." Jani didn't sound like she believed it.

The lantern's reservoir was only a quarter full by the time they reached the far side of the maze. Butu snuffed the fire as soon as he was sure they had reached the long tunnel. The squad started lamenting their lack of oil only minutes after the light was gone. Only Butu could see the tunnel despite the darkness. To him, the slope was gentle, and the floor was smooth. His squadmates seemed doomed to find every hole and jutting point of rock along the way, stumbling, tripping and sometimes even falling hard, scraping elbows and knees.

Jani and Lujo and I didn't have this much trouble the first time! Butu thought, picking Retus up again. He couldn't help but notice how the other sordenu's arms had gotten thicker.

"Shanubu!" Retus muttered. "It's almost like the Urgarun curse is still working, but all it can do to us now is make us bruise our shins."

"The city is well-lit," Butu assured them cheerfully. "It's not as bright as sunlight, but it's brighter even than a triple full moon."

At last, they reached the edge of the city. The Urgarun Wail burbled under the bridge, echoing like the weeping of a small child. Butu, Lujo and Jani took several steps onto the bridge before Butu noticed the rest of their squad had stopped walking. They stared speechlessly at the magnificent crystal walls and gates and at the buildings beyond them.

"It's incredible!" Blay breathed.

"That's the view from outside," Jani said, sounding a little sad. "The inside is — well, you'll see."

Butu let Jani and Lujo explain the salt and the corpses and the falling buildings and all the other things they had discovered on their first trip down here. He kept his eyes open for any Akdren presence, and he was happy to see Tirud did the same. They found no lanterns or oil walking into the city, or, blessedly, any Akdren at all.

While they talked their way through the city, Butu let his mind wander idly to thoughts of Amber and Paka, musings about the kingmaker and king — anything but what he was looking for.

Then he found it.

It was gone an instant later, but at least he knew which way to go.

I was right. There's a gate on the far side of the city.

"We're close, now," he called to them, pointing. Everyone closed in a little tighter and followed him, past the large palace.

This part of Urgaruna looked like a city destroyed by fire and reclaimed by the desert, but instead of sand dunes, towering stalagmites of salt marked the passage of time. When they reached the edge of the city, Butu at first mistook the towers of the fallen gatehouse for two huge stalagmites. Only the gap in the crumbling city wall betrayed them.

Butu crept across the slick salt until he reached the edge. Below, he could see light reflected from the waters of the Urgarun Wail. The iron drawbridge on the far side of the underground river had corroded almost entirely to rust, revealing a cave barely above the mirror-like surface of the river.

CHAPTER 48

The Wail was a few dozen feet wide here. Butu stared down at his reflection in it. He brushed his head, noting the white sheen of salt that had settled on him.

"There's no way we're jumping over that," Blay said.

Phedam tossed a chuck of rock salt into the water. Its ripples bent in a steady current.

"I can swim across with a rope," Tirud offered.

Blay shook his head. "A chant would be faster."

Butu looked at the cave mouth resolutely and started chanting softly. "Water and sand, sand and water, it's the same to cross either. Sand and water, water and sand, crossing both's like crossing land."

Lujo and Retus joined him for the second repetition.

Tirud motioned them to silence. "That's too dangerous. If it fails, you might all drown."

"A bridge would be better," Jani said. "That way we can all cross."

Blay nodded, and the three of them recited stone-shaping chants, instead. It took much longer than usual. When they were done, though, the squad could cross on a narrow crystal footbridge.

"Any enemies on the other side?" Blay asked Butu.

"No," Butu and Tirud said at the same time.

"I'm sure Butu can sense what's in the cave, but how do you know?" Phedam demanded.

"There are no signs here — no clothes or weapons. If they'd tried to swim across fully clothed, they would've drowned," Tirud explained, and Phedam subsided with muttered apologies.

Butu could sense much more about what waited for them there. *Is this what Pisor achieved at Urgaruna?*

"The Urgarun children are waiting for us," Butu said softly, but if anyone heard him, they gave no sign.

"Let's go," Blay said, leading the way. "Watch your step," he said as he stepped over the remnants of the rusted drawbridge. "There are probably pieces sharp enough to cut."

The mysterious light was even fainter here than in the rest of the city — about as bright as the light of one of the moons.

"Shanubu!" Tirud hissed when his eyes had adjusted to the gloom.

To all appearances, they were merely statues of children crafted from sandstone. They cowered or ran or stood frozen in terror, horrified by whatever had come through the iron gate. Most looked like old second-cyclers or young third-cyclers, though one first-cycler peeked fearlessly through a doorway on the far side of the large chamber.

Perhaps a hundred in here, with many more in the other rooms. The youngest ones were the best-defended, but they fared no better.

"A thousand years isn't long enough," Jani murmured, echoing Butu's musings.

"They look like they were killed by simam," Phedam noted.

Tirud nodded grimly. "Even sordellas couldn't have done this to a first-cycler."

His meaning was clear. *Only a king could do this.*

A statue knelt before them, a child caught in the act of getting up. A hand reached out for them, palm up. As if under compulsion, Retus reached out to help him up. As soon as he touched the hand, it crumbled, raining a fine dust on the floor. Retus jerked his arm back.

The squad formed a half-circle around the crumbling statue. A shiver inched up Butu's spine as he watched the statue's arm melt toward its body.

Sand poured out of the shoulder as the arm vanished, falling with the measured order of sand in an hourglass. The head and body melted quickly after that, the child's frozen, fear-contorted face vanishing. In moments, a pile of dust marked the place where a king had killed a child with Pisor's magic. Butu saw the shock in all their eyes, mirroring his own.

"What are we unleashing?" Phedam muttered.

"Asked like a true third-cycler," Tirud said, sounding not quite pleased.

"Is this a good idea?" Retus asked plaintively.

"Another worthy question," Tirud said. He let out a deep breath as if he knew the answer better than he cared to admit.

No. This is a terrible idea, Butu thought. *If we find Pisor, we should find a way to get it as far away from here as possible. Mnemon was right. No one should have this kind of power.*

Blay cleared his throat. "We have no choice. This war between the clans will continue until a new king is made. The kluntras aren't just going to leave Pisor behind and return home."

"Whatever happens, we shouldn't let Philquek get it," Lujo said firmly. "That leaves Aesh or Jusep."

"Our orders are to deliver it to Aesh," Blay reminded them.

Lujo pointed at the pile of dust and then waved his arm to take in the frozen faces of the Urgarun children around them. "This is beyond any orders. If I'm going to end up in some story, it's not going to be as one of the sordenu who helped make the next Pepis the Tyrant."

"He's right," Retus said. "Tirud, Jani, you know more about the two kluntras than any of us. Who would harm the fewest people?"

Jani shook her head but said nothing.

"I'm too old to be kingmaker." Tirud sagged enough to look the part. "I have little say in this."

But I can be the kingmaker if I want, Butu thought. *Most of the squad could, but do any of us want that?*

"We can discuss it later, if you'd like," Blay said. "We haven't even found Pisor,yet, and it looks like we have a bit of ground to cover. We'll split into teams. Tirud and Butu, go that way. Phedam and Jani, go that way. Lujo and I will take the third way. Retus, you'll stand watch here. Let us know if you see anyone coming this way."

They saluted and obeyed, gingerly stepping around every other statue they neared.

It's another of Blay's delaying tricks, but the Akdren won't even pretend to be interested in our opinions. They'll just kill us.

Tirud and Butu were barely out of earshot of the others before they saw the first of the warnings.

"Look." Butu pointed at grooves in the floor near an arch into another chamber, similarly filled with statues.

Tirud read the words softly, "If you would be kingmaker, remember this."

"This was made with magic, not a tool," Butu observed, tracing the smooth lines of the words with his finger.

"Come on," Tirud said, a twinge of awe in his voice that Butu shared.

We're raiding a tomb. It's no wonder the Akdren didn't come back here to look. He passed statues of younger children, clinging to each other with mouths wide open in frozen cries. *No one survived.* He licked his lips, tasting the strong salt in the air. *And we're going to make another king, who could do something like this.*

There were warnings carved next to every entrance. "If you would be kingmaker, remember this" and variations on it were the most common, but they also saw "If you would be king, remember this place," "Pisor was a curse, not a gift," "Power is the bane of humility" and many more.

"Did Mnemon carve these?" Butu asked, but Tirud did not answer.

There were just as many statues in the other halls and chambers, and the children seemed to get even younger. Aside from the statues and a few pieces of stone furniture, most rooms were empty. Cloth had long since rotted away, and metal objects had corroded to scraps.

The carvings turned into taunts. "You'll never find it." "It isn't here." "It's gone to Nekomis." "I found a way to destroy Pisor."

At last, they neared a room with no exits. Fragments of large, humanoid statues made of basalt and marble lay scattered around the entrance. Butu sensed the stone cribs before they reached the room, each with its own small statue sleeping peacefully inside.

"Golems," Tirud said when he saw the first blocky head.

Butu thought of the sentinel that had once guarded Jasper. *Did the king who buried it do something like this to the Ahjea children?*

"A nursery," Tirud added.

A shallow pile of black, brown and red marbles highlighted the center of the room. On the far wall, another carving chanted, "They sleep, you weep, you made the king who made them sleep. You weep, they sleep, Pisor in his hands, and so you weep." Butu knelt and examined the marbles. Each was carved into the shape of a sleeping infant's head. He tossed one to Tirud.

"So now we know how Mnemon spent the decades after he disappeared. But where's his body?"

"Maybe it rotted away like everything else," Butu said, sitting down on the stone floor.

Tirud shook his head. "Even after a thousand years, his bones would still be here. Mnemon obviously spent a lot of time in Urgaruna, but he didn't die here. Maybe he took Pisor with him, or maybe there's some secret to destroying it and he found that."

Butu considered this, rolling a handful of marble heads between his hands. After a long moment, he shook his head. "No. If Mnemon had destroyed the Sword of Kings, he would have made sure everyone knew about it. He didn't want the clans to go to war over Pisor." Another pause. "I think I know why he let Pepis the Tyrant rule instead of unmaking him."

"To make sure the Turu remembered the tyranny of kings?"

Butu let a double handful of the marbles fall through his fingers as he spoke. "Maybe a little, but imagine this: You're a kingmaker who wants to do more than just unmake the king. You want to put an end to kings forever, or at least for as long as possible." He held up one marble, then dropped it into the pile and mixed it up. "The hard part is getting far enough away from the king that he can't just track you down and bring you back."

"So he came to the cursed rock."

Butu shrugged. "Wherever he went, the king isn't going to want anyone to know his kingmaker is out there somewhere beyond his protection, especially if he knows the kingmaker has Pisor. He's going to kill everyone who knows the truth." Butu paused in his playing with the marbles and held up a blank one with a grin. "The longer Mnemon let Pepis rule, the fewer people knew what happened to the kingmaker and Pisor. By the time the king died, Mnemon's trail was so old no one could've followed it."

"How did he get Pisor away from Pepis long enough to escape with it?"

Butu picked up a double handful of marbles and held them out for Tirud to see. "From everything we've seen, he had the power to shape rock, and maybe he could do the same with metal. He made a false Pisor and switched it with the real thing. He probably had help, too — sordellas or others young enough to use magic but old enough to think for themselves."

"Like our squad."

"Yes," Butu said, digging idly in the pile of marbles. They were cool to the touch, and very few of them were granite or sandstone.

They're probably worth a fortune, except for their shape.

"But where's the sword?" Tirud muttered.

"I don't know, and after what I've seen here, I'm not sure we want to know."

Tirud snorted a laugh. "It sounds like Mnemon's plan is still working."

"Of course it is. It's the only part of it that doesn't rely on magic." Butu stood up.

"Unless you count the treaty we broke to be here," Tirud said. "We should report back."

Butu took one last look at the frozen, sleeping forms of the youngest Urgarun children as they wordlessly left.

If Mnemon was foolish enough to leave Pisor in Urgaruna, it would be in a place like this nursery. He'd want anyone who found it to know what he knew about kings.

CHAPTER 49

The way back was faster, and a little less eerie. The corpses' backs were not as twisted as their faces. In the entry room, Blay and the rest of the squad waited. Jani looked sad. Phedam and Retus, grim. Lujo looked furious, and the way he looked at Blay told Butu all he needed to know about why.

"Find anything?" Blay sounded impatient.

He just wants us to find Pisor so he can help make Aesh or Jusep king, Butu thought bitterly.

Tirud shook his head. "And you?"

"Nothing but statues." He glanced at the dark ceiling. "I wonder how the battle is going?"

Butu heard the tremble in Blay's voice. *No,* Butu amended, remembering his time alone in the shanjin with Nolen — when he had been in command. *Blay is every bit as afraid the Akdren will capture us as the rest of us are. But when you're in charge, you can't let your fear show.*

Tirud shrugged. "It's a siege, not a battle. Nothing will be decided today."

"Unless simam arrives," Phedam corrected. "Or unless we find Pisor."

"Are you absolutely sure you've lost the power to feel metal?" Blay asked slowly.

"Yes!" Lujo snapped. "How many times are you going to ask?"

Blay ignored the outburst. "How about the rest of you?"

Retus shook his head without turning away from the bridge. Butu said nothing.

"It might help if we didn't have our swords in here with us," Phedam suggested with a shrug.

"Good thinking," Blay said. "Lujo, I need you to try one more time with the swords outside."

Lujo almost exploded in fury. "No, corporal! My magic is gone. Gone!" Lujo balled his hands into fists. "All Zhek's grand plans and all that practice in the shanjin failed. I can no more find Pisor down here than you can."

Blay flushed with obvious rage and took a step toward Lujo. Tirud moved between them, meeting Blay's gaze.

"Blay, please. He's done enough magic for one day. They all have. Half of them haven't slept. Butu still reeks of piss from his night with the snakes, and Lujo's ordeal was just as bad if not worse."

Butu felt sick to his stomach at the memory. Lujo took two steps away from Blay before crumpling to the floor with his head in his hands. Jani gave them both worried looks. Blay didn't spare either of them a glance, but he didn't argue, either.

Tirud continued. "A few hours of sleep would do all our tempers some good. Maybe the magic will work again, or maybe we'll notice some clue Mnemon left that we're too tired to see now."

Blay said nothing for a long time, weighing Tirud with his eyes. At last, he nodded once. He even managed a smile that didn't seem forced. "Very well. I'll take first watch."

"I'll take second," Tirud said at once. "Retus, can you manage third?"

"Yes." Retus frowned. "Just explain to me how I'm supposed to tell time down here so I know when to wake all of you."

Blay barked a laugh. "We'll just have to guess, I suppose. Get some sleep, squad. That's an order."

They found a chamber nearly devoid of the dead Urgarun children. The ground was hard and not quite cold. Butu wanted to talk to Jani and Lujo about the nursery and what he had worked out about Mnemon, but he was asleep almost before he lay down.

"Corporal," Tirud's voice trickled into Butu's dream.

Blay snorted awake. "Yes?" he asked muzzily.

"The Akdren are back," Tirud whispered.

"Where?"

"The palace stairs, but they're fanning out."

Butu rolled over and leapt to his feet, his sword clattering to the floor. He picked it up and started buckling it on. "Should I wake the others?"

Blay looked to Tirud in the dim light.

Tirud shook his head. "Not yet. It's a lot of city to search."

"If they think they have Pisor, why are they coming back?" Butu asked.

"I don't know. Go back to sleep," Tirud said. "The second watch just started, and it might be a long time before any of us sleeps again."

And when that sleep comes, it might be the sleep of the Urgarun first-cyclers, unless we find Pisor. Butu managed a salute and lay down again. He licked dry, salty lips. *If the Akdren don't have enough supplies to withstand a siege, we don't even have enough to survive more than a few days.*

Sleep stubbornly eluded him. He couldn't stop thinking. Why had the Akdren come back? Where had Mnemon hidden Pisor? If they found Pisor, what would they do with it? It wasn't like they could sneak past the Akdren army. Someone would have to make a king, and someone would have to be made king, but who?

At last, Butu gave up. He stood up, buckling on his breastplate and sword. He made eye contact with Tirud and silently, sulkily motioned back into the corridors. Tirud nodded, understanding. Butu walked back amid the statues of the dead Urgarun children, Mnemon's inscriptions taunting him wherever he went. He tried to ignore them.

Maybe he sealed it in the walls or floor somewhere in Urgaruna. It's a big city. Even a second-cycler could spend weeks looking for it.

Butu suddenly tripped over a loose stone and sprawled onto the ground. He winced as he picked himself up slowly with scraped hands. He supposed one day he would get used to these daily failures of magic and the pains they brought.

Maybe not. Maybe that's why everyone wants to be king. It's not about ruling Turuna but regaining what you lost with your childhood. Would I go as far as Jusep, Aesh, and Philquek have to get my magic back?

Butu stopped walking as something flickered at the edge of

his awareness. His heart pounded in his ears as he put a hand on the hilt of his sword. He was not alone.

"Don't think about the magic hiding you from me," he chanted loudly as he drew it out of the sheath. "Don't think about what will happen if your magic fails."

No young third-cycler flickered into sight, but Butu hadn't expected one to. He and Lujo had managed to avoid the Akdren, after all. But an enemy with fingers in ears was less of a threat than one with sword in hand — especially one young enough to use magic. Butu walked around the room at a measured pace, still chanting.

There.

He turned, swinging his sword at neck height. The blade flashed through empty air, but he had expected that. A second, third, and fourth swing would have gutted, hamstrung and decapitated his hidden foe. But the intruder dodged, spun and leaned sideways out of his reach.

"Show yourself!" Butu shouted at his opponent.

"I'm unarmed," Amber said as she materialized. She looked terrified, but she was indeed unarmed.

She has more magic than any of us. She could easily sneak away with Pisor.

"Amber! What are you doing here?" Butu demanded.

She was trembling and breathless, eyeing him fearfully. Butu put away his sword, and she visibly relaxed.

"Sorry," Butu said. "I thought you were another thief looking for Pisor."

"Like you?" she asked. She still looked wary, but her lips twitched with some amusement.

Butu ignored the jibe. "How did you even find us?"

She took a deep breath. "You know the marble I gave you? It's a very minor miraman. Child or adult — if you give it to someone, you can find them no matter where they are."

Butu clasped the pouch of marbles at his belt.

"That's how Beker followed me in the shanjin. It wasn't any use to us once we were lost together. I gave it to you because..." She trailed off, blushing. "I don't really know why I gave it to you. In the shanjin, you were kind to me. You saved my life and brought me back to my clan."

"They're not looking for us. They're looking for you," Butu murmured.

She tilted her head in confusion. "For me?" The realization struck her. "Oh, you mean the soldiers. Yes. They're supposed to protect me, but I snuck away."

"If they find us, they'll kill us."

Amber let out a deep breath. "I know. I'm sorry, but I had to come down here."

"Why?"

"To find you," she said cheerfully. She couldn't meet his gaze though. "And to find Pisor."

"We can't let your uncle have Pisor," Butu said.

"But he's sick. Pisor is the only thing that can cure him, but only if he's king."

"He broke his word to you, Amber. His sordenu were going to execute Lujo and me."

She frowned. "I'm sure he didn't mean for that to happen. I've heard sordenu can be rough on people they think have broken the treaty, but I can't imagine them killing anyone without orders. One time, my brother told me ..."

"Some of the ones who did it were there," Butu interrupted. "They knew Philquek's orders."

She blinked but recovered from her shock quickly. She pointed a finger at his chest. "Do you think Aesh or your kluntra would make a better king?" she demanded.

He took an involuntary step backward. "No." A pause. "I don't think anyone should be king. You've seen the city. You've seen this." Butu gestured at the statues. "I'm not going to let anyone do something like this again."

"I've also seen what's going on outside, and you haven't," she countered. "The Akdren are in trouble. We're trapped in Urgaruna with little food and less water, and there doesn't seem to be any way out that doesn't end in a desperate fight against the Kadrak."

"Which you'd probably lose, right?" Butu was beginning to understand.

Amber shrugged. "We can't get out, and the Kadrak aren't going to leave until they force their way in. They want Pisor, and they're convinced it's somewhere in Urgaruna."

"You could just surrender and let Aesh al'Kadrak have it," Butu suggested.

She shook her head, beads swinging back and forth. "The Kadrak and Akdren are old enemies. If a Kadrak becomes king, he's not going to show mercy to the Akdren who almost got Pisor before he did."

"Maybe we can sneak out and give Pisor to Jusep. He's an ally of the Kadrak, but he doesn't hate the Akdren as much as they do."

"You'll never make it out. There are thousands of Akdren in Urgaruna."

"We snuck in," Butu reminded her.

Amber raised her eyebrows at him but said nothing.

After a moment, Butu rubbed his shaved head with one hand. "Okay, so sneaking out of a fortress in the middle of a siege would be a lot harder," he conceded. "But what are you suggesting we do?"

"Make a king."

"What if I'm under orders not to?"

"Then give Pisor to me. I'm sure Philquek will make a good king, and I'll make sure he lets you go free after he's done killing everyone outside the rock." She gave him an impish grin out of place with the subject.

Butu shuddered.

"Sorry." Her smile was sad, now. "That's the way things are, right now. There will be a king whether we make one or not."

And this way, we might be able to choose a king who won't be a tyrant. If I were kingmaker, who would I make king?

Butu tried to push the thought aside. "But we don't even know where Pisor is."

"I do."

Of course. Her magic is only starting to fade. Butu reached a decision. "Tell me where to find it."

"Yes, tell us," Blay's voice said from outside the room.

CHAPTER 50

How did he sneak up on us?

Blay held his sword at the ready as he stalked closer. "Consorting with the enemy is a very serious crime, Butu." He turned his attention to Amber. "And using magic in war is a capital one."

He must have been hiding around a corner. The stone walls block my magic senses.

"Another interrogation?" Amber rolled her eyes. "I thought you'd be bored of this game by now."

"If she'd wanted Pisor, corporal, we couldn't have stopped her from taking it," Butu said, trying to sound calm and reasonable.

"You still can't," Amber muttered.

Blay's sword moved to her neck. "Watch me."

She flinched but didn't back down. "If you kill me, you won't find Pisor before those Akdren sordenu reach you."

Blay turned his attention to Butu fractionally. "Do you still think she's an innocent girl who doesn't mean us any harm?"

Innocent, no. And a good thing for us, too, or Philquek would be king already, Butu thought, but instead he said, "She has a point, Blay."

Blay nodded once, but his sword didn't move. "Show us where to find Pisor, and we'll let you return to your clan."

It's nearly the same offer Philqueck made Lujo and me.

Amber didn't seem taken in by it, either. "No, I don't trust you," she told Blay flatly. "You'll just kill me as soon as you know where Pisor is."

"If you don't, we'll kill you before the Akdren take us."

"Put up your sword, Blay," Butu said, patience taxed too far. "No one is killing anyone, here."

Blay's eyes bulged. "You don't give the orders."

"No," Butu said, "but I remember the ones we have, and if you kill Amber, our mission will certainly fail."

I really wish she'd stop smiling when I say things like that, Butu thought when he caught Amber's smirk and Blay's answering sneer. *She has the brain of an envoy but the face of the worst gambler in Turuna.*

"Corporal, please," Butu pleaded.

Blay slammed his sword into its sheath with a growl. His hand never left the hilt.

Butu turned his attention to Amber. "How do you want to do this?"

"I trust you to keep your word. I'll whisper Pisor's location to you, and you won't reveal it to anyone else in your squad until I'm gone."

"We'll wait until we're alone at the entrance," Butu told her. He glanced at Blay, whose scowl deepened. "That way I can guarantee your safety."

A grin spread across her face. "You'll make a pretty good kingmaker."

"He's not a kingmaker," Blay said.

Amber regarded him levelly. "Then you'd better choose another kingmaker from the rest of your squad before the Akdren find you. It seems like you don't have many choices there." She returned her attention to Butu, looking brighter. "I'm ready when you are."

Butu looked to Blay, who nodded. They left the corporal behind. Butu and Amber walked past the frozen terror of the Urgarun children until they reached the entry room.

Tirud still stood watch. He turned when he heard them. His eyes widened slightly when he saw Amber. "Flag of truce?" he asked.

"Something like that," Amber said.

"Your clansmen are looking for you."

"I'll try to get rid of them for you," Amber assured him.

"Could you leave us alone for a few minutes, Tirud?" Butu asked. "We need to talk privately."

"Blay knows, doesn't he?" Tirud asked.

Butu nodded.

"Very well. I'll keep the others from overhearing."

Amber watched Tirud leave. When he was out of earshot, she stared hard at Butu. "I want you to promise me you'll make a king who won't just kill everyone who came here for Pisor."

Butu cocked his head but didn't say anything.

"I knew I couldn't keep that promise anymore," she explained. "That's why I decided not to be kingmaker."

Butu thought about that in silence for a moment.

"Well? Do I have your word?" She sounded more earnest than impatient, but only just barely.

"You meant to give Pisor to Beker, didn't you? You weren't actually lying to us."

"Yes," Amber said in a voice choked with suppressed tears. "We worked it out together. Anyone who kills for Pisor will kill with it. He's going to want a kingmaker loyal only to him."

Butu nodded. "The king stays king as long as his kingmaker doesn't think he's a tyrant."

"No." Amber shook her head vigorously. "The king stays king until the kingmaker stops being kingmaker. Why take Pisor from a kingmaker who has already unmade the last king he made?"

"Better to replace him with your own kingmaker."

"Exactly. The king almost always chooses the kingmaker. But what happens when the kingmaker actually chooses the king because the king can't pick and choose his kingmaker?"

"Such as when he's surrounded by enemies with no way out and few children within reach," Butu supplied.

"Something like that," she said with a small smile. She sobered, then. "But then it works the other way. What if it isn't the king who is the tyrant? What if it's the kingmaker?"

Butu hadn't quite considered that, but it fit with some of the other things he had been thinking about Pisor while they were in the shanjin. "The king still gets the blame."

"Even though it's the kingmaker's fault."

"If either of them is a tyrant, you have tyranny. And from what we know of the Time of Kings, that's usually how it turns out."

"Not always, though. Sometimes they both had enough wisdom to rule well. Your eyes are open. If you can find someone in your squad you can trust to see like you do, maybe the first king in centuries won't be like the last one Turuna saw."

Who of the squad would make a good king?

"What if they won't let me be kingmaker?"

Amber gave a small laugh. "Don't give them a choice. Once you've touched Pisor, they can either let you make a king or kill you."

"Right." Butu didn't think his squad would kill him for touching Pisor. He had some doubts about Blay, maybe, but not many.

"It's a promise, then?"

"What is?"

"Any king you make won't kill everyone who came here for Pisor."

"Oh that. Yes, of course." Butu thought about the wording of that. "I don't want anyone to get killed, really. If we can find a peaceful end, we'll take it."

"I knew I could trust you." She leaned forward and kissed him on the cheek, and then she told him where to find Pisor. "Good luck, Butu."

"Wait," he said as she turned to go. When she looked at him, he pressed the miraman marble into her hand. "Next time, I'll find you."

She blushed. "Aren't we getting a little old for hide-and-seek?" she asked, but she clasped her hand around the token. Moments later, she was gone.

CHAPTER 51

"Tirud, she's gone," Butu called.

Blay came into the room, instead. "Well?"

Butu's mind raced, trying to dream up a believable deception. "I can lead you there, but we'll need Lujo." *I can sneak away while they're asleep.*

"We'll wake him." Blay sounded almost eager.

"Let him sleep. The Akdren won't come tonight."

Blay shook his head. "We can't know that."

"She won't lead them to us! I already told you…" Water from Blay's finger silenced him.

"Philquek isn't an idiot," Blay said, rubbing his goatee. "He at least suspects her reason for coming down here. The search party is here for Pisor even more than it's here for Amber. They might have seen her leave this crypt."

That, at least, made sense. *It also means that she could be in danger for betraying her clan.* Butu pushed the thought aside.

"We'll wake Lujo, and then we'll retrieve Pisor," Blay concluded in a reasonable tone.

Butu tried to think of an equally good reason not to, but nothing came to him right away.

Blay's smile told him the corporal had seen through his ruse. "Whatever that Akdren girl may think, you will not presume to be kingmaker."

"Whatever you say, corp," Butu said, trying to sound nonchalant. "Let's go wake Lujo."

Blay looked around the entry chamber as they left. "Where's Tirud? It's his watch."

"Here, sir." Tirud stepped through one of the other entrances, tightening his belt. "Just took a short rest break while I could."

Blay relaxed. "As you were, then. Butu, with me."

Lujo woke at a whisper from Blay and without disturbing anyone else's sleep. The dim light hid Butu's disappointment at this.

"Lead on," Blay whispered to him.

Butu briefly considered creating a din. Maybe a loud "yes, sir" would wake them. Or perhaps he could trip and fall on Retus or Phedam. He wanted the whole squad there, even if it meant one of them caught him in the act of seizing Pisor. That would put Blay even more on his guard, though.

Instead, Butu simply nodded and walked carefully toward the nursery. Blay and Lujo took in the scene with a glance — the broken golems, the stone cribs, the sleeping infants. Neither completely hid his horror and revulsion. Butu considered it a comfort. The nursery still made him feel slightly ill. He glanced at the circle of grisly marbles at the center of the room.

Mnemon should have sealed it at the heart of the rock where no one would ever find it.

"I feel something," Lujo announced in a groggy voice. "I can't pinpoint it, though."

"Butu?" Blay prompted.

"One of the cribs," Butu said. "She didn't say which one."

"Shanubu!" Lujo breathed. "There's dozens of them." He didn't sound like he relished the prospect of dirtying his hands with the dusty remains of so many Urgarun infants.

Not that I blame him.

"He couldn't have done it without disturbing the body," Blay reasoned. "One of them is probably a stone copy. We should be able to tell the difference. I'll look over here. Butu…"

"I've got these," Butu said in an almost cheerful voice, trotting over to the row of cribs nearest the center of the room.

"Right. And Lujo, take that row over there."

"Yes, sir."

They walked around the nursery, examining each infant statue in turn. Lujo disturbed one by accident. It crumbled before his eyes. After a moment of stunned horror, he continued the grim search.

Butu crept closer and closer to the circle of marbles, stepping over the broken golems as he pretended to check each infant in its crib. The other two were nearly to the far side of the nursery and had their backs to him.

Just a few more.

"Wait," Lujo said, turning slowly. "It's behind us."

Shanubu!

Butu surged forward even as Blay turned around.

"Butu, halt!" Blay commanded even as Butu's arm dove deep into the pile of head-shaped marbles.

Lujo stood frozen in place, watching, but Blay ran forward, his hand falling to the hilt of his sword. Butu dug deeper, searching for Pisor's hilt. His fingers grabbed something sharp, instead. He yelped as blindness seized him as surely as it had that night on the obstacle course.

Butu wanted to jerk his arm out of the pile of marbles, but instead he gripped the blade of Pisor gingerly and pulled it free. He blinked in the gloom, feeling wet drops fall from his fingertips and onto his pantleg. The cuts didn't close right away, or even appear to be trying to close.

It didn't even leave me a small talent like Blay's. All that practice with Lujo and Nolen and all the punishment from the other sordenu, and what do I have to show for it? Nothing. Well, nothing except a sword that has caused a war and might make a tyrant.

As his eyes adjusted, Butu saw the tiny streams of blood running from his fingers and down the blade of Pisor before dripping onto the thousands of marbles carved to look like infant heads.

Blay appeared next to him, saw the cuts and frowned. "That was stupid." The corporal's hand was no longer on his sword. "Let me see." He sounded genuinely concerned.

Butu backed away from Blay, holding the Sword of Kings like a miraman talisman. Pisor was exactly as the legends had described — a blade without decoration, a hilt with no pommel. It was a sword so crude Butu could have made one just like it with a few minutes of chanting and considered it a botched job.

Or I could've if I still had my magic.

"He touched it," Lujo murmured, eyes wide. "That means he's kingmaker."

"Not if he gives it to another child, no," Blay said. "You can use magic, too."

A little eagerness flashed across Lujo's face, and Butu's heart sank.

Lujo would enjoy being kingmaker, and that's dangerous. Maybe he could grow into it, but he might try to make the world into one of his stories. A king could do that, and he'd probably have to if that's what his kingmaker wanted.

"If he touches Pisor, he'll lose his magic," Butu warned them. "We won't get out of here unless he can open a tunnel for us again."

Blay didn't look convinced.

"It's true!" Butu insisted. "I'm as blind as Tirud, right now."

"Give Pisor to Lujo, Butu. No more tricks."

Lujo's eagerness had turned doubtful. "He might be right, corporal. The legends say Pisor's touch steals away a child's magic."

Blay puffed out a breath. "Our orders are to keep the Akdren from making a king. As sordenu, we all have a duty to do that."

"Are you hiding any other orders from us?" Tirud asked from the entrance to the nursery.

Jani and Phedam tailed him. Phedam's eyes widened as he spotted Butu with Pisor. Jani looked exhausted, as if she hadn't slept at all.

Anger flashed across Blay's face at the barb, but he contained it. "Not this time." He turned to face the trio. "Aren't you still on watch, Tirud?"

Jani and Phedam looked surprised and glanced at Tirud.

"Yes, but Retus is there, now," Tirud said. His expression became grave. "Matters have become more complicated. A squad of Akdren are heading this way. I think they spotted our bridge."

"How long do we have?" Blay asked, looking severe. The others' faces echoed his.

Tirud shrugged. "Retus's sling might give them pause. Not long, though."

Even if Lujo started his tunnel right now, we'd never get out of their reach in time.

Blay took a deep breath, closed his eyes and held out a hand. "Butu, I need you to give me Pisor."

CHAPTER 52

Butu took a step back, closer to Tirud, Phedam and Jani. "Why? Our orders are to make Jusep king."

Blay met their shocked stares one by one. "Only for a little while — long enough to bring Pisor safely to Jusep. It's the only way to save the Ahjea."

"You expect me to make you king only to unmake you? You know how that will end," Butu said.

"Yes." Blay's eyelid twitched.

"Do you want to die?" Jani asked.

Blay set his jaw. "I am the servant of the Ahjea. I will die gladly for my clan, if it is necessary."

"That's not the same as wanting to die." Jani buried her hands in her armpits, her eyes wide at his words.

Butu felt disgusted. "I'd sooner Pisor fall into Akdren hands than make you king, Blay."

How can I tell you, Blay? Butu thought of the Urgarun infants around them, of the city and the Wail and all the other terrible things a king's wrath had wrought. *I don't want to make the kind of king who would do something like that.*

"How can you say that?" Blay sounded wounded to the core.

He isn't a bad person. If he really wanted to be king, he could've killed me and had Lujo make him king. But if he were my king, he would keep secrets from me. He'd lie to me about important things the way Philquek lied to Amber about not executing us.

Butu raised Pisor. "If I make you king, I can see only two results. You might keep your word of honor and lay down your life to bring Pisor to Jusep. But if you're loyal enough to die for the

Ahjea, I know you well enough to know you'll make sure I die with you so Jusep can choose a new kingmaker."

"You're a sordenu, Butu." The corporal grimly pushed his sword back. "You must be willing to sacrifice everything for the Ahjea. The kluntra might reward you by letting you remain kingmaker. It's not my decision to make, nor is it my place to question the decision."

Butu waved the argument aside. "The second possibility is you'll decide to remain king. You're ambitious, Blay. We know that."

"I'm a loyal sordenu," Blay said firmly, one hand reaching up for his goatee.

Retus? Probably not old enough, and he's too inexperienced to be a good kingmaker. Phedam? He knows war and is smart enough to learn the rest, but he's too much of a follower for the job.

"I'm not going to make a king just to unmake one," Butu announced. He stepped away from Blay so he could see Tirud and Jani as clearly. Jani's hands clasped at her side, and Tirud looked ready to run. "You're all my squadmates and my friends, and I'd rather die than kill any of you."

Tirud is a teacher and a natural leader, but he's also a spy, and I don't know much about his life before he joined our squad. That leaves Jani. She's old enough and understands Pisor as well as I do. She also knows politics better than I do.

Butu walked around him and stood before Jani. He held the sword up, resting it in the palms of his hands, which still bled freely. Sweat appeared on her forehead. Butu hesitated.

Am I just picking her because I've already eliminated the others, because she and I had ... have feelings for each other?

"Jani. No one deserves the power of Pisor as much as you do," Butu said. "Rule well, Queen Jani pi' Ahjea."

Tirud frowned as Jani took a step backward, shaking her head violently. "No, Butu. This is a bad choice."

"Shanubu, it is," Blay muttered, but he didn't intercede.

Butu frowned in confusion. "What? How? This makes sense. Even though you're a ku, Jusep won't object because he still thinks of you as his brother's daughter. You're smart, and you know politics better than anyone here. Who would make a better queen than you?"

Jani shook her head. "We've known each other since we could walk! We've been friends, sweethearts and squadmates. I'm not comfortable with the…relationship you're offering me. You'll have an obligation to kill me if I become a tyrant, and I'm sorry if that doesn't appeal to me." She put her hands resolutely behind her. "No, I'm not sorry, actually."

"But you won't do that! I know you better than that, Jani," Butu pleaded, thrusting the sword at her. She stepped away from him. "I wouldn't offer it to you if I doubted you."

"Butu, enough," Tirud said, stepping between them and placing a hand on his shoulder. "You found Pisor, so you have a right to choose who becomes king, but can't force someone to do it. Jani has made her choice, and whether or not you agree with it, you must not reject it."

"You're saying I don't really have a choice."

"You always have a choice, Butu, but so do the ones you offer to make king." He leaned in close to Butu's ear. "I heard your promise to Amber."

Butu looked up at the red-skinned sordenu, who removed his hand from Butu. "Would you help me keep my promise, Tirud?"

"Promise? What are you talking about, Butu?" Blay asked.

Tirud licked his lips nervously, staring at the sword. In his face, Butu saw desire and fear, and most importantly, understanding. He nodded once, sharply.

"And if I offered you Pisor, would you accept it?" Butu asked, lifting Pisor. "Would you rule as king, if you had that choice? Would you put an end to this war and prevent others like it?"

Tirud wrenched his gaze from the unremarkable sword, looking around at everyone. Fear warred with pride behind his eyes.

Please, he thought. *If it's not you, we're not leaving here alive, and thousands of Turu will die before the day is done.*

Tirud froze, suddenly, looking at something behind Butu. Then the emotions melted, coalesced into something Butu couldn't quite name. His posture straightened, and he turned back to Butu.

"Yes," he said. "I will be king."

His hand closed around Pisor's plain hilt, and Butu's Turun sight returned instantly, causing him to let out a sigh to match everyone else's.

He stepped away as Tirud lifted the sword and looked down its blade, noting every mar and imperfection. Butu half-expected him to explode or start glowing, but he just stood there, blinking and staring at the sword with an awe out of proportion to its dull appearance.

"How do you feel?" Lujo asked, breaking the silence.

Tirud blinked, and tears fell from his eyes. His face looked a cycle younger as he smiled.

"I feel like a king," he said in a hushed voice. Then he straightened even more and held Pisor high over his head, face a mask of exhilaration. "I feel like a king!" he cried, and with a great booming roar, all the infants in their cribs exploded into clouds of dust and became a whirlwind around him.

Butu shivered.

"Long live the king!" Lujo cried, and the others took up the cry.

CHAPTER 53

"Let's go out there and stomp those Akdren flat!" Lujo's whoop rose above the cheers. "Nothing can stop us now!"

Everyone stopped, and Butu looked at him in horror. "No," he said firmly. "He will keep the promise."

The vortex of sand collapsed around Tirud, making spiral patterns on the stone as it settled around him. He drew his Akdren blade, and it became a replica of Pisor.

"You're right, Butu." He nodded past the twin swords at the kingmaker. "First, I'll collect Retus and get all of you to safety."

Tirud flickered out of the room. Mere seconds later, he returned with Retus.

He doesn't look like he's been in a fight, Butu thought. He opened his mouth to give voice to his curiosity, but Tirud pressed Pisor's hilt into his hand and winked. *There was never an attack. Tirud only said that to trick Blay into revealing his intentions to us.* Butu closed his mouth. *Or to trick me into making him king.*

Tirud glanced at the ceiling. "The top should be fine. I can't feel any caves or tunnels that go all the way up."

"Top?" Retus said, swaying a little.

Tirud walked over to one of the walls and touched it. The stone groaned as it bent and twisted itself into a staircase leading up. He shared a grin with Butu.

"Make sure there's enough air in there," Lujo warned.

Tirud nodded.

They watched in amazement as the stairs multiplied, slowly climbing up through limestone and then through sand until they could just make out a distant light that had to be the shanjin. A great wind blew from the city beyond the Urgarun Wail, buffeting them with sand and salt for a second before Tirud blocked some of it.

Tirud walked up the first few steps, staring at the great tunnel before him.

"Shanubu," he breathed, then laughed. He turned back and held his hand out to Jani, who stepped forward and started jogging up the steps. Retus and Blay followed, then Phedam and Lujo. Butu was the last to grasp the new king's hand, and Tirud lifted him up as if he was a doll.

"I'm not sure if I can ever thank you for restoring what was lost to me as a child," Tirud said. "I never really knew what magic was."

Butu clasped him on the shoulder. "Get us out of here without breaking the promise, and I'll find a way for you to pay me."

They chuckled and ran up a dozen steps before Tirud closed the tunnel opening behind them. Everyone slowed, huffing and puffing, a few hundred steps up, and the exit looked no closer. Tirud laughed at them and raced to the entrance before coming back down, barely sweating.

"He's as bubbly as a child," Lujo grinned. "He didn't look very winded at all."

"Yeah, well, this is a lot of steps," Retus said, bending over.

"We're safe now," Blay said. "We can walk it." And he suited action to words, but this time, "Fought the Kanjea in their orchards green," came from his lips.

With a grin the squad fell in line. Tirud kept step with them.

"Saw the sweetest fruit that I'd ever seen."

Time passed easily, then, despite the climb. They reached the top sweaty and thirsty, the sun noticeably above the horizon. Tirud picked at the ground with his sword, staring from the cloudless sky to the ground, far below. He disappeared in a puff of sand suddenly. Butu assumed he was scouting.

"Is this the top?" Retus asked, slumping on a rock.

"No," Lujo said, squinting over his shoulder at the peak, more than a thousand feet above them. "That's the top."

"He didn't say what top," Phedam noted.

"I don't think I could lift my foot up even one more step," Retus moaned.

Tirud reappeared. "I found a way up."

"Tirud," Blay said. "You don't think we'll be safe here? We can post a watch, if there's a way up."

Tirud shook his head. "You can't see from here, corp," he said. "Come on, it's not that far."

With barely a mumble of dissent, everyone rose to their feet and followed him a short distance to a sheer cliff. Phedam muttered something about how he wouldn't have to climb mountains if he sowed wheat, and Lujo snorted.

As they approached, a huge slab of basalt slid out of the rock face like a giant step.

"You still don't have to climb it," Butu told Phedam, and Lujo outright laughed.

"Shanubu," Phedam answered, shoving Butu.

"Get on," Tirud said, and they did. Jani's eyes were wide at all this magic being used, and when with a groan the ledge rose up the side of the cliff, snapping and cracking, everyone except Butu and Tirud fell to their knees to hold on. The sight of the ground dwindling away beneath them rapidly was disconcerting.

As their platform rose and twisted around the great spire of the mountain, the entrance to Urgaruna came into view, and the massed army before it. The Kadrak had spared no troops, Butu noted. Four cavalry companies and eight sordenu, each at least three times the size of an Ahjea one. From up here, he couldn't tell where the Ahjea's Tem company was.

Zhek is down there, Butu thought. *Tak and Chewlip and them. I hope they're all right. I hope we don't hurt them. Well, maybe a one-on-one with Zhek would be all right.* He pressed his lips together.

A banner blazing out behind a group of horsemen made Butu look more closely there, but he couldn't make out features on the marble-sized soldiers below.

But that's probably Aesh al'Kadrak and Paka. I hope we don't hurt you either, shumi.

"It must be a thousand feet, at least," Retus marveled, interrupting Butu's thoughts. He looked around. Everyone had regained their feet again, standing gingerly on the trembling surface.

"That's small for a mountain," Lujo proclaimed. "Where I'm

from, we have mountains where snow falls all the time. The drifts alone must be a mile deep. Travellers speak of a Turun village guarded by golems made of solid ice..."

"Here we are," Tirud interrupted, and their platform came flush with the top of the rock, whining to a halt and then leaving them in awed silence.

They looked out, expecting a flat table of rock looking out over the shanjin wasteland. Instead, they found a playground race track with basalt obstacles. At the center of the playground stood a tiny basalt replica of Urgaruna's crystal palace. The wind was strong and wild enough to encourage them to pile onto the top of Urgaruna just to get away from the edge.

"Corp, can I talk to you for a moment?" Tirud said.

Blay nodded, and joined the king. After a moment's hesitation, Jani said, "Come on, let's see if we can find some water up here."

They wandered through the buildings and hanging bars and other relics of childhood. Retus broke the silence.

"It's barely eroded," he said, touching the black surface of one of the obstacles.

"We're high above the sand," Jani noted. "Even the big sand-storms can't throw much sand all the way up here, and it almost never rains this deep in the shanjin."

Butu looked around this hidden playground. "It's like Sentinel's Finger."

"Or Iaje's Island," Retus said suddenly.

"What?" Butu asked.

Retus shrugged. "Amber mentioned it one of those times I was stuck with her. There's an island in the Riphil, home to crocodiles and alligators, with a rocky ridge on it. Only kids can get there because they have to walk across the backs of the animals."

"I guess everyone has a place like this," Lujo said.

"Everyone does," Tirud said, and they turned to see him and Blay approaching. "There's a spire off the coast in Kanjea territory. Children need a refuge, I guess." He cleared his throat. "I'm going to, ah, take care of things. I'll return as soon as I can."

"Good luck," Butu said, and everyone echoed him.

Tirud smiled at them, then leapt off the edge of the cliff.

CHAPTER 54

"All this magic," Jani said after a few minutes of standing around doing nothing.

"What?" Butu asked, looking away from where Blay, Retus and Lujo stood near the edge, watching the battle.

"We've broken the Treaty completely." She looked worried. "Without it, everyone can make sordellas again." She gestured around at the playground. "More places like this will be arenas, if kids are even allowed to come here. Unless Tirud wins over everyone, today's battle will just be the opening for a greater war."

"I'll try to keep the Treaty of Mnenom alive," Butu said. "I don't think any clan wants to see sordellas again."

"Tirud's almost reached the Kadrak army," Retus said from the edge of the rock. Butu used the interruption as an excuse to get away, but Jani followed to watch.

"They've sent riders with a flag of truce to meet him," Phedam said, pointing.

"Shanubu, where is he?" Jani said. "I can't tell one from the other up here."

"Behind their army, see the lone figure? Looks like a cactus?" Lujo said, pointing.

Three horsemen, one wielding a white flag, approached Tirud. A hundred feet away, they stopped. Butu looked around for the standard-carriers, the sordenu who marked where Aesh and Paka were. That small group of horsemen rode hard from one of the flanks. But they were too late.

The white flag fell, and its bearer kicked his horse into motion. Galloping at breakneck speed, sword shimmering in the morning sun, he rode directly at Tirud. They saw Tirud flinch before the cloud of dust from the horse's hooves obscured him. Meanwhile, one of the other horsemen raised his arms, and a dozen more leapt forward. Aesh was still too far away.

The dust rolled away, revealing Tirud holding his sword. The horse lay on its side, and the cavalryman knelt in the sand, headless. *The first casualty of the new king.* In front of Tirud, a slightly larger than man-sized statue stood.

"Golem," Lujo breathed.

"Just like a first-cycler," Amber said.

The dozen new horsemen galloped in, bows out. Thirty yards away, they turned their horses and began to circle, kicking up a huge cloud of sand. The sun glinted off a dozen arrowheads as they fired almost level at Tirud.

Arrows flew and then turned to splinters as they neared him. A moment later, the swordsmen arrived, but their swords shattered themselves in mid-swing rather than strike the Turun king. Tirud made no motion to retaliate. Instead, he started walking toward the Kadrak army, the golem melting back into the sand.

Butu pointed to the standard-bearers. Aesh had arrived to take command, but instead of parlaying like his lieutenant — *no one else would be stupid enough to fight under a flag of truce,* Butu thought — he wheeled his horse back one rank, and trumpets sounded. They could hear them faintly up here.

"Form up," Phedam said, eyes closed. "Cavalry flank. Sordenu close ranks." He opened his eyes wide. "They'll hurt themselves more than him!"

"Haven't they figured out he's the king?" Lujo asked. "Only a fool would stand his ground against him. Everyone knows kings are almost invincible."

"They know," Butu assured him. "They're testing Pisor's legend the way Philquek did. Except instead of trying to figure out how to make a king, they're looking for a way to fight one."

Another long, low trumpet note reached them, and the sordenu marched forward. At thirty yards, another trumpet blew, and the sordenu broke into a run. Butu felt sorry for those who would reach Tirud first.

Can he defend himself from a charge without killing anyone?

The ground exploded in a ring around the king, smashing fists of sand into the sordenu's ranks. Many fell down, but more kept coming. Blinded for a second, though, to everyone except the group at the top of the rock, Tirud sank into the sand. The Kadrak army swirled around the place where the king had been only a minute before, and after a few seconds, came to a standstill.

"Where did he go, and what is he doing?" Phedam asked. "He can't've left us up here with his kingmaker still in danger."

Butu scanned the milling sordenu, and then looked at the two companies of cavalry, who, with the other two companies, formed the points of a square around more than a thousand useless sordenu. He looked down farther.

"Oh, shanubu," he muttered. "That phutra Philquek."

Jani gasped as she saw the Akdren pouring out of Urgaruna. More than a hundred were on the ground already, and the frantic sounding of trumpets brought a Kadrak cavalry company around, even as a few hundred sordenu peeled out of the mess Tirud had left them to respond before all of the Akdren escaped.

"It'll be a bloody melee," Phedam murmured. "Where's Tirud?

Jani pointed to a spot beyond the Kadrak camp. "Look."

What had appeared to be a fog along the ground rose thicker, growing redder as it drew the finest grains of sand from the shanjin. It billowed and reared, parts growing larger while others flattened, bulging and roiling in a sudden, shear wind that whipped the Kadrak banners.

"Shanubu!" Lujo cried.

"No, simam," Jani said sullenly. "Butu, he's going to kill everyone."

Butu gripped Pisor in his hands, staring out over the sands at the gigantic red storm. Lightning crackled in its wine-dark depths, and the sands shifted near it, glittering like mirages from the heat.

Tirud, you promised, Butu thought. *If that so much as touches one of the Kadrak, I'll have to do what I hope never to do.*

Half the Kadrak had returned to stall the Akdren refortification, but the other half had seen the simam. They hesitated no longer than a fraction of a second before they wheeled their horses in retreat or ran, weapons dropped into the sand like so many shiny bones. They passed the standard-bearers, Aesh and his two companions, and a handful of other captains and generals, who stood their skittish horses, mouths agape at the sight. Heads bent together in a worried conference.

"Can it get us up here?" Retus asked.

Jani shook her head.

"No," Phedam murmured. "The Urgarun children will have their revenge on anyone outside the rock, though."

"Shanubu, Butu," Retus cried. "Stop him!"

"Wait," Lujo said, and they all looked at him. "The simam hasn't moved."

That much was true. Butu felt a wave of relief wash over him. *Tirud is just using it as a distraction. He has everyone's attention, now.*

Seeing the Kadrak army running toward them, any Akdren at the top of their wall had run back inside, no doubt shouting about the simam approaching. The ones on the ladders fled upward. The front line, already gearing for skirmish, heard the shouts, looked back at the deadly red wind, and froze for a heartbeat. Then everyone ran for the same cover. Kadrak and Akdren alike huddled in whatever hole they could find. Before long, even the standard-carriers ran to hide, and three horsemen waited at the edge of it all, staring up at the immobile storm.

"That thing is huge," Lujo said in an awed voice. "Can you imagine what it looks like to them?"

They didn't answer. From the front of the storm stepped a lone man surrounded by six tall, angular figures. He held a sword like an officer ready to call for a charge.

"Golems!" Lujo breathed. "Even newborns only have one guardian golem."

Tirud paused for a moment, a diminutive figure before the enormous red, crackling storm behind him. Anyone else standing where he was would look like the children in Urgaruna. The golems around him flexed and bent, showing off their tremendous strength. Butu felt awed, and he was leagues away.

It doesn't help to know that he could be here in a handful of seconds, Butu thought, grinning madly. He lowered Pisor. *That should do it, Tirud.*

Tirud seemed surprised the army was gone, but he rallied his golems and in a heartbeat was in parlay distance with the three horsemen. A brief exchange, and the three men dismounted and slapped their horses aside. The skittish beasts ran back toward Urgaruna.

Two of the golems disappeared as the four men approached each other. Then three golems picked up the Kadrak leaders, Tirud took the lead, and they raced for the top of Urgaruna.

CHAPTER 55

"It'll take a while for them to return," Blay said suddenly from behind them. He held out a finger. "We all need water."

Butu watched the four figures approaching Urgaruna while the rest of the squad took turns drinking water from Blay's outstretched finger. Finally, they came close enough to identify.

"It's Zhek and Paka," he said, with mixed excitement.

"Your shumi?" Phedam asked.

Butu grinned. "Yeah, and our favorite lieutenant."

"Come drink, Butu," Blay said. "It's all for nothing if you die of thirst."

Butu had forgotten how long it had been since he had had anything to drink until he got the first taste of the water. He drank greedily until Jani cleared her throat, to which the rest of the squad laughed.

"They're halfway up the spire," Phedam said, leaning over the great drop.

"Halfway up or halfway down, have to go all the way 'round," Lujo chanted. "Halfway down or halfway up, the vale below is just a cup."

"What?" Retus said.

"Must be a mountain thing," Butu added, grinning. "Race around the valley?"

"Yeah," Lujo said. "There's this perfectly circular valley. They say it used to be a volcano ..."

Jani's brows had knit together a moment before, and now she said, "Get out of sight. It's best if they don't know we're up here."

"Why?" Retus asked.

"To keep the kingmaker a secret," Jani explained. "Butu's Tirud's only weakness, remember?"

"But how?" Lujo asked. "My magic doesn't..."

Jani pointed at the basalt palace. "You don't need to be invisible if you have that."

"Paka can probably still sense most of us," Butu warned.

"I'll stay out in the open to watch Aesh's kingmaker," Blay said. "I'm far too old to be mistaken for a child."

Does he intend to protect us or betray us? Butu wondered. *Of course, letting him stay here is even more dangerous. If I die, Blay can deliver Pisor to Aesh's kingmaker. He and Zhek are better swordsmen than anyone in our squad.*

"And the rest of us will watch over Tirud's kingmaker," Lujo said, clasping a hand on Butu's shoulder as they walked to the basalt palace together.

Just inside, the space seemed larger than it was. They all stood, tense and ready. Butu leaned on his forehead against one wall, hand gripping Pisor's hilt until it turned white.

I don't want to die. He glanced at everyone. Jani and Phedam conversed in low tones and Lujo whispered to Retus — probably the rest of his story. Butu felt very alone.

What does it mean, that I'm thinking of my friends as betraying me? No one here would, even Lujo. Tirud is out there, and he won't want me to die. Paka is out there. Has he changed too much to be my shumi? Blay could try, but Tirud knows to watch him. Zhek probably will try, the thought made his blood boil a little, *but everyone will be watching him.*

That only leaves Aesh al'Kadrak, and no one knows anything about him, so they'll be watching him.

Butu walked over to his four squadmates, who stopped talking as he approached.

"Lujo, Phedam," he said in hushed tones, "if I get killed up here, you should take the sword. But please choose your king carefully."

They stared up at him. Lujo looked serious, now, but Jani was shocked.

"You're not going to die," she said. "We'll all protect you. Tirud especially."

"Tirud will have to get Philquek for this battle to end," Butu reminded her, "and in that time, Aesh will be with us. I'm worried about Blay, and Zhek is coming." He took a deep breath. "And I don't know how much Paka has changed."

Jani opened her mouth, probably to call him silly, but closed it and knit her eyebrows. She nodded slightly.

Lujo nodded. "If I get the chance to take the sword, I will bear it for you, Butu."

Butu murmured his thanks and went back to the wall, where he closed his eyes until he sensed Tirud and his companions reach Blay.

"Blay, where are the others?" Tirud asked.

He doesn't mean to keep us a secret. Why?

"They're resting in the shade of the buildings." Blay sounded off-balance, like a sordenu who had just been dressed down by a general for obeying the orders of his sergeant. "Should I bring them out here, your majesty?" The formal address sounded strange in Blay's mouth — at once awkward and deferential.

Of course, no one has used it in hundreds of years.

"Yes," Tirud said with barely a hesitation.

Butu sensed there was a lot about the situation Tirud wasn't telling Blay — a lot he couldn't say in front of Aesh and Zhek.

"Yes, your majesty!" Blay shouted.

A moment later, Blay appeared inside the basalt palace.

"All of us?" Jani whispered.

A look of panic crossed Blay's face as he struggled with the possibility that Tirud's orders were part of a show for the kluntra's benefit and not ones he expected Blay to follow to the letter. He opened his mouth, but no words came out.

"Lujo and Retus will go first," Jani said, making the decision for the stricken corporal. "If Tirud asks after others, Phedam and I will go out. If he says something that makes it sound like it's just the four of you who were resting here, Butu will stay hidden. Otherwise, he'll come out last."

They all nodded. Lujo and Retus followed Blay out.

"Ah, here are two of them." Tirud sounded pleased. Someone spoke in a soft voice. "Where are the others?"

Either he hasn't considered the risk, or he knows something about this situation we don't.

"Where is your cousin, Zhek?" Aesh asked.

"She must be here somewhere," Zhek said. "Jani. Jani, where are you?"

Jani made a tiny indignant sound and clenched her hands into fists. "Stay here unless he calls you," she whispered to Butu before slipping out of the shadow.

"We're coming," Phedam announced.

Jani and Phedam slipped out of the shadow and into the open.

"I am not your cousin, Zhek al'Ahjea," Jani growled at the kluntra's son. "I am Jani ku Ahjea — third in command of the Tem-35 sordenu squad."

"Where's Butu?" Paka's voice asked. "Where's the kingmaker?"

Tirud's told them about me, Butu thought with a sigh. *Either he has a reason, or he's a fool who won't be king for long.*

He stepped into the light. "Here I am, shumi."

Paka's face lit up in a great grin, and Butu forced himself to share it as he felt Zhek's melting glare on him. The surprise was the excitement on Aesh's face, excitement that softened into a tight grin as Paka raced to his shumi and they clasped hands. After a second, Paka wrapped his other arm around Butu.

We haven't been apart that long, and he's almost my height already.

Aesh was shorter than Butu expected — shorter, in fact, than everyone except Butu and Paka, and Butu was only a couple inches shorter. He looked much younger than Jusep, as well, and his arms and legs were as scrawny as the rest of him was gaunt. Though the Kadrak kluntra wore a military uniform of nearly the same color and make as Butu's, it was covered in ribbons and medals. Gold and silver jewelry dripping with gems covered Aesh's neck, ears and fingers. The most prominent of these was the thick golden crown on his head.

Aesh came to Urgaruna dressed like a king, and he expected to leave as one.

"Is it true you gave up your birthright and became a ku so you could join a dangerous mission to recover Pisor and bring it to me as a bridal gift?" Aesh asked Jani casually. Butu noted the Kadrak kluntra met her eyes solemnly. He was not eyeing her body as

Nolen and Lujo had joked he would be.

She glared daggers at Zhek, and she visibly struggled to find the right way to express her fury.

Before she could speak, though, Aesh laughed lightly and looked at Zhek. "It was a clever lie, al'Ahjea. Not that I believed it for a moment, of course, but I understand why you told me it. You thought I meant to take her hostage to use her as a lever against your father, but you were wrong. You were always meant to be the hostage." Zhek jumped at the news, and Aesh's voice became light steel. "A man will abandon his nephews and nieces, but he will not abandon his heir without good cause. No, she was merely an excuse to bring you to me."

CHAPTER 56

The Kadrak kluntra ignored the lieutenant's discomfort. He placed the full force of his gaze upon Jani, then, and she shrank a little before it. He seemed to command almost as much of the area as Tirud did, without the magic.

"I mean no offense to you, Jani, ah, ku Ahjea. I have my spies among the Ahjea sordenu, so I have heard what you endured to refuse my proposal." He spread bejeweled hands. "Such beauty as yours is rarely paired with as much strength and courage as you possess. I withdraw my proposal, for I am not worthy of you. You deserve no less than a king for a husband." He bowed slightly.

Is that how a king is supposed to talk? Butu half-expected Jani to slap the Kadrak kluntra, to spit or sneer at him, but instead, she smiled at the flattery. Tirud looked away as if pretending not to hear, far more embarrassed than Jani looked.

"I won't force anyone to marry me," Tirud said. He glared at the Kadrak kluntra. "Most especially a fellow ku."

Aesh looked horrified. "I didn't intend that you should, your majesty, nor do I pretend to understand the desires of one of the minds that found Pisor where an army of Akdren could not."

"I would think you'd be angry that Jusep and Zhek betrayed you by sending us to Urgaruna," Butu said to the kluntra. His boldness was rewarded with angry glances from Zhek and Blay.

Aesh betrayed no irritation. He smiled. "My nephew is right to idolize you, Butu." Paka's mouth opened in an O and Butu felt his cheeks warm.

The kluntra gestured theatrically. "Your squad has bested all the great clans, which means you and all your companions have great courage and resourcefulness. In truth, Jusep acted on my orders, as you acted on yours — to ensure the Akdren did not make a king. I would have preferred if you had brought Pisor to me so Paka could make me king, but I believe you did the right thing to make a king instead of letting the Sword of Kings fall into Akdren hands. Philquek would have destroyed the Kadrak without hesitation, while an Ahjea sordenu would be more likely to consider my clan an ally."

"Speaking of which, we're missing one negotiating party," Tirud observed. "I'll be back soon with Philquek."

Tirud and his golems sank into the stone beneath his feet. Aesh continued drawing members of the Ahjea squad into conversation, flattering them so blithely he almost sounded genuine. Butu said nothing, watching each of them in turn.

Blay stood a little apart from Zhek, and Butu sensed he was wrestling with his loyalties. Retus and Phedam looked exhausted, like they would just as soon curl up and sleep as recount their adventures. Lujo was in his element, here, describing the squad's journey in grand detail with barely a grain of truth while Aesh listened with interest and Paka stared in amazement.

Jani stood close to Butu. She picked at the hilt of her sword as if considering whether she would need it. Zhek pretended to be interested in Lujo's tale, but Butu caught him casting furtive looks at Pisor and angry looks at him. Butu tried to keep his face calm.

He knows enough to risk everything. Butu felt a spark of irritation. *Let's get this over with!*

He gestured to the small palace behind them. "You must be hot after so much time in the shanjin sun," Butu said. "Let's relax in the shade until the king returns."

"An excellent idea," Aesh agreed, breaking off his conversation with Lujo.

"Yes," Zhek said, and the smothered look of triumph on the lieutenant's face told Butu what would happen.

Butu did not wait for anyone else, but turned his back deliberately and walked past Jani.

"If you'll follow me," he said, somewhat louder than he wanted.

"What are you doing?" Jani whispered as she caught up to

him. "Aesh or Zhek could murder you right now!"

"They wouldn't think of it, under a flag of truce," Butu said solemnly. "We're just going to get to the shade."

Jani glanced warily at Zheck, but she fell back half a step and followed him. Butu consciously tried to find where everyone was behind him, and was thrilled when thinking about it didn't make the effort fail.

I am truly an adult now, he thought. *Now if only I can get the height to be one!* Though the short kluntra appeared quite formidable.

Retus and Phedam passed them quickly, racing without magic and enjoying it. Lujo continued the story of squad Tem-35 after Aesh and Paka stood up, but that kept them far to the rear. Blay flanked Zhek, not three paces behind Butu. His skin prickled at the knowledge.

I want to be wrong, he thought. *Shanubu, let me be wrong. What would it accomplish? Even if he gets Pisor, no one here will make him king.*

Butu walked calmly, but his heart pounded in his chest. He forced himself to let Jani catch up to him. He kept his hand away from Pisor's hilt, but it took a force of will.

If I touch my sword first, of course he'll attack. He'd only be defending himself, and I'd be in the wrong. If I'm right and I wait, though, he might succeed.

Retus and Phedam had entered the tiny palace, shouting and making echoes. Blay and Zhek still paced each other, and Aesh, Paka and Lujo were even farther behind.

Butu felt Zhek's sword leave its sheath a heartbeat before Paka gasped, shouting a warning.

My shumi was watching for me, too. Butu smiled. *He listened to Jusep's lesson, too.*

Zhek needed two quick steps to reach Butu. Jani turned as Blay's sword leapt from its sheath, and Butu didn't have time to think about why his sword came out second. The conversation at the rear halted as soon as Paka spoke, and hands went to swords even as boots scraped the ground, trying to run.

None of them could have warned me in time. His smile turned grim. *None of them can save me.*

He wheeled and brought Pisor up as fast as Karp ever had moved, blocking Zhek's hard over-arm chop in a perfect X that any weaponsmith would cringe at. Zhek's blade snapped where it touched the unornamented Sword of Kings. The broken blade twisted in the air, struck a basalt wall and landed, spinning, on the ground.

Zhek stared at him with mouth open, clutching the broken sword dumbly. Butu met his gaze.

"I've learned to see," he said softly. "That won't work on me."

CHAPTER 57

Then Jani pushed Butu away from Zhek, placing herself like a shield between them. Jani leveled her sword at Zhek, first, and Blay arrived next. Zhek raised the broken remnant of his sword as if he meant to fight them with it, but Paka ran up with childish speed and touched it, turning it to powder that glittered as it floated to the ground.

Lujo and Aesh looked equally angry at Zhek when they arrived with swords drawn, and Retus and Phedam ran out of the palace with hands on their swords. Butu could almost sense the murder in the air.

They could call it execution for treason.

"Wait!" he shouted. "Let him live."

They didn't stab Zhek on the spot, but they didn't take their eyes off him, either.

"He just tried to kill the king under a flag of truce." Aesh's voice was cold, and his sword quivered in his shaking hand.

"It was a test. I was never in any real danger." Butu hoped the half-truth sounded like truth. Aesh's eyes narrowed in disbelief.

"Why else would Tirud bring you to Butu and leave you while he went somewhere he couldn't protect his kingmaker?" Jani asked, picking up his train of thought. She sheathed her sword and looked at Zhek severely. Of all of them, Butu thought she looked the angriest. "Go to Jusep and explain to him why, when a friend of the Ahjea was made king, you thought it best to kill him and seize Pisor for yourself. Go to him and explain why you've disgraced the Ahjea like this. If you're lucky, he'll only remove you from the line of succession."

271

The fight went out of Zhek. At a command from Blay, Phedam and Lujo stripped the armor and weapons from Jusep's son and bound his arms and feet in his shirt and pants.

Tirud quirked an eyebrow at the bound Zhek when he, Amber and Philquek arrived. The ancient Akdren kluntra sniffed at the drawn swords, especially Aesh's. Everyone sheathed their swords hurriedly.

"Has there been trouble?" Tirud asked mildly.

"Nothing we couldn't handle," Butu said.

Philquek glared at Aesh, who gave him a weak, bitter smile.

"Fine," Tirud said, after staring hard at Zhek's beaten expression. "He can explain to his father what happened."

"He will," Jani said sternly. "If I have to say it for him."

Aesh and Philquek each snorted, and stared at each other afterward. Tirud's lips pressed together.

"I see you need no introduction," he said dryly. "You know why you're here."

"Because your majesty summoned us?" Aesh asked.

Philquek scowled at Aesh, but his voice was deferential when he addressed Tirud. "What are your terms?"

"It's fairly simple. I am the king of the Turun."

The two kluntras met each other's eyes for a moment. They nodded.

"The rest of the clans ..." Philquek began.

"You will inform them," Tirud said. "I will be busy. Urgaruna, here, will be my seat of power."

"So no clan loses any territory," Aesh said, bobbing his head in agreement.

"All the clans are to withdraw their armies and return to their own territories without fighting each other. Anyone who stays in Urgaruna will have to forsake his clan and swear to serve me. In return, I'm granting amnesty for all treaty-breakers."

"The treaty doesn't hold now that there's a king," Philquek said.

Tirud took a deep breath and winked at Butu. "The clans will keep the Treaty of Mnemon. Punishment will be severe to any who break the Treaty."

"Agreed," Philquek said. "Too much blood has already been

spilled in this war. My men will return to their homes, your majesty."

"I can withdraw my army, or simam will kill most of my clan's soldiers," Aesh noted. "I must commend you, your majesty. You've thought of ... many things. You'll make a fine king."

"If we're agreed, I'll return you to your men and oversee the withdrawal from up here," Tirud said.

"Would you be opposed to me leaving a Kadrak fosterling here in Urgaruna?" Aesh asked as he approached the basalt outcropping.

"Who did you have in mind?"

Aesh smiled and looked at Paka and then Butu. "My nephew is friends with your kingmaker. They've already been separated once. I'd like to reunite them."

Tirud considered this briefly. "Very well."

Philquek suddenly broke in. "And let Amber stay with you, as well. She's become friends with your kingmaker, too. If Turuna is to be a kingdom, again, she could learn much as a part of your court."

"If she wants to stay."

Amber grinned and nodded vigorously.

"It's settled, then." He turned to his squadmates. "You have the same choice. I won't keep you here if you'd rather go back to Jasper."

"I'll stay," Lujo said at once. "If I turn my back on a chance to serve the first king in centuries, I'll never forgive myself."

"I'm staying," Jani said.

Blay knelt down in front of Tirud, his face solemn. "I will serve you even if it costs me my own life, your majesty."

Tirud looked embarrassed by the display.

"I don't have much choice, but if everyone else is staying, I don't have any reason to leave," Butu said.

"You have a choice, too, but I'm glad you've picked the least awkward option."

They looked at Retus and Phedam expectantly. Surprisingly, Retus spoke first.

"I'm glad I've had this adventure with you, but I've had enough excitement to last a lifetime. I think I'm going to see if Pater will let me return to my father's herds."

That left Phedam. Butu thought he saw tears in his eyes.

"I'm tired of adventure, too, but you're the only family I have left. I'll stay, but I think my soldiering days are done."

"You're welcome, always," Tirud said, and the rest of the squad murmured similar sentiments.

"You'll need more than sordenu," Aesh warned. "I'd be glad to send some of my advisors to help you rebuild Urgaruna."

"Me, too," Philquek said, glaring at Aesh.

"I'll consider it. For now, return to your armies and go home."

Philquek stepped onto one outcropping, and Aesh and Retus stepped onto another. Retus carried the bound Zhek over one shoulder like a sack.

"There," Tirud said, before the platform started moving. He gestured, and as they watched, the simam's red cloud became still. "It'll be some time before the dust settles, but its heart is quiet."

The kluntras nodded, more awe in their faces at his command of the deadly wind. The platforms descended.

"Let's go back to the shade," Tirud suggested. "It'll take hours for the Akdren to leave Urgaruna."

"I'm hungry," Phedam complained. "There's no food up here."

"The Kadrak still have supplies. I'll bring some."

Before they could respond, he ran off the edge of Urgaruna and down the sheer cliff face. They watched him become a tiny figure on the shanjin before returning to the basalt palace.

"What's it like in the sordenu, shumi?" Paka asked timidly.

Butu laughed. "Where do I even start?"

He told Paka about the training and the other sordenu. He told him about finding water and the sandstorm and how he had met Amber. When he got to the part where the squad was uncovering the well, Phedam abruptly left the palace. Butu told Paka about Nolen's death, but the memory was still too fresh, and his voice cracked.

Lujo broke in to tell Paka about how Jani, Tirud, and he had scouted around Urgaruna, brushing aside Jani's many corrections. He told Paka how he had suggested sneaking into Urgaruna to steal Pisor and had just explained how they had tricked Philquek into thinking they had given him Pisor when Amber finally corrected him.

Jani explained how she had returned to the Ahjea to let them know their squad knew where Pisor was. She dwelled a little longer on Zhek's attempt to keep her from leaving with the rest of the squad. She told him about how they had rescued Butu and Lujo before sneaking into Urgaruna and of all the terrible things they had seen there.

When Phedam returned, Blay took over the story, describing the events that came before Butu made Tirud king. When the story was done, it was dark. A blue moon and a yellow moon hung in the sky among the stars.

Tirlum and Galdera.

Tirlum was the wandering blue moon. It rose in a different part of the eastern sky each night and disappeared to the north for a month before reappearing in the southeastern sky. Galdera was the yellow moon of hope. It rose in the west and set in the east, getting smaller as the night wore on until it disappeared completely. But most nights, it appeared in the sky again long before the sun rose as a promise that the night would not last forever and that day would come again.

Butu could find no sign of Zheldesa — the green moon — or Quemney — the black moon that blocked light instead of shedding it. Butu remembered the stories about how each of the four moons had been made. They were all miramani, of course.

Magic made the first children, and the children made everything else. Every star, every moon, every mountain, every river, every kind of animal and plant, and everything of beauty in the whole world is the wish of a child made manifest.

And now that power lay in the hands of an adult.

Have I made the right choice?

CHAPTER 58

"They're mostly trail rations, but it's better than nothing," Tirud said from the entrance of the palace, and Butu was surprised he hadn't sensed him sooner. His golems carried armloads of wrapped bundles. "Come eat outside where there's at least moonlight," Tirud suggested.

"Can't you make light like in the city underground?" Lujo asked.

Tirud shook his head.

"Then how did the Urgarun make it?"

"How did they make Pisor do what it does, and why couldn't any king destroy it?" Tirud countered. "Maybe there are limits to the miramani a king can perform, or maybe there are mysteries in Urgaruna that've been hidden for thousands of years that will explain Pisor. That's the other reason why I'm making it my capital — to solve some of those mysteries."

They filed out into the open and sat down in the cooling air.

"Like what happened to Mnemon after he hid Pisor?" Butu asked.

The golems brought them the bundles of food and water.

"Exactly. If he'd died in the city, the salt should have preserved his body like the others."

"And whether the Urgarun refused to unmake Pisor or whether they couldn't," Jani said.

"Right."

"If you could destroy Pisor forever so no more kings could be made, would you?" Blay asked thoughtfully.

Tirud considered this for a long moment as they passed food

around the circle. "I'm not sure, yet. It would be interesting to have a chance to make that choice, though. It's the kind of choice the leaders of my birth clan would meditate on in the orchard."

Lej, Butu remembered. *The fruit that lets you see the situation the way you would see it when you're older. Can Pisor do that, too?*

Silence fell over the top of the rock as they remembered how hungry they were. Butu ate his fill for the first time in days. He felt all the fear and tension of the last few months leaving his body. At once, he realized how exhausted he was. He yawned and stood up.

"I'm going to sleep."

"Good idea."

Soon, they were all on their feet, collecting the remnants of the food and joking softly with each other about how tired they were.

"I have a question," Jani said to Butu as they settled into the basalt palace of the Urgarun children. "How did you know Zhek was going to attack you?"

"I got my Turun sight back when I made Tirud king. Mnemon could still shape stone after making a king, so it makes sense that I'd keep whatever talent I'd've kept as an adult," Butu explained.

"No. I mean before that. I think you knew what he'd do before you suggested resting in the shade."

"I knew he wanted to be king, but he doesn't think ahead. It was adult magic."

"Adult magic?" Amber asked.

"Yes," Butu said, remembering Tirud's explanation in the shanjin. *He wasn't talking about blood priests at all.* "If you don't think about what you're doing and why, you're like sand. You get blown around by every little gust of wind — every whim and feeling that comes along — and even adults without magic can shape you into whatever they want you to be."

"If you would be wise, you must keep your eyes open," Tirud murmured.

"And if you would sleep, you must close them," Lujo grumbled.

Silence fell over them, then, and Butu drifted into sleep.

He woke to the distant sound of sordenu marching chants. Butu rose and went to look over the edge of the cliff. Tirud, Blay and Jani were already there. Below, the Akdren army marched west, back toward the Riphil, with the Kadrak army several miles ahead of them.

As they watched the withdrawal in silence, the others came out to join them. The sun was hot in the morning sky by the time Tirud broke the silence.

"Let's go down into the city."

They gradually turned away from the cliff and followed Tirud to another basalt outcropping, which descended back to the shanjin. From the surface, Tirud lowered them into the earth and back to the nursery of the Urgarun children's sanctuary. They crossed the marble footbridge into the dim quarter of the city.

Tirud surveyed the fallen city as they walked.

"I'm not yet certain I should keep the name of my adopted clan," Tirud said.

"Will you go back to being a Kanjea?" Jani asked.

He hesitated. "No. I'm thinking of taking the name Tirud pi'Urgarun. I suppose we are all Urgarun, now."

Tirud waved a hand vaguely at the ruined building. The eternal tears of the Urgarun children suddenly stopped falling from the ceiling, and as the dull translucence of salt melted away from the crystal buildings, the ever-present light brightened until it rivaled the sun except without the heat.

"It's so beautiful!" Amber breathed.

"Is that the palace?" Paka asked, pointing at the gleaming crystal building at the top of the enormous dais.

"Yes. And you can have whatever room in it you want," Tirud promised as they walked toward it.

"Really?"

"I'd prefer you let me have the throne room, but other than that, yes."

"Of course."

They walked on a little while until they reached the stairs.

"I'll go pick one out," Paka announced as he broke into a run.

He vaulted the stairs in twos and threes. Butu couldn't help but smile.

"Do you wish you could still do that?" Blay asked as the rest of them ascended.

"Sometimes," Jani admitted. "It's not so bad once you've learned how to do everything without magic."

"I'd give anything to go back," Blay said, touching his goatee.

"Even everything you've learned and experienced since your mirjuva?" Tirud asked.

"Maybe not that, but just about anything else," Blay said at last, taking his hand from his face with a grimace.

"How soon before the other soldiers loyal to Tirud come down here?" Phedam asked. "This city feels so empty."

"It takes more than soldiers to fill a city," Amber said. "We need craftsmen and traders and people to provide food."

"And tailors," Butu said, pointing to the bottom of his pants, which were now nearly an inch too short for his legs.

Finally!

As they reached the top of the stairs, they heard a clatter and a muffled cry. They exchanged brief looks and then ran to the source of the noise. Paka sat on the floor, looking extremely confused about something. Butu reached him first.

"What's wrong, shumi? What happened?"

Paka looked up at him, showing him scrapes on his hands that were already healing. Very softly, he said, "I fell."

Butu held out a hand to Paka. "Then let me help you stand up again."

Four Moons Press

Invites you to read a sample
of a forthcoming novel

By Eric Zawadzki and Matthew Schick

available at

fourmoonspress.com

COMING IN SPRING 2012

ABOUT THE AUTHORS

Eric Zawadzki

Eric spent his Midwestern childhood reading fantasy, so it probably isn't surprising that he came to idealize stories of going to a far-off land. When no wizard showed up to tell him he was the heir to some otherworldly throne or the only one who could defeat the nefarious designs of a dark god, Eric took this whole questing hero thing into his own hands.

While backpacking alone in Poland without so much as a phrasebook, he met many strangers who gave him advice and directions. One family even took him in for the night, feeding him and asking him about his travels. No bandits or wolves, but that's probably for the best. He still has nightmares about that wolf-man from The Neverending Story.

He lived for a time among the majestic mountains of Colorado before seeking his one true love, Beth, on the frozen wastelands of Minnesota. They married on a beautiful spring day and are in the process of living happily ever after.

Matthew Schick

Indiana had a slogan in Matt's childhood: "There's more than corn in Indiana." Driving around the state, he agreed — there were also soybeans and vast, flat skies. He found inspiration because there was so much room for it, inspiration to explore, to fill himself with variety, and to write with them in mind.

He now lives in Charlottesville, Va., with his lady, whom he met while working as a journalist in Hawaii. He ended up in Hawaii after doing similar work in Colorado and Virginia, and going to college in Wisconsin. In his explorations, he has found people, food and experiences that made each place an inspiration for the worlds in which he writes.

. . .

The words of a prophecy brought Matthew and Eric together for the first time when they were only fourteen. Not ones to fight destiny, they quickly began a collaboration that has endured for nearly twenty years — flourishing even after they discovered girls, went to different colleges, and lived half an ocean apart. Fate briefly brought them both to Minneapolis, only to fling Matt away again, but they concocted a scheme to finally publish their works and throw off the prophecy altogether.